CRIME PAYS

THE TRIPLE CROSS

THA TWINZ

Copyright © 2013 Tha Twinz

This novel is a work of fiction. Any resemblances to real people, living or dead, actual events, establishments, organizations, and/or locales are intended to give the fiction a sense of reality and authenticity. Other names, characters, places, and incidents are either products of the author's imagination or are used fictitiously, as are those fictionalized events and incidents that involve real persons and did not occur or are set in the future.

Published by:
Prestige Communication Group, LLC
PO Box 1129
New York, NY 10027
Email: Info@prestigecommunicationgroup.com

ISBN-10: 1490986456
ISBN-13: 978-1490986456

Crime Pays Credits:
Written by: Tha Twinz
Edited by: Zach Tate, Salih Israil, Tonia Taylor-Bragg
Cover Concept by: Baby Born
Cover Graphics by: Marion Design

Printed in the USA

Dedication

This book is dedicated in the loving memory of our beloved niece Sabine Maisha Bragg... Although you are no longer with us; in our hearts and minds you are always there! We miss you sooo much!

Acknowledgement

To team PCG - thank you so much for all your hard work, sacrifices, and level of professionalism. As a result, the CRIME PAYS? trilogy is now a huge success across the country. Like apple pie and baseball, Crime Pays has become an all time people favorite... Now how real is that! You guys did a hell of a job, THANK YOU!

To our family and friends -Now, you know it's way too many of you guys to name but do know that we appreciate your love and support.

To all the bookstores, vendors, and distributors around the country - Thank you so much.

And last but not least, to our loyal readers -It was you that has made Crime Pays? what it is. Thanks for your love and continuous support. Because of you PCG will continue to put out nothing but GREAT work.

Tha Twinz

ONE

It was 3:00 a.m. and a caravan of seven black passenger
vehicles sped down a dark country road in the Georgia
Mountains. Each truck was filled with military-trained members
of the Cuban gang Los Marielitos, which had terrorized the East
coast for over 3 decades.

This late night excursion was led by a Cuban named Mostro.
His skin was black as tar, and his appetite for spilling blood was
insatiable. He found killing better than sex; the bloodier, the better.
His truck stopped on the roadside of two huge ranches that sat on
20 acres of fenced-in farmland. The homes were separated by a
corn field.

The immaculate home on the left belonged to Self, a homicidal
sociopath who had sent many Marielitos to their death. The one on
the right belonged to Bobby Lee, a redneck militiaman who was
Self's brother from another mother. Bobby Lee and his now
deceased brother Wilbur had killed Marielitos in New York for
Self when they joined the war to assist Manny Black. A war that
left them with 4.5 million dollars of the Marielitos money, and no
one was the wiser.

The caravan of Marielitos stopped their trucks at the midway
line between Self and Bobby Lee's houses. The team leaders for
each truck stepped out and met the cigar smoking, camouflage
dressed, skinhead leader Mostro, who had his signature machete in
hand. He pointed his weapon of choice west, in the direction of
Self's house and said, "*Uno.*" Then he pointed east and said, "*El
gringo,*" telling his soldiers that the white man he had been trying
to find for over a year lived there. He laughed loudly, knowing
nothing but crickets and livestock could hear him. "*Quiero sus
cabezas!*" he yelled, telling his soldiers that he wanted the heads of
the men he came for.

"*Viva la Marielitos!*" his men chanted and the phalanx of armed
Cubans rushed out of the trucks and hopped over the wooden
fences prepared to satisfy their general's appetite for blood.

*****

Beep! Beep! Beep! Were the subtle sounds of Bobby Lee's
alarm, letting him know that someone hit all three trip-wires to the

perimeter around his six bedroom ranch. It couldn't have been a false alarm or some form of animal that had tripped it. For the alarm to go off meant someone was approaching his property from a hundred yards out and tripped more than one wire.

He quickly rolled out of bed, leaving his young, naked, second cousin, who was going to be his bride someday. She was twenty years his junior, ready to have children, and ever since he became wealthy, he was the apple of her eyes.

"*Squuut, squuut, squuut,*" he kissed loudly, summoning the three, vicious pit bulls that belonged to him and his three brothers who were sleeping in the other rooms. "Go and get 'em boys," he ordered his dogs after opening the glass sliding door and sending them into the night.

He filled his jaw with a fresh wad of Redman chewing tobacco and picked up his carbine rifle.

And he waited.

When he didn't hear the dogs growling or quickly returning, he waited some more. Then he heard the painful cries from two of his dogs. He rushed to his night table, pulled out an air horn and squeezed it three times.

"This is it, boys" he yelled from his bedroom. He opened the trunk that lay at the foot of his bed and threw his carbine next to his sleeping beauty. When her head snapped up he said, "Wake up, Missy. We gots some fixin' to do."

His bride-to-be quickly jumped up and slipped her naked crotch into a pair of jeans while he dug into the trunk and removed the gear he had for such an occasion. He slipped on a pair of camouflage fatigues, tossed a bulletproof vest over his fragile bare chest, and then removed an M-16 machinegun from the bottom of the trunk. With his machinegun cocked and loaded on the bed, he quickly tucked two .357 Desert Eagle handguns into the handmade leather holsters on his hips. He then placed two hand grenades into the side pockets of his fatigues and filled his hands with as much ammunition as he could.

In the other bedrooms, Bobby Lee's brothers scurried for their clothes and weapons. Rich, the twin to Wilbur, who stood 6'5" and weighed more than 250lbs, grabbed three handguns, placed two grenades into his pockets and picked up his crossbow. He slapped green paint unto his face, put tobacco into his jaw with his filthy hands and made his way out of the house and into the woods.

Andy, a scrawny brother that drank too much moonshine ran into his mother's room with two AR-15's. "Wake up, Mama," he told the eighty-five-year old. He locked her door, sat in a seat at the foot of her bed, and faced the door in her room, protecting the leader of the family. William-Larry, the twin to Bobby Lee yawned with calmness. He scratched his testicles, not caring about whatever was coming his way. After sliding on only his boxer shorts, his cowboy boots and his cowboy hat, he sucked his teeth and slid a toothpick into his mouth. Then he rushed to the front door, opened it, and held up the Remington rifle that was leaning against the doorframe.

As Bobby Lee slid his glass porch door open, a bullet smashed through the opposite door. "What in tar-nation?" he uttered to himself when he saw three men, twenty feet away, running towards his house. "Missy, past me midnight," he yelled to his woman before stepping onto the porch and firing rapid shots of his M-16, cutting the three men down.

"Be careful, baby," Missy warned after handing him an M40AR sniper rifle with an infrared scope, allowing him to see into the night.

He looked through the scope and counted more than ten men creeping in different areas of his property. Three flash-bang grenades went off, lighting up the woods, fifty yards towards the back of his house. He sat the rifle down realizing that a dozen men were coming for him. Instantly, he was grateful that he and his family were prepared for such an event.

*****

Self awoke to the thunderclaps of Bobby Lee's flash-bang grenades. The pulse of the strobe light that he used as a silent alarm was going off.

"Peaches, wake up," he called his pregnant wife Joy by her nickname as he shook her. His first child was in the room next door. He rushed to the strobe light switch in the corner of his master bedroom suite to cut it off.

"What happened?" she asked with sleep in her voice.

"Get your gear and strap up. We got company," he told her.

She sat up in bed and mechanically reached into her nightstand for the Mac 11 submachine gun with the extended clip. She had been forced to train with the weapon. She looked over to her husband and calmly said, "Master, don't let nobody come in this house." She grabbed another extended clip and wobbled out the bedroom in an effort to get to her son.

"Self got this," he said with his full, platinum and diamond smile, always referring to himself in the third person. He rushed into his huge walk-in closet and panic room, grabbed an aviator jumpsuit, and slipped his feet into a pair of steel-toe camouflage Survivor boots. Within seconds his tall 240lb frame was strapped with two Glock 10 automatic handguns, a 15" Tanto blade and an AK47.

He hit a red button on his light switch and the twelve halogen lights on top of his roof came on, making the perimeter around his house bright as day. Then he looked out. To his right, about twenty feet away from his house, close to his horse stables, one of his flash-bang grenades went off. A man screamed in Spanish. Someone's foot was stuck in one of the bear traps he planted.

He heard the man's screeching cries, recognized the Latin accent and knew his enemies had returned. "Marielitos," he huffed before he took off.

Self sprinted at top speed and ran in the direction of the horse stables, knowing the best defense was a great offense. Someone began shooting at him but he kept running. Changing directions made him a harder target, but the bullets kept coming. So he ran faster.

He reached the woods, dropped flat to the dirt and controlled his breathing. His face was inches from a pile of smoking horseshit. With each inhale the stench that he'd grown accustomed to invaded his nostrils, and then he heard them.

Two men foolishly tried to help the other trapped man remove his mangled leg from the sharpened claws of the bear trap. Self stood slowly and looked around for the others that shot at him, but no one was there.

There had to be others. Those three couldn't have tripped his perimeter, he thought. "The house," he said before quickly standing. He aimed his AK and fired shots, exploding the head of one and dropping the other two before they knew what hit them.

He ran as bullets from a fully automatic machine gun rained down on him. He turned and realized that more than one man was up in his trees. "Self trees?" he said to himself with confusion like someone had committed the ultimate violation. He lifted his AK and the weapon did a sprint of rapid fire into the trees.

"Over here!" he heard someone yell. His shots gave away his location, so he ran.

Shots came closer to him. After returning fire he cut through the woods, heading back to his house. Up ahead, four men were running towards the front door. The men stopped short, aimed their weapons at the bright rooftop lights and shot them out. Self pushed faster.

The familiar discharge of his wife's gun came from inside. He kept his rifle high, aiming at the back of the heads of the men that were entering his house. Less than ten feet away he slowed, fired with steady aim and hit two of them. The other two quickly scrambled around the house, firing back.

Self rushed into his yard, jumped over the dead bodies and dropped his empty AK. As he ran around his house he removed his handguns. He reached the back of the house and was met by other soldiers kicking at his steel, reinforced door.

"Kill de *puta*!" a Cuban yelled when Self suddenly appeared.

Self raised his gun and they raised theirs. While back peddling, he pumped shots into the Cuban's. Suddenly, one of their shots hit the center plate in his bulletproof vest, lifting him off his feet. He fell back, certain that his rib had broken. But that wasn't the first time he took a shot to his vest. He staggered forward, emptied his clip, holding his gun behind him, before hearing someone yell out in pain. Then he rushed around the corner. He ran through the sliding glass door to his master suite. When he got inside he heard the rapid fire of his wife's gun in the hall. He dropped his empty clip and reloaded.

More than eight Marielitos were coming in the front door when Self reached the hallway. At the opposite end of the hall, four more made their way through the back door. The window from his mother-in-law's room crashed in slivers. Then the sound of her .38 revolver went off in calculated shots like Self had taught her.

"Not here, motherfucker's," he heard Eva yell before several shots silenced her.

Self rushed into the hall. He saw the small crowd of killers at the front door, quickly slid his hand into his pocket, and tossed a grenade at them. "Ahh," Self yelled when two shots hit him in the chest, and one in the leg, sprawling him to the floor. His grenade went off, scattering the pieces of his enemies at the front door.

Seconds later, Joy rushed into the hallway with her baby in one hand, and her gun in the other. She tucked her baby, aimed her gun at the men who were pouring in from her backdoor, and squeezed the trigger until her gun was empty.

"Master!" she yelled for Self when the gun cracked back, waiting for a new clip.

Self's eyes opened. His ears were ringing but he could read his wife's beautiful lips as she barked, "Get up!"

He slowly sat up.

"*Whaaaaaaaa*," his one-year old son cried out to deaf ears.

Joy ran to a China umbrella basket at the end of the marble tiled hall, retrieved her husband's tool of choice, and rushed back to him.

"*Whaaaaaaa*," the baby cried louder, his ears ringing from the deadly noise.

Self was checking his military grade vest when Joy rushed up to him and handed him a .50 caliber Desert Eagle. He squeezed the handle tightly as she turned, hearing a noise coming from the backdoor.

"Oh my god!" Joy suddenly cried out.

"*Whaaaaaaa*," the baby bawled, making matters worse.

BONG! BONG! BONG!

Three quick shots aimed at Self entered Joy's midsection. She held her baby as she collapsed to the floor.

Self looked down at his wife in total terror. He glanced at the shooter and split his skull with a barrage of bullets before emptying the clip into two other gunmen that stood directly behind his first victim.

"*Whaaaaaaa*," the baby cried from the littered marbled floor.

The door to Eva's room opened down the hall as Self leaned over and grabbed his son.

"*Whaaaaaaa*," his son screeched, maybe trying to give him a warning.

Self stopped and suddenly felt someone behind rushing in from the front of the house. He quickly turned and raised his cannon, but it was empty.

*****

"Now look at what the good lord done bought us," Bobby Lee chanted to himself while standing at the backdoor looking through the scope of Midnight. He saw a mob of Marielitos rushing towards him in the night. "Brothers!" he yelled out to his team. "It's killing time, and Mama these vermin we cants eat."

Bobby Lee inhaled deeply as he tightened the suppressor on the tip of his tool. He spat a wad of tobacco onto the dull hardwood floor, opened the folding stock of the gun, adjusted the cheek piece, and pulled the bolt back–filling the custom 12 round magazine. He then lifted the scope to his eyes and fixed his vision all across his property again. This time, he saw what looked like more than twenty-five Marielitos rushing onto the property from all sides.

The men approached with hungry footsteps, running to and fro, clad in army fatigues like they were rushing the front lines of war. And they were. The Marielitos were looking for payback, but they wouldn't get it if he could help it.

"I'm in my early forties, with a lot of life before me. An' a moment came that stopped me on a dime…" he sang loudly, keeping in tune with his favorite song by Tim McGraw. Slowly he adjusted the focus from his professional rifle scope, lining up the heads of Cubans in his sight. Like a pack of hungry wolves invited to a feast, the Cuban sprinted with a heated passion to kill.

"I spent most of the next days, looking at the X-Rays," William-Larry loudly continued the rest of the verse, leaning against the threshold of the front door with the butt of his Remington rifle nestled in his shoulder as he took aim. He wiggled his lean body against the strong post, across the hinges and took in a deep breath of the warm August night air to stay calm like the military had taught him. The invaders of his property were fifty yards away and coming fast.

"Oh, they done started something," Andy announced as he quickly filled an old mayonnaise jar with liquid courage.

He put the hot drink of liquid muscle to his lips and bounced on the tips of his toes as his Adam's apple bobbed with each gulp. When the jar was half done, he wiped his mouth with the back of his hand and rushed to take care of his number one priority. Over the sweet melody of his brother's voice, he rushed back to his mother's room.

"What in da hell?" she asked in shock when he came back through the door without knocking. The elderly obese woman quickly sat up in bed with a Remington .45 Colt in her veiny hand, aiming at her door.

"It's me, Mama!" He said with annoyance. She should have known better.

His mother reached over to the night stand, placed her glasses on her face and opened her eyes wide while looking at him. "What?" was all she asked. He ignored her fussing over her house dress and the run in her stockings. "We gots to go," he advised, rushing to her side. "What's that?" she asked, bending her ear towards the door. Andy helped his mother off the bed and into her rocking chair. He reached into the trunk at the end of her wooden king size bed and removed a Mac-11 sub-machine gun and placed it into her hands. Then he stopped and bent his ear towards the door while reaching for his jar. His brothers were still singing loudly and he shook his head before sucking down a large gulp of homemade moonshine.

"What happened?" his mother asked as her eyes followed his.

"*Live like you were dying*," he uttered the name of the song to himself before putting the mayonnaise jar back to his lips.

"*Huh?*" his mother asked, checking if the clip was full and then slamming it home and cocking it back. "Whatya say?"

"Live like you were dying," he yelled and pointed to the closed door. "They singing Tim McGraw's live like you dying, Mama!"

She chuckled and calmly said, "Den I reckon somebody dying."

Back at the front door, William-Larry huffed before lying on the floor. He quickly opened his bi-pod and adjusted the scope mounted on top of his life insurance. He took aim finding ready targets. Then he fired, easily finding targets that rushed closer to his line of fire. Rapid gunfire instantly came back his way. The Cuban's were not the usual shooters. William-Larry fired again, and again shots came close to his location. He quickly concluded that his new enemies had to be military trained.

"These fuckers ain't afraid of dying!" he yelled to his brother.

"I know!" Bobby Lee yelled from the back door before squeezing his trigger. With the slight whoosh from each squeeze, the heads in his scope exploded with a crimson mist. Bobby Lee's exhaled as each shot he fired signaled who wouldn't be going back to Cuba. After the fifth man dropped, and the trained killers saw the direction the shots were coming from, they aimed their weapons towards the back of the house, but Bobby Lee was gone.

*****

If it was hard for someone who was 6'5" and weighed 250lbs to disappear into thin air, then someone forgot to send Rich the memo. As the surviving twin brother to Wilbur, who had died at the hands of the Marielitos, Rich had been waiting for this day for a very long time. Out of Self and all his brothers, it was he who had spent the most time in the outdoors. It was he who aced all Green Beret test and became an instructor for the U.S. Special Forces. It was also he who was closer to Self. And like Self, he trained and trained some more, then waited for civil war to hit the mainland. Now that the Marielitos had come to kill him and his family, it was combat time. The more he sweated in peace was the less he would bleed in war. He had no intention of bleeding.

He ran from the house and did a fifty yard dash in seconds. Quickly, he dropped to the soil, made himself one with the moist earth, and waited. His palms dug into the ground, feeling for the vibrations of just how far away his enemies were. Within seconds he felt the subtle tremors he was waiting for. As he had expected, several Cuban's were frantically running towards the house from all directions, and five of them were just feet away from him.

He sank deeper into the cow manure beneath him until the thump of a man running towards him vibrated the ground under him. He swiftly reached for the razor sharp arrows in the black leather pouch on his back and then eased the bow off his back until the arrow was firmly in his hand and resting near his right cheek. As the Cuban trespasser ran near to his head, Rich quickly rolled onto his back and reached his hand out, tripping the runner. Like an anaconda emerging himself with his meal, Rich covered the Cuban's body with his and he pushed the razor sharp tip of the arrow into the soldier's leg, severing the femoral artery.

"*Ayeee, Ayee*," the Marielito wept.

"*Shhh*" Rich raised his arrow and stopped below the Cuban's chin. "*Shhhh*," he beckoned while slowly sliding the tip across the man's windpipe.

The runner would never run again. His eyes closed and Rich rolled off of him, using the night and bright stars to shield him from the rapid gunfire that was bursting all around him.

"One down. All left to go," he whispered while crawling on his belly, making his way to the other men violating his private property.

He inhaled the dew and stench of manure while surveying the area. Men were scattered all over the property. To Rich, this meant their military training was subpar. They were probably a guerrilla group, a rebel unit or a bunch of hungry souls being fed by the Marielitos. For Rich they would be child's play, but he couldn't risk standing and being in the line of fire of his brothers.

One by one he counted how many men were in his direct view until he stopped at sixteen. Mimicking a crab, he stayed low with his stomach touching the dirt and quickly scuttled away to the side, moving towards the men ahead. One hand and knee alternating in front of the other, he slivered closer to the men heading in his direction. He slowly rolled onto his side while removing four arrows from the satchel on his back and didn't hesitate to fill the bow.

"My turn," he breathed out before letting an arrow go and another quickly following behind it.

"Cono!" one of the attackers yelled as Rich got to his feet, standing in the middle of four soldiers.

"Hi!" he yelled, startling his enemies and trying to use shock value to his advantage.

"Come!" one of the soldiers yelled as he charged Rich.

"Go!" Rich said before sending the tip of his arrow through the brave ones torso. With the same speed he used to plunge the arrow, he removed it, spun to his right and plunged it into the neck of another. He then dropped his bow to the ground.

"Si!" one of the soldiers said, his eyes darted down at the threat to his life. He looked up at Rich and then charged him yelling, "Marielito!" while lifting his gun to end Rich's life.

Rich ran, leapt with his right knee leading, and slammed it into the soldier's jaw. He then removed the knife from his hip and quickly sliced the Cuban's throat. Footsteps were behind him. Rich flipped the blade, held his fist at the butt of it and slammed the approaching Cuban in the heart. He spun again. The last man stood with an M-16 assault rifle. Rich's feet left the ground again. With a leap, and the base of his blade nestled into his palm, he descended and aimed the blade for his enemy's left eye. Before sliding his blade into the socket like a key into a new lock, he chopped at the M-16, sending it to the ground. After the Cuban's eye and frontal lobe of his brain was sliced in half, Rich quickly withdrew the blade and reached out and yanked at his victim's coat, stopping his body from falling. He then silently helped the corpse down with his left hand, while using his other hand to saw the knife into his victim's chest.

More Marielitos were just a few feet away and hadn't realized that their comrades were dead and that they would soon be joining the grave. Rich flicked the blood from his knife, slid it into its holster and then pulled another arrow from his satchel. It was killing time.

*****

Self's ears rang and his body shook from the shots he took to his midsection.

"A hum du Allah," he breathed while looking down at his chest, thanking God for saving his life. This was the second time his body armor had saved him, but the pain sent him to the floor. "Cock suckers," he grumbled, disappointed that it was the Marielitos who shot him again. "*Gotta be more on point,*" he mumbled.

The late summer wind moved the scent of cordite through the air. Sweat dripped down into his eyes, but that didn't stop him from seeing the four Cuban soldiers who were rushing into the house. With the salty taste of blood in his mouth, Self struggled to pull himself up. From a deep squat, he placed his back against the wall and used all the power in his legs to stand. His breathing came in uneven spurts, and he opened his eyes to see death staring at him.

"Ju de one day call Self?" Mostro asked before spitting in his face.

Self's eyes widened. Where did Mostro come from? The pitch, black face in front of him with the gold-tooth smile startled him, but for some reason, in that second, Self couldn't feel any pain.

"You enjoy dead?" Mostro asked Self, who thought he was dreaming.

"What?" Self asked. This was not the time for talking.

Mostro placed something between Self's legs. His black face glistened with sweat and his scowl cracked into a sinister smile.

"*Whaaaaa,*" Self's son wailed on the floor next to him.

Self followed Mostro's eyes down to his own crotch. First he glanced at Mostro's bloody blade, just inches from him. Then he looked down at the small bloody ball before him and was sure he was seeing things. After all, Self had killed many. He had tortured. He had pulled a man from the inside out, and with the help of the militia, he could kill, skin and eat a man if it meant his survival, but this was different. He stared down into the dead eyes of his mother in-law and realized it was Eva's severed head down at his feet.

"Nuhhhhh," he gasped.

"*Siiiiiiii, puto,*" Mostro laughed while walking away and heading towards Joy's crumpled body. He reached down, snatched a fist full of her hair and turned her lifeless head to face Self. "*Siiiiii.*"

The baby screamed louder. Self's eyes darted from Mostro to Joy's dead body.

Mostro stood while lifting Joy's body up to his waist with one pull. "Pantera!" he yelled over the gunshots outside and the sounds of his men running into the house. "Pantera!" he yelled again. When Self didn't respond, Mostro vented all of his anger. "*Viva la Marielito!* Today, de blood of Pantera will awake. Today all de enemy of Marielito will die. Pantera free Cuba. Pantera love Marielito." He pointed his blade at Self and yelled, "You kill, Pantera. Mostro kill every trace of you, Self."

"*Wha-wha-whaaaaa,*" the baby cried.

Mostro looked over to the baby, turned Joy's head towards her bawling child and he shook her head in a savage rage. "Pantera! Pantera! Pantera!"

"Fuck, Pantera!" Self coughed out loudly. "Let her go!"

Mostro snapped his evil gaze at Self like what he was suggesting was impossible, like it defied logic. Then he laughed. "I come to remove *tu familia*, de way you remove mine." He slapped the sharp blade against his chest and yelled, "Pantera *mi hermano, puto!*"

"Shit," Self uttered to himself. Mostro was Pantera's brother. There would be no turning back for him.

"Pantera," Mostro said calmly before spinning his machete in his free hand. "Ju attack de Marielitos? Ju kill me *hermano*, Pantera? " he asked Self before lifting his machete.

As Self looked on, he lost his breath when Mostro hacked at Joy's neck with his sharp blade. Self closed his eyes, but his ears continued to work well. Over his son's screech Mostro cursed with each swing and thump as he hacked through Joy's spine. When Self felt the thump of Joy's headless body hit the floor, he reopened his eyes.

"Look!" Mostro yelled, holding Joy's blood soaked head inches from Self's face.

Self raised the empty cannon and aimed it at Mostro's head squeezing the trigger three times with all the strength he could muster, but gun was empty.

"Ju *basura*," Mostro called him garbage. "*Finito!*" he bragged and then tossed Joy's head to his soldier. "Wrap them up. *Rapido!*" he ordered for them to hurry.

Self was stuck in a trance of immobility. The only thing that worked well was his eyes. He traced the steps of the Marielito solider that dropped the two heads of his heart and soul into a trash bag before quickly running out the door.

In the distance he heard the footsteps of the last two men checking each room of his house, probably making sure there were no surprises hidden. He glanced towards his bedroom, hoping they only looked inside and didn't walk around snooping for more than humans. If only he could find the energy to make it there. Somehow, some way, he needed Mostro to slip, and he would take it from there. Once he reached his bedroom, he could make all his pain go away.

"*Whaaaaaa!*" the baby screamed, pulling Self from his trance.

Mostro's deranged glare looked over to the child like he forgot that the only remaining bloodline of Self was still there. He looked at the small child like it was a distraction, he spat with disgust. "*Cono!*" he yelled before looking over at Self, then back down at the baby. Again his scowl turned into a huge smile.

Like a skilled soccer player, Mostro shuffled an imaginary ball from side to side as he quickly made his way to the baby.

"*Whaaaaaa,*" the baby wailed.

Mostro shuffled the invisible ball behind his leg and spun around. He dodged an imaginary defender before lifting his heavy combat boot and kicking with all his might, smashing the baby's skull and silencing him forever.

"*Goooooal. Goooooal,*" he yelled like an announcer at a soccer match. Then he quickly skipped back over to Self laughing. "Ju ready to die?" Mostro asked Self.

The heat of anger drained down from Self's pulsating skull and flowed throughout his entire body. With each heartbeat, his body throbbed, sending ripples of new energy with each wave. He slowly slid his hand down to his side until he found the handle of his blade and curled each finger around the thick handle.

Mostro scanned the room, looking at Self and then at his soldiers. He snapped his finger twice to get the attention of the soldier that was carrying a body bag. "There," his bad accent said as he pointed to the floor. He looked at Self, making eye contact. "For you," he pointed to Self, knowing he was going home with the notorious killer. "Castro done!" Mostro raved. "Raul *finito*. When Primo and Gato see ju body in diz bag? We party." He traced his chest with his finger in the sign of a Holy cross, looked up to the ceiling and said, "Pantera. For you."

Mostro attempted to step closer. Self used the last bit of energy he had left to push himself off the wall, fell to the ground and then rolled onto his back. He barreled inches away from Mostro and quickly sprung up into a kneeling position with one knee before planting his sharp blade into Mostro's right foot.

"Hmpt," Mostro grunted instead of screaming. He quickly swung his machete down, catching the edge of Self's shoulder blade, but that didn't stop him. Self quickly removed his blade from Mostro's foot and pushed him back while standing. He swung the blade, ready to decapitate Mostro, but the animal moved too fast. "No good," Mostro chuckled as his blade clanged against Self's blade, stopping him from slicing his neck.

Self struggled harder to turn the blade just an inch so that he could sever Mostro's artery, but the animal was much stronger than he looked. That's when the thought entered Self's mind. He had never considered it ever in his life, but this was different. Mostro would have to pay. *Run to fight another day,* a thought Self had never fathomed before ran through his mind, and that's what he did. He dropped his blade into its sheath and quickly kicked at Mostro's back, sending him lunging forward.

"Get him," Mostro ordered struggling to get his footing.

A wide-eyed, balding soldier lifted his handgun, turned to a fleeing Self and shot with precision.

Self grunted as the back of his vest was peppered with slugs.

"*Cabo! Dejar!*" Mostro yelled to get out, but the soldier didn't have the experience that Mostro had. As Mostro hobbled out the house, the soldier had something to prove. and rushed behind Self with speed.

Self hurried into his bedroom, slammed the door behind him, and slid the deadbolt home. Immediately he heard the sound of the soldier trying to kick the door in. He had spent years of preparation and hard work for the day the Marielitos came. He was certain they would come one day, but Bobby Lee wasn't so sure. Nevertheless, they both prepared for civil war, and their militia lived for it. Now that he was in the midst of this war with old adversaries, he knew what to do.

He stumbled to his knees, quickly crawled to his walk-in closet, and then dived in. Beneath the shelves of furs, his wife's shoes in plastic containers and racks of designer clothes was a horizontal, three-inch bar. A bright yellow, cast-iron lever was installed for just this type of occasion. Self grabbed the lever with his bloody hand and pulled down hard.

The thick, steel pocket door was released, shutting him in with enough pressure to crush a man that was caught between the door.

"Beep...beep...beep," a faint alarm and slow strobe light flashed, telling whomever flipped the alarm that in ten seconds all the artillery around his property was armed and ready to go. Like skilled hunters, Self and his brothers had designed his panic room, so on such occasion, he could protect his family. Now that he was all alone, the room would protect him, but he was losing blood fast.

Like rice farmers in the orient, Bobby Lee and Self planted one hundred and twenty 12-gage shotgun shells with chargers an inch underground, making a perimeter that circled both their homes. With much effort, Self rushed to the circuit to trip those chargers and detonate those shells. Once the switch was flipped, he would have an additional minute before the dynamite he and Bobby Lee had planted in the walls would explode and leave the house in rubble. Self struggled to the switch and hit it.

"*Rapido! Rapido!*" Mostro yelled to whatever Marielitos were left as he ran off the front porch.

The way Self rushed into the room alerted the cold blooded murderer that something was wrong. He was certain of two things. There was no way a warrior like Self would retreat. And if Self was anything like him, the landmines that went off earlier were just the introduction to the explosives his enemy had access to.

"Come," Mostro said to one of his soldiers, beckoning him like a father to his son. He quickly limped across the huge lawn. He had close to fifty yards before he could reach his vehicle, but he moved quickly. The soldier rushed over and Mostro grabbed the back of the man's collar, using him as a crutch. "Run. *Pronto*," he ordered.

With all his might and the help of his soldier, Mostro rushed ahead while using the man's collar like a yoke on a horse. The first of the loud popping sounds went off behind him near the front door. The ground erupted and one after the other, the shotgun slugs blasted from under the earth and into the sky, hitting every living thing that stood between them.

"*Arrgh,*" the solider groaned when he was hit.

Mostro quickly stepped to the side, pushed the soldier down on top of popping ground, and protected himself by standing on top of the man's body. The shotgun shells went off all around him, and the bodies of the Marielitos crumbled like a building demolished from an explosion.

Self only had 30 seconds before the dynamite in the walls exploded. In the opposite corner of Self's closet was a flat steel plate. He removed the plate to reveal the circular handle of a hatch that led to a tunnel under his home. He had nothing in his tank of energy left, but he turned the handle, freeing latch, and moist air rushed upward into his face. He leaned, head first into the entry of the tunnel, grabbing each rung of the steel ladder until he lost his grip.

Within 30 seconds, the sticks of dynamite would remove any trace that he ever lived there.

TWO

The blast and mushroom cloud was a hundred yards away from Bobby Lee, but it shook the earth under his feet. Bobby Lee knew it could only mean one thing. Self couldn't handle the barrage of soldiers that came his way, so he and his family went to the panic room.

"Ya hear that?" William-Larry asked, running from the front door towards Bobby Lee at the back. "Self farm done bought the farm."

"Hush," Bobby Lee ordered before putting his long range scope to his eye. Inside the sight enhancer he saw Self's house burning to the ground. Memories flashed through his head of Self and his family buying the land with Manny Black's money and building each house to Joy's specifications. He thought of the tunnels they spent close to a year building. One tunnel linked both houses. Then the thought of their training in Montana and how Self converted to Islam, but loved living with rednecks and pushing his body to its limit. Now that the farm was on fire, Bobby Lee prayed that Self and his family were safe.

Bobby Lee sighed, knowing the life they had in Georgia was over. He must have killed ten men tonight, and they were still coming. He turned to William-Larry. "Dem squirrel fuckers still coming? How many you put down?"

"Many," William-Larry said flatly, like the men who were shooting into the house weren't there.

"Rich out there hunting, huh?" Bobby Lee thought out loud. Then his impatience turned into exhaustion. He looked into his scope, shot a man dead like he was target practice and then yelled, "Andy!"

Andy came stumbling out the back room with a jar of moonshine in his clutch. "Aye, you felt the ground shake? Self let dem chargers off. Probably a slaughter up there. Wit' him being alone and all."

"Self can take on an army," Bobby Lee reminded.

"Yes, sir. Best we ever seen. Knife, stick, gun, rock. He get the job done," William-Larry chimed in.

"So, we holding out?" Andy asked his big brother.

Bobby Lee knew what had to be done. They had many drills on what to do if this day ever came. He held up his index finger and spun it around in a circle. Then he whistled loudly before yelling, "Missy!" He turned to Andy. "We bring Ms. Molly out. Take Mama to Montana. Take her home. But let the dogs out before you go." He turned to William-Larry. "Set off a flare so Rich won't get hit."

Missy rushed into the hall with two duffle bags at her feet and one strapped over her shoulder. When the men heard the thump of the bags they all looked down and then back up to Missy. She shrugged before asking, "What?"

All eyes looked down at the bags. They were not filled with the cash and ammunition that was previously prepared.

"What?" she asked again when all went silent.

Bobby Lee pointed to the bag. "*Missy*," he grumbled as a warning.

She sighed, looked out in the direction the Marielitos were coming, and said, "My shoes? I am *not*, on this God's green earth, fittin' to leave my shoes behind. Me and Joy done spent too much money for them to go up in flames. Y'all worry about the killin', and I'll carry the extra weight. Cause we leaving."

Bobby Lee knew Missy was the perfect woman for him. He kissed her and said, "Get Ms. Molly going. We tired of playing wit' deez squirrel fuckers."

"Roger that," Missy said with glee. She was able to keep her shoes and had time to join the fun. She kissed Bobby Lee's lips and then rushed off.

Andy swallowed the last of the courage in his jar and hugged his brother. "See you in the mountains. I'm taking mama down the tunnel. Let the dogs out. Kill some Cubans, and then hittin' the road to Montana, correct?"

Bobby Lee nodded.

"What about the cash?" Andy asked about the $150,000 they had in a safe in the tunnel that led to the barn twenty-five yards away.

"Willie a meet you in Montana wit' Missy," Bobby Lee ordered.

"Hell I am," William-Larry protested between firing shots.

Bobby Lee popped off a couple of rounds through the back door and then yelled to the roof, "Missy, what you waiting on?" Then he turned to his brother. "Willie, you goin'. Now get!"

"And where *you* going?"

Bobby Lee knew what had to be done. "Don't know. Me and Rich gotta see 'bout Self. Then headed to the Carolina's or maybe New York. Self's call."

"If he still around," William-Larry said and Bobby Lee shot him a look of disappointment. He shrugged and uttered, "He ain't get here yet."

From the roof Missy yelled, "Good golly Ms. Molly!"

William-Larry quickly loaded his weapon and ran to his room to gather his things and head for the tunnel. Bobby Lee reloaded and slung the duffle bags with his wife's shoes over each shoulder before heading into the kitchen where the door to the basement that led to the panic room and tunnel was located. Then he leaned his back against the wall and waited for Ms. Molly to do her work.

*****

Rich was crawling his way towards a group of soldiers until the sky lit up in a bright, white light from the family's distress flare."Damn it," he grumbled while burying his face into the ground. He was too close to the line of fire, and with that flare going off, it meant a lot of killing was about to commence. He froze until darkness was back to where it was supposed to be. Then he quickly crawled backwards until his foot hit something.

Laying in the darkness with his face buried in the ground was a young Cuban soldier scared to death. He didn't move so Rich thought he was dead, but then he knew better. In war, some soldiers are accustomed to shooting, but others don't know what to do when the prey is shooting back.

It's no fun when the rabbit gets the gun.

"*Adios, mio,*" the young soldier cried with both his arms tucked under his.

It was only a matter of minutes before Ms. Molly was going to sing. Rich quickly turned and crawled until he was lying next to the soldier like two lovers in the bed. "Open your eyes," he whispered, his lips inches from the young boy's nose.

The boy's eyes opened in shock. He was so afraid he hadn't sensed Rich come next to him.

"Your weapon. *Pistola,*" Rich sweet talked.

The boy looked down at his waist, and then handed his rifle over. Rich nudged his chin at the .45 handgun on the boy's waist and he handed that over too. Rich checked to see if it was loaded, pulled the hammer back to single action, and then shoved the barrel into the boy's eye socket.

"*Pronto.* Who sent you?"

"Mostro, general.   Primo, *Nueva York. No sey,*" the boy pleaded.

"Okay," Rich said softly. He only had a moment to spare. He pulled an arrow from his satchel while turning the boy onto his side.

"No.No. No. No," the boy begged at the sight of the arrow.

"*Shhhhh,*" Rich beckoned before slowly sliding the sharp, four headed blade into the young boy's heart. "It's okay," Rich assured as the boy grasped his last breath. He covered the boy's face with his hand while twisting the blade and then started towards the house.

*****

Ms. Molly was a Browning M2, 50 caliber machinegun, best suited to shoot anything from man to aircraft. Missy was in a canopy on the roof with Ms. Molly locked and loaded. She squeezed the trigger and the air was filled with the thunderclaps as Ms. Molly unleashed a stream of rounds at the trespassers. Bobby Lee set the chargers off. He pulled the lever for the chargers in his yard and shotgun shells exploded all around the property.

"Whooooo haaaah!" Missy yelled from the roof as she cut down the men on her and Self's property.

Bobby Lee peaked out the back window and saw bodies scattered on his lawn. The litter of ten Pit-bulls was outside savagely biting at the necks of the men Missy shot. Andy had done his job. The lawn looked like a scene in a war flick and Missy wasn't letting up.

Bobby Lee waited until he heard the "kling" of the barrel signaling that it was empty and called out, "Missy! Let's get to goin'!"

Missy met up with him at the basement door and stopped short. "Got my shoes?"

He grabbed the bags from a corner and told her, "Get."

Missy smiled, pulled a .40 Glock handgun from the small of her back and said, "You da best," before following him down into the basement where the hatch to their tunnel was open.

As they rushed down the rungs of the ladder Missy asked, "What about Self and Joy? We going to check on 'em, right?"

Bobby Lee closed the hatch above them and followed her down. "*We* sticking to the drills we done did a hundred times."

Once in the tunnel, Bobby Lee hit the switch to ignite the house. His cell phone vibrated and he put it to his ear hoping it was Self, but it was Rich. "I got it," he said after listening for a moment. He stopped short and looked down one side of the tunnel, and then the other. He pointed in the opposite side of the tunnel and ordered, "Go on ahead, Missy."

She shook her head in protest. "I'm coming with you."

He dropped the bags of shoes at her feet. "You can't. We done been over this."

She looked down at the bag of shoes, kicked it in frustration and rushed to his arms. "Bobby Lee, you know I can be of use."

He looked at his watch and then into her deep blue eyes. He spat his tobacco and took a deep breath of stale, humid air. "Woman. do as I say. Mama and dem boys needs you."

"And I need you." she said, just stating a fact.

"I'll be there. Let me and Rich get Self and Joy and we meet up. Get."

"You sure?" she double checked, never willing to defy her man.

He looked down towards the end of the tunnel where Self and Joy should have been coming from and silently prayed to see his brother's massive size and heavy beard, but no one was coming. "Go, Missy. The house is coming down. Go!"

"Let me wait here," she begged.

"Go. Call me when you on the road," he answered his lady.

Missy kissed him long and hard. "Okay. Kill 'em fo' they kill you," she pleaded before grabbing her bags. She took one last glance at him and ran down the bright tunnel.

Bobby Lee started his way down the tunnel in the opposite direction and within seconds he could feel Rich right behind him. Bobby Lee hadn't heard a single footstep. That's just how Rich was—by the time you knew he was there it was too late.

"Not sure he made it," Bobby Lee thought of Self and uttered to himself out loud. Memories of how Self had made the Atlanta news for having a major shootout with the Marielitos on a major thruway after raiding a gun store popped into Bobby Lee's mind. He had met Self after he was released on Federal parole. Self had wanted to join their militia. At first Bobby Lee thought Self was a nut, until he saw his appetite to learn and his willingness to kill anything at any time. Then Manny Black called Self, and since that was Self's brother, together they went to finish the war that Manny started resulting in Bobby Lee losing his brother Wilbur, the twin to Rich. Manny made them rich beyond their greatest expectations, but the price of war was too expensive.

"I can hear him," Rich informed Bobby Lee as they neared Self's property.

Rich rushed ahead. When Bobby Lee caught up to him, Self was lying on his back with a line of blood on the cement floor. His left ankle was dangling from the prong of the ladder.

"Get him up," Bobby Lee told his brother.

Rich kneeled and slung all of Self's 250lbs over his shoulder like it was a sack of potatoes.

"We got you brother," Bobby Lee softly told Self.

"Joy gone," Self whispered. "And my babies. Marielitos. Fucking Manny," he exclaimed before passing out.

Bobby Lee knew what had to be done. He was going to do what he should have done from the start. Clean up the mess, so it could never hurt them again.

THREE

High in the mountains of Colon, Panama laid the Black family compound. The massive house that combined three residences into one had a Spanish style tiled roof, 15 bedrooms in all, and Puncho was still building onto the property. Palm trees lined every corner of the landscape, and there was a 360 degree view of the mountains and the ocean in the distance.

Manny Black had come a long way from doing armed robberies in Brooklyn. In his lifetime he went from petty stickups, to cold blooded murder, and then he met Pantera, the East Coast leader of the Cuban gang, the Marielitos. After committing a murder for the Cuban beast, he gained much wealth, a love lost and his street empire named The M3 Boyz. They were a group of murderous kids in Harlem, led by Manny Black and his now deceased brother Rico, and enforced by the God, Self. After being fed by the Marielitos, Pantera changed the game. He wanted Manny's head on a platter because Manny fell in love with and went on to marry the woman that he raised as his daughter, but Manny and Self had another plan. With the help of his own soldier, Pantera's head ended up on a platter and the war was over—so they thought.

With every kilo of cocaine and heroin Manny Black's team sold on the streets, his money was well invested in MB Enterprises—a holding company, now worth well over 30 million dollars. At the helm was his brother, Edeeks Gonzalez. Not of relation, but a brotherhood nonetheless. For the past two years things had been quiet and Manny's life consisted of running his company, loving his girlfriend Racheal, and raising his son, Manny Jr., the young child that was initially raised by his enemy Pantera.

Four times a year Manny visited the compound that he built with his only surviving blood kin, Puncho, to relax and do absolutely nothing. This day was no different. Manny played hard and he spent that day lying out by the huge, infinity pool, overlooking the hills of South America. Lil Manny swam laps while Manny's sexy, glamorous woman lounged pool side in a bikini, reading the latest edition of Vogue. The nanny stood at the pool's ledge watching over Manny Jr., and three of the compound's staff from Panama stood around in all white uniforms of slacks and collared shirts.

Life was great and had been going well until Manny felt the vibration of his global phone against his stomach. "Speak," he answered when a number from South Carolina registered on his caller ID.

"Hey, Boss," Bobby Lee greeted in a flat unusual tone.

Heat invaded Manny from his chocolate toes and up to his crotch. "What happened?" he asked calmly while wiping his handsome face and running his hands through his pitch black curls.

"They came."

"They-*they*?" Manny asked, fearing the worse.

"Yes, sir. Dem squirrel fuckers."

"How many?"

Bobby Lee grunted then said, "Too many."

"Need me there now?"

"No. This is a heads up."

"Where's Self?"

"Not good."

Manny sighed, "Alive?"

"Both farms gone," Bobby Lee explained.

"And him?"

"Not too good."

Manny yelled into the phone, "Is he dead or alive?"

"Alive. But needs to heal."

"Put him on the phone."

"Not gonna be able to do it."

Manny's heart raced; he felt like he was ready to kill again. Self was his trust worthy brother, confidant, and the one person he knew he could rely on to look death in the eyes and win. "Can he talk?"

"Not sure if he don't want to or if he can't."

"Where's Joy and the baby?"

"Gone," Bobby Lee said before his voice cracked.

"Gone, *gone*?"

Bobby Lee swallowed hard and said, "Resting. The mama too."

"Nah, don't say that."

"Fraid so," Bobby Lee said with his voice cracking from emotion. "Can you imagine what we will have on our hands when Self comes to?"

The news blind-sided Manny like a truck hitting a pedestrian at a crosswalk. He immediately buckled and dropped to one knee. The tears overruled his anger. He clutched the phone tightly until his knuckles whitened. "*Nooooo*," he cried. Because of his participation in crime, he lost a brother, a son and his son's mother. Now another side of his family was dead, all because of the same old Marielitos coming back to haunt him. His world was quickly spinning out of control.

"You there?" Bobby Lee inquired.

"Hit me back," Manny mumbled before ending the call and dropping to both knees. His head was spinning, his heart was racing and he couldn't breathe.

He passed out. The news of Joy's and Eva's death was just too overwhelming. The moment he hit the floor, all heads at the pool turned his way.

"*Señor* Manny?" the nanny Macca yelled out.

Racheal looked over, dropped her magazine and rushed over to his side. "Manny!" she yelled with panic. "*Baby?*" she called out, fearing the worst. She looked over her slim shoulder at Manny's brother Puncho who was at the back of the house talking on his phone. "Puncho!" she screamed.

"What?" Puncho asked in frustration until he saw his brother lying on his side. "Manny!" he yelled before dropping the phone and rushing over.

"Manny! Manny!" Macca yelled, holding her fat, round face. The older, chubby, Columbian matriarch was a true mother to Lil Manny, and one of the most reliable people in big Manny's life.

Puncho ordered Lil Manny out of the pool and rushed over to his brother. He dropped his head close to Manny's mouth to see if he was breathing. Once he felt the slight wind leaving his brother's nostrils, he opened his palm and smacked Manny with all his might.

"Get the fuck up, bro. I need you around," Puncho begged. "Come on, man. Not like this." He smacked Manny again and said, "Come on, bro! Wake up. Wake up."

Manny's eyes fluttered and then opened. "*Que*," he asked with weakness. He raised his back off the scorching ground and looked up at his son. "What...what happened?" he asked no one in particular.

"You-you," Racheal stuttered. "You were on the phone one minute and then the next, you were slumped onto the ground."

"You okay, *hermano*," Puncho asked with much concern.

"Back up," Macca demanded. "Give him air."

Manny stood, but the place was still spinning.

"Get him something to drink," Macca said to the Panamanian staff that was right there, ready to serve.

Manny stared at his little brother, who looked very much like him, except for a longer face and glasses. *No,* he thought while remembering his brother Rico, whom Manny's ex-assassin wife killed. Then he thought of the way Puncho had built their Panamanian businesses, which included a private jet chartering business, a host of real estate, and a chewing gum factory in just a matter of years. Then he thought of the massacre of his Georgia family and instantly started snapping his fingers.

"Tell Macca to get Lil Manny," he ordered Racheal. To Puncho he said, "Get us a plane ready. We leaving now."

"Now?" Racheal asked over her shoulder as she walked away.

"Now! Now-now-now!" he yelled.

"Why?" she asked, more out of concern than defiance. She had a way of putting up a protest and instantly wearing Manny down to see things her way, but it was clear that today was not the day for that.

"We just gotta go," he answered with his voice cracking.

"Are you okay?" she asked.

"Ju okay?" Macca chimed in who was now helping Lil Manny get out of the pool, and opening a huge beach towel so he could dry himself off.

"What's up, *hermano?*" Puncho whispered when he was out of earshot of Racheal and Macca.

"They killed Joy, and her mother. And the babies," Manny regretfully explained.

"Marielitos?" he asked.

Manny nodded, and then looked away at his son.

"Whoa, whoa, big bro. Why you leaving? You need to be *staying.*"

"Gotta get home."

"So you moving *to* the drama? *Right,*" Puncho answered sarcastically.

"What the fuck you want me to do?" Manny yelled.

Racheal with her cellphone to her ear asked Manny, "Why are we cutting our vacation short?"

Manny locked eyes with Puncho and then looked over to Racheal. "Business," he lied.

She smirked and said, "I'm on the phone with New York, and as the vice president of the company, I get updates on the hour, so you have to come better than that, Manny. Everything with business is well. Who were you on the phone with before you took your spill? You were crying, Manny. And we're not doing *that* bad with business."

Some things were not Racheal's business. Although she found out about Manny's criminal background from an obsessed detective named Baylor who was determined to put him away for the homicide of a snitch, Manny never pillow talked and most things were not for her to know.

Manny grabbed his son, held him tight and told Racheal, "Other business. We have to go. Pack so we can leave now." She walked away and he then looked over to Puncho and asked, "Is the plane ready? And can you get the driver over here to take us to the airport?"

Puncho nodded. Because of him, the Black family had a charter plane service. He hatched the plan to Manny many years ago when money was flowing and he hadn't turned back since. The business had struggled terribly in the beginning, but Puncho believed in his vision and pressed on. Now that they were the premiere chartering service in Panama, diplomats and wealthy executives called Puncho when they needed a private plane. He walked away from his brother and put his phone to his ear.

Manny was distracted by thoughts of Joy and Self until Puncho said, "Cubans? *Where*?"

"What?" Manny asked while Puncho talked to someone on the other line. "You say Cubans?"

Puncho signaled Manny to wait. "Now?" he said into the phone. "No. Wait."

"*Que paso*?" Manny asked, annoyed.

Puncho frantically searched through contacts in his phone. "Cuban's," he said with panic. "At the airport. Just flew in from Miami. Three of them. They want to meet with me personally. They like the service they said and want to discuss future business."

"Marielitos. Here? *Fuck*!" Manny stomped the concrete.

Puncho nodded rapidly. "Yes. Fucked. They about to get fucked if they came to play with me."

Manny doubted his lil brother could shoot a man like he had done so many times before. "Who you calling?"

Puncho licked his lips, nodded rapidly again and answered, "Chango. I'm calling Chango. And the *policia*."

"Police?" Manny asked with disgust. "We don't fuck with police."

Puncho beat his chest and yelled, "*My* police! I'm not a kid, Manny. That's the last time I'm going to tell you that." He spoke into the phone while Manny waited impatiently. When he was done, he looked at his big brother and said, "You in Panama. *My* country. I'm going to handle this. You can ride along if you want."

Manny was not allowing another brother of his to die. He told Puncho, "Hey, Mayor of Panama. Get my guns out the pool room when you done being tough."

*****

After much argument and protest from Racheal, Manny and Puncho jumped into a customized, matte black, four-door jeep Wrangler and headed towards the airport with the excuse that they had to tie up some last minute business before they left. As they descended the mountain that held the compound, an old Chevy Impala raced up the mountain towards them. Manny quickly checked if his Sig Sauer 9mm handgun was loaded.

Puncho rested his hand on the gun. "This my people," he told his older brother.

Manny stared at the car and held his gun tighter. He was certain Puncho was not prepared to handle serious trouble. His younger brother just wasn't built that way. His brother Rico was the wild one, and Manny was wild and yet a thinker. Puncho? All brains.

When the doors to the Impala opened, a huge Panamanian stepped out from the driver's side holding an AK47 like a LA gangbanger in the movies. His round face was the color of a brown paper bag, he was in his early thirties, and his slick, black hair was three inches above his scalp and needed to be groomed. He had to be at least 300 pounds with his pants sagging, and his face was in such a grimace that it would probably hurt if he smiled.

The passenger door to the Impala opened and out stepped one of the blackest men Manny had ever set his eyes on. He was the complete opposite of the driver. Slim and trim with well-manicured dreadlocks dangling in front of his serious face. At a closer glance Manny made out two long scars on each side of his face that favored tear drops rolling from the bottom of his eyelids down to his lips. He stepped forward with a short Samurai sword in hand and then he stopped short. He stared into the sunrays and before tossing on a huge pair of designer Oakley sunshades. Then he looked up and argued in Spanish with the sun. He pointed the sharp blade at the sun and made a promise to get even.

Manny nudged his chin towards the darker man. "Who that?" Then it hit him. "*Chango*," the brothers said in unison.

"Yep," Puncho affirmed.

Manny sighed. His world was spinning out of control and the last thing he needed was someone who was just as out of control around him.

The obese driver stepped to Puncho's side and Puncho let the cool air from the AC out. "Culo," Puncho greeted the man, whose named appeared to be ass in Spanish.

The man nodded, confirming his name, but he didn't say a word.

"The Gods tell me that blood will spill today," yelled Chango from a distance. He walked over to Manny's side of the truck and tapped the closed window with his sharp blade. Manny rolled the window down halfway before Chango said in a guttural tone, "You Manny Black? Big Manny Black? *El jefe bola grande*." Chango paused, looked over his shoulder at no one but air and said, "I'm talking to de boss." Then nodded, took a bow before the invisible friend, and said, "Yes." He then turned back to Manny and said, "Your son. He belong to me. No one win. But baby safe with Chango. I go to *Nueva York*. Yankees," he said with a huge grin that revealed dark gold frames around his two front teeth.

"What are you talking about?" Manny asked, unable to comprehend.

Chango's head snapped to the side like someone called his name, but no one was there. He nodded to the invisible entity, telling it he agreed. Then he chuckled and pointed his thumb at Manny. "He no know. He will know wha' he no know." He turned his attention back to Manny and said, "Chango me Chango. Rougher than Rambo. You have son, right?"

Manny looked over to Puncho with a smirk of disappointment on his face.

"Answer the man," Puncho said, not used to giving his brother orders.

Manny shook his head in frustration. "Yeah. Manny Jr."

"I know long time," Chango said in a tone that suggested that Manny was silly for doubting him. He leaned in closer to Manny and said, "He safe with Chango. Never worry."

Manny looked down at his watch thinking that Cuban's were hunting for him and time was not working on his side. "What about going to the airport?" he asked, losing his patience with Puncho's silly friends.

"*Si*," Puncho responded and nodded at Chango and Culo. "Head back to the car and follow us. Let's see what they got waiting for us."

Puncho's friends made a dash to their car and pulled off, taking the lead. As the Impala sped from the valley below the mountain and through the city, Puncho struggled to keep up with the 100 MPH speeds.

Manny broke his silence and asked his little brother, "Where you find these clowns?"

Puncho laughed. "You need to get off this little brother shit, *hermano*. What? I'm good enough to learn from you and turn crumbs into a bakery, but not smart enough to pick good soldiers?"

Manny pointed to the car ahead and said, "This dude Chango? You serious?"

Puncho took his eyes off the road and looked over to his brother. "Tell me something bro."

Manny sighed, feeling like the entire trip was going to be a waste of time. "What's that?"

"If I introduced you to Self, or our brother Rico…God bless him…, but let's stick to Self. Your man. Your brother that you probably love more than me."

"What?"

Puncho nodded. "I know, *hermano*. I don't take it personal, but I know the way Self killed and almost died for you that you gonna love him more, so cut the bullshit." He banged against the steering wheel for emphasis. "But if you didn't know Self and the way he talk and move, and everything gotta be his way, would you think the beast was a clown or on some funny shit?"

Manny thought of his brother's words and had to admit he was right. "Okay. I get it."

Puncho smiled. "Don't doubt Chango. And I won't doubt Self."

"Say no more," Manny said in Self's fashion and began missing his brother even more. He had to get home.

Puncho raced through Panama until he reached the private airport that they built from the ground up. When he pulled up, a police car and blue passenger van were facing each other at a hanger where a small white jet was parked. On their knees were three men with their hands interlocked behind their heads and looking arrogant despite their circumstances. Two portly police officers stood over the men with pistols cocked and their eyes nervously looking down at the three submachine guns lying at their feet. At a closer look, the husky man in the middle had a blood soaked shirt on from being hit in the head with the butt of the policeman's gun.

Manny tried to get out of the truck and Puncho stopped him. "No." "My way," he said, telling Manny he was not in charge for once.

Puncho never spoke to the officers or exited the jeep. He simply nodded at the men in uniform and they nodded back, receiving his silent message. Immediately they yelled at their prisoners in Spanish before scrambling the Cubans into the passenger van.

Manny sat quietly in the passenger side of the jeep with his gun cocked, just in case. His mind was totally distracted with thoughts of Joy and the rest of Self's family dying, but he had underestimated Puncho. He had no idea that he had rubbed off on his little brother to the point where Puncho had his own goons and police officers on his payroll. And since they were following the police van into the mountains, it was certain that their captives were not going to jail.

Through the back streets and then the countryside, Puncho trailed the police van for twelve miles until they reached the top of the Panamanian mountains. When the caravan of cars came to a halt, the police opened the van's sliding door and dumped the prisoners onto their bellies. Puncho handed the officers a stack of American bills wrapped in a white handkerchief before they saluted him and drove away.

Manny stepped out the truck and kept his distance. He was going to allow Puncho to be a man. His curiosity on how his little brother would handle the situation was eating at him, so he looked on. Chango and Culo stepped out of their vehicle and begun handling the Cuban's with extra care.

"We clean the earth," Chango was talking to the sun again. "So sun give the light. We wet the land so the sun grow the food. Thank you," he said to the sun, before smiling at the men and feeding them water to wet their thirsty palates.

Manny didn't travel all those miles in a hot jeep to be polite and feed his enemies. Puncho's men couldn't handle it, so he walked over to the Cubans with the anger of Self's family dying raging through him. His blood was on fire. "Fuck the talking, fuck the water. And fuck y'all if you Cuban's are looking for me. Start talking!"

Three pairs of eyes looked Manny up from head to toe, and all three men chuckled with indifference, telling him that he was a joke. One of them, the most handsome and well dressed, shook his head. The others continued to chuckle while staring at the soil under them.

Manny drew his gun and pointed it, but two things stopped him from pulling the trigger. He was tired, and he wasn't certain that the men were even Marielitos. But what were the chances of that being a coincidence? Manny didn't believe in coincidences.

"*Hola*," Chango said as he stepped up with a smile to the well-dressed Cuban that was on his knees with his hands in cuffs. "Ju come to kill Puncho?" he asked calmly and Manny couldn't tell if Chango was totally sane or not.

The six Cuban eyes quickly moved to the right, listening to the sharp blade twirling in Chango's hand.

"Why you here?" Puncho yelled, too emotional for the task.

"You Marielitos?" Manny uttered and all eyes shot back to him.

The prisoners remained silent. A chubby one in the middle spat on the ground and looked at Manny with disdain this time.

It's them, he silently told himself.

Chango stood next to his prisoner and smiled up at the sun again. He then looked over to Manny with a full, wide grin showing all of his teeth. His head shot to the side like someone was next to him whispering in his ear. "*Noooo*," he whispered to his imaginary friend. Then he put one finger to his blackened lips. "*Shhhhh*," he quieted the voice and then started to shake his head. "He no know," he told the ether while looking over at Manny.

Chango quickly grabbed the dapper Cuban by the back of his well-groomed hair and dragged him off to the side. He shoved the man to his knees, meticulously placed his slanted blade right at the center of the man's chest and sliced in and down until his prisoner's, bloody intestines were spilling from him.

Culo rushed over, aimed his machinegun at the bloody Cuban and let a burst of shots ring into the dying man, silencing his groans. He then looked at the other two prisoners. "Who da fuck answering questions now?" he yelled.

The Cubans remained silent and stood fast with their lips sealed.

Manny walked over and put the gun in the face of a slim Cuban who was wearing a pink polo shirt. "You here to kill me and my brother?"

"Hmpt," the chubby prisoner grunted. He and Manny locked eyes and he sighed. Then he licked his parched lips and said, "*Viva! La! Marielitos!* Manny Black!" he spat on the floor and laughed at Manny and Chango.

Manny raised his pistol, but hesitated again.

The chubby Cuban continued. "We come to kill, but know we can die. Mostro, Gato and Primo lives on, and more babies are bor…"

Culo silenced the Cuban with his weapon, cutting him down with hot slugs.

Chango grabbed the face of the survivor and placed the slanted blade at the top of the prisoner's left check. Then he twisted his wrist like he was turning a key into a lock and plucked out the man's eye, sending a stream of blood all over his pink polo shirt.

"*Arghhh,*" the man yelled, rapidly squinting.

"Ju talk?" Chango asked.

The prisoner opened his mouth only to cry louder. Chango twisted the blade, plucking out his other eye, leaving two eyes sitting in the crimson dirt below, looking up at him. The prisoner quickly grew silent, accepting his fate.

"*Final!*" Chango said, telling everyone he lost his patience. He nudged his chin at Culo and backed away before Culo shot into the Cuban's head, exploding it.

Puncho turned his back to the gore. Chango walked around him with his face inches from Puncho. "*Jefe,* they no talk." He then looked over to Manny. "War, Manny," he chuckled. "You know war. But you no know dead. Chango dead."

Manny understood. Something had changed. Chango detected that Manny was defeated and Chango was right. Manny couldn't squeeze the trigger. Maybe he gotten lazy, spoiled, or just naively thought that the war would have died with Pantera. *When will it end*? He thought to himself.

Puncho took a deep breath, and then asked Manny, "You alright? Chango killed the fucker because—"

"He's loyal to you and they wasn't gonna talk regardless." Manny spat on the floor. "Too many of these motherfuckers to deal with. These motherfuckers keep multiplying. They're an army."

"Then we need to build an army," Puncho said before walking away.

Manny looked over at Culo and Chango dousing the bodies with gasoline before dropping car tires on top of their heads and lighting it.

He had Self, and Puncho had Chango. The two generals of the army they would need to defeat the Marielitos.

FOUR

When they got back to at the Black family compound, Manny was lost in his own thoughts trying to figure out if he was really ready for war and what had just happened. His business was worth more money than he could spend. He had finally made a breakthrough with his son. In the beginning it was hard for Lil Manny to make the transition of his mother dying, leaving Pantera who spoiled him rotten, and then moving into Manny's disciplined environment. Now that time had healed their wounds and with the help of Macca, Manny had finally gained Lil Manny's love and respect.

After Edeeks made Rachael vice president of his company, Manny and she had a rollercoaster ride of a relationship. It was because of her that Manny grew soft. She penetrated his vulnerabilities and pleased his sexual desires. What more could a man ask for? But they always argued. Racheal's life was a mystery. The only family member he had ever met was her sister, Ann. According to Racheal, Manny couldn't meet her parents in DC unless he was ready to make her his wife.

These thoughts were at war in Manny's head while everyone was packing to go home. He wasn't even sure if he wanted to go. He wasn't sure of anything. Even Panama wasn't safe. His wealth could move him anywhere in the world, but that would suggest leaving Self behind and that wasn't happening. It was Self that pushed him to excel in the crime world, and Self who terminated anyone that got in their way. Then when the war started, Self helped to dismantle the Marielitos while Manny eliminated all those who got closer to him, even his wife Xia.

Pantera trained her to be an assassin. Although she killed his brother Rico, and Manny killed her to save his own life, he longed for her still. Through the prison time Manny did, the attacks in and out of there that he endured, and then coming home to find Xia alive after he pumped slugs into her, he thought of her passionate love. The way they laughed together, and how she didn't sweat the petty things that the average woman does. They were cut from the same cloth and together the sky could have been the limit. In a perfect world she would be there to watch her son grow, but her world was controlled by the Marielitos, and now Manny had to make moves because of the same vicious group of killers.

*****

The G7 private jet that left Panama carried Manny, the nanny Macca, Puncho, Racheal, Culo, Chango and Lil Manny. Each person on the plane was lost in their own thoughts except two of them. Lil Manny looked at Chango and smiled. His behavior was unexplainable to everyone except Chango, who wonderfully sung old Panamanian songs to the boy. His voice was amazing and had everyone mesmerized. Since his son was happy, Manny didn't care. Based on Chango's loyalty to him and Puncho, and the murders he committed on their behalf, Manny had totally dropped his guard. The only thing that bothered him about Chango was the inner peace he himself felt in his spirit when the crazy man was around. To break off from the deadly images dancing in his head, Manny picked up the phone and called the president of his company—the man he could trust with anything.

"Yo," Manny solemnly said into the phone when Edeeks answered.

"*Fewwww*," Edeeks sighed when he heard the tone in Manny's voice. "What happened now?"

Manny quickly grew irritated. "*Hermano*, do you like to annoy me, or you picking up some bitch ways?"

"Bitch…*ways*?" Edeeks mumbled into the phone. "What is this a boss-worker conversation, or me and Manny convo? As a matter of fact…" Edeeks raised his voice, "Fuck what it is, Manny. I got bitches running around this bitch all crazy, *our* place of business; because they heard Rachael is on her way back. So forgive me if I'm a bit concerned why a multimillionaire, who has a luxurious compound that he overpaid for, is cutting his vacation with his gorgeous vice president short. Something must have happened so I'm asking what the fuck is the deal?"

"Watch your tone, *hermano*," Manny warned.

"Watch…*my*…tone…," Edeeks slowly repeated before he sarcastically asked, "What chu gonna do, Manny? Put a bullet in my head? That bully-fear shit is old and tired. So you gonna tell me what happened or we gonna stay on an international call bullshitting?"

Manny's knuckles grew white from squeezing the phone so hard. He was losing control of everything around him. He knew that he was on a secure line, otherwise he would have hung up, but that didn't stop him from unleashing his wrath on anyone that disrespected him, especially the man he made rich enough to last him a few lifetimes."Listen bro, right now *is not* the time for your disrespect. I called to tell you that I was coming back and your tone is like I work for you."

"Really, Manny?" Edeeks whined. "That's another thing that's getting old. Do I really work for *you*? You don't work *with* me. I don't answer to you unless you want to have a dick measuring contest, and your bitch, that *I* made vice president is the only one that can run this company besides me, and that's only when she ain't off putting your dick in her mouth or ass or whatever the fuck y'all do. You have no idea what it means to be caught up in your shit or the pressures that come down on me for running shit for you."

"You wanna quit, faggot?" Manny was losing his cool.

"Now I suck dick?" Edeeks barked at Manny's ultimate disrespect. "Only if you knew."

"Answer the question," Manny pressed on.

Edeeks sighed again before quietly saying, "No, Manny. But I'm done. You may have to fire me. It's probably best for us all."

The thought of Edeeks abandoning him sent Manny into a new rage. Through clinched teeth he softly said, *"Puta!* I don't need this shit. First these motherfuckers try to destroy Self, they took Joy and Eva away, and the baby, and then came down here to get rid of us and you want me to deal with your shit?"

"What-wha-*what*?" Edeeks stuttered. "Who? When? What happened?"

"The Marielitos, motherfucker," Manny whispered into the phone. "Just now."

"Awwwww," Edeeks moaned. "This shit is never gonna stop."

It was Edeeks who handled hiring lawyers and Manny's legal affairs. It was he who supported Manny while he was in prison. It was he who had to pay millions to politicians and the PBA when Cuban bodies were being found all over the city and all eyes were pointing to Manny and his M3 crew. He was an unwilling active participant in an ongoing racketeering criminal organization. Now that all the heat had been gone for years, he didn't like the thought of Manny going back to war. There were no more politicians to buy, and Edeeks's life had been too compromised for him to get involved.

"Sorry, *hermano*," he said.

"Oh, I'm your brother now?" Manny responded with sarcasm. "I had no idea."

"Yeah. Don't forget that. We landing soon," Manny sighed and then changed his tone to an exhausted one. "Can you please have two cars ready at Teterboro when we land?"

"Yeah, man. Will do," Edeeks mumbled and ended the call.

Manny put his phone away wondering what in his life did he have control of.

*****

The flames that were burning above Self and Bobby Lee's homes were like a candle burning on both sides of the stick. That candle was the tunnel, and the entrance and exit was the ends of the stick. In the middle was Bobby Lee, Rich and Self. The two blood brothers rushed to stabilize an unconscious Self, lying him down and making sure his breathing was maintained.

Rich removed the body armor and quickly checked Self's entire body. "Ankle might be broken."

"Okay," Bobby Lee said as he was scrambling to clear the tunnel. "We'll make a stint when we get to the barn, load him up and then we move."

"I can make him a cast when we get on solid ground," Rich reminded him.

"Get it done," Bobby Lee instructed. "And set everything right, cause when he comes to, he gonna be angrier than a possum tangled in a hornets' nest."

Rich squatted down over the scent of burnt wood, the crackling of fire above their heads and the temperature of the tunnel warming up. He slung Self over his shoulder, stood with the extra weight like it was nothing, and they moved. Like a bunch of kids running through terrain that they knew their entire lives, Bobby Lee and Rich dashed through the tunnel. They cut through the smoke that bellowed from their property, and kept moving until the tunnel grew colder and the noise of the fire destroying both properties subsided. They reached the rungs of the ladder that led to their barn.

"You go up first," Bobby Lee told his brother. "I'm right under giving you a boost."

The sound of a single dog barking from above let them know that the coast was clear. Andy had done his job. By the time Rich hiked up the stairs with Bobby Lee pushing up from under him so they could stop struggling with the rungs of the ladder, Self started to come to. The men climbed out from the tunnel and into the barn filled with hay, tractors, and bay for car repairs. In that bay sat a dusty Toyota Tundra pick up on 30 inch, high impact tires. The brown custom paint was the color of dust. Huge fog lights that could light up an entire field were mounted all along the top, and a tool box filled with artillery and rations sat in the extended cab.

Bobby Lee and Rich lay Self in the back and he whispered, "Mostro".

"Come on with it," Bobby Lee snapped at Self, trying to pull him out of his haze.

"Probably suffered a concussion from the fall," Rich said as he opened the back door to the pick-up truck. He reached into the back seat, flipped the bottom cushion over and removed a laptop and an object that was the size of a kite, but shaped like a five-point star.

Bobby Lee looked at what was in his brother's hand and said, "Send her up so we can hit the road." Then he patted his leg, "Bucky," he called the last, attack pit bull that Andy left behind to protect the exit hatch of the tunnel. The dog rushed over and sat, still on guard. Then he looked over to Self who was squirming around in the back of the cab. "Self!" Bobby Lee yelled. "You got a broken ankle, not a broken spirit. Get up, man!"

Self's eyes opened. He blinked slowly and then faster. His eyes opened wide and then both of his hands slowly rose to his forehead. "Cocksucker tried to kill the GOD." He sat up quickly and yelled, "Joy! And my babies!"

"Gone," Bobby Lee said as calm as a therapist while trying to hold back tears. Self's son was like his nephew and one of the joys of his life. The thought that he was gone forever, at the hands of the enemies who he should have massacred in the past, hurt like hell.

Self shook his head and then wiped his eyes. He shook his head again. "Watched this cocksucker. Name Mostro. Talk to the God like he know Self."

The sound of small propellers and a rotating engine interrupted Self's conversation and Bobby Lee's thoughts.

"The drone?" Self asked as he struggled to get out of the truck's cab.

Rich had the laptop open and the huge five point star levitated off the ground with the help of the four propellers attached to it. He tested the mobility of the small flying object, and the screen showed everyone in the barn. Instantly he used the arrows of the laptop's keyboard to move the drone and at top speed it flew out of the barn.

"Send her down the route out of here, and see if Sheriff Banks and his minions rushed to the house yet. It may take an hour before he even realizes that half the town is ablaze."

"I'm on it," Rich stated.

The small camera on the drone sent back images of dead bodies littered on the property. Rich hovered the small aircraft over the place he and his family called home and then back to Self's ranch and eventually their soon to be escape route.

"Clear," Rich reported.

Bobby Lee stepped in front of Self. "Now we got two options. Option one is us hightailing it up to Montana and starting all over, right in the heart of our militia so we know if these squirrel fuckers come for us, half of the U.S. armed forces is right next door. Option two is us holding up in N.C. until you recuperate, and then head to the apple so we can finish this once and for all."

"And those are the best options you giving him?" Rich scoffed, knowing the answer before Self said a word.

Self hopped down out of the cab and stood on one leg, hopping to get used to only using one. "Self taking the option to twist every single Cuban shit back," he growled. "Until Self tired of taking lives. And this God isn't getting tired. His name Mostro. That's all Self need."

Rich smirked at Bobby Lee, telling him that the answer was obvious.

Bobby Lee shrugged, "Can't make decisions without considering the team." Then he turned to Self and lowered himself a little so he could look up into Self's eyes. "You mad. Real angry. That don't work in war. So *you* can't make any decisions without considering the team. Over-stand that? You my brother, but strategy over strength."

Self snarled, "You make the strategy, and let Self know when Self gone lay down the strength."

Bobby Lee understood him clearly. If someone killed Missy he would launch biological warfare on an entire town just to guarantee everyone involved was dead and gone. He spat out all the tobacco in his mouth, stuffed a new wad inside and chewed. "Hmmm," he hummed while examining Self. "Okay, brother. We go to war."

*****

Alpine, New Jersey had always been a safe place for Manny Black. The grand, luxury homes and highly secure neighborhood was the rest haven to many of New York's Black elite. Just minutes across the Hudson River, Manny's Estate was the one place he felt that he could be himself. But for the first time in a long time, he arrived home and felt his house was not a home. He felt vulnerable. It wasn't far from where he lived that he ended the life of Pantera and his late wife Xia.

Everyone from the plane walked into Manny's foyer. For the newcomers their eyes searched the twelve foot ceilings, the massive chandeliers, the antique furniture and the spaciousness of Manny's dwelling.

"America," Chango uttered with pride as his eyes took in the marble floors and the gold plated silverware on the dining room table that seated fourteen comfortably.

"Land of opportunity," Culo uttered in amazement. "Ju make it here, Yo. Ju make it anywhere."

Manny was unimpressed and too distracted to pay attention to his new fans. He stripped down, rushed up and into his master suite to shower, and when he returned, Puncho and his crew were in the den waiting. Manny walked in and all three men stood.

"Where you going?" Manny asked Puncho with alarm.

Racheal walked around, singing away her nervousness and Puncho's eyes cut to her. "Hilton Times Square," he responded. He nudged his chin at the two other men. "We got two rooms there."

Manny thought of the five other bedrooms that were just growing dust. "I got plenty of room." He eyed Puncho's body language and said, "What' sup?"

Puncho squirmed, his eyes looking towards Racheal in the other room. "*Hermano*, no disrespect, but you know my vibes about her."

"Why don't you have those same vibes every time we in panama?" Manny asked in her defense.

Puncho stabbed his thumb into his chest. "Because that's the Black family compound, and my name ends with Black and me and papa built that shit."

"And this house is owned by a *Black*, and I run this shit."

"Seriously?" Puncho asked, knowing that everyone knew that Manny didn't have a clue about what was going on in his house.

He only slept there. In an effort to avoid an argument, Puncho said, "Look, *hermano.* I'm tired, and I couldn't sleep here if I tried to. So we gonna get a few hours' sleep and get with you tomorrow."

Manny sighed. He had too much on his mind to deal with Puncho's suspicious feelings about Racheal. From the very first day Puncho met her he told Manny that he didn't trust her. Most women were after something. Money, sex, security, or an easy mark to be an ATM for them for the rest of their lives. In Puncho's eyes, Racheal maneuvered her way into Manny's business, then his bed, and then his head. At times she controlled his mind and Puncho didn't like that. Women come and go, but brothers are there for life. And the one thing that always dug at Puncho was upon first meeting Racheal she didn't ask questions about the type of man Manny was. Instead she asked all the wrong questions. Everything was all business for her, and Puncho didn't like that. He didn't feel she could properly take care of his brother.

"Ok, Lil bro," Manny agreed in defeat.

On the way out the door, Chango stopped before Manny placed his open palm against Manny's heartbeat and listened intently before he started to dance from side to side like a puppet on a string. He moved to Manny's rhythm, and then smiled. He then looked over his shoulder and said to no one, "*Si.* I know-I know." Then he looked into Manny's eyes, tapped his chest and uttered, "Life. Like clock. One day it stop. No fear," Chango warned.

"Thank you," Manny said dismissively.

He led his brother outside to a Chrysler 300 that Edeeks had sent for them. He said his farewells and watched the car pull off. He turned and walked back to the house wondering what Chango was talking about.

"What the fuck?" he said as his feet froze atop the gravel in the driveway when he looked into his house.

The lights that were just on were now out. Panic set in. He didn't have a gun, baseball bat or even something to throw at an intruder if they were on the inside waiting. Instead of waiting to see what happened, he ran to get closer to his weapons and his family. He barged into the house from the side door that led to his kitchen. He rushed to Macca's quarters on the ground floor. When he burst into her room she was applying aloe to Lil Manny's sun-burned back.

"*Que paso, jefe?*" she asked her boss what was wrong.

"Umm, nothing." He winked at his son. "Love you, son," he said before closing the door and looking like a paranoid fool. He remained silent, hoping if someone was in the house they would reveal their location before he became a moving target.

Nothing moved. Then he heard a noise coming from his master suite upstairs. He walked lightly, closer to the sound, in fear of losing Racheal. He reached the top landing and cut the corner and found the culprit coming straight for him.

Racheal walked down the hall towards her man holding a bottle of Courvoisier Rose with a glass in the other hand. He glanced at her hand and let his anxiety die down, but something else about her was distracting him.

"You like it, baby?" she asked as his eyes were locked onto her silk, peach teddy. The scent of Angel perfume, mixed with her sparkling skin, plus the way she had her hair up in a bun caught all of his attention. "Here," she told him before handing him a full glass of the liquor. "You're *so* stressed," she whispered before licking the side of his neck. "You want me?"

He welcomed the affection. It was the only peace he had in his life for the moment, and if it was up to the Marielitos, it may be the very last time he would be with his woman. "Yeah," he answered.

"Sssssss," she hissed, fumbling inside of his pants. "You need me to be *nice*," she whispered, just stating a fact. She squeezed his semi-hard cock while licking the side of his face like it was her favorite flavor. When his length started to grow in her hand she encouraged him. "That's right baby. That's right. I'm gonna ride this dick and make my man feel better," she promised. Then she stopped.

She poured him another glass and put it to his lips, encouraging him to drink. Then she took a swig from the glass, poured some more and started to descend with glass in hand. Manny's eyes trailed down looking at the top of her head. She looked up at him as she placed his stiffness in the glass and stirred her drink. She then held his dripping cock in her hand and licked the sides of it, keeping her eyes locked on his.

"You like it," she teased. She deep throated him, deeply inhaled the scent in his pubic hairs, and on her exhale she slowly maneuvered her lips to tightly grip his shaft until she was at the tip. "Muah! *Awww*," she celebrated, smacking her lips.

Manny looked down and was reminded why he was addicted to her. Every slurp, smack of her lips, and the sounds of her gagging told him what he wanted to hear. She was there to please him, Mr. Manny Black. The man he was sure she wouldn't look twice at if he was still a petty thief in Panama. He grabbed the back of her head, clutching the thin tracks of her $3,000 weave, loosening her bun and choked her with his inflated cock.

"*Ughhh*," she groaned with her throat full. She repeatedly slammed her throat into his dick, making him fuck her throat at a rapid rate.

"That's right, *Mami*," He chanted. His mind was far away from the loss of Self and his family. It wasn't on the Marielitos. Nor was it on the danger that was lurking to end his life. He welcomed the wave of heavenly pleasure that traveled from head to toe. Racheal's hot mouth, the smacking noises of her lips moving and the scent of her perfume had all his senses going into overdrive.

As soon as he felt the electric pulses of an orgasm traveling up his spine, Racheal stopped. She stood while pulling on his full erection and asked, "You love me, right?" Manny's sleepy eyes closed and he nodded rapidly. She stroked his tip. "We're not in danger are we?" she whispered before planting sweet kisses on his earlobe.

"Nah, come on, Mami."

She knew when he was lying. She clawed at his chest, slowly turned her back to him and slid his stiffness towards her ass. With the finesse of a professional stripper at a world famous club, she bent over and made her butt cheeks move up and down while holding his stiffness between them. Then she put his tip by her asshole and rubbed his cock up and down her wet slit. She slid his tip into her wet hole and grabbed the back of her ankles, bracing for the painful pleasure that was on the way.

He plunged himself deep inside of her, grabbed her hips, and pulled her body into him, meeting his flesh with hers.

"Um. Um," she grunted. "Whoa," her voice trembled. "*Arghhhh*, Manny!" she bawled when he started bucking hard into her center. "Fuck me, *Papi*," she panted. And that's what he did.

Manny slid himself into her wet fold, sinking deeper. Faster. Deeper. Pushing away all his pain with each pleasurable stroke. He fed her well, and when his orgasm knocked that it was coming, Racheal was right in tune.

"Shit!" she cried. "I'm cumming, Manny. *Ohhh…yes!* Sprinkle this pussy with your cum," she grunted through clinched teeth while humping back into his thrust.

He couldn't take it anymore. It was too good. He exploded into his woman like he always had, feeling the pleasures of life unfold with the stars that were bursting behind his eyelids. When the last drops of his wakefulness were released, his eyelids became heavy. Racheal pulled his pants up and grabbed his hand with the tenderness of escorting a child to bed the night before school.

"Come on, *Papi*," she said softly, escorting him to their bedroom.

Exhaustion settled in when Manny's head touched the down pillows. He had no idea how long he would be able to sleep. Life had a way of always throwing death at his door. Now that he was about to sleep, he silently prayed that his eyes would open for many days to come.

*****

By the time Manny's eyes were closed for the night, Racheal's phone began to vibrate. She sent the call to voicemail, and cut her eyes to Manny to see if he stirred awake. She then removed herself from the giant canopy bed, covered her naked body with a flowing, scarlet silk robe that shielded her from the breeze of the August night, and quickly moved from the room to the hall where she fumbled with her phone.

"Where are you?" she whispered, heading for the front door. The caller answered and Racheal uttered, "Damn." She quickly headed to the kitchen and disarmed the security system before opening the side door to let the visitor in.

"Hmpt," the visitor grunted with disapproval when she looked down at Racheal's attire.

"Ann, don't start your shit," Racheal warned in hush tones.

At MB Enterprises Ann was introduced as Racheal's sister and was hired as a finance executive. With her lanky frame, chocolate skin, and a giant mole on her cheek, she looked nothing like her sister. At the time Manny had just terminated a Cuban employee, due to his paranoia. Racheal had recommended Ann, and he hired her on the spot. Manny had taken one look at her short hairdo and masculine presence and knew she was nothing to play with. Since then, Ann had done all she could to have full control of Manny's financial information. She was hired as his personal assistant, and with Racheal's help she quickly moved up the ranks. As an executive she had managed to cut the fat in the finance department down to three employees, all whom were handpicked by her. What no one else knew was that she and Racheal had other plans for MB Enterprises, and a personal relationship that would keep their bond tight for life.

"When did you guys fly in, and what happened in Panama? I just flew in from Virginia," Ann said, with her eyes darting all over Racheal's body.

Racheal saw her gaze and immediately relaxed. "Not sure. He received a call, and then he just passed out. It was the strangest thing. I knew it was bad news because he turned white. And he looked like he wanted to cry. I'm sure I saw a tear fall."

"Did you see something that showed that he has some type of problem?" Ann inquired.

Racheal shrugged. "I never saw him afraid before, and *I know* Manny was really alarmed. Then, then he rushed us to pack so we could get out of there and lied that everything was okay. He left Lil Manny and I at the compound with the staff while he was gone for a few hours. We had a couple of sociopaths fly back with us too, so I know there's trouble in paradise."

Ann gripped her chin with her index finger and thumb. She twisted her lips into a smirk while staring at the marble floor. "Hmmmm," she hummed. Then she eyed Racheal's robe and nakedness again and asked, "Are you staying focused on our agenda?"

Racheal looked out the window at the full moon. "Of course," she answered, but Ann wasn't satisfied.

"What's in his head, baby? Did he look for more property like he wanted to move over there? Where's he most vulnerable now? What's changed?"

Racheal looked back out the window and then down to the tile that favored a huge chessboard. "I'm his vulnerability," she answered. "The only thing I know of and no. He has no plans of moving. They have a big ass compound out there. I sent you the pictures. He's staying right here."

"This is coming to an end very quickly. You ready for that? Your head still in the game, because I know where all the money came, went and where it is right this second. I made an app for my phone that tells me when the money moves." Ann leaned forward. "So again, is your head in the game and are we going to be able to meet our agenda and end all this?"

Racheal nodded. She found refuge in the marble floor again.

"Come here," Ann ordered.

Racheal quickly obeyed and softly tiptoed her way to the breakfast nook where Ann sat behind an octagon table. Ann looked up at Racheal's eyes and then down at her feet before licking her lips and softly whispering, "Come closer, baby," She guided Racheal to the table and eased her butt on top of it.

"You crazy," Racheal whispered apprehensively, worried that Manny would walk in the kitchen at any moment.

Ann slid her hand inside of Racheal's robe and began to softly caress her leg. "You're sure you're staying focused on what's *really* important?" she asked when Racheal hesitated.

Racheal grew limp to the seduction. "*Yes*," she gasped, as Ann opened her legs and sat between them.

"He did this to you before, right?" Ann asked, pushing Racheal's chest down until her back was comfortable on the table.

"Don't go there," Racheal begged, weakened by memories of when she had first made love to Manny in her Brooklyn apartment, and he had indeed spread her open on the table and feasted between her legs.

"Yes," Ann said and softly tapped at Racheal's clit. "I *will* go *there*. Right…in…here," she mumbled while her finger slid between Racheal's lubricated folds and curved upward to her G-spot."

"Oh shit," Rachael moaned.

"That's right, baby," Ann chanted, licking the sides of her legs and working her way to Racheal's center. "That's right."

Like she had done many times before, Ann sucked at Racheal's pubic hairs and licked her finger every time she withdrew it from Racheal's wet heat.

"Aye," Racheal whimpered. "*Whoa…whoa…I—I. Eeeeeeee,*" she squealed when Ann licked her clit softly while pulling at her G-spot with her middle finger. The more Racheal squirmed and grabbed at Ann's hand, the more Ann sucked on her clit, teased the lips, and softly plunged her tongue deep, then inched it out of her secret lover.

For Racheal, this was nothing new. Long before there was an MB Enterprise, she and Ann were teenage lovers. Manny Black and his enterprise was just another mission, another way to pay the bills and meet their agenda.

"Suck it," Racheal whispered as her legs began tremble. "*Ohhhhh*, you make me cum…so…*haaaaaard*," she bawled before grabbing Ann's head and cumming harder than any man would ever make her.

"Feed me," Ann begged before slurping hard at Racheal's love hole, drinking all that squirted into her mouth.

"Racheal!" Manny yelled from the bedroom.

Racheal jumped off the table like it was on fire. Ann sat back and relaxed, chuckling softly.

"Here. Down here," she said, quickly moving as far away from Ann as possible while fixing her robe.

Manny walked into the kitchen barefooted in a black robe and a sub-machine gun in hand. "Oh," he said when he discovered Racheal on the other side of the marble island. He looked over to Ann. "Oh, what's up sis?" Then his eyes shot up to the ceiling. "Why y'all in the dark?"

Racheal looked over to Manny with guilt all over her face and then she looked over to Ann for an answer.

Ann calmly folded her legs and leaned back a little further before looking Manny directly in the eyes. "Oh, no reason. Guess we just got caught up in girl talk. I didn't even notice." She nudged her chin at his weapon and said, "Were you expecting an army?"

Manny squinted at Ann, looking intensely at her. There was no way she could have known that an army of men stormed Self's farm, so he quickly dismissed her inquiry. He let the gun drop to the side of his leg and said, "Nope, I just get crazy when my baby's not lying next to me, that all."

"Awwww," Ann said affectionately. "You two are a solid couple. I just love it."

Manny smiled, and then shot Racheal a look that told her to hurry up. "See you later, Ann," he yawned. "I'm going back to bed."

Ann stood during Manny's departure. She walked over and planted her palm on Racheal's ass and whispered, "Make sure you stay focused. You still on birth control, right?" Racheal looked away and nodded. Ann headed to the back door and whispered, "See you at the office, baby." She blew Racheal a kiss. "Find out what you can. *Viva la Marielitos*," she bragged and walked out the door, laughing.

Ann's last words shook Racheal back to reality. She had to stay focused. There were too many stages of their plan left for her head not to be in the game. She just had to figure out how to explain being two months pregnant.

FIVE

The following morning Manny walked into MB Enterprises with his son, Racheal, Puncho, Chango and Culo in tow. The Lincoln Building at 37th Street and 7th Avenue was home to Manny's headquarters. The towering building held tenants as important as the U.S. Federal Government, foreign ambassadors, and lawyers that represented the residents of New York City.

"Whoa, Mr. Black," said Larry the security guard. The ex-marine who wore a tapered crew-cut at all times, and whose chest could stop a Mack truck, towered over Manny and his entourage. "You have the whole family today, huh?" Larry had a delayed gaze at Chango, who wore a camouflage suit and boots and was busy talking to himself. Then he recognized Puncho. "Puncho, my man," he said with familiarity. He opened his huge arms like he wanted to hug the entire crowd, and then said, "Okay, everyone follow me."

Manny chuckled at Larry's antics. He wasn't the head of the heavily armed security men who sat behind thick bombproof glass. He was only head of security for MB Enterprises, and had proved his loyalty to Manny in the past.

When the entourage exited the elevator, a chorus of "Good morning, Mr. Black," begun then there was a pause of silence. It took a moment before everyone realized that Racheal was in tow. Everyone greeted her, and then many of the employees rushed her with their hands filled with papers.

"Okay! Okay!" Racheal said to calm the small crowd gathering. She didn't bother to tell anyone from the entourage goodbye or even notice that they had all walked into the office together. She was like a racehorse at the gate. As soon as the chime to the elevator rang and the doors opened, she was off, racing to snatch, grab, and sign papers that multiplied during her absence.

Puncho looked at the small commotion that unfolded and leaned in closer to Manny. "Who runs this company again?" he teased. "And if she does this when it comes to your money, I'm supposed to believe she don't run shit in your crib?"

Manny stared into his brother's eyes, smirked to allow his silence to say all he needed to say, and then he walked away, heading to his office.

Standing in the atrium of MB Enterprises and stopping Manny in his tracks was a tall African woman with chalk white teeth and a mocha, oval face. Her head was shaved clean at the sides and down the center were big, burgundy box braids that flowed down to her small butt. As Manny grew closer, her gleaming white smile grew wider. "Top of the morning, Mr. Black," she greeted with her British accent.

"Nzinga," Manny said before kissing both her cheeks. Every time Manny looked into her eyes he got caught up in her beauty. If she wasn't already Edeeks's mistress, Manny probably would have made her his wife. She doted on him like she was his mother anyway.

She reached up to adjust his Hermes tie, and then patted the lapels to his Savile Row suit. "Has either Lord Manny or yourself eaten breakfast?" She asked with a smile.

Manny looked away and knew what was coming next.

"Fine then," she said, knowing her boss like the back of her hand. "I'll have crumpets, porridge and a spot of tea delivered to your desk, sir."

"Good! Good, you do just that," a tiny voice that was behind Nzinga said with a firm tone.

Nzinga turned around as a short, Asian woman that looked like she just stepped off a high fashion runway stepped forward with a stack of folders.

"What's up, Toki?" Manny asked his office manager.

She did an annoyed smirk and then answered, "Cash for Gold! You want storefronts splattered across the United States, yet you're nowhere to be found? *Really*, Manny? Who does that?" she complained and Manny knew then that he was back in his office for sure.

"What do you need me to do?" he asked Toki.

She looked around to see if Racheal was near and said, "Leave me in charge when you and the Mrs. decide to disappear. Then we can really get some things done around here."

"I'll keep that in mind," he answered before making a left towards his office and stopping short.

"Hey ah, Manny," a deep baritone voice came from behind him, and he knew Larry wanted to talk.

Manny turned to find Larry standing there, checking the perimeter with his eyes and probably silently begging someone to get out of line. Larry was an adventure junkie with military

54

connections up the whazoo. He had became friends with Manny after revealing to Manny that he knew about his entire life, time in prison and his war with the Cubans. From that day on, Larry had been dying to get in on the Marielito action.

They stepped out of earshot of Manny's entourage and Larry asked, "So how bad is it?"

Manny often wondered how Larry could tell when something was wrong. "What makes you feel something is wrong?"

Larry sighed for patience. Manny was insulting his special forces training. "Okay," he breathed out, calling upon himself for more patience. "You go to Panama, a semi-hostile nation, for vacation, of all things. Then you cut it short. Little Manny is in tow instead of with the nanny, Puncho is here looking as nervous as a Catholic priest in a day care, and you show up with these two other fellows who…one ain't too right in the head, but he's seen some action, maybe even put a few men down." He took a deep breath. "Now tell me, do I have to get armed to the teeth cause Castro's boys may be coming back to town?"

Manny thought about his past and the future he wanted. Larry knew about the last war, so what was the sense of hiding anything? He took his own deep breath, looked Larry in the eyes and said, "The Cuban's can always try to come, but this time, they may already be here."

Larry tapped the .357 auto-magnum on his waist and said, "Well now we talking. We are now in alert code red," he said with pride and walked off like he was ready to frisk the whole building.

Manny stepped away, feeling safer, and now that he was at the office, he hoped he could get some work done. He was just about to cut the corner to his office when he heard someone calling his name. He immediately cringed at the sound.

"Boss! Ohhh Boss," Edeeks joked from down the hall.

It was Edeeks who was actually the boss of MB Enterprises. In the beginning, Manny had the great ideas, but as an MBA grad, Edeeks had the business sense. Manny invested his money from crime into various businesses that he and Edeeks founded, and while he was busy hunting and being hunted by the Marielitos, Edeeks was forming corporations that ended up making them more money than they had ever imagined. Without Edeeks' business sense, and his knack for selecting a proficient workforce, Manny's visions would have never materialized.

"Boss! Boss!" Edeeks was persistent.

"Yo!" Manny snapped back, annoyed.

Edeeks was always fluctuating in weight, depending on how things were going with his wife. Since he wasn't able to keep his dick in his pants, his marriage was on the outs again and he was eating down the house. When his weight was down he could easily pass for the twin to actor Andy Garcia, but the way he had gained the pounds, he looked more like a tub of Cherry Garcia.

"*Yo?*" he asked Manny with sarcasm. "This is MB Enterprises! A place of corporate business, worth over thirty million dollars and the founder is addressing me with 'Yo'?"

Even Chango quickly grew annoyed at Edeeks and stepped forward. He stood next to Edeeks, sniffed him like a dog checking out a new person and looked him in the eye. "Ju got business with *El jefe?*" he said, intimidating Edeeks.

Edeeks turned beet red and quickly stepped back. "Ah...Manny?" Edeeks said, while pulling his head back and twisting his face like he smelled something rotten, but Chango stepped closer. "Manny! I need to talk to you," Edeeks pleaded as Manny ignored him and cut the corner, heading into his office.

After cutting the corner, Puncho walked into Manny's massive office space first. The office was the size of a large loft. The wide open space was filled with a massive glass and chrome desk on one side of the room, and the other held an entire lounge set with an 80" TV against the wall. In the back was a walk-in closet, full bathroom, sauna and smoking room for his occasional cigar.

Manny walked over to his desk, Chango and Puncho gravitated towards the TV, and Culo stood in amazement, wondering how his whole family could live comfortably in Manny's office.

"Can you dig it, Yo?" Culo said extremely loud. "Can—you—dig it?"

"Yes," Chango chuckled. "It's dug."

Culo waved his hands over his head, spun around and said, "Manny. I want to be you when I grow up, Yo."

Manny was growing tired of Puncho's crazy friends, but he gave Culo a thumbs up, hoping that would quiet him.

While everyone was off into their own worlds, there was a tap at the door. All heads turned to the entrance as Edeeks slowly cracked the door open and stuck his head in.

"Mind if I come in?" he asked Chango instead of the owner of the office.

Chango winked at him and nodded that it was okay.

Edeeks stutter stepped inside and stood at the entrance with fright on his face. "Ah, can I come in?" he asked louder, directing his question at Manny, but staring at Chango and Culo.

Manny plopped down in his seat and barked, "Stop fucking playing."

Edeeks quickly slid into one of the two chairs that were parked in front of Manny's desk. "So…ah…um, what's going on now?"

Manny quickly stood. "That reminds me." He pointed to Puncho, snapped his fingers and whispered, "Close the door." After his little brother followed his order, Manny walked up to the television, grabbed the left corner and pulled it forward.

"O-yeh. Good Morning America," Chango complained that he was watching the show after Manny swiveled the television away from his line of vision.

"Oh boy," Edeeks grunted, really annoyed now. If Manny was moving the TV it only meant one thing.

Puncho walked over to Manny with his neck twisted to the side, eager to see what his brother was doing. It was brilliant, and he wasn't surprised to see that Manny had a hidden mahogany panel behind the wall beneath the brackets that held the TV. When Manny opened the wooden, trap door, it revealed four deep drawers that disappeared into the wall. The entire drawer held an arsenal of weapons. Manny quickly removed two Glock, 10mm-fully automatic handguns with extended clips.

"God bless America," Chango celebrated after he stood next to Manny and slid his hands around the handle of a Mac 11 sub-machine gun. He quickly gathered up three extra clips. Manny looked at Chango with a smirk. Chango shrugged, not wanting to be left out of the party. "Since I'm here, *Jefe*," he said to Manny before he scooped up a .357 revolver and quickly tucked it into his waist.

"Manny, we need to talk," Edeeks said with nervousness.

Manny ignored him.

Culo walked over, examined the arsenal of handguns and sighed with disappointment. "AK, Yo. I need a AK-forty-seven, Manny."

Manny stared into his eyes with scorn, wondering if Culo thought he could just call up a delivery person to drop off a major assault rifle.

"*Hermanooooo*, we need to talk," Edeeks said more firmly.

Manny looked over to Edeeks and patted his waist to make sure his weapons were tucked away neatly. "What's up?" Manny snapped.

"Business!" Edeeks snapped back with authority.

Chango looked over at Edeeks, put one finger to his black lips and whispered, "*Shhhhhhh.*"

Edeeks fidgeted in his seat and made sure he no longer made eye contact with Chango.

Puncho grabbed a Sig-Sauer .9mm handgun and Manny looked at him and asked, "You know what you doing?"

He nudged his chin at Chango and Culo and asked, "You still doubting me?"

Manny turned his attention to Edeeks. "What's up?"

Edeeks stood. "When you ready to talk, come to my office."

Puncho felt the vibes coming from Edeeks and walked over to Manny. "Yo, *hermano*, these guys want to go sight-seeing. We out. Call me the minute you need me or you hear something. We gonna start at Yankee stadium."

"You sure?" he asked, still being the protective big brother.

"Look at these guys," Puncho bragged about Chango and Culo. "What I got to worry about? Just call me if you need me."

Manny no longer felt vulnerable. Once he was in the office he was certain he was in the safest place on earth.

After side stepping all the employees that wanted his time, Manny walked into Edeeks' office wondering what the urgency was about. He did not want to hear another speech from Edeeks telling him to run away from the Marielitos. He stepped into the office and found Edeeks standing over his desk looking down at a ledger full of numbers. "What's up?" he asked before sitting.

Edeeks looked down at Manny and shook his head in disappointment. "What happened to the Manuel Oil Project?"

Manny thought about the oil rig and drilling operation that he was financing off the coast of Louisiana. It had taken months to seal the deal, and big check after big check went to the management, licenses and certifications of the rig, but Manny had gotten so caught up with everything else that he hadn't been on his job concerning the business.

"Why? What's up?"

"What's up?" Edeeks asked sarcastically. "That business just killed our profits this year. Either you're retarded, or just don't give a fuck about pissing away millions."

"Watch your fucking mouth."

"We talking seven million fucking dollars, Manny!"

The pounding in his head started to beat through his skull. "What the fuck are you talking about?"

Edeeks repeatedly raked his fingers through his hair. "I'm talking about this company being a joke. This shit had to be a fluke. We made millions too easy. We're in over our heads because I can't keep doing this."

"Doing what? What, E?"

Edeeks plopped down in his chair and sighed. He was exhausted. The loss of seven million proved that Manny was not a great businessman. He had great ideas, but Edeeks was overworked and it just didn't make sense to him anymore.

"Do you know what it's like to be holding your interest together, Manny? Only *you* can up and leave his business and responsibilities for an entire month because you know Edeeks will take care of it. Think about it. Your money, your business, your commissary account when you're in jail? The commissary accounts of your soldiers still in jail, their families, your family, your homes, your..."

Manny's temper couldn't be contained. "You want to quit! Good, take your half and I'll run this shit myself!"

That made Edeeks head snap to Manny. Then all his anger died. The thought of Manny running the company meant they'd be broke for sure. Edeeks started to laugh. He laughed so hysterically that Manny had to wonder if he was being punked or if there was some kind of inside joke going on. Then Edeeks started to cry. Vicious sobs shook his heavy frame.

"What the fuck is this?" Manny uttered, and then looked around Edeeks' massive office, waiting for the surprise cameras to come out.

"What's this, Manny?" Edeeks questioned between sobs. "This is a mess. This is love, Manny. The shit you feel you're entitled to." He shook his head while tears dripped on top of the ledger. "Nope. *No mas.*" He quickly wiped away his tears, took a deep breath, and on the exhale he asked, "You know the type of pressure I'm under? Because of you?"

"Fuck all that!" Manny wasn't trying to hear it. He stood, dialed Ann's number and when she picked up he barked, "Get in Edeeks office. *Now!*"

Within minutes Ann waltzed into Edeeks office with a stack of folders in hand. Surety was etched into her face and confidence in her strut. She looked Manny in his eyes and asked, "I take it that this is about the Manuel Oil Project?"

"So you know what I called you for, huh?" Manny snapped.

Ann sighed before saying, "Yes, the same project that I've been chasing you around about for the last few months. Said project for which you asked me to violate company policy—the policy that you created and reprimanded others about—and sent off checks for contractors, drillers and speculators without the right approval or inspections. *That* company, right?"

"That same exact company," Edeeks chimed in while pulling himself together.

Ann grunted and then followed with, "The same exact company that I sent you text, emails and followed up with your vice president about?"

"I was busy," Manny mumbled.

"Ha," Edeeks disagreed.

Manny knew he was out-numbered. "So when I'm out handling business, this is the shit that goes down?"

"You weren't available," Ann said.

"Handling business? What business, Manny?" Edeeks wanted to know.

Manny didn't have an answer. He was usually out trying to come up with new ideas, working on a project or slacking off with Racheal at his side for weeks at a time. In his defense he said, "*My* business. The shit that made MB Enterprises."

"Ack hm," Ann cleared her throat.

"*Really?*" Edeeks asked.

His private business was only for Edeeks. He didn't mind the disrespect from Edeeks, but from Ann it wouldn't be tolerated. "You know me?" he said to her.

She stared him in the eyes and said, "Very well. Better than you know."

Manny squinted. If she was a man, he would have hit her in the mouth for the tone she used. He nodded. "Good. You can clear out your desk and leave all the documents on my desk. Just because I'm with your sister doesn't give you a pass."

"You can't be serious," Ann stated.

"Yo, what you doing?" Edeeks yelled out.

"I got this," Manny lied.

Ann crossed her arms. With no fear she asked, "Are you certain you want to make an irrational move like this?"

He knew for certain that he was going to regret the decision, but there was just too much going on in his life, and Ann felt that she was in charge, and if everyone felt like he was the one slacking, he needed to set an example. "I said what I said. Clear it out."

She looked at him with indifference and asked, "So I'm fired?"

Manny nodded.

She shrugged "In that case, go fuck yourself, Manny Black. You couldn't do half of what I do in your best year. So, good luck. Fuck you again, and please don't ask me to come back." She spun off and then stopped short. "And Manny. When shit hits the fan, don't beg me to help you."

"Don't threaten me," he yelled, too loud for his own liking.

She turned all the way around and put both hands on her hips. "Or what, Manny Black, you fucking degenerate?"

Edeeks shot out of his seat. Ann didn't know how violent Manny could get. Edeeks wrapped his arm around her shoulder and said, "Ann I'll fix this."

She laughed. "Some things can't be fixed or taken back, Edeeks. Good luck, for now," she chuckled while walking out.

"What the fuck is that supposed to mean?" Manny snapped.

After letting Ann out, Edeeks closed the door. He turned and, rested his back against the door while folding his hands under his butt. "It just gets worst with you."

Manny had enough. He stood and made his way towards Edeeks. "*Man*, do what the fuck you gotta do. I got bigger problems."

Edeeks nodded repeatedly while stepping out of Manny's way. "Yes. You do," was all he said as Manny walked out the door.

*****

Racheal's office was a mini replica of Manny's. The only difference was she had no spa and her massive corner office was decorated in beige, peach and cinnamon pastels. The double doors opened to peach carpet that led to a massive circular glass desk that sat on an elevated platform at the end of the room. This was her throne. Her high desk allowed her to look six inches down on all visitors. She insisted that her modern office furniture, the drapes and location of the two chairs in front of it be placed the exact way the president of the United States sat in his oval office. She even had a tall American flag in the corner to intimidate her male business associates. As she sat at her desk trying to make sense of the mountain of computer files in her cue, Ann burst into her office without knocking, and then quickly closed the door behind her.

"This asshole just fired me!" she announced to Racheal.

"Who?"

Ann smirked at how clueless Racheal could be at times and said, "Are you serious right now? Who else? *Manny!*"

"*What?*" Racheal was flabbergasted.

Ann walked over and sat on the beige lounge chair that sat against the wall. She refused to sit in front of Racheal's desk and look up at her, so she patted the seat next to her. "Can you come over her please, your highness? This shit has to go down today."

"Why?" Racheal asked without moving from her computer.

Ann slammed her hand against the pillow and said, "Not today. We need to move the money *today*." When Racheal didn't move she asked, "Do I have to snatch you by your weave to get your ass over here?"

Racheal's head snapped towards Ann as she stood. She stepped down off her throne and walked over to the couch and had a seat, lady like and proper. "What did he do? And what did you do that caused him to just want to up and fire you?"

Ann's eyes narrowed, "You're not taking this degenerate's side are you? You gettin' shit twisted?"

Racheal squirmed in her seat before answering. "No. Something had to happen for him to fire you. He has no clue on what's happening in the finance department and neither does anyone else besides me and Edeeks."

"Well I hope your boyfriend's head is in the game too."

"Don't call him that," Racheal snapped. "His head is where it always is."

"On pussy!" Ann confirmed.

"Where we need it to be so he can be clueless and we can get our agenda met."

Ann smiled and clapped her hands. "Great. Glad to see you're focused, but I need phase one to be sped up today."

"What's the rush?"

"He just fired me! Are you deaf or not paying attention? I won't be there to make the transfers for the other three phases."

"And it will take him months to figure out where everything went and is going and he still won't be able to understand it."

Her explanation wasn't good enough for Ann. "So what happens if that bitch Toki takes my place? She's been clocking my position since day one. Or what if Manny trips and a bullet goes into his head?"

"We already have a contingency for that, but you're right."

"So now what? Do you see why we need to do this today?"

Racheal nodded. "If something happens to Manny, Edeeks will control everything anyway, but he needs to get that in writing."

"And you can take care of him, for sure?"

Racheal smirked like she should never be doubted. "He can't move in this company without double checking with me." She stood, adjusted her skirt and asked, "Why not kill one phase, speed things up and just do two phases for the same amount. Today?"

Ann bit her bottom lip and said, "Then we need to spend half the day covering our tracks and part of the night. How you going to explain your absence to Manny? And be careful of greed, we still have the others to answer to."

"Yeah, the others," Racheal huffed.

Racheal got lost in her thoughts for a moment. "Get all your files and take the two laptops. Meet me at the parking garage in a half hour. I'll take care of Manny and we'll head to the house to handle business."

"You want me in this man's home, who just fired me?" she asked like Racheal had lost her mind.

Racheal nodded again. "Let me take care of Manny. Just meet me there in the garage in a half hour."

Ann stood and kissed Racheal on her cheek, "Sometimes I think you get off on this shit."

As Ann walked out the door Racheal answered, "I do."

*****

Nothing was going right for Manny. He was on shaky ground and didn't care or even know how to make his life fall back into place. There was nowhere to run away from his responsibilities and the only place that was safe from the Marielitos was his office, and even in there he was being attacked. As soon as he flopped down into the chair behind his desk, Racheal walked into his office sobbing. She was not a crier. Unlike other women, it wasn't her style to cry over every little thing, and the way she was sobbing uncontrollably told Manny that something was seriously going down.

"What happened?" he asked as she approached his desk.

"Do you love me, Manny? Are you capable of loving anyone, Manny?"

"Here we go," he mumbled. "What's that supposed to mean? Do I *show* you that I love you?" he asked with his temper rising again.

She cried longer and louder and then she blew her nose and yelled, "Listen asshole! Do! You! *Love* me?"

This had to be the week from hell, but Manny wasn't gonna catch a break. He didn't even recognize the woman before him. "Yes."

"Then don't lie. Do you want a future with me? Do you *really* want me as your woman? I *really* need to know, Manny. Lives depend on it."

"What are you talking about? The thing with Ann was—"

"I'm not talking about Ann!"

"Then what are you talking about?"

"I'm talking about me—us."

"So what's the big deal?"

"Big deal?" she huffed like he was an idiot. "I'm pregnant asshole. With *your* baby inside of me. I've never been pregnant before. I need some *fucking* answers!"

Instantly a migraine worked its way between Manny's temples. It felt like the whole building was falling down on him. First the Marielitos being back in action to kill him and his brothers, then him losing millions because he was slacking on his job, and now he had another child on the way. He already felt he wasn't doing a great job as a father as it was. Then when it came to being what Racheal would want him to be, he was certain he would fall short. He loved being with Racheal, but he didn't think he was capable of being in love ever again, but he could never tell her that. She was the one person he counted on to help him put his company back on track if Edeeks ever decided to leave MB Enterprises. He was partially at her mercy.

"Okay, so now what?" he asked. He had no clue why she was crying so much. He didn't want to personalize her actions, but with women, there was no way of telling what was really going on in her mind.

She softly asked, "Can you just answer a few things so I can make sense of what the hell is going on in my world?"

"Like what?"

She sobbed harder and asked, "Why did we leave Panama? Is your life in danger?"

Manny didn't want to talk. What went down in the streets, stayed in the streets, but with Racheal things were different. He wasn't getting any younger and he needed to move on. He was finally tired of playing games and decided right then and there that he was going to open up to her, but just a little bit. "Yes. My life is in danger."

"Fuck you, Manny. If you're in danger, then I'm in danger. Who wants to kill you?"

"I never said anyone wants to kill me."

"Stop playing games with me. Do you think it's the Cuban's again?"

Manny's head started throbbing. He didn't remember ever telling her about his war with the Marielitos. "*What?*"

"I'm not stupid, Manny. You told me the reason why you went away to prison, and I checked it out when we first started dating. Plus, that time when Detective Baylor kept telling me things to make me stay away from you. Stop playing with me. Are you involved with anything illegal that has someone wanting to kill you, or is it the Cuban's again?"

"No. Nothing illegal."

"So it is the Cubans?"

Telling her things she needed to know because she worked and lived with him was one thing, but telling her everything was not ever going to happen. "No. Not sure," he lied.

She looked deep into his eyes and asked, "No? You sure? Was any of their money involved with starting this company and is it money that you owe them? Is that why they keep coming after you?"

"You a reporter or some shit? Why you always interrogating me?"

"*Stop*, insulting me, Manny!" she yelled loud enough for the whole office to hear. "I'm having your baby and there's shit I need to know! We're in this together. I'm having your child."

His hands started trembling. It was like everyone was after him. "No. Relax."

"Do not, tell me to relax. Answer me, Manny!"

There was no way she was getting more information out of him. "Just don't panic. I have a small issue I'm gonna clear up."

"Are you using the law or a gun this time, Manny?" she demanded to know. "This is the type of shit I need to understand if I'm going through with this pregnancy."

His face turned into a scowl. "What you mean *if?*"

She stood. "What the hell is happening to you? We just left Panama—rushed out of there—probably because someone is trying to kill you. Then we came back home with a couple of psychopaths, and then you come here on some new bullshit and fire one of the best employees you have. *Genius!*"

"I did what I had to do to create a productive work environment."

"And firing my sister was going to do that?" She stood and stomped away. "You're such an asshole. Stay away from me, Manny. Macca and I will take care of Lil Manny, but don't bring any danger to our home! Just stay away from the house."

She slammed the door and Manny wondered if he was in the Twilight Zone. Everything was going wrong, and Racheal was basically telling him that he was homeless and he agreed. There was no sense in bringing danger to his child and pregnant girlfriend.

She was right, and he hated that. "Fuck!" he said to no one. "Another baby…" he mumbled and then picked up his phone.

*****

Only five people had access to the phone that was ringing in Bobby Lee's hand, and most of them were with him in a North Carolina bunker getting Self and his brother Rich ready for a trip to New York City. So when he saw the 212 number come up on his phone, he knew Manny was calling.

"What's up, Boss," he answered, as he had since the day Manny made him and his brothers' millionaires.

"I need to end this shit," Manny uttered.

"It's just starting, brother," Bobby Lee assured him.

Self was up and limping around, packing all the heavy artillery they could find into the back of a Chevy Tahoe. When he heard Bobby Lee's tone, he knew it was Manny on the other end. That's when he did what he never did before.

"Let me talk," he demanded in first person. "What up, Slick?" he asked Manny.

A sense of relief from all his worries washed over Manny when he heard Self's voice, but the tone was off. He had never heard that tone before. It sounded like Self was upset with him. "Hey, brother."

Self grunted. "Brother? Yeah, Slick. Joy, Eva, Babies gone. Self got serious business to handle in N.Y."

"You know—"

"Save your speech, Slick, and your money. Self don't need it." When Manny made his first two million, he cut Self a check for half of it. Then when they robbed Pantera, the leader of the Marielitos for millions, Self and Bobby Lee split that down the middle.

Manny kept reminding himself that Self just lost his whole family, so he walked on eggshells. "Whatever you need, I got you."

"Whatever Self need?" Self asked with sarcasm. "The God need to put some holes in a few heads so this shit can end. One of dem holes gotta go in the head of an animal that go by Mostro. You know that faggot? Self gonna push him off the planet, Slick."

"Know him?"

"Indeed, Slick. He Pantera brother. Blood brother. You started this shit, and dem is yo' people. All Self need to know is where to find this Mostro. Self gone knife that piece of shit in pieces."

"We on the phone, bro'."

"Fuck that!" Self barked.

Manny didn't know the person on the other side of the phone. Self never liked using phones and when he did, he always kept talking to a minimum. Now he was lashing out. The line was clear, so Manny wasn't worried about that. What disturbed him was how Self was yelling at him. That was new. "When I see you we can talk."

"*Talk*?" he spat out like it was an evil word. "Self ain't talking when Self turn the apple out. You started this shit and Self gone end it. Self will deal with this whole shit accordingly. Give us a few weeks so Self legs and shit is right, and we be there. Nuff said," he ended the call and left Manny listening to nothing.

Was there anything Manny knew how to do right? He had no clue. Everyone around him was disappointed, and for the first time since his brother Rico died, he was lost.

*****

Racheal walked out of Manny's office and headed straight for the elevator. Toki rushed behind her and asked, "Will you be back today and will finance be preparing that wire transfer?"

Racheal stopped short and looked Toki in her eyes while searching for an answer. "Um, no. I have an urgent matter to deal with, and yes, the transfer is a go. Please make sure you communicate with only me in this matter."

Toki frowned. "That's odd. Soooo, you *don't* want me to run this through financials?"

This bitch won't quit, Racheal thought and quickly concluded that the conversation would flow better if she spoke Toki's language. She pointed down to Toki and said, "You may be the director of finances or even CFO by morning, but you didn't hear it from me."

"*Really?*" Toki asked with eyes wide open from excitement.

Racheal put on a plastic smile, held both hands out like a crossing guard and said, "No promises. A lot has to be worked out and Mr. Black has to handle things. Ann was a bit much," she said in an effort to plant a seed that Toki shouldn't be "much" either. "But we'll let you know," she said while turning her back on Toki and heading for the elevator.

As Racheal left the Lincoln Building, she wrapped her designer shades around her eyes to block out the sun and the rest of the world. She hustled uptown on Seventh Avenue until she reached 40th Street, made a left, and headed west until she was close to the corner of Eighth Avenue at the parking garage that was overshadowed by the New York Times building. She heard the faint beep of Ann's vintage BMW 2000 and hopped in.

"You have the files?" she asked Ann as the AC struggled to turn from warm to cold.

Ann cut her eyes at Racheal, asking without asking, if she was serious.

"Okay," Racheal surrendered. "Floor it. He's not coming home, but if he does, I want the hard part out of the way."

"Everything changes after today," Ann warned.

Racheal pushed her shades to her forehead. "If you can't do the time, don't do the crime."

They both cracked up with laughter as they entered the Lincoln Tunnel.

*****

"You gonna lose focus for how long exactly?" Bobby Lee asked Self with pity when he hung up the phone on Manny.

"Who fault is this?" Self barked, getting angrier by the second.

Bobby Lee leaned against an old rusty barrel that held drinking water for the bunker and he spat tobacco before calmly saying, "Ours."

"Speak. Self ain't tryna hear all dat, but go 'head and run your jibs."

"*Well*...you could have just taken a minimum wage job many years ago. Bounced around into a so-called 'good job,' collected a pension and got yourself a sure-fire gold watch at the end with a kick in the ass before they filled your position with some fucker for lesser pay and more hours."

"Bullshit!" Self spat, but he was growing calmer. "Might as well do life in the pen for some shit like that. That ain't living."

"*Hmmm*," Bobby Lee hummed. "Well then, this all started when you and Manny decided to put bullets in the heads of these squirrel fuckers for money and drugs. Then it got hotter when you and me and Wilbur—God bless 'em, decided to kidnap a piece of work for the amount of four million dollars, that—by the way, is getting real low after we gotta get us some more farms. Somebody force you to do all that?"

Self removed his blade from its sheath, pulled out a sharpening stone, and began to sharpen his blade while shooting evil grimaces at Bobby Lee.

"Got something you need to get off your chest?" Bobby Lee said, inching his hand closer to the butt of his gun.

"Indeed," Self answered. "They murdered Self queen and Self seed."

Bobby Lee spat another trickle of tobacco onto the ground. "Yes, sir The life we live. We must reap what we sow. A tough pill to swallow, but kinda the way everybody else must feel when we on the other side of the trigger, correct?"

"Don't matter," Self said. "Mostro's Self's."

"Yes, sir. Ain't nothing gonna stop that, if I can help it."

"Me too," Rich added himself in, dropping a leg brace for Self's sprained ankle.

Bobby Lee softly said, "But that still don't kill your anger, and no matter how many you kill, and families you destroy, it still won't bring back your family."

"So when Wilbur died, it was okay?" Self asked, trying to send words with teeth on them by hitting Bobby Lee's weak spot.

He whistled and said, "I'm disappointed in you."

"Answer the question!" Self barked, trying to justify his anger.

Bobby Lee bobbed his head like he was listening to a Hip-hop tune. "War doesn't discriminate. As you know, when we lift our weapon we understand that they didn't make only one gun. The same person you shooting at, is shooting at you. That's war. We at war now. We were at war when Wilbur passed, and we're going to continue to be at war until we die or this thing comes to an end."

"And how we do that?"

Rich walked over with sweat dripping off his head from carting all the artillery. "The nature of war is motivation. We need to give the enemy an incentive to be motivated to stop."

"What? Get medieval and place their heads on stakes?" Bobby Lee suggested.

Rich actually gave it some thought. "Historically that was effective, but with this enemy we're dealing with something is different. If we remove the enemy, another emerges. If we kill the soldiers then more come. This enemy has to be handled either through negotiation or surrender or a truce."

"No negotiation," Self demanded. "No surrender. No retreat. No mercy."

"So what do you suggest?" Rich asked. "Anger rests in the bosom of fools, so whatever you suggest, keep your anger out of it."

Self went into deep thought. "Self find Mostro. Self remove Mostro head. Self hang it from a lamppost in Times Square. All Marielitos know not to fuck wit' Self."

Rich said, "Or they become more passionate about killing you."

"Whatever is wrong, you need to pull it together," Bobby Lee warned Self. "It's gonna make you sloppy, and then we gonna have to bury you."

"Not before Mostro go," Self promised. "After Mosto go, Self look forward to dying. Self aint got shit to look forward to anyway."

"So you're going to war ready to lose?" Rich asked with disappointment. "I can't rely on you if anger is fueling your moves."

"Self is ready."

Bobby Lee spat his tobacco and sighed, "Self *is not* ready. Let your leg heal and then get your mind to heal."

Self placed his palms against his eyes in surrender and everyone gave him his space. He was going to need it for all the killing he would have to do to get to Mostro.

*****

In the confines of Manny's study, Ann had two laptops open with a range of files from MB Enterprises on the screens. Racheal ran upstairs to change into a white, velour Juicy Couture sweat suit.

"Where are we?" Racheal asked as she held onto the back of Ann's chair and stood over her. She stared at the screen on the left and said, "Good, those numbers get moved to..."

"Just watch me, baby," Ann bragged. "Are you sure you want to move two phases right now?"

"This is what we planned. You're gone from the company, so we need to get this done before someone takes your place and I won't be able to cover the tracks from the others or Manny. If we do it this way, right now, no one will be wiser. Let's get it done."

"Okay, it's getting done, boss," Ann replied and began to unravel what they had taken over a year to plot.

On one computer screen Ann had a listing of shell companies that she and Racheal had created that stretched across the globe. With the touch of a few key strokes and with Racheal's guidance Ann transferred the total of three million dollars from MB Enterprises and into thirteen different companies. Every hour the money was bounced and hidden in companies that spanned from the UK, to Greece, Ireland, the Cayman Islands, Morocco and Switzerland. After the transactions were done eight hours later, the money stopped at Belize in a company that only Ann and Racheal had access to. Manny would be none the wiser, it would take years for Edeeks to trace it, and if the U.S. Government checked into it, by the time Racheal was finished drafting papers that Manny would sign, it would look like he was stealing his own money and it was all legit.

"All done," Ann announced before cracking her knuckles and intertwining her hands behind her head and kicking her feet up on the desk and crossing them at the ankles.

"I know just what we need," Racheal said before walking out the study. She returned with two champagne flutes and a bottle of Dom Perignon. She popped the top and poured the bubbly. "Congratulations on becoming three million dollars richer while out-smarting the U.S. government."

"You make it sound so criminal," Ann uttered with a chuckle.

Racheal touched glasses. "Cheers," she said before gulping down the entire glass. She poured another glass and said, "*You* of all people know that it is, but after we move the other six million, then we can really celebrate. This is only the beginning."

Ann looked up from the seat and crammed her neck back to look up into Racheal's eyes. "You're so smart."

Racheal looked down at Ann's awaiting mouth and bit her bottom lip. "And you're always down to take care of me and have my back."

"Ride or die," Ann boasted.

Racheal slowly moved her hand from the back of the chair to Ann's neck. She slid her fingers into Ann's shirt, flicked her lace bra to the side and softly wrapped her pointing finger and thumb around Ann's nipple.

Ann inhaled deeply from Racheal's soft touch. "*Hhnnnn*," she groaned while caressing the hand that fondled her erect chocolate nipple. "Kiss me," she begged before Racheal leaned over and inhaled Ann's exhale.

Sensuously, Ann sucked Racheal's tongue, feeding on her need to have her all to herself. At first, small pecks. Then, hungry sucking. Finally she stood, and pulled her lover to her. She reached into Racheal's sweat pants.

Racheal broke away. "You been banging on that computer," she warned, not wanting the dirt from the keyboard inside of her. She kissed Ann harder while unbuttoning her top. "Come on."

She grabbed Ann's hand and in an effort to avoid Macca, they scuttled up the stairs and into Manny's master-suite.

"You sure he's not coming home?" Ann asked when they entered the massive double bathroom that was divided for him and her. His side was a half a room distance away.

Racheal shrugged before planting kisses on Ann's neck, close to her ear. "I want *you*. Manny's not coming. He does what I say," she assured.

That was enough for Ann to hear. She slowly unzipped Racheal's sweat top, freeing her firm breast. "You like sucking them, don't you?" she asked Ann.

Between Ann's licks and nibbles on Racheal's breast, she said, "I like those millions you made us, but I like you more.

Racheal leaned over and kissed her neck while Ann feasted on her breast. "*Ohhh, yeah*," she moaned before saying, "If you didn't control financials, I couldn't have done it. We're a good team."

Ann reached up, cupped Racheal's mouth and said, "*Shhhhh*. I don't want to talk, I want to *fuck!*" She pulled down Racheal's sweat pants and it revealed her wet flesh.

"*Aye*," Racheal whimpered when Ann took control and kissed on her neck, then her nipples. Ann slid her tongue down to her belly button until it stopped on her wet mound. "*Ummmm*," she moaned when Ann used her lips to softly pull on her clit. "*Sssssss*," Racheal hissed when Ann nibbled between her thighs, the back of her knees and then got down on her knees and kissed her feet.

"Let me worship you," Ann begged while Racheal looked down and blushed.

"You know exactly what to do," Racheal said with appreciation as she was helping her lover stand.

Ann broke free from her lover's clutch. As she walked over to the large standing shower, she removed her clothes, revealing her chocolate, lanky frame.

Racheal quickly followed her lover. They stepped in, sealed the door shut and fumbled with the shower controls while passionately kissing and enjoying flesh against flesh.

"Oh!" Racheal yelped at the cold water that flowed before the warmth and steam settled in.

"Let me warm you up baby," Ann said with her seductive whisper.

She quickly rubbed body wash into her hands, removing traces from the keyboard while Racheal looked on. Then she rubbed the chilled, silky cleanser onto Racheal's shoulders, smoothly caressing her skin down her left rib cage and then around to her back.

"Ummm," Racheal moaned while Ann gently moved her breast against the heated marble walls while she caressed Racheal's back.

"I got you, baby," Ann promised while sliding body wash down the crack of Racheal's ass and then cupping her vulva. "You know…" she whispered. "I make this pussy jump," Ann reminded her.

"Uh. Huh," Racheal grunted while her body began to spasm, obeying Ann's words. Every time Ann moved her cupped hand forward from her lover's ass to her clit, cleansing it with each swipe, Racheal's love folds contracted, making her wetter by the moment. "Uh. Huh."

Steam rose in the shower removing any vision through the glass to the outside. The bathroom was filled with the scent of tropical fruits and coconut as well as the body heat of their passion and the hot water that washed over their glistening bodies.

Ann gently pushed Racheal forward into the tiles. Her finger slid between Racheal's inviting velvet lips. Softly she explored with two fingers, one tapping at her clit from behind, and the other gently stabbing into her center.

"*Aye*," Racheal whimpered. In shallow trembling breaths she moaned. "*Ga-nnnn. Ummmm.* Hmpt. *Ohhhh*, shit!" she rejoiced when Ann slid three fingers inside of her and used them to alternate between clit, her deep hole and wet folds.

"Want me to suck it? Huh, you freak bitch?" Ann growled.

Racheal slammed the shower wall twice and demanded, "Yes! Yes! *Yesssssss.*"

Ann dropped down to her knees while opening the crack of Racheal's ass. She slid her hungry tongue deep between the comforts of Racheal's buttocks. She licked at the place that separated both holes while her thumbs dug into the round mass of Racheal's ass and she separated them.

"*Ga-nnnn. Ummmm.* Hmpt," Racheal buckled.

Ann slid her tongue into Racheal's wetness, planted her face deep between both cheeks as the water trickled over her nose. Then she plunged her tongue deep into her lover before licking her way pass the drooping folds until she stopped at the pointy tip of Racheal's clit.

"God! *Dayuummmmmm*," she screamed when the fireworks went off behind her eyelids and her center contracted into ripples of deep pleasure.

"I'm sucking this wet pussy dry!" Ann promised. The passion turned her into a monster of lust.

Ann drank every drop of Racheal's dew. When her thirst was quenched, the two took turns washing each other and skipped drying the other off. They were too busy rushing to get to the bed.

.

Six

After spending the night in the office, Manny woke up motivated the following morning. He was convinced that the only way to put his life back together was to find out who this Mostro was, then eliminate him, Gato and Primo, whoever they were. Three lives was a small price to pay for him to put this war to an end and finally get a peace of mind, but where could he start? In the past, the method of getting information out of a person was to give them unbearable pain. No matter who it was, everyone had a pain threshold that would make them consider selling their mother out, but these new Marielito soldiers were different. It had to be a new regime, and the monster named Mostro had to be behind it. So how could he catch Mostro or the ones named Gato or Primo that the men in Panama called out? Manny had no idea, so he aimed his green Range Rover in the direction of the only team he had.

Manny drove to 42nd Street in the heart of Times Square and parked between Seventh and Eighth Avenues in front of the Hilton Times Square. Chango came bopping out of the hotel entrance with a giant Gucci duffle bag. Manny scanned his rearview mirror and silently prayed that the phalanx of police officers would not stop the strange looking man in Iraqi fatigues. If they knew the amount of weapons Chango was carrying, they may have called in the National Guard to arrest him.

"*Que paso, hermano?*" Puncho asked when he sat in the front passenger seat.

"New York!" Chango yelled as he and Culo climbed in. "I love it!" he said before going into a Reggaetone rap about his experience there. When he started to sing, Manny checked his rearview mirror wondering how such a beautiful voice came from a psychopath.

"He good right?" Puncho laughed asking Manny.

"Better than good," Manny said while turning off 42nd Street and heading for the Queensboro Bridge. "He's in the wrong line of business."

"I know," Puncho told him. "That's how I met his sick ass. I was supposed to be his manager and start a record company for him, and then some clowns tried to extort me, then Culo and Chango made them disappear."

"Ayeeeeeee, dey scream out when I pinch they balls wit' de pliers," Chango bragged.

"Yeah," Culo chimed in. "Then he put a drill through dey forehead. This motherfucker sick, Yo."

Manny wasn't sure what he was dealing with, but they were all he had until Self and Bobby Lee showed up. He turned to Puncho and asked, "Why they call him *Culo*? He an ass?"

With the exception of Manny, everyone in the truck burst in laughter. Then Culo looked out the window, lost in memories.

Chango patted Culo on the shoulder and said, "*Mi hermano*, he used to get fucked in the ass as a baby by this *pato*."

Manny didn't like to hear about child molesters. "What's funny about that?"

"Nothing," Puncho uttered.

"Ain't shit funny, Yo," Culo grumbled.

"*Si*," Chango jumped in, still laughing. "But this motherfucker save all his money. He buy AK-forty-seven. Then he make the *pato*, de *pato hermano*, de *pato* lover, and other brother bend over the hood of the car, and where he shoot dem, *Jefe?*" he asked, Manny.

He answered, "In the ass."

Culo clapped before laughing. "Right up the ass hole. Hot slugs and I wish I could do it every day."

"Right in the *culo*," Chango celebrated. "Dats why I name him *Culo*."

The men laughed while Manny plotted. He was certain everyone in the car had killed before, but his gut kept telling him that Puncho should not be with him. "Puncho I want to drop you off at the office. Want you to stay there."

Puncho sighed, "Stop with the little brother shit." He pointed to the back of the truck. "These are *my* soldiers. What else I got to do to prove to you that I'm ready for this?"

"Chu brother is a man," Chango said with authority.

"Alright then," Manny huffed with reluctance. "But this is not a game."

"And the Gods are in charge," Chango chuckled. "Nobody die today, *jefe.*"

Manny didn't want to doubt that, but he had other plans for the Marielitos.

"Where we going anyway?" Puncho inquired when they reached Queens on Van Dam Street, on the other side of the bridge.

"Places the Cuban's used to own. They may have kept those businesses and I can catch one of them slipping so I can find out who Primo, Gato and Mostro is?"

"*No se,*" Chango was talking to himself again. Then after mumbling a long paragraph he tapped Manny on the shoulder and said, "De tan man. He know evil. He feed on death. The tan man can tell you what you want."

"What tan man?" Manny asked. He was losing his patience with Chango's antics. "What the fuck are you talking about?"

Chango shrugged. "De tan man who work for the government. That's all they tell me?"

"Who told you?" Manny snapped.

"Don't ask," Puncho warned, but it was too late.

"You won't believe it, Yo," Culo advised.

"De Gods," was Chango's last words. He sat back in the truck and his body language told everyone that his word was final.

"Shit," Manny breathed out. Who was he to argue with the Gods?

For the whole day Manny made one turn after the other that didn't help him find who he was looking for. As Chango predicted, Manny's efforts of driving to the old Cuban business from years ago was a waste of time. Most of the places where he and Self had killed Marielitos in their other battles were gone, owned by African's and there was no trace of anyone that even looked Cuban. Now he felt more vulnerable.

"Where these guys be at?" Puncho wanted to know.

"Everywhere," Manny said hopelessly.

Culo remained quiet. He was too busy enjoying the sights of going through every borough in New York.

Chango looked at Manny and smirked. There was no sense in trying to explain to Manny that his answers were coming from someone else. So Chango sat in the back seat and sharpened his blade. What he knew, was that he was going to use it real soon.

*****

Sleep never came easy to Manny, and that night was no different. Although he owned an estate, he felt like he was homeless. He couldn't risk bringing the Marielitos' heat to his home, but he was sure it didn't matter. The way Mostro killed Self's family said it all. Everyone that was close to Manny was a potential victim, so Chango insisted on sleeping outside of Manny's house in a rented Jeep Cherokee. "For the baby," Chango insisted, and Manny wasn't going to argue.

Once again Manny was on the hunt. Back when all the drama with the Marielitos began, he used to cruise around until he lucked up. So to get a peace of mind, he drove around again the next day, wishing and praying that some type of lead to the Marielitos would come his way. He even played with the thought of putting himself in the open so they could come out to get him, but he didn't want to fight a war he couldn't win.

"*Chucha!*" Manny cursed while sitting in the parking garage of Kennedy Airport with his head banging against the steering wheel. Then his phone rang. He looked down at the new local number and said, "Yes."

"We here," Bobby Lee said. "Bronx. Parking lot of Home Depot on Gunhill Road. Black Ford F250 and Black Cargo van. We'll do some shopping. Your ETA?"

Manny glanced at the clock in the truck. "Give me twenty."

"We'll be shopping," Bobby Lee said before killing the line.

A sudden sense of calm enveloped Manny. He was sure he could go to war with Self and Bobby Lee by his side, because from sun up to sun down all they did was train for civil war. They understood combat, military strategy, and most importantly they had killed for Manny before. Then he thought of Self. When he visited Georgia a few months earlier, Self was happy to be a father. He had taken Joy from being a stripper, to building her a catering business. Then she developed real estate and frozen food products while he stayed at home and took care of his son with the help of his mother-in-law Eva. Now they were all dead, over a war that Manny created. He could only imagine the level of anger Self was holding inside.

A million thoughts raced through Manny's mind as he sped along the Van Wyck expressway until he reached The Whitestone Bridge. From there, he headed north towards Connecticut until he was on the New England Expressway. Finally, the Gunhill Road exit was on his left and he cut across three lanes of traffic to get onto the exit ramp. After two stoplights and a sharp left turn, he pulled into the massive parking lot of the Home Depot. Way off to the left, and tucked deep inside the last row of commercial trucks and vans, was the vehicles that Bobby Lee had described on the phone.

Manny hopped out his truck with anxiety disturbing his acid-reflux. He looked into the trucks, but no one was there. As he approached the entrance to Home Depot, he ran off a list in his head of everything he thought they were buying. Mac-lite flashlights to make silencers, pipes for pipe bombs, PVC pipe and fittings for bigger explosives, fertilizers, flammable chemicals, and gear that would help them with camping, just in case they had to go on the run and live off the land. And he was almost right. He walked into the store and found Self, Bobby Lee and Rich each with a full shopping cart at the register.

"Just in time," Bobby Lee said before spitting a wad of tobacco on the store floor. "Pay the lady," he told Manny while tucking his cash back into his pocket.

"My man," Rich said with a smile as he embraced Manny with a hug.

Manny broke Rich's embrace, and turned to a clean shaven Self, who walked away like Manny wasn't there. Two things told Manny Self wasn't okay. First, Self was a devout Muslim. He converted when he did time for killing Marielitos in the middle of an Atlanta freeway. Now that Self's long beard was off, Manny wondered if the deaths had caused his faith to sway because Self did not play when it came to his beard. The other reason was Self's nonchalant attitude.

"Don't mind him," Bobby Lee said while pointing his thumb at Self, who walked out the store. "He's a bit sour. What he witnessed, some people never come back from."

"Well, I got 'em," Rich assured Manny as they pushed the carts out the store.

Manny paid the bill and took a deep breath as they walked out the store. Self leaned against the truck waiting. When Manny approached, Self led him by a tree near the gate that circled the shopping center. He palmed and planted Manny's head in his chest and held him so tight it was hard for Manny to breathe.

"As Allah is Self witness, Self going to cut Mostro in pieces," he declared with his voice cracking from emotion. "He held her head up to Self face, Manny. You know the God's happiness came from Peaches. He was on a different mission, Slick. This cat different from the rest of them Cubans. That's why Self got to remove parts of this cat. Self gonna cook his heart and eat it like a real warrior should. If we run down on this cat, remember…he belong to Self."

Heat drained from Manny's head on down to his toes. He loved Joy. She was his only real sister. A down to earth woman who was driven to love her man with all she had. Because of that she loved Manny too. Her mother Eva was a firecracker. A woman who didn't know how to make Joy into a woman like Self did, but one that gave Joy the will to survive any odds. Then there was baby Self. Too smart for his age, and did everything he saw his father do. They were all gone forever. All at the hands of the man Self wanted to personally destroy. Manny wasn't getting in the way of that.

"He's yours, Self. Whatever you need, it's yours," Manny promised.

"You can't give Self what Self need," he spat. "Self going to meet up with Self family. *After* Self destroy Mostro." He turned and looked down at Manny's eyes, "Where we find him?"

Manny looked away, wishing Rich or Bobby Lee would come over. The air was thick with tension. "I don't know."

"Then let Bobby get on his computer and find them," he said and walked away.

Manny walked behind Self wondering if Bobby Lee was the man that Chango was talking about.

"Where y'all holding up?" Manny asked the group of men when he reached them.

Bobby Lee nudged his chin south. "Down yonder. Place called Throgs Neck? Saw a house for rent on the net, so we took it. Three floors. Space for each of us and a garage. Private and near the water."

"Okay. I'll follow," Manny told him.

Bobby Lee shook his head. "No sir. You follow Rich. I gotta shop for some grub to feed these two giants."

"Say no more," Manny said and Self looked over to him, knowing that was Self's tag line.

Manny followed the cargo van back to the New England Thruway headed for the Throgs Neck Bridge, and got off at the last exit. The small Bronx neighborhood was littered with boats and houses that looked like they belonged in a fishing town in Maine. When they arrived at the desolate house, which was going to be their base camp, Manny knew that if anyone came looking for them, they would see them coming a mile away.

After unloading all the items from Home Depot, they waited for Bobby Lee to return. When he did, they set up a grill for barbeque.

"They came hard," Bobby Lee told Manny. "Set off *all* the trip wire. To get that many soldiers requires some serious money, and this can't just be about revenge. Somebody want us out the way, but why?"

"That's what I can't figure out?" said Manny. "We did them a favor by removing Pantera."

"How you know that?" Self asked.

Manny shrugged. "It makes sense."

"That's what Eduardo said," Bobby Lee reminded them how a top official handed Pantera over to them to save his own life.

"Yeah, that's what he said," Manny agreed. "When they came for me in Panama—"

"*When?*" Self spat out.

Manny locked eyes with Bobby Lee wondering why Self didn't know.

"He wasn't himself," Bobby Lee offered an explanation.

Manny turned to Self. "The day they came for you. Three of them. How they knew where I was at is driving me crazy. It's like they got somebody in my camp feeding them."

Bobby Lee held up his laptop. "Easy. You a legitimate businessman now. Real easy to trace you."

"So what happened?" Self asked.

"They came to the airport and Puncho got these guys," Manny said while shaking his head. "Chango and Culo."

"Who names themselves asshole?" Rich inquired.

"*Exactly,*" Manny chuckled and then quickly grew serious. "But Chango…he's…demented. Talks to himself—"

"*So,*" all three men said in unison, showing that they were guilty of the same thing.

"Nah," Manny said raising his hand. "He really doesn't talk to himself. He talks to…some people that no one else can see."

"Oh," came from Self. "*And?*"

"And he handled his business for Puncho. He's official. Took the Cuban's out. They wouldn't talk so Culo cut 'em down and they did the tire burning thing."

"*Nice,*" came from Rich.

Manny shook his head knowing what Rich was capable of. "And before they left, the Cuban's mentioned Mostro and—"

"Gato and Primo?" Self cut him off.

Manny felt validated. "Yeah! That's who I've been looking for, for the past few days."

"So where's Chango and the ass now?" Bobby Lee asked.

"Hilton Times square. But Chango got this weird connection with Lil Manny…" Manny looked up to the setting sun. "…you would think Chango was his father and not me."

"Are these guys in?" Bobby Lee pressed.

"Way ahead of me," Manny answered.

"Get 'em up here," Self ordered. "We meet 'em in Pelham Bay Park. See what they feel like. And while they coming you can tell Self what happened in Panama."

Manny picked up his phone and tapped Puncho's number. He wasn't sure he could handle Chango and Self together, but he was soon going to find out.

*****

Manny hopped into the cargo van with the rest of the crew from Georgia and parked near the New England thruway, next to Pelham Bay Park. When Puncho arrived they all used the recess of the dark trees to hide them from passersby.

Puncho greeted Self and Self received more love than Manny did. Culo introduced himself to the group, and received mutual love and respect, but Chango wasn't too sure. Like an animal introduced to a new habitat, he hesitated to step forward. Instead, he looked at his own camouflage uniform, and then inspected the same pants on Rich, and the black fatigues on Self and Bobby Lee. Then he tried to see what type of weapons they had concealed, but nothing appeared. Then he started talking up to the sky with both hands raised high.

When his hands dropped, he walked over to Rich and said, "Knife man. Me Chango!" He stood there waiting like he wanted Rich to bow before him. Rich, forever the gentleman, smiled and nodded at Chango instead.

Satisfied with Rich's response, Chango walked over to Bobby Lee and gave him a big hug. "Thank you," he said to Bobby Lee. "Ju give more than people give. But ju be *mucho bueno*," Chango promised and then turned to Self. "Hmpt," he grunted and walked away, standing off to the side by himself.

"Satisfied?" Manny asked Self.

"He harmless," Self reassured everyone about Chango.

"So how we gonna fish out these Marielitos?" Puncho asked the group.

Bobby Lee locked eyes with Manny, nudged his chin towards Puncho and asked, "You sure about this?"

"No," Manny replied. "But he wants to get dirty. They wanted to kill him too, so…?"

Bobby Lee sighed, "Okay. Let the Special Forces man figure this out. I just want to kill me some squirrel fuckers and end this cause somebody gonna pay for friggin up my farm. And I needs to get back to Missy and mama."

"What do we know?" Rich asked.

"Military men," Chango said to the sky. "Cuban. Marielitos. Good soldiers."

"Correct," Rich agreed. "So someone with some serious money is paying for these mercenaries."

"Primo or Gato. Mostro is like the field general," came from Self.

Chango started laughing and Self shot a grimace that showed he was offended. Rich saw the negative energy brewing and asked, "Chango, what you think we should do?"

He placed his hand on his chest and leaned back with his laughter. "Me? Chango?" His smile disappeared. "Me go to Cuba and go to war. Then go to Miami and kill Marielitos one by one. Me? One year and everybody *finito*."

"Ohhhh…kaaay," Rich breathed out before looking at the other men. "Right now we need Intel. We can't go to Cuba."

"They may not even be in New York," Puncho offered.

"Somebody up here paying for my farm!" Bobby Lee promised.

"So," Rich said, trying to keep everyone in focus. "We know they hold up in New York. We know they have two leaders." He pointed to Bobby Lee and said, "You can run a search on those names and see if you make a hit. Try police records." Then he turned to everyone else. "What else?"

"That killing Pantera was better for them, so why they after us?" Manny asked.

"How do you know that? I wasn't there," Rich asked.

"Eduardo said so," Manny answered.

"What if the squirrel fucker lied and played us the whole time?" Bobby Lee asked Manny.

"And lose all that paper?" Self inquired. "Who give up four-point-five mil like that? They came cause Mostro is Pantera brother and Mostro started the beef, probably thought shit was gone be real sweet. If we ain't prepare for these ducks, it would've been sweet for them. Now it's gone be sweet for Self. Real sweet."

"Somebody that stands to make more than money is involved," Bobby Lee said.

"Did you let Eduardo live?" Rich asked like he was already disappointed.

"Sure did," Bobby Lee answered, disappointed in himself.

Rich turned to Manny. "Did you check his last known address?"

Manny dropped his head to the ground. "Nah. I figured he moved like everything else they owned."

Rich nodded. "Okay, so we know a top official from the Marielito's lives in New York and he's still alive. He gave up information before, maybe he'll help out now."

Bobby Lee quickly opened his laptop.

Rich asked Manny. "You remember where he lived?"

Before Manny could answer, Bobby Lee said, "Got it right here. Could never forget his pretty boy name or address. I sent flowers to his woman. Never done that before so I remember." He fidgeted with the keyboard and yelled, "Yippee Ki yae, motherfucker. I reckon he gots the same address."

Manny stood. "His ass is mine!"

"No, at sun up," Rich said. We go in three vehicles. Scope it out and figure out if we can get him to talk. If he sends us in the right direction, we go to war and end this."

"So it's on," said Manny.

Chango walked over softly clapping his hands. "So we ready for war?" he asked the group.

"Hell yes," Bobby Lee answered.

"Ho-kay," Chango said with his strong accent. He walked until he was two feet in front of Self and loudly said, "Mi pleasure to go to war." He pointed at Self. "But not with him. He too angry."

"What the fuck?" Self uttered.

"Chango, chill," Puncho begged.

Chango shook his head. "He no good. Something wrong. He useless."

Self jumped up and kicked at Chango's head. Chango ducked under his leg, planted a jab of knuckles near Self's groin and Self stumbled.

"Everyone back up," Rich ordered.

"Break this shit up!" Puncho screamed.

Bobby Lee spat out a wad of tobacco and said, "Puncho you too young to reckon when two bulls can't be in the same pen. So, they'll work it out. Let men be men."

Self threw calculated punches and Chango ducked or side-stepped every single one of them. "He no focus," Chango yelled. Then he dodged to the left, bounced on his feet and did a roundhouse kick that landed in Self's chest.

"He good," Bobby Lee announced while enjoying Chango's show. "But can he shoot?" he asked out loud, knowing that it was only a matter of time before Self would do what he did best.

"You fucking with the God?" Self asked, winded. He wasn't healed yet.

"No *habla*," Chango answered, telling Self he didn't want to talk.

Self moved in, faked left, Chango flinched and Self landed a stiff jab to Chango's midsection, and then doubled up with right hooks, making Chango stumble backwards.

Self landed a blow to Chango's jaw, dropping him instantly with a punch that would have put most men to sleep, but Chango hopped back up. He rushed in, flipped to the side and did a roundhouse kick to Self's face and then he doubled up on blows to Self's head. Quickly, he kicked him in the shin of his bad leg, dropping Self to one knee. Self tried to rush and grab for Chango's midsection, but Chango side-stepped and did another roundhouse kick to the back of Self's head, sending him stumbling forward to the ground.

"Get up soldier!" Rich barked, showing whose side he was on.

Self sprang to his feet. After he stood he was calmer. He took several deep breaths while eyeing Chango. Then he reached to his side and pulled out his massive knife.

The gold frames in Chango's mouth appeared when he saw Self's knife. Instantly he reached to the small of his back and withdrew his small Samurai sword. He held the blade to his chest, looked over at Self and asked, "Ju sure, *amigo*?"

Self didn't move. He stared long and hard at Chango, lost somewhere else. When he returned from the trip in his mind, he exhaled in defeat and put his knife away. Then he held out his empty hand.

Chango looked over at Self long and hard, but he didn't put his knife away. He walked over to Self, hesitantly shook his hand, and then slowly backed away.

"Self good now," Self declared. "Focused."

Rich walked over and put his arm around Self's shoulder. "Yes, finally you are." Then he looked over to Chango. "Thanks."

Chango wasn't convinced. "Tomorrow we see."

Manny and Rich exhaled with relief when the fight was over. Rich felt the tension of both camps release and said, "So the crack of dawn we move as one?"

"*Si mi hermanos*," Chango sealed the deal.

"I need some steel!" demanded Culo. He looked over to Rich and asked, "Army man. You got an AK-forty-seven over there in that truck?"

Rich shook his head. "Nope. SIG five-sixteen's. Fully auto with a hundred clips. Box of hand grenades, a dozen pistols, full body armor for six, and sticks of dynamite. Just in case."

"We gots five SIGs. Enough to go around," Bobby Lee bragged about the machineguns that could shoot six hundred bullets in under two minutes. "Got a couple of Bushmasters with drums too," he continued, explaining that he had automatic shotguns that held twenty shells in a round drum.

"Okay!" Culo celebrated. "Give me the SIG with five clips."

"Bushmaster," Chango requested.

"So it's done," Bobby Lee declared. "Tomorrow it's huntin' time. Somebody paying for what they done to my farm," he reminded them yet again before spitting out his tobacco.

"No surrender, no retreat?" Self asked aloud like he always did when he was going to war.

Manny heard the familiar mantra and smiled. "You fucking right, *hermano*."

SEVEN

At the crack of dawn the caravan was on the hunt for the Marielitos. Chango and Self were in the cargo van with Self driving. Bobby Lee, Rich, and Culo were in the Ford pick-up truck, and Puncho and Manny drove the rented Jeep Cherokee.

Manny had slipped. He had forgotten to check the one Marielito that helped him in the past. Eduardo had double crossed his boss in an attempt to gain a higher position. With Manny eliminating the top man in New York left room for Eduardo to flourish, but where was he now? Manny needed to know. When they reached Long Beach, Long Island, the familiar neighborhood with its oceanfront streets, immaculate houses and old money brought back many memories for Manny. But it seemed too farfetched for a leader in the Marielito gang to leave himself that vulnerable and still live there.

Manny picked up his phone and called Bobby Lee, the computer geek. "You sure this house belongs to Eduardo? *Still?*"

"Look," Bobby Lee uttered with finality. "I'm looking at the Department of Buildings website and this guy is the same owner for the past ten years. He even had an extension added onto the property. Then I checked if the taxes was paid, and guess who paid it?"

"Got you," Manny said, but something didn't feel right.

They parked on different areas of the block and waited for hours. All eyes were on Eduardo's house, but there was no activity. No doors opened, no cars came or went. Nothing. Then Manny spotted an older Latina wearing a maid's uniform pulling up.

"I got something. A minivan," Manny said into his phone.

"I see it," Bobby Lee said. "Now what? Don't see any Eduardo."

"Fuck it. I'm going to wake his ass up," Manny said as he exited the jeep, carefully pulling a baseball cap over his face.

"Not without me," Bobby Lee said into the phone while climbing out the minivan.

As the two men quickly moved to catch the maid before she shut the front door, Manny looked over his shoulder and saw Self quickly gaining on them.

"They killed Joy," Self said for an explanation with his palms up, like he was begging for mercy.

At that point Manny didn't care. The older lady was slowly closing the door behind her. As it was about to seal them out, Manny placed his foot at the center and kicked his way in.

"My God!" the lady screamed out before she hit the hard floor face first.

Manny stepped over her, removed his weapons and started to climb the winding stairs in front of him. When he felt the stairwell giving and heard it creaking from behind, he knew it was Self's massive body that had his back. At the top of the stairs four bedrooms appeared with a bathroom between a pair of rooms. Manny headed for the room with the widest door. It was open. He peeked inside and saw a woman in a peach, satin nightgown sitting on a brown leather bench in front of her antique king size bed.

"*Jesus!*" she gasped. Then she looked at the two men and said, "No money here. We have no money."

"Where's Eduardo?" Manny asked.

The woman's head snapped up to Manny and her eyes twinkled with familiarity. "I know you," she mumbled and she took a deep breath while holding her chest. She pointed to Self and said, "You too." She pointed to herself and said, "It is me, Aida. Put away your pistols. I fed you two with my own hands. My daughters played around you," she reminded them of their visit years ago.

She clearly remembered the day the two men had held Eduardo at gun point and was invited into her home instead. That day, as Eduardo had her prepare food for them and himself, he told them all they needed to know to kill Pantera.

"You want Gato? He do bad business," she asked.

"Yeah, whoever that is, we want Gato too," Self said with urgency.

"*Gato?*" Manny asked, confused.

She nodded rapidly and then waved them off. "Eduardo's friends call him Gato. His mama named him that."

"So your husband is Gato?" Self said flatly, putting pieces together.

"*Husband?*" she asked with disdain. "Gato stopped being my husband long ago, the bastard. He's a whore. A weak man. After making a little money he forget about his wife. He think money can fix everything. He no good." She stood and her eyes sparkled with a great idea. "You want to kill him?" she asked with a smile before whispering, "I have good insurance for him. Please cut his balls off. The bastard. Then he can stop embarrassing me by making babies that are not mine."

"Where is he?" Manny asked.

She held up her hand for him to wait. She walked over to her antique cabinet and removed a business card. "Here," as she handed Manny the card. "You can find him there. Go after five o'clock. He's always there. He drives a blue Infinity truck, but you know Eduardo."

Aida assumed Manny and Self were in constant contact with her husband, but she was wrong. Manny looked down at the business card. It read, "Alpha Scrap Metal & Recycling, 233rd Street and Provost Avenue, Bronx NY."

"I'm not gonna have to come back here, right?" Manny asked.

She walked over to him, touched his shoulder and looked into his eyes. "Not if you do the job right. I'm going shopping for my black dress today. Can you do it?"

"Guaranteed," Self said.

Aida smiled. "Good. Now let me walk you out so my daughters don't get scared."

That was too easy, Manny thought as they left the house. Then his phone rang.

"Well?" Bobby Lee asked.

"Eduardo is Gato. Same person," Manny answered. "Where are you?"

"Back of the house. Still inside," Bobby Lee chuckled. "Drive away from the beach, pull over and tell Rich where you are. I'll be there in a minute.

"Okay," Manny said with a million thoughts running through his head.

*****

"The cocksucker flipped the script," Self grumble. "Never leave a man alive that will kill you another day."

All the men were huddled in a McDonald's parking lot, hovering over cups of coffee.

Manny nodded. "Eduardo sent the hit to cover his tracks. He sold Pantera out, and now that he's making money, he's trying to cover his tracks?" Manny asked, unsure that he was the only one with that conclusion.

"Mostro kept yelling out that faggot Pantera's name when he was gutting my fam," Self said with disdain.

"Okay, so how he know about us?" Rich inquired.

Bobby Lee shook his head. Things didn't add up that easy. "With the army he assembled, he could have sent a rocket through your door and ended it that way."

"It was personal," Manny chimed in. "A hit on all three of our places at the same time? That was more than getting even for Pantera."

"And they asked for me in Panama. This shit is bigger than Nino Brown," Puncho added, quoting one of his favorite movies.

"I think this shit is a triple cross by Eduardo," Manny insisted.

"But what's in it for him, to send a hit on us?" Rich asked. "He already got what he wanted by now. If anything, why not keep his secret to himself?"

"Maybe he no sleep," Chango added.

"Guilty conscious," Puncho translated.

"No. He sold us out and he's cleaning up his dirty work," was Bobby Lee's theory.

"But Primo must have approved it, because everyone keeps mentioning his name too," Rich argued.

"Man Eduardo-Gato, or whoever the fuck he is this week, could of sent them, telling them it's coming from Primo," Self added.

"When do I get to shoot somebody?" Culo felt left out.

All eyes looked at him, stunned. Then Self said, "Exactly. When Self gonna set his ass free? What up with that address she gave you?"

Bobby Lee spat out his tobacco and rocked on his heels. "The place is legit. It's not too far from where we staying. Based on Google maps, it's a ghost town. It looks like a little private village of scrap metal."

"Can we go now?" Self asked impatiently. "Let's drive through, see what he working wit', lay out our strategy and then lay his ass out so he can drop into the God's hands."

Rich nodded his approval.

"Let's do it," Manny uttered. "I need this thing to be over."

"We need mask," Culo added.

"Great idea," Bobby Lee said. "Let's do that now."

The crew jumped into their rides and worked their way back to the Bronx. After purchasing ski masks from Modell's Sporting Goods, everyone jumped into their vehicles ready to kill. What they failed to remember was that many went to kill and ended up dead.

*****

In the middle of a winding Bronx back road that favored a scrap metal and junk yard city laid Alpha Scrap Metal & Recycling. The curved road was bustling with a dozen forklifts racing from one side of the street to the other carrying everything from car engines to metal bins of computer parts. The noise was loud, the scent of the air was filled with diesel fuel, and the men who were working had one thing in common. They were all Latino.

Manny drove by the business twice, looking for Eduardo. There was a junk yard on both sides of the winding street, both belonging to Alpha Scrap Metal & Recycling, and both had trailers that were used as offices with suspicious men looking at the Jeep driving back and forth.

At five o'clock on the dot a Cadillac CTS sports car pulled into the parking space in front of the scrap metal yard and the man Manny was looking for hopped out in his usual, tieless suit.

"That's him!" Manny announced into his cellphone when the tall, handsome frame of a balding Eduardo stepped out the car. Manny double checked his gun and then grasped the extra clips. "How you want to do this?" he asked Bobby Lee in a hurried tone while slipping his mask on. Eduardo was across the street, briskly walking towards an office door.

"Let's wait it out," Bobby Lee suggested.

That wasn't the answer Manny wanted to hear. Right there was Eduardo, the man they called Gato, just a few feet away. Since he ratted out his crew before, Manny was convinced that he would talk. They had history, and Eduardo was a coward, but Manny would fume in silence. It was too important for them to move as a team.

Puncho's Jeep Cherokee was twenty feet away from the entrance to Eduardo's office. Across the street and close to a half of city block away, was the cargo van with Self and Chango. Parked at the intersection on the corner, behind Manny, was Bobby Lee, just a few feet away from the other office that belonged to the scrap metal business.

Within minutes of Eduardo's arrival, the bustling of forklifts carrying cargo came to an end. The only activity on the streets was an occasional car passing through the winding road. Manny didn't take his eyes off the door his enemy went through. He was surprised when six Latino workers rushed out of the office that Eduardo had entered.

"Anything happens, stay in the truck," Manny warned Puncho. "I need you to drive us up out of here."

Manny predicted the future. Right before his eyes two forklifts came speeding out of the scrap metal yard, headed towards Self and Chango. Dangling from each forklift was a passenger with a machinegun in hand and Cuban bandanas wrapped around their wrists.

Manny tried to grab his cellphone, but there was no time. Chango hopped out of the passenger seat, letting the heavy slugs of his automatic shotgun go.

"Fuck!" Manny yelled and rushed out the truck.

The soldier who rode the forklift on Self's side the truck was not there to play games. He sent a full clip of hot rockets bursting into the driver's side windshield, but Self was gone.

"Party time!" Chango yelled through his mask before he removed the head of the forklift driver. The forklift and its passenger swerved recklessly. *"I want to live in America!"* Chango sang as his slugs found the body of the reckless passenger. Then he had to duck. Fast.

The young soldier who was blasting into Self's side of the truck turned his weapon to the passenger side, sending a bullet through Chango's dreads, but thankfully not his head.

Manny jumped out, ready to assist Self and Chango when two men on a forklift carrying assault rifles were headed for Bobby Lee. Suddenly the door to the office opened and Eduardo stepped out, not ready to talk or negotiate, but to greet Manny with the hot fire that was quickly leaving the .45 caliber gun in his hand.

"*You?*" Manny yelped like he was insulted that Eduardo would try to kill him. He let the hammer to his .10mm fire off as many rounds as he could while running for cover, but his efforts were useless. As he stepped around the front of the jeep, two men ran out from across the street, blasting AK47's and peppering his vehicle.

"*Arrggh!*" Puncho screamed before dropping beneath the dashboard.

Manny's eyes ballooned out of his mask. His brother was hit, but he had no time to check on him. Too many bullets were flying his way. He spun, empting his clip while Eduardo ran back into the office to avoid being hit. Then he reloaded and fired at the two men who were firing at him. Each waiting to see who fell first.

When Self saw the forklifts coming his way with the sharp, long hands of the lift heading for his windshield, he slipped on his mask and yelled, "Back door," but Chango laughed. He was busy slitting a hole through the top of his mask so his dreads could flow out of it.

Self rushed to the back door of the truck, patted the two .50 Desert Eagles on his hip that never failed him before, and then gripped the handle of the Sig Sauer 516 machine gun—tight. He flipped the single shot lever, and turned to his right to come around the van. A single tap dropped the driver of the forklift and a double tap dropped a soldier who was too busy trying to kill Chango to realize he had just died from two bullets to his heart.

"Self!" Chango yelled out while crouching from the other side of the van. "That chu, *amigo*?"

Self's sight was on the gunmen across the street that were firing at Manny. He crouched down, aimed for the spine of the shooter that was closest to Manny, and fired. Then he fired again then he stood and ran to the front of the van.

"Emphatically, it's Self. The God *you should* be looking up to the sky and smiling at and calling out to wit' yo' crazy ass," he answered back and then took off running to save Manny.

Chango chuckled while firing in the direction that Self ran in, giving him cover.

Manny was outgunned until the shooter closest to him fell. He didn't need to know why. He spun, put two shots into the head of the other shooter that was coming for him, and then aimed his empty weapon at another soldier that was coming his way. Thank God it was Self.

"What in tarnation?" Bobby Lee uttered when his binoculars revealed two forklifts scattering with machinegun toting cowboys.

"Am I seeing this right?" Rich asked as a forklift headed towards Self. The other one had to travel the furthest to get to him.

"Dey coming our way, *gringo*," Culo warned from the back seat.

As the armed men on the forklift sped their way, Bobby looked at the men shooting into Puncho's Jeep. "It's killing time." He slipped on his mask and turned to Rich. "Sniper these fools."

"From here?" Rich asked.

Bobby Lee looked at the ten foot distance between him and the forklift. "Better move quick. Act like its rabbits."

Rich quickly reached to the back seat, grabbed his Remington .226 from the arsenal of weapons he left next to Culo, and put the sight to his eye.

"Close your ears," Bobby Lee yelled to Culo.

In the crosshairs of Rich's scope was a teenager with long hair dangling over one side of his face driving the forklift. Rich put the cross on the driver's left eye, exhaled, and fired, splitting his head into two. Rich moved his hand to the left, set his sight on his next target, and he took a deep inhale. A crimson mist of the driver's blood sprayed the gun-toting passenger, and as he impulsively wiped the splatter of wet flesh and bone from his face, a hot slug from Rich's rifle entered his nose and another one quickly entered his heart.

"*Whoooo!*" Culo yelled from inside the truck like he was watching a movie. "That shit was dope, Yo!"

The forklift swerved left and off the road. Bobby Lee removed his fingers from his ears and yelled, "You gettin' rusty, Rich. You gettin' rusty." He grabbed a handful of 100-round clips, tossed them into the right pocket of his fatigues, pushed a fresh wad of tobacco into his mouth, and then he adjusted the hole in his mask so his spit could exit. "Let's go make 'em pay for what they done to our family."

*****

Manny was catching his breath when Self reached him. "This mother...fucking, *puta!*" he yelled while pointing at Eduardo's office. "That faggot either got tipped off by his wife, saw us, or he just lucky, but he in there."

"You see Mostro?" Self asked, hoping no one was confused about why he was there. He ducked around the van, fired two shots and quickly ducked back around to avoid the massive gunfire. "Let me know 'bout Mostro," he reminded Manny.

"Gotta get these motherfuckers up off us."

"Got a grenade?" Self asked.

Manny smirked. "Come on man."

Self ducked around the end of the van and quickly returned. "Next time we bring grenades."

"Puncho got hit. I still didn't get a chance to check on my little brother."

Then instantly the gunfire stopped.

"Somebody controlling these bitches wit' a radio or some shit. How they just stop like that?" Self wanted to know. "Tear they ass up as soon as you get the chance," he instructed Manny.

The door to Eduardo's office opened and the army of workers who were just hauling scrap metal earlier, were now armed to the teeth and ready to fire hot metal at Manny and his crew.

"Move," Self yelled to Manny. He lifted his machine gun and started firing towards the office while trying to make his way behind the jeep.

Screams of pain and fear came from the armed men pouring out of the scrap metal yard across the street from where Manny and Self were with their backs up against the jeep. There had to be at least twenty of them. Rapid fire was coming their way. Suddenly the attention of the Cubans was quickly diverted.

Chango was blasting away to the left of Manny and Self, while Bobby Lee and Rich blasted from the right.

Culo exited the truck and was mesmerized by the object of his affection lying in the middle of the street. He threw the machinegun Rich gave him in the back of the truck and took off running into the street. Lying on the ground, just a few feet from the massive gunfire was an AK47. It belonged to one of the men who were shooting from the forklift, but he wouldn't need it anymore. It was better used in Culo's hands, and that's exactly what he did when he gripped it.

"My shit right here," Culo celebrated before squeezing the trigger. A hot flash left the Russian nozzle and planted itself into the asphalt below him. "My turn!" he yelled out to no one and aimed down the road where the Cuban's were pouring out of the office. He fired shots, hit his mark, and then ran over to every AK47 he saw on the ground so he could remove the clips for more ammunition.

Rich ran towards Self and Manny with a machinegun slung across his body and his sniper rifle in hand, picking off every shooter that got closer to Manny and Self while Chango did the same. Everyone was trying their best to kill the Cuban's and stay alive. Then all shooters were interrupted.

Sirens from the West screamed from a mile away. Then the powerful exhaust of three black armored vans came from the back of the winding road. The vans roared as they entered the gun fight, and when one of the Marielitos entered the middle of the street, the first van plowed him down and dragged the body until it stopped in front of Eduardo's office.

The three vans screeched to a stop and Manny, Self and Chango rushed away and hid behind a black metal dumpster.

"What the fuck is this?" Manny asked while reloading and seeking cover.

The sirens grew closer.

"*Policia!*" Chango yelled out, but that didn't stop him from reloading his gun with a new clip.

The police sped on the scene. Gunfire was random and not a full assault. It was like everyone took a collective pause. Suddenly the side doors to the first armored van opened. Two men dressed in all black, full body armor and motorcycle helmets jumped out. In their hands were M-16, big barrel machineguns that could stop a tank. One of the men launched a grenade into the police car, instantly causing it to explode and catch ablaze.

The other man rushed out into the middle of the street and began to empty his long chain of bullets into anyone who was in his way.

"Who is that?" Manny asked.

"Enemy of Self enemy is Self friend," Self chanted while crouching low.

Gunfire erupted. The Cubans who were busy trying to kill Manny now fired at the men in body armor.

Instantly, the side doors to the other vans opened. Three men in full body armor poured out the last van and ran into the street firing. Out the doors of the middle van, revealed the one person everyone there feared or despised. It was Mostro. He limped out the middle van with only a machete in his hand. On each hip, he had a big chrome, .41 revolver like a cowboy in the wild west.

"*Shaaaaay tahaaan!*" Self growled at the top of his lungs when he spotted Mostro, calling him Satan. He took off into the middle of the street, making himself an open target.

"Party time!" Chango yelled before running into the street behind Self. He dropped to his knees, then fell to his stomach, and shot away the knees of the two men in full body armor.

Self gripped his Desert Eagle and carefully aimed at Mostro, who was heading for the office, but he missed.

The gunfire from Self and Chango was like an announcement to the Cubans. They turned their guns back on all targets and started firing.

"So who the heck we killing?" Bobby Lee asked Rich.

Rich lifted his rifle. "Anyone that didn't arrive with us."

"Okay," Culo answered and ran behind a dumpster before firing his weapon.

On the winding road of 233rd Street it sounded like a civil war irrupted. The police arrived, quickly reversed out of the gunfire, and set up a perimeter a half a mile away. Self tried to shoot his way towards Eduardo's office, but the men from the armored vans were trained assassins. Their bullets were calculated and came too close.

Manny ran across the street from the office and hid behind a disabled forklift. Too much was going on. He had expected a shootout of some sort, but this was impossible to handle. Gunshots were coming from every angle and wouldn't let up. It was all happening in a matter of seconds, but for Manny, much of it was happening in slow motion.

Bobby Lee, Rich and Culo began to retreat. Rich was doing a better job of taking men out from a distance. Bodies littered the sidewalks, streets, and driver seats of forklifts, and the gunfire hadn't stopped.

Self was determined to end it all that day. The man he needed to kill was a few feet away and instead of focusing on getting to the office, he pulled Chango with him to kill the men that stood between him and that office.

Eduardo's office door flew open. Two gunmen came running out with their guns blazing in Manny and Self's direction. Manny ducked lower and grabbed his cellphone. He saw Rich a block away, but couldn't communicate with him.

"Yo!" Bobby Lee said with a slight chuckle when he answered the phone.

"The real black dude that came in the armored vans? That's Mostro! Tell Rich to take out the dudes in the van."

"Tried that," Bobby Lee explained "But they were helping us. We sent a few rounds their way, and far as we can tell, the tires are armored, the van definitely, and they on the other side of our view. We gotta get around em."

"Throw a grenade!" Manny suggested.

"Not wit' the police up the road," Bobby Lee explained. "When we leave. And *we are* leaving, we may have to use 'em on a few cops to get gone. And we don't need the F.B.I on our tail, but after this...the president might get a call." Bobby Lee paused. "That's him there coming out? Who he got horse collard?"

Manny put the phone in his pocket and peeked across the street. Mostro exited the office dragging a limp Eduardo by the head.

"Fuck this," Self uttered and removed his mask after dropping his machinegun to the street. He wanted Mostro to know who was going to kill him. He removed his two pistols from his waist and inched his way to the office.

"*Viva la Marielitos!*" Mostro yelled when he limped out of the office with Eduardo in his hands. All the shooting stopped. "*Gato es el ratai,*" he yelled, telling his men that Eduardo was a rat. He grabbed the back of Eduardo's head, removed his machete, and with one strong whack, severed his head. "Bye bye!" Mostro said when he let the head and body drop to the ground.

Self raised both cannons, aimed towards Mostro and fired.

Mostro's head snapped from side to side, feeling the slugs drop too close. When he looked up and saw Self he growled. Then he threw his machete towards the armored van so his men could pick it up. Quickly, and looking like he had practiced it a million times before, he removed the two pistols from the holsters on his legs and aimed at Self.

Both Self and Mostro were moving closer to each other while exchanging shots. Both men wanted to see the end of the other, but none of their shots hit their mark.

Suddenly the spot light of a police helicopter lit up the street. One of Mostro's shooters from the armored van aimed his gun high and sent a massive burst of lead into the belly of the copter, causing it to wobble and dive left until it was out of sight.

The closer Self moved, the more Mostro and his men sent shots his way. Again he was outgunned and at a disadvantage. Trying to shoot Mostro was suicide. Self wanted to chop him into pieces, so dying in an effort to kill Mostro was not part of the plan.

After emptying his revolvers, Mostro limped into the safety of the second armored van. Within seconds the powerful engines roared. The front tires of the first van rolled over the bodies of the men that Self and Chango killed and all three vans made a U-turn.

Bobby Lee, Culo and Rich saw the armored van's coming their way and shot at the windshields, engine blocks, and tires, but nothing could stop them. They would need a rocket launcher or a tank. Mostro's caravan sped away, and Self took off, heading for the cargo van.

"No chase," Chango warned after jumping in the van on the passenger side.

Self ignored him and sped past Manny and Bobby Lee and the crew. He wanted Mostro badly. He needed to kill him more than anything he ever needed to do in his life. Anything less meant disappointing himself and not honoring his dead family, and that wasn't going to happen.

He sped around the back roads, just feet away from the speeding vans. Up ahead was the exit ramp to the New England thruway, a Hess gas station, and the intersection of 233rd Street. At the intersection was a phalanx of police cars and trucks, blocking the way out, but that didn't stop Mostro. His armored vans plowed through the roadblock, and kept going.

"Turn, turn!" Chango advised and Self listened. He wouldn't make it through the barricade or the tight opening the armored vans made. The cargo van didn't have that type of power, and he would be captured and that wasn't an option either.

"What the fuck is he doing?" Manny yelled when he saw Self haul ass and chase behind Mostro with Chango as his passenger.

Behind him the roar of the police engines grew closer until the Marielitos sent hot metal their way.

Manny looked all around, praying for an escape but before he had to leave, he had to get his little brother to the hospital.

He rushed over to the jeep Cherokee and found Puncho. "*Emmpt. Emmmmpt,*" Puncho groaned.

"Hang in there," he warned his brother. "Don't stop fighting, we gonna get you—"

Gun shots came whizzing by Manny's head. He ducked quickly, returned fire and then soon realized that the police were done waiting. He ran for cover from the gunshots of the Marielitos, and the police trying to move in, finding himself being pushed away from Puncho.

"We gotta get out of here," he said into his Bluetooth.

"Head's up!" Bobby Lee responded in Manny's ear as he and Rich backed their pickup towards Manny.

"Duck low, Manny!" Rich said and Manny dropped to the ground.

Manny looked around and there was an older, portly Cuban with a .9mm running his way determined to kill him. Like a deranged killer, the man recklessly aimed at Manny, not knowing how to shoot correctly, but he pointed and repeatedly fired shots. The stench of asphalt, motor oil and sewage seeped into the back of Manny's throat while he frantically looked around, but he was pinned down. Sirens were approaching quickly. Closer. Closer. Then more gunshots erupted.

While Bobby Lee drove, Rich was in the back of the cab with a strap around his waist that hooked him in so he couldn't be thrown from the truck. He sprayed random shots around Manny until he dropped the deranged shooter and then he sent a few shots at an oncoming police car.

"Move! Move! Move!" he yelled to Manny.

With much effort Manny pushed up off the ground, grabbed his gun and stopped short. He looked over to the Cherokee that held his little brother, then his head snapped to the images down the road of the sea of flashing red and blue lights.

"Let's get!" Bobby Lee said over the Bluetooth, snapping Manny out of his fantasy of rescuing Puncho.

Manny did a full sprint, dived into the back of the pick-up, and Bobby Lee pulled off before Manny's body hit the flatbed of the truck.

"You good!" Rich told Manny as he hovered above him.

On both ends of the winding road police barricades blocked off the exits. Bobby Lee headed east towards the beginning of the industrial path of Provost Road and then made a sharp left. Shallow woods with spacious tracks of trees lay ahead. Bobby Lee made his own road by driving down a walker's path, speeding through the darkness with nothing to guide him, but his fog lights and his will.

"Where's he going?" Manny yelled to Rich holding on for dear life as the truck bounced up and down. For him, one more hard bounce and he was going to be airborne out of the truck.

Rich was crouched down holding on for dear life too. He had his eyes closed, trying to avoid the dust that was tapping at his lips and mouth. "I don't…know…the Bronx!" he said between the high bounces of the truck.

Manny wasn't sure where Bobby Lee was going, and he didn't care. There were no police trailing them, and by his calculations they were either going to end up on a highway or a swamp, and both of those were better than police custody.

After the bounces came far and few in between, Bobby Lee found a dirt road that ran opposite a service road and killed the lights to the truck and drove faster.

All was quiet over the Bluetooth connections, and Manny feared the worst for his brother. Two things ran across his mind and that was either they would all be in jail together and he could look after him then, or he was going to get away and then he could take care of Puncho from a distance.

Suddenly the bright headlights to the truck came on when Bobby Lee turned onto a thruway. Manny peeked and saw a sign that read, "Welcome to Connecticut".

EIGHT

"What the hell was that?" Manny screamed a few hours later when everyone was safely back together. They all met up in the Bronx except for Puncho and it was driving Manny crazy. "This shit...*is not*...adding up!" He screamed out to the group while pacing across the hard wood floor like a mad man. He turned to Bobby Lee, "Bro, can you get on that computer. I need to know where they got Puncho," he softly asked with a worried tone.

"I'm on it," Bobby Lee said before opening his laptop.

Rich chimed in., "Follow the dispatch for the ambulances and then cross reference to the hospitals."

Bobby Lee cut his eye at Rich. "Who taught you?" he asked, silencing his little brother instantly.

"Mostro in N.Y, and he Self's," Self declared. Puncho wasn't Self's concern. He was interested in nothing but killing Mostro and cutting his enemy into pieces. "Where he laying his head, boss?" he asked Rich.

Rich shrugged. "I'm flabbergasted that we just had a gun battle in the middle of a New York City street, and we're here talking about it. Let me get some time to process it."

"America," Chango said, grinning.

"Word, Yo," Culo agreed.

"Well get to processing. It's just the beginning," Bobby Lee uttered while tapping away at his computer. "You ain't seen nothing yet. Compared to how we had to handle these squirrel fuckers before? That was just a warm up," he warned, speaking from experience. "And when it comes to the N.Y.P.D? Well...I don't want to send them boys' caskets to they mamas, but they just ain't ready for that kind of street war, and no matter what happens, we got to get our asses back to the mountains. No matter what happens. Dead or alive."

"We live," Chango said. "Good day."

"Somebody *please* make sense of this shit for me?" Manny cried.

"Boss?" Self asked Rich, looking for some sense out of the madness they were in.

Rich caressed his jaw. "What do we know? Eduardo is—*was* Gato. He sold out his organization to you guys, and someone is cleaning things up. Hence the reason they came for us and him.

Mostro terminated Gato to make a statement, and that should leave Primo as the top guy."

"Unless there's another player?" Bobby Lee offered.

"Is there even a fucking Primo?" Manny asked in frustration.

"There is a Mostro," Self added.

"Doubt if he's the head of this army," Rich concluded.

"No, Primo," Chango said as he sat in the lotus position, nodding with surety.

"How you know?" Self asked, accepting Chango into the family.

Chango shook his head. "Man no die from tire burning and call out man name who no live."

"*What?*" came from a confused Self. He snapped his fingers at Culo who was dozing off to sleep. "Translate that shit."

"Huh?" Culo said before coming to. Then he closed his eyes and somberly said, "Put gas and a tire on a man's ass and light that bitch on fire. When he screaming out a name, we know that name belong to somebody, Yo," he explained before closing his eyes for the day.

"Then there is a Primo," Rich concluded.

"Now we back to square one!" Manny yelled in total misery. Puncho was on his mind and he wasn't thinking straight.

When Bobby Lee was done tapping on his computer, he looked over at Manny and said, "Albert Einstein hospital."

"*What?*" Manny asked.

"Who?" Rich inquired.

"Where they took Puncho," Bobby Lee explained. "Critical condition."

Silence enveloped the men. Everyone was lost in thoughts of their reality. Then Chango opened his arms wide and yawned. "He will live," he said calmly like he had a direct line to God.

"I gotta check on him," Manny started to panic.

"Cancel that, Slick?" Self told Manny. "They gonna have heat *way* up his ass. Little homey wasn't cut out for this. So you gotta deal wit' that."

"*Now* you need to tell me this?" Manny asked, losing his temper.

"Better now than never. Wake up, Slick. This war shit…" Self faded off into his own mind. "…anybody could go."

"We needs to get on the same page," Bobby Lee noted.

"What chu need—"Chango stated before getting into a conversation with his imaginary friends.

Everyone looked on, starting to get used to it. When his conversation was over, he looked at the group like it was perfectly normal to talk to invisible entities.

"We need to understand de beast understand?" He wanted everybody's undivided attention and he got it. "I watch de movie. *El cinema, Scarface. Los Marielitos* was de *escoria* of Cuba." He turned to Manny and asked, "*Como decir escoria, in de English?*"

"*Escoria* is scum in English," Manny translated.

"Niggas nobody want," came from a dozing Culo.

"Tank chu," Chango said in his best English. He sat up in his meditative posture a little straighter like he was a professor giving a lesson. "To go from scum, to be man, chu must prove a lot. When we go to war we fight against man proving he man. We...we will gladly die for that. I say we go to Cuba."

"Not happening boss," Bobby Lee spat out with his tobacco. "For too many reasons."

Self stood and rechecked his weapons. "Mostro is in New York and we wasting time."

"This ain't like last time," Bobby Lee reminded Self. "These squirrel fuckers are a different breed. They don't lie down," he stressed. "They killed their own, you see that?"

Rich had a solemn mood. "They are human. Just trained and motivated by something."

"Or someone," Manny chimed in. "Gotta see Puncho."

Self said, "And we need to find that someone right now so Self can chop the monster in pieces."

Rich took charge. "Ok, so we know that Mostro is in New York. We need to tap into the police blotter and do investigatory work on where the vans came from and if any of the Marielitos lived." He turned to Manny. "Find someone that can go check on your brother, someone reliable that can handle business and deal with any police questioning without giving you up. The spotlight is going to be on you. Go back to the office and lay low there." To the rest of the group he said, "We need to lay low, do intel and do what we have to do to track down whomever Primo is."

"Sounds like a plan," Bobby Lee said, making it final.

*****

Manny didn't have a home to go to so he went to the safest place he had at his disposal—his office. There was nothing odd about an executive walking into the Lincoln building at midnight and making the most of his shower, steam room, pull-out bed and entertainment center, but nothing worked that would relax him enough so he could sleep. Thoughts of Puncho getting shot and being in critical condition ran a marathon through his mind. The guilt of him putting his brother in the hospital shook Manny awake.

He put the TV on, and every local channel was highlighting what they called, "Bronx Massacre." Every news channel was broadcasting and showing images from the bloody mess that he helped create. He was obsessed with thoughts of going to the hospital, but that meant getting through hospital security and police officers who knew Puncho was not alone in the shooting. So visiting his brother was out of the question.

Sleep fought with Manny all night. Finally, by 3:00 a.m. he dozed off, but was back up at 6:00 a.m. He awoke with a solution to his problem of making sure his brother was okay. He was going to send the one person he knew always took care of him and would keep her mouth shut.

By 6:30 a.m. he had shaved, showered, and dressed in a gray windowpane suit and a purple shirt with a purple and platinum tie. He slipped on black wingtip shoes, Cartier glasses, and diamond cufflinks that gleamed from the recess lights above. By 8:00 a.m. he had called the office of his best employee, knowing she was there before anyone else.

"Top of the morning, Mr. Black," Nzinga answered her extension when Manny called. "You must have spent the night again? I didn't see you come in this morning."

Her voice was a relief. "Can you come to my office at once?"

"Be right there. *After* I order your breakfast from the cafeteria."

Within twenty minutes, the food servers were entering Manny's office with a food cart covered in white linen. Behind the waiter was Nzinga dressed in a cranberry, linen, one-piece dress with drooping cleavage that displayed a solitary ruby pendent. Her peep-toe, high heels that strapped at the ankles made Manny wonder what she saw in Edeeks and why he hadn't chose her as his woman when he first came home from prison.

"Top of the morning, sire," she greeted before dropping a copy of the *New York Times* and *Wall Street Journal* onto his desk like she had done so many times before. She pointed to the news on the television. "Cuban's on the telle all night?"

Manny nodded slowly and remained silent until the food servers were gone. "I need to speak with you about that."

"You do?" she asked with an arched eyebrow as she sat across from him.

It wasn't the first time she saw Manny in trouble with the Marielitos. Thanks to Edeeks and his pillow talk, from the very beginning of MB Enterprises Nzinga knew Manny was a thug with a good head on his shoulders. The last time the Marielitos were after him, and he needed to seek refuge at Edeeks's home, it was Nzinga who helped. After they developed a closer relationship, it was only a matter of time before she knew all his personal business anyway.

"I need you today like I never needed you before," he confessed.

She crossed her long legs and shifted in the seat. "Whatever you need. I'm at your disposal."

"It's about Puncho."

"Is he well?" she asked with urgency.

Manny's stare went to the carpet. "No. That's what I need you for. He's in Albert Einstein hospital. In critical condition. I need you to go check on him, please."

"Are you in bloody trouble? What do *you* need before I go there?" She asked, always worrying over him. "Have you been eating a decent meal? And this Cuban thing on the news? Are you back in trouble with them? Is it related and how do I best protect you when I arrive at the hospital?"

Nzinga had so many questions, but Manny knew she could be trusted, but the less she knew, the better. "No. Just take care of my brother. I can't go. You understand?"

Nzinga stood abruptly. "Let me clear my schedule. Then I'll be promptly leaving." She looked over at the rumpled bed and said, "Let me get someone up here to tidy up, and Manny," she stated while leaning in closer. "You're always welcome at my home, if you need a place to stay, you know. Edeeks and I are done. Been done for a long time now. He's back with his wife and I've moved on. FYI."

Manny nodded that he understood. If he was interested, so was she. Thinking straight was hard enough to do, so thinking with his dick was out of the question.

Nzinga smirked at his solemn expression and then smiled without showing teeth as she backed her way out of the office.

Manny exhaled a sigh of relief and waited.

*****

Racheal hurried into Manny's office at 9:00 a.m. "Baby are you okay?" She rushed behind his desk and looked down into his eyes. "Where have you been? Have you heard the news—where were you last night?"

The last thing Manny needed was another one of her interrogations. He looked over at the freshly made couch that held the bed he had slept in last night and said, "I was here."

"All night?"

"All night," he uttered.

"Cubans were killed in the Bronx. They used the word Marielitos."

"*And?*"

"*And?*" she snapped back sarcastically. "Those are the people you had problems with before. Stop playing with me Manny."

He shrugged. "So. They have problems with a lot of people."

"Like who?"

"You ain't see me in days and this is what you come up with?" he asked, quickly losing his patience.

"Where's Puncho?"

His head eyed at her. "Why?"

She looked away. "Um…I had a dream about him. He was in trouble. Is he okay?'

"I don't know how he's doing," he didn't lie.

"Was he with you yesterday?"

"What's with all the questions?"

"I know you, Manny. I walk in here dressed very well. You haven't noticed and that means you're worried. So tell mommy what's been going on with her man? I don't know why you never confide in me. I'm here for you Manny."

"I want to come home to the house I bought, and sleep in the bed I bought for me!"

She smirked and quickly grew angry. "You rush us from Panama. You get all cagey. You tell me we in danger, and I hear that the same people that you had problems with in the past were killed and shooting at the police up in the Bronx, and you don't expect me to protect our children?" she asked, brushing her hands against her stomach. "Thanks for asking if me and the baby are okay. I hope this isn't an indication of how you're going to behave during this pregnancy."

Her pregnancy had in fact been on his mind during all the drama. He wanted a daughter and a real life badly. He just needed to end this war and there was no way of explaining that to Racheal so he remained silent.

In her state of emotional instability she looked down at Manny, saw that he was remaining silent, and lost it. "Okay, Manny," she yelled and turned on her heels. "*Fine*! Have it your way!" she screamed and stormed out his office.

"This bitch is crazy," he uttered to himself and placed his forehead on his desk.

*****

At noon Nzinga walked into Manny's office wearing a smile that instantly uplifted his spirit.

"He's okay?" he asked.

Nzinga nodded and her smile morphed into a smirk followed by sobbing. "He's not well and he's in a coma. He was shot in his head, you know? I had to act like I was his sister. Then the police began to ask questions and tried to interrogate me, but I was having none of it."

"What did they ask you?"

"The simple blokes asked for you and I informed them that I had no idea of your whereabouts. Then they wanted to know personal things about your patterns of behavior. Again I was of no help to them." She paused and then said, "Puncho started mumbling something about Mariel?" She cleared her throat and asked, "How much trouble are you truly in? Is this company at risk based on your past criminal behavior? Not judging. I just really need to know. I feel that I should know, Manny."

"Why?"

"I love it here. Love you…" She looked up and around the room. "…bloody in love with all this."

"You have nothing to worry about."

"I take it then, that you need me to continue to be responsible for Puncho?"

He nodded. "Yeah. I won't forget what you're doing for me."

She reached across the table, held both of his hands, and closed her eyes. "Jesus take care of this man," she prayed out loud. Then opened her eyes saying, "It's not too late you know."

"For what?"

"To give yourself to the Lord."

He looked away in shame. "One day, but not today."

She held his hands tighter. "Manny, you have changed my life. Never forget that, but we all must do what we have to do." She stood. "I'm going back to the hospital at the end of the day. Just call me if you need anything else."

"Nzinga," he said and she stopped short to look over her shoulder.

"Yes, Manny," she said seductively.

"Thank you. For everything."

She closed her eyes and then looked to the ground. "Don't thank me, Mr. Black. When the day comes, you will see that you are the one that I should be thanking. So save your gratitude and just continue to allow me to look after you. That is thanks enough."

She walked out denying him the opportunity to ask what he did that was so great that she needed to always thank him.

*****

At 3:00 p.m. the direct line in Manny's office rang, waking him from a nap he had dozed into. "Hello?" he answered.

Larry excitedly said, "Boss. You have Captain Baylor on his way up with three officers. *Them* I can keep away, but he's on his way up."

Manny hung up the phone before Larry was done with the warning. He rushed to his private compartment behind the TV and stashed away the three guns he was carrying. As soon as he snapped the TV back into place his two doors flew open.

"Mr. Manny Black!" the detective who had arrested and got Manny sentenced to eight years in prison announced his arrival. Behind him were a group of three, young detectives who shadowed Baylor's every move.

"Baylor," Manny said flatly. "You here to harass me again? Think maybe this time you brought a warrant with you."

As he always did when he came to harass Manny, the detective pushed items from Manny's desk onto the floor before having a seat. Then he propped his feet up on the edge, crossed them at the ankles, and smiled. "No, Manny, you scum bag. I'm not here to harass you." He looked around the office. "You made some changes. Nice."

Manny stared at the dark, round pock marked face in front of him with the unlit cigar dangling from the corner of his impolite mouth. Then he stared at the layers of fat in Baylor's neck and the way his face drooped. He sighed and sat across from Baylor and said, "Make it quick."

Baylor shook his head. For a split second, his eyes grew sensitive and then his menacing stare quickly returned. "No, Manny Black. This time I think you want me to take my time." He nudged his chin at the phone. "Go ahead. Call your overpriced lawyer before your flunky Edeeks walks in here with his threats."

Manny didn't want to play his game. He knew why he was there so he wanted Baylor to hurry and leave "So let me guess. Cubans acting up in the Bronx, and you wanna come down here fucking with me?" Manny's eyes looked over at the three detectives who were admiring his art, the statues in his office, and nosing around. "God forbid if Castro dies, I should expect the whole fucking force to be in my office breaking things, huh?"

Baylor followed Manny's glare, turned in his seat and said to his minions, "Fellas. Have a seat."

Like trained pets, the eager officers quickly sat in the lounge area only a few feet away from his arsenal of weapons.

Baylor kicked his feet back up on the desk and said, "No, the Cubans in the Bronx that I'm sure you had something to do with is not my business today. *Today...*" he paused for effect. Then he uncrossed his legs and stood, looking over Manny while reaching for his handcuffs. He dropped the cuffs on the desk and said, "Today I'm finally arresting your ass for the Murder of Vallejo 'Packy' Pacquio."

The detectives pulled their guns and quickly rushed over to Manny.

"Want to call that lawyer now?" Baylor asked.

Manny was furious, but he wouldn't let Baylor see him sweat. Not again. The case he was being charged for was many years old. Baylor was the detective who arrested him for charges of being affiliated with the M3 crew, then he had arrived on the day he shot his wife, so Manny knew Baylor would love to see him begging and pleading for his freedom. That wasn't going to happen.

Manny arose from his desk like a man that was still in charge. He was certain that they had no evidence. While Baylor and his flunkies looked on, Manny calmly reached for his phone, pressed a number, and when Nzinga picked up, he said, "Have my lawyer come down to Central Booking and post my bail, and bring me a fresh suit and a plate of food. Also…"

Baylor snatched the phone out of Manny's hand and stared into his eyes as he said, "Too much evidence this time, Manny. I got you on tape. Turn around now. You have the right to remain silent. Everything you say or do can be…"

Manny didn't hear anything else out of Baylor's mouth. He had promised himself that handcuffs would never touch his wrist again and now they were being forced on—tight. The words "*have you on tape*" were ringing through his head. His problems with Pantera and the Marielitos was due to Pantera having him on video tape committing murders and trying to blackmail him into committing more murders and making more money. Now his life took another turn due to another video tape, but he didn't believe it.

"You bluffing," he said to Baylor, but something was seriously wrong.

Baylor looked like he wanted to cry. Like he was disappointed that he couldn't toy with Manny anymore the way he had done for years. Now that his investigation was over and he had Manny in his grasp, he had no words. The usual shit talking Baylor was silent. He shook his head. "No, Manny. We have you this time. You killed Packy, a confidential informant that put two of your soldiers away, and then you..."

"Captain!" one of the detectives yelled out, trying to tell Baylor that he was giving up too much.

Baylor looked the young man in his eyes and reprimanded him with, "Been doing this before you were born. Go down and get the car."

For Packy, shit, Manny said to himself. Just then he realized just how serious the arrest was.

Edeeks burst into the office, saw Manny in cuffs, and started to turn. "I'll call Joe," he said without looking at Manny or anyone else in the room.

"Right on time," Baylor mumbled to the fumes Edeeks left behind. Then he turned to Manny and said, "Loyalty like Edeeks is hard to buy. He must be really afraid of you. Love doesn't last that long. Especially with how rich you made him."

Manny knew someone was speaking, but he heard nothing. Instead, he focused on the solemn eyes of his employees as he was escorted out. Everyone poured out into the hallway looking at their boss being led away.

Nzinga defied Baylor's authority and walked up to Manny. "Keep your head up and represent us well. Trust in the lord." She kissed Manny on his cheek and whispered, "Puncho will be okay."

"Step aside!" Baylor growled at everyone from MB Enterprises. He rushed Manny out of the office, but when he reached the elevator bank he ran into a blockade.

Larry was blocking the entrance to the elevator. At each of his sides were two armed men Manny never saw before, dressed in suits with earpieces in their ears. "Slow your roll, Captain," Larry told Baylor.

"You about to obstruct justice, boy?" Baylor asked Larry.

Larry pointed at Baylor and said, "You have one more 'boy' in you before you're going to need the whole force to contain me, and you won't be making it out alive. *Now,* I didn't see a warrant."

"You used to be on the job?" Baylor asked, questioning if Larry was ever a police officer.

"Much higher rank than patrol," Larry answered. "Government."

Baylor and his men were stunned. "And you're willing to be arrested to support this scumbag?"

Larry smiled. "Just doing my job." He extended his hand. "Now can I see that warrant, or I'll have to stop you from kidnapping my employer."

Baylor looked over to his detective. "Hand it over and save this fool from getting shot."

The young detective pulled the warrant out and handed it over to Larry, who read it and then locked eyes with Manny and shook his head. There was nothing he could do.

Manny smiled. The love Larry showed proved that he was doing something right. "Walk us out Larry," Manny ordered. "Keep things calm as we're walking out of the building."

"Don't waste your time security man in trying to walk us out, that's not happening!" Baylor barked.'

Manny turned to Baylor and barked back, "*Puta!* You run the police, but *this* is my building." He then looked over to Larry and said, "Do as I said."

"We will see about that," Baylor said and it was a battle of who controlled Manny more.

Larry and his two goons rushed ahead of Baylor's entourage, clearing the way to the elevator and trying to make sure Manny walked out safe. As they took Manny out, the lobby to the Lincoln building was not swarming with people like Manny had expected. Baylor and his boys tried to look too dignified in walking Manny out in cuffs, but no one paid them any attention. The attention was on Manny and some of the tenants from the building asked if he was okay and some heckled Baylor and his minions for arresting a businessman.

"You lousy bums should be out chasing real criminals," a well dressed man in a business suit said in Manny's defense. Little did they know that Manny was the exact type of criminal the police lived to arrest.

The detectives swiftly guided Manny to an awaiting car and drove off with sirens blaring.

"I wish you were still on parole," Baylor said in the backseat with Manny. "This way I know you would rot on Rikers for a while. The fact that you managed to get off so soon is beyond belief, but those lazy bastards at parole will do anything to get out of working."

Manny was equally grateful he was off parole. The reason was Sheriece Taylor. She came into Manny's life as his parole officer, but quickly fell for his corporate appeal and expensive zip code. After a rocky affair, Sheriece left heartbroken, but also a homeowner thanks to Manny.

During his ride to Manhattan's Central Booking, Manny replayed how many times he had been arrested and had taken that same ride, but this time was different. He had been as creative as possible to avoid the law, make a fortune, and stay legit. He promised himself that if he received bail, he was never returning to prison. The authorities would have to find him in another country or gun him down in the streets. Then he wondered exactly what Baylor had on him, and knew exactly how to play the game.

"Baylor, I'm going to invite you to dinner when I get out of here in a couple of days."

Baylor grunted and said, "I *really* have you this time, Manny."

"You got shit, Baylor. A grainy video of some bullshit and of someone else doing some shit you wish I did."

"You're not that smart, you hot shot executive," Baylor fumed. "You can't beat hundreds of years of police work. I got you Manny. So good." "You probably reenacted a scene with one of your snitches but you don't have *me*." "Yeah, I got you," he bragged. "Bodega video camera has you buying a can of Skippy. The victim had Skippy all over the entry wound, so I take it you used the plastic jar as a silencer so no one could hear the shots—smart, but the video from the building next door has you leaving the crime scene. He ratted on your soldiers—motive. You killed him while out on a date with your now vice president, and when she finds out, I may have a new witness against you."

Baylor pointed out the window. "Take a good look at the world. It's your last time seeing it. Once we drop you off, we're heading up to the Bronx to get a better look at things. You didn't tell me your little brother was shot in a Cuban gun fight. I need to put you at the scene. I *know* you were there," he chuckled.

"When it rains...*it pours*," Manny thought to himself.

Just as Baylor was gloating about where he was sending Manny and what he was going to do to him, his phone rang with an old fashion ring tone.

"Baylor here," he answered. "Yes, I have him in custody. Right next to me, on our way for him to be processed."

Baylor grew eerily silent and Manny looked over to watch Baylor's face twist into several different expressions.

"Who is this coming from?" Baylor demanded with panic pushing his words. "Is someone over there going to give me some damn answers when I arrive?" Manny heard him demanding. "This is *my* collar. I worked hard on this case, gathering evidence for years and you're pulling this shit?" Baylor screamed into the phone. He must have been reprimanded by the person on the other line because he quickly grew obedient when he said, "Yes, Sir I can do as I'm told, but...okay it will be done," he ended the call, punched his hand in frustration and said, "paper pushing, brown-nosing bastards!" He tapped his driver and instructed him, "Take us to headquarters."

Instead of being led to the local precinct, Manny was led to the police headquarters at One Police Plaza in downtown Manhattan. "What we doing here?" He questioned when the unmarked car came to a halt within the confines of the massive structure that's owned and fortified by New York's Finest.

"Not many scumbags get escorted here. Only the top of the scumbag food chain takes this ride. Looks like you must be getting a gang of new charges coming to your rich ass," Baylor uttered. "Consider yourself important. Now get out of the car. I got orders to follow. For now."

Right there in the car, Manny pushed hope to the side and came to the conclusion that the image he created of himself as a successful businessman had come to an end. He was going through the criminal justice system, and for him to survive that ordeal, he might as well get into criminal mode. He was out of practice in being a young thug, but if Baylor was going to take him in, he wasn't going to go in so easy.

"Get out the car!" one of Baylor's flunkies ordered Manny.

All three men were outside with the door open, waiting for Manny to step out. Manny resisted getting out, just for the sake of resisting and Baylor's flunkies quickly reached in and yanked him out. "Don't like this bullshit," he grumbled through clinched teeth.

"No one cares, hot shot," another of Baylor's boys said.

Manny cleared his throat and said, "You know what's sad about you fuck boys?"

Baylor smiled like he wanted to be entertained with Manny's misery. He chuckled and said, "Tell us asshole. Go ahead, let it out on your last day of freedom. Tell us why you mad?"

Manny shook his head. He knew what he was up against and wasn't going to give them the pleasure of compromising himself. "You guys go to college to put your life on the line every day, for crumbs." He looked at Baylor's flunky and said, "Your bosses, the public, your wife that's getting fucked by the thug, that stupid bitch don't even respect you, and you think you better than me? You only a hero to the N.Y.P.D when you die. You ain't better than me! No, you just stupid and needed a job and you think a badge and gun gives you power?"

"More power than you, right now, asshole!" one of the detectives snapped.

Baylor wrapped his hand at the center of Manny's cuffs before telling his men, "You guys go up ahead. I'll take it from here."

His men knew not to question him. They shot Manny evil snares before walking ahead. Baylor stopped short and Manny's thoughts were filled with panic, certain he was being set up. *Is Baylor down with these Cuban's?*

Baylor pulled on the cuffs and turned Manny around before whispering, "This arrest is the icing on the cake for my retirement party, cocksucker." He leaned in closer so their eyes locked. "If you think I give two fucks about your future, you're not as smart as I give you credit for."

"Good, then let's go to court so I can beat this case and you can retire looking like the sorry motherfucker that you are."

Baylor pulled Manny close to what an outsider would see as intimate. "Listen to me, Manny. This is my job. Not my life. Me and you are not that different. You and me both have a job and that's crime. You get rich off of it, and I have to arrest your dumb ass based on evidence you leave behind. You leave the crumbs, and I follow the trail."

"Just like a rodent," Manny spat.

Baylor pulled him even closer. "I have my job, Manny, and you have your job, and whoever does their job the best stays ahead of the game, or out of jail. Where you fucked up at is you can't stay away from cameras, and where I always win is I have years of police experience on my side." He changed his tone to one of compassion. "Manny, I got you on video. Anyone can see it's you. Direct evidence. Or what you guys call, red handed. Dead to the right. you're done."

Baylor shoved Manny forward and he asked, "Where you taking me?"

"Someone *way* too high for me to question wants to talk to you."

Manny grunted. "I said too much to you pigs already. Nuff said, I'm done."

Baylor pushed him forward and said, "Well then do some listening, asshole, cause I don't want to be here just as bad as you do."

He escorted Manny through the brightly lit corridors of police headquarters. The trip was like traveling through a fortified maze of hallways, staircases and elevators. Finally after being shuffled to a floor scattered with a bunch of empty offices, Manny was led into a dimly lit room where a clean cut, handsome man with Mediterranean skin stood in front of a white projector screen. He looked like he belong on the cover of a fashion magazine instead of doing police work. Manny was sure the man's suit had to cost as much as his, and that was the price of a small car.

"*Hola, amigo*," the stranger greeted in perfect Spanish. He looked over to Baylor and ordered, "Remove the cuffs and kindly leave the room, please."

"Hmpt," Baylor grunted before doing what he was told. "I'll be on the other side of the door," he stated as a matter of fact.

"No. You won't. That won't be necessary. We will take it from here. You can leave the building," the suit ordered.

Baylor looked over to the stranger in the suit and fidgeted. He was confused, like he was in a land where they didn't speak his language. "*What*? This is *my* collar," he protested.

The suit ignored his tone and looked down while shuffling papers. Without paying a drop of attention to Baylor, he said, "Duly noted. Now leave. For good. Please don't encourage me to express that we can handle it from here again."

Manny rubbed his wrist in an attempt to regain circulation. An eerie silence gave way to tension that could be cut through with a knife. Baylor was behind him, but Manny could bet his freedom that Baylor was chewing on his cigar extra hard and squirming on his feet.

"Gonna miss you, Baylor. See you soon," Manny said with a deadly tone, not being able to resist the urge to stick it to Baylor one last time.

Baylor grabbed the door and yanked hard, but the door stopper stopped it. He struggled to slam a door that was slam proof. Thereafter, the suit cleared his throat and asked Manny, "You hungry, Mr. Black? Would you like some form of refreshment?"

"*Refreshment*?" Manny asked in disbelief. This was unlike any arrest he had ever encountered. The hunger in a bullpen-holding cell was like no other, and instead of baloney and cheese with stale coffee, Manny wanted to test just how much trouble he was really in. "Sure. Two Spinach and feta wraps, Tums, and a liter of water, Ph. balanced."

The suit looked over to Manny with annoyed eyes before lifting his cell phone. "I need someone to go down to Starbucks and pick up two Feta wraps, Tums and a bottle of water."

"Ph balanced," Manny demanded, trying to make a joke out of the situation, but the suit shot him a look that told him he wasn't there to entertain.

"A regular bottle of water," he reinforced over the phone. After placing Manny's order, his beady eyes looked down at his papers, and then he looked over to Manny. "You haven't asked who I am. Or what you're doing here," he said with overconfidence.

Manny sat back and crossed his legs at the ankles in front of him, making himself comfortable. "I know you're someone I won't like. I know you either will or can make my life more miserable, and I know your interest will be for me to help you in some way, or my enemies have sent you to try to terminate me."

"Try?" he asked.

Manny nodded. "I don't die so easy."

The suit nodded. "That is absolutely correct. Just the way we like it," he answered confusing Manny.

"We?"

The suit smirked and held up a finger for Manny to wait. "In due time, Mr. Black. Relax."

There were several different options of who the man could be, but when Manny fished for an answer, he sort of agreed to all options Manny offered. What really threw Manny off balance was when the suit stopped talking. He totally ignored Manny while preparing for his presentation. Then another shock came to Manny when his food arrived by way of a gorgeous Latina with a small badge hanging off her hip.

"*Buenos noche*," Manny told her, testing the waters to see just how important the man in the suit was.

The Latina's head turned his way, causing her hair to brush against the full, round mound that stopped at her waist. She smiled, placed the brown paper bag onto the table before him and responded. "*Buenos noche, Señor.*" She then removed the items from the bag like a waitress before walking out the room, leaving a trail of perfume behind. Suddenly the suit took a new interest in Manny.

"Now what would Racheal say?" the suit questioned as Manny slowly lost his appetite.

Racheal? He knows about Racheal? Manny asked himself.

The suit stopped shuffling papers and watched Manny chew his food.

Manny finished his food, and then paranoia set in. *Did they drug me? Nah. He needs me,* Manny reasoned. *I just hope he ain't Marielito.*

"All done, Mr. Black?" the suit asked.

Now that Manny had a full stomach and the Tums to help with his acid reflux, he stood and said, "Yes. Now you can take me to Central Booking so I can get to arraignment. I'm no snitch, so fuck *you*, Baylor, and every pig in this building."

The suit sighed before shaking his head. "Tsk, tsk, tsk. I never asked you for anything, Mr. Black. I've only offered you comfort."

"Not on a homicide," Manny reassured him. "The only comfort on a homicide is a plea to a short sentence and I'm not copping out."

The suit shrugged. "Well, you can sit in a holding cage all night long, or you can sit here while I watch a few photos."

He ignored Manny's presence once again.

What was Manny going to do, leave? The suit dimmed the lights in the cramped room, walked over to the screen, and hit a button on the remote. Instantly, a huge photo of Pantera, the man who started the war with Manny popped up.

Manny sat back down and squirmed in his seat.

"Roberto Sazon," the suit announced, pointing to Pantera's picture. "But you know him as Pantera. Is that correct?"

"Keep talking," Manny answered, refusing to incriminate himself.

"We're almost sure you were the trigger man that caused his demise. We're also aware that you were his hired gun and formed the street gang the M3 Boyz. As the leader of the gang we believe that you generated a great deal of fortune. Pantera provided the heads that you had to take off and you were possibly provided drugs and cash in exchange. Not to mention the sum of close to four million dollars before you may have killed Pantera's money man and accountant, on the same day Pantera died. Let's also not leave out that MB Enterprises, which is a great business I might add, was formed with fruit from the poisonous tree. Seed money from illicit activities that aided in the formation of the business that you developed. That's racketeering, but we're not interested in bringing charges against you for any of that."

"*We*?" Manny asked. "Again you said *we*. You F.B.I?"

The suit chuckled, "Pardon my manners Manny. My name is Alvaro Santa-Maria. Special agent."

"Who do you work for?"

"*People*. Powerful people who are interested in the future of Cuban-American relations," he answered swiftly. Then he hit the remote again and a picture of Eduardo. "Eduardo Morales is his real name. You know him as 'Eduardo or Gato.' He was a confidential informant for my agency for quite some time, but..." he hit a button and Mostro's picture came up. "We have reason to believe that this man—Pantera's blood brother—Manuel Batista Sazon..." he paused and chuckled. "It just hit me that the two of you have the same name and his first initials. Funny."

"You C.I.A.?" Manny asked with total confusion sending his mind spinning in circles. Alvaro was too calm for Manny's taste.

He smirked at Manny like he was insulted. "No. Much higher than that. My orders come directly from the Commander-in-Chief."

"The President?" Manny asked and suddenly had the desire to use the toilet.

"That's correct," Alvaro answered. "As I was saying, we have reason to believe that this man, Mostro, beheaded Eduardo in the Bronx. We also believe that you and your cohorts were there, primarily this man..." Alvaro hit a button and Self's picture came up. Then another picture revealed what was left of both farms. "Your brother Puncho, was hit in the exchange of gunfire. We have the right to charge him with acting in concert with every homicide committed that night, and his lack of cooperation is angering many of my lesser law enforcement agencies, so he will probably rot in a Federal prison."

Whoever Alvaro was, he was no Baylor and no petty beat cop. He knew Manny's crimes well and Manny was sure he was never seeing the streets again.

Alvaro saw the look of defeat on Manny's face and asked, "Do I have your attention now? Or do you still want to leave?"

"Keep talking," Manny uttered.

"Thank you. The way we have it, you were a soldier for Pantera. You engaged in a few homicides for him, and everything was well until you became romantically involved with this woman..." Alvaro hit the button and Xia's picture appeared. First, one of her full figured face, and another of her dead, finely shaped corpse after she received plastic surgery. "We're almost certain you killed her too."

Alvaro sat still allowing the image of the one woman who actually understood Manny to stare back at him. Manny's emotions swirled. He remembered shooting her and then coming home from prison to see her come back from the dead as a whole new person, only for him to have to kill her for sure.

"The woman—*your wife* Xia, was a trained assassin, but I'm sure you know that. What you may not know is she often visited Cuba for the sole purpose of terminating hostile politicos. It worked to our interest so we didn't mind if she cleaned up the garbage."

"What's this about?" Manny asked, defeated.

"This is about world power and those who control the levers of change. My employers," he said with pride. He hit the remote and a picture of Fidel and Raul Castro appeared. "These dictators have had their time. Communism isn't beneficial to many. After Fidel passes, which we're certain will be soon, Raul will sell to the highest bidder, and the Marielitos will try to be the brokers of making Cuba a paradise for tourism and use their influence for political leverage. We're talking *trillions* of dollars. That's what the Marielitos are truly about. When the Castro regime falls, they will return to Cuba, and expect to be rewarded. Or they will assist in the fall."

"And where do you fit in all this?"

Alvaro chuckled and placed his palm to his chest. "*Me?* I'm truly indifferent, but, my employers intend on having significant influence in the next regime, which brings me to this man." The picture on the screen changed to a photo of a balding, well-tanned man with a grey crown of hair and a neat, grey goatee. "Do you know who this is?"

"I have no idea," Manny responded with his full attention on Alvaro, who had basically explained to him that he was never seeing freedom again.

"This is Jose Miguel Gomez. Soon to be Florida's Senator Gomez," Alvaro paused and said, "He is also known as Primo. The current leader of Los Marielitos."

There he was. The man Manny and his crew needed to get rid of. The one who was the cause of Self's family being destroyed and the leader who had to die.

Alvaro studied Manny's face for a reaction. When he didn't see any recognition in Manny's eyes, he was embarrassed. "You have no idea who this is?" he asked with surprise. "Guess I just pulled the rabbit out of the hat?"

Manny remained calm. There was no comprehension of what was going on.

Alvaro was a great poker player. His face gave no clues to clear up Manny's confusion.

"So…what do you want?"

Alvaro saw Manny's puzzled expression and said, "We have a missing link. Gato was very helpful, but now he's gone. It's in the best interest of my employers that all the missing pieces of the puzzle add up, and the one thing we are in the dark with is what went on in Delaware, and many other pieces that are still relevant to us today. Things off our radar, and places that aren't good for us to be openly associated with. If we understand many of the missing facts, then we can end much of the Marielito stronghold. We cannot afford for Primo to win his seat or gain more political influence, but if he can be tied to a criminal organization, and we have a direct witness…or if he's terminated by a street thug, based on his criminal activities…well then, he is defeated and our agenda is met. He will be in town this week…"

Alvaro stopped short and let the silence sink in, and Manny's brain was on overload. After he slowly grasped at the pieces of the puzzle he was given, Manny tried his best to make sense of it all.

"So, according to you, I was the trigger man for Pantera. Now you want me to be the trigger man for you—*your employers*?"

"You said that, Mr. Black. Not me."

Manny nodded. "Or be a snitch to fill in the blanks?"

Alvaro answered, "And receive full immunity from all current and pending charges and investigations associated with you and your conspirators. Keep your fortune, and maybe have a future in Cuban politics. Who knows? I've seen crazier things. We believe that you'll be a natural. You're a leader, Mr. Black." He signed and then offered, "Or you will have no choice but to battle a full indictment from every law enforcement agency known to man. In due time of course. Just enough time for you to think over our offer."

Manny looked over to Alvaro with complete helplessness etched into his face. The offer was too easy. His mind contemplated over the options Alvaro put on the table. It meant he could walk away from the life of crime, end the war with the Marielitos, and save Puncho from spending eternity in a Federal prison. Then for some strange reason he thought of his Bugatti, the million dollar car he rarely drove. He had spent millions and made even more. Then he thought of Racheal. What would she think? She was pregnant with his second child, so now he had two children who would never see him again. Then he contemplated the chance in front of him to bring his enemies down, and then there was the arrest for Packy. The snitch that caused his main soldiers to be rotting in prison right at that moment, and the reason why he was being arrested.

He weighed the pros and cons of his situation, but the code he lived by gnawed at him. "Everybody talk gangster until it's time to stand up and be a gangster," he mumbled.

"What was that?" Alvaro asked, not sure he heard Manny right.

Manny cleared his throat and said, "You live by the code. You die by the code."

"*Code?*" Alvaro chuckled. "The code is a myth. Made by the invisible Minister of street ethics. The top men get to the top by playing ball, compromising and selling each other out. I see it every day."

Manny stood. "Rather die on my feet than live on my knees."

"*Really*, Manuel Black?

"Really," he answered.

"Thought you were wiser."

"Was going to say the same about you," Manny replied.

Alvaro smiled and reached his hand out to shake Manny's. "You have made your choice, Mr. Black. Now you must live and die with it." He reached into the side pocket of his blazer, removed a business card, and handed it over to Manny. "Call me if you change your mind."

Manny stared at the card, hoping Alvaro could be identified with a government agency, but the card only had a phone number in bold letters. Manny thought that was odd. *Just a phone number?* he thought while flipping the card over to the back, hoping there was more information, but there was none.

Alvaro picked up his phone. Within seconds, two Latino men in dapper suits stepped into the small room and stood at ease at the back of the room. Alvaro nodded to the men, pointed in their direction, and told Manny, "Your ride awaits you. Hope to hear from you soon."

"Seriously doubt that," Manny said with the weight of the world pressing down on his shoulders and getting heavier by the second. His freedom was gone.

The men in suits carefully placed black handcuffs onto Manny's wrist and checked if he was okay with the level of tightness.

"Farewell, Mr. Black. We *will* meet again. I'll be waiting for your call."

*****

Manny was led out of Police headquarters and placed into a black armored Van, not that different from the ones Mostro showed up in at the shoot-out. His mind whirled. He sat in the comfy, individualized leather seats starring at nothing but the portholes in the van. There were no windows and he didn't know if he was around the corner or in a different state.

Is Alvaro a powerful Marielito? He questioned himself during the ride. Maybe he is Primo and wanted to throw me off? He's Latino, the girl with the badge was Latina, and the two men in suits that's in the front of the van are Latino. Since when does a government agency from the president have all Latin employees? His mind asked him. "Chucha!" he cursed in frustration. With handcuffs on his wrist and being led to God knows where, Manny was convinced he was on his way to be killed by the Marielitos.

After a few turns and the van traveling for a short distance, it came to a stop. Manny heard the two front doors open and close. Then someone was fidgeting with a key in the side door that led to him. Then the door opened and he sighed at the sight of the familiar Supreme courthouse at 111 Centre Street, right across from Manhattan Central Booking.

"You look happy to see the place," one of the men said with a chuckle.

Little did he know, Manny was at one of the safest places in New York City. He knew from past experience of the Marielitos' determination to kill him in or out of jail. During his eight years of incarceration, he had too many knife fights and attempts on his life by Marielitos in the prison system. Now that he was being led into the state courthouse, and not the Federal one, there was still hope that he was able to receive a bail, or at the very least, still have his street cred protect him once he was back in the system.

"Have a good night, Mr. Black," one of Alvaro's men said after Manny was passed over to a correctional officer.

The plump woman in a dark blue uniform eyed the departing men in suits, and then she slowly inspected Manny's custom shoes and designer clothes and tie. She carefully read his processing papers again before typing his name and date of birth into her computer. When Manny's criminal history came up on the screen her eyes bulged. She looked him over with eyes of extra caution and held her hand up. "Hold up," she told him. After a brief whisper into the phone she hung up, took two steps back and then watched his every move with her finger on the panic button on her hip.

A few minutes later a steel door opened and two captains in white shirts, along with two large, black officers walked in. One of the captains had a long, freckled face with a Hollywood smile that civil servant health insurance paid for.

He adjusted his glasses and approached Manny like a gentleman. "Good evening, Mr. Black," he said softly. "Welcome to my facility. I'm Captain Warren."

Manny looked down at the extended hand. From experience he knew that in the Department of Corrections, the same hand that greeted you wouldn't hesitate to beat you. He pushed his hands into his pocket and looked the captain in the eyes.

The captain smirked and followed Manny's lead and pushed his hand into his own pocket. He then started rocking on the tips of his toes. "Okay, Mr. Black. Have it your way. My officer's and I will be escorting you to protective custody."

"Protective custody?" Manny asked. That got a rise out of him. Protective Custody, or "P.C." as the inmates called it was for the weak, the broken, or the informants that were hiding from their partners in crime that they were now telling on. "I'm good. I'll take my chances in population," he told them. "I don't have to worry about being protected from anyone in your jail."

The captain looked over to his subordinates with worry. He swallowed hard and said, "Well...Mr. Black. Based on your history in the system. We are not putting you in protective custody to protect you from the inmates. We're putting you there to protect the inmates and staff from you. No offense."

Manny shook his head in disbelief. Because he fought fire with fire and shed the blood of the Cubans who were trying to shed his blood, he was still being labeled. It had been too many years since he was released from prison, but in the eyes of the system, once a criminal, always a criminal. He was too tired to even care.

"Do what you have to do," he informed the captain.

A unified sigh came over the correctional officers. "Step this way, please," the biggest of them said politely.

The stages of fingerprinting, picture taking and giving his personal information was all a blur for Manny. He was placed in a holding cell the size of a small living room. The officers were given strict orders that no other inmate was to be placed in the cell or to have any contact with Manuel Black.

"*Chuchaaaa*," he softly cursed when he found himself back on the hard, steel bench of a holding cell, in the bullpen staring at the ceilings that he swore he would never stare at again. When he was released from prison he had made the promise to himself that before he allowed himself to be taken into custody he would rather die in a hail of gunfire from the N.Y.P.D. Now that he was back, too many thoughts from the past and the present were wrestling for his attention. Too many questions were invading his mind. Too many emotions swirled from his heart to his head, but guilt wasn't one of them. He had made up his mind right then and there that he was going to die in prison. His greatest nightmare was prison becoming his home, but hope wrestled with his decisions.

What he couldn't figure out was if Alvaro knew so much, then why hadn't the F.B.I, the C.I.A or any other law enforcement agency step in and arrested him a long time ago. Too many questions and too few answers. Whatever the case, he was determined to spend every dime he had to save Puncho and give Little Manny the best life possible while he was dying behind bars. Lastly, he had to get word to Self about Primo and why Primo had to die, but how?

Manny wasn't used to getting any sleep, and if he couldn't do it on a Hastings, California King sized bed with a gorgeous woman lying next to him, then sleeping on a hard, steel bench wasn't going to cut it. The moment his eyes closed he heard rattling of the bars that kept him captive. "Mr. Black!" a tiny, black female officer who struggled to get the gate open called. "You have to see the judge in a few hours so I have to transport you upstairs."

He was moved from one holding cell to another until he was beneath the arraignment courthouse.

"Yo, that's Manny Black?" an inmate yelled from one of the cages. Manny's street cred from the M3 Boyz had always followed him.

"Yeah!" Manny yelled out from the lonely holding cell, knowing what would happen next.

The chatter from cell to cell for those who knew the legend of Manny Black began. The inmates were yelling out his name like he was their hero. Others who were escorted pass his cell, looked at him with awe, while some stared with envy and hatred eating at their cores because they were in the presence of the hustler who made it.

By mid-afternoon three correctional officers approached his cell. A large, black, bald man politely asked, "You're Manny Black, right?"

Manny nodded.

"I got 'em," the correctional officer called down the hall before quickly opening his cell. Manny stepped out with apprehension. The officer put his hands behind his back and opened his legs, standing at ease. He looked down to Manny and said, "Ahh…um. Joe is…Joe is here. He asked me to take you to him."

The other inmates in the cages next to Manny grumbled and made demands, but they were ignored. The only thing the correctional officers were focused on was Manny. They cleared the halls while escorting him through the building, and moved quickly until they were on a floor that was designated for the officer's lounge.

Standing tall, and fully tanned with his hair slicked back, wearing his $4,500 shoes, $7,000 tan business suit, and brandishing his million dollar smile, was Manny's criminal lawyer, Joe Tacopica. Next to him was a short, flat-chested blonde holding a new suit, shirt, tie and shoes.

"You still wear the same size, right?" Joe asked.

Manny nodded, and Joe nodded to the guards.

The tiny female officer approached Manny with a hot, aluminum take-out plate that was covered. "This is for you," she said in a tone that was best suited for her supervisor. She then grabbed the suit from Joe's assistant, and told Manny, "This way please."

Joe bounced his arched eyebrows, making a joke of the entire fiasco, and Manny wasn't surprised or impressed. He was used to the drill. Joe was one of the most influential lawyers in the world. Whenever police and judges were arrested, it was Joe's number they called before they called their families. This was the only reason why he was seeing a judge in one day instead of two.

After Manny was well fed and directed to a bathroom where he could wash up and change into his new suit, he returned to Joe and his assistant feeling like a new man.

"This way, sir," Joe said before leading him into a private conference room.

The snug space was the size of an apartment's closet. The only thing that separated Manny from his lawyer was a short wooden desk that bumped against both their bellies.

Manny made sure they were alone before he showed how annoyed he was. "What took you so long?"

Joe's eyes widened with surprise. "I was held up by U.S. Attorneys in the hallway. This is a state case, but for some reason, the U.S. Attorney's office is all over you. They were like sharks looking for a bloody caucus until I showed up." He leaned in closer and whispered, "F.B.I get in touch with you? Any idea why the feds are on you? You talk to anybody?"

Manny thought of Alvaro Santa-Maria. It was clear that he wasn't F.B.I and it appeared that he even had a low opinion of them and was insulted that Manny suggested such a thing. So for Manny, he believed Alvaro's words.

"No," he answered. "Some guy from some other agency wanted to talk, but I didn't," he told his lawyer. "I doubt if they gonna release me on bail for this case."

Joe frowned and stood, "You wouldn't want to bet that, right? I saw a new Ferrari with my name written all over it." He buttoned his blazer and then revealed, "They have some grainy video of someone that looks like you, and can even maybe be a relative of yours, but that doesn't make it you, and as you know, they have to prove what they have first. You're a law abiding citizen, who employs people all over the world. You help families get fed, and that's what the judge needs to know." Joe chuckled, "By the time I'm done reaming the N.Y.P.D with freedom of information motions, and the DA's office with my discovery motion, I'll probably get the video suppressed and they got no evidence. No evidence—"

"No case," Manny answered with a brand new smile. Hope had quickly returned to his heart.

Joe brushed lint off his shoulder and said, "Get someone over here with a half a mil so they can post your bail. I expect my payment in cash. Sent special delivery." Joe smiled and Manny knew he was actually going home. "The judge and I smoke Cuban's together from time to time, no offense, and when his wife was diagnosed with cancer? Guess who was sending specialist to see her?"

A tear welled up in Manny's eyes. "Thank you, Joe," he said with his confidence slowly returning.

Joe waved his finger. "Don't thank me, yet. I still don't know if the AG's office has a trick up their asses for you, but when you do thank me, make it in cash."

Lawyers, Manny thought. Always out for the money.

A few hours later Manny's name was called and he walked out to face the judge.

An unkempt, scraggly looking man with auburn hair stepped forward and announced himself as the district attorney on the case. He expressed how Manny was a flight risk due to his extensive criminal history and a fortune that could take him anywhere he wanted to go. He suggested a five million dollar bail along with a surrendered passport.

Joe explained that Manny was innocent until proven guilty and suggested that the judge should set the bail for two hundred and fifty thousand before going on a tirade about Manny being an upstanding citizen.

The older, Jewish man on the bench, slammed the gavel and signed papers as he said, "Bail set at a half of million dollars. The defendant will be detained until said amount is posted."

Joe said, "Your honor, my firm will vouch for that amount."

"Whatever," the judge said, twirling his gavel.

Manny was going home. With Joe's law firm vouching for the surety of Manny's bail, the cuffs were removed and Manny walked out of court a free man—for now.

He shook Joe's hand and thanked him again for making his dream of freedom come true. Joe and his assistant walked off, leaving Manny alone in the bustling hallway of 111 Centre Street.

Again, having money came in handy, but Manny didn't fully believe it was real. Based on what Alvaro told him, he was certain that at any second someone from one of the many law enforcement agencies was going to slap a new set of cuffs on him and put him back in jail. As he gathered his cellphone, money clip, and house keys, he grew more and more nervous by the second.

Let me just catch a cab and get home, he thought to himself.

With each steady step to the front door, which was just a hundred feet away, Manny's nervousness grew into full blown paranoia. His head snapped from side to side, looking for white men in suits, ready to apprehend him. He looked through the glass on the doors, searching the crowd of pedestrians walking in front of the building.

When he stepped out of the front doors and onto the gray, dirty courtyard, he still couldn't believe his luck. He was out, when just a day ago his mind was set on dying in prison. Life was funny. As he approached the sidewalk, a long, white, stretch Humvee limousine pulled up to the curb.

Manny's shifting eyes watched as the passenger doors of both sides of the vehicle opened. He thought his eyes were fooling him when the passenger stepped out.

It was Mostro, dressed in a white tuxedo with a black cumber bun around his waist. A bright smile spread wide under the dark Ray Bans that covered his deadly eyes. The tip to his black cane tapped the asphalt three times before three men dressed in jeans and motorcycle jackets rushed to exit the other side of the Humvee.

"Dis way, *senor Blackito*," Mostro growled with his heavy accent. He bowed like a valet while his open palm gestured for Manny to get in. "I want to send you to meet me hermano Pantera."

This Motherfucker is bold and crazy Manny thought to himself.

Mostro's young soldiers moved discreetly onto the sidewalk where Manny stood. One of them had chinky eyes and was light skinned. The other was too pale to be considered Cuban, and the last, a shabby dressed man with dark skin and deadly eyes waved at Manny.

The leader of the three, Manny thought when the dark man's arrogance made him first on Manny's list to kill. Terminate him, and the other two would lose their courage, Manny foolishly hoped.

The street was filled with parked police cars, Department of Corrections vehicles and unmarked police cars. Too many members of law enforcement were coming in and out of the courthouses, so if Manny stayed still and didn't move, he was sure that he would be safe, but he couldn't do that. He was dealing with the same animal that gunned down his own men and two police cars filled with officers. Mostro was unpredictable.

"Maybe another time," Manny said to Mostro before walking off. He looked over his shoulder and yelled, "You mine. You can tell Pantera I said hello."

Mostro tapped his cane on the ground with frustration and said, "Ju finito, puta." He then ducked into the limo and left his three soldiers on foot to follow Manny's trail.

While Mostro's limo followed Manny down the street, he quickly crossed its path, rushed to the other side of the street, and started walking in the opposite direction. The limousine stopped short, but the police car behind it made its brake light quickly go off and it started to move.

By crossing the street and walking in the opposite direction of the Humvee, Manny was now walking towards the three men who were trailing him. They quickly closed in on him and he had nowhere to go. Manny had to think fast. The darker of the three kept smiling at him while he tightly held onto whatever was hidden in his front jacket pocket.

What was he to do? Although the bustling street was filled with law enforcement, Manny couldn't pull himself to call out to them for help. Then as he was nearing the pale Marielito, just twenty feet away, the man flashed a big revolver, showing Manny what was in store. Manny felt like his end was near until he saw a police car coming down the block towards him.

He shuffled off the sidewalk and into the street. He raised his left hand like he was hailing a cab, and the police cruiser slowed before it came to a halt. He quickly glanced over the roof of the police car. The killers who were closing in on him a moment ago continued to walk past him. The chinky eyed killer, who was on the other side of the street, saw Manny stop the police cruiser and he quickly turned and walked away in the opposite direction.

"You need something?" the driver of the police cruiser asked Manny while suspiciously eyeing his expensive suit.

"Yeah…" Manny uttered while looking at his enemies stop at each corner of the block. He was still trapped between them. All he had to do was point the armed men out, or find an excuse to jump into the police car, but that was against his code. He started this war, and he had to figure out a way to finish it, not call the police when he was in over his head, but he didn't have a problem with using the police to buy him some time.

Manny looked into the police officer's eyes and asked, "Can you tell me the way to the subway? I'm lost."

"What?" the officer asked, not believing that was the reason he was stopped.

Manny looked over the roof of the car, still scoping out his enemies. "The subway," he told the police officer. "I need to get to the subway," he lied.

"Oh," the officer replied before bending his elbow and pointing over his shoulder. "Back that way," he pointed in the direction of the chinky-eyed killer who was leaning against the lamppost—

waiting. "Head straight up this street behind me and you can't miss it."

While the officer was giving his directions, Manny didn't pay attention to a word he said. He was too busy stalling so he could find an escape route. Both corners had a killer leaning against a light pole, and the darker Marielito inched his way back up the block and was directly across the street buying food from a hot dog stand.

"So, you got that buddy?" the officer asked.

Again Manny frantically looked around. His eyes met his salvation before he stepped away from the police car.

"Hey! Did you know your—"

Manny left him in midsentence. He moved as fast as he could, walking up the street that the officer directed him to.

The Marielito across the street dropped his hot dog so he could trail Manny. The other at the corner sprang up from the lamppost, not believing his luck of Manny coming his way. He pulled his jacket back, revealing the butt of his gun.

Manny moved faster, looking for a break and praying that he could somehow make it out alive. As he was approaching the Federal courthouse at the corner, a sea of white police caps and light blue shirts came pouring from the side entrance of 100 Centre Street.

"Traffic!" Manny said too loud for his own liking, and getting the attention of the small group. He hoped the Marielito soldier feared the law and wouldn't try to gun him down in front of the police. Based on the way Mostro moved, that was a strong possibility.

Manny quickly ran up and emerged himself into the group, ignored their suspicious glares and strolled along with them like he was with them. He took his time and kept the pace of the group while awaiting a new opportunity to flee.

As the group of traffic officers crossed Worth Street at the corner, Manny trailed them as he was shadowed by the tall courthouse buildings above. All three Marielitos slowly walked behind him, not letting him out of their sight. To Manny's left and across the street, a small triangular park in Foley Square separated Centre Street and Lafayette Streets. At the northern tip of the park, the sign to the J and Z subway lines beckoned like a beacon of hope.

Like a thief after a midday heist, he took off into a mad dash and strived into a full sprint, surprising his enemies, car traffic and pedestrians alike.

Running from drama was not something Manny was used to, but he was outgunned and outnumbered, and not ready to die. For the first time in a long time, he was about to take the train, then he realized that he didn't have a MetroCard. He wasn't ready to go back to jail for jumping the turn style so he ran to the glass box with the attendant inside.

"A Metrocard! Keep the change," he said as he shoved a hundred dollar bill through the slot of the subway booth.

As the attendant was sliding the Metro card through the slot, Manny heard the pitter-patter of the three men running down into the subway. Quickly, he rushed through the turnstile, foolishly hoping for the men to follow the rules and get a Metro card too, but he was wrong. The chinky-eyed killer pulled out his silenced weapon and aimed it at Manny.

Manny ducked, and then ran while recklessly dodging from side to side until one of the bullets hit a passerby instead of him.

"ARGHHHHHH," was the loud chorus of cries that came from passengers who ran for cover in every direction once they witnessed the shooting.

It was on!

Manny ran down the long subway platform with straphangers all around him screaming and running for their lives. He dodged behind the steel pillars of the subway, taking a glance and waiting for some kind of advantage. When he quickly ran to the end and out of platform, he jumped down onto the tracks, heading uptown. He glanced behind him and the Marielitos had their guns drawn, running faster than he was. No trains were coming so Manny ran into the abyss of the subway tunnel, seeking protection in the darkness, but the Marielitos didn't stop.

Running down subway tracks in designer shoes was not Manny's idea of a great plan. He was a moving target, running in a straight line. He hopped over the deadly third rail of the middle track, hoping an express train would come and crush his enemies, but no luck. He cut over to the third track that headed downtown, and heard the rumble and rattle of a train quickly approaching the station. Then he felt gunshots whizzing by him.

All three men stood their ground, took aim and started shooting at Manny. He ducked behind a dusty pillar and froze. Then the ground under his feet shook.

The train was approaching.

The Marielitos restarted their chase and Manny took off into another full sprint. Again he was rushing to the end of the train track. He crossed over to the opposite track. The blaring horn of the approaching train startled everyone but that didn't stop the Marielitos from sending more shots his way.

The downtown train was speeding into the station while the Marielitos' shots were getting closer to his head. He stood in the path of the oncoming train with only one option. If his body couldn't move quickly enough he was going to be splattered all over the station by the oncoming train.

Manny ran to the edge of the platform with the headlights of the approaching train illuminating him. The conductor's horn blared. Manny placed both of his hands on the dirty pavement of the platform. He lifted his body with all his might, and the train sped by, just missing his heel by centimeters.

Now that the train made a wedge between him and the Marielitos, he ran at top speed out of the subway.

Back onto Centre Street the answer to his escape appeared. Manny raised his hand and a yellow cab pulled over. Manny quickly jumped in as one of the gunmen appeared in the middle of the street. "Alpine, New Jersey. Floor it!" Manny yelled to the driver.

NINE

Manny walked through his front door and the warmth of his home comforted him, as he rushed across the marble floor towards sounds in the kitchen.

"Oh!" Ann yelled out before placing her hand to her chest from fright. "You startled me," she said, looking over Manny's newly rumpled suit. "You look a mess." She eyed him from head to toe. "Got a 'get out of jail free card,' Manny?"

She stood in his kitchen, wearing his cranberry silk pajamas, and had the nerve to insult him.

"Manny and Macca here?" he asked, showing his priority.

In an exaggerated motion she looked at her bare wrist, stared at an imaginary watch and then tapped her wrist and looked over to him with a smirk. "School, Manny? Are you okay? Seriously?" she chuckled at his ignorance.

"Where's your sister? And why aren't you at work?" he asked with a look of disgust on his face.

She smiled, sipped out of his personal mug, and answered, "You fired me. Remember?"

"So, why the fuck are you in my house?"

"She asked me to stay over because she doesn't like to be at home alone. So...I'm here." As Ann placed the mug on the island, she sarcastically said, "I'm sure she'll be glad to see you." Then she pointed up towards their bedroom suite and said, "She's in the bathroom with her head in the bowl. I think she has some kind of stomach virus."

He turned his back to Ann and decided to deal with her later. The only person he owed an explanation to was Racheal and that was going to require a lot of sweet talking. He rushed up the stairs realizing how much he loved her. It took his arrest for him to snap out of his selfishness and come to grips with how supportive Racheal had been over the years. Based on his talk with Alvaro, he knew his time was limited. He had destroyed so many lives, and Racheal was the one person who didn't deserve any pain.

Ann was right. Manny walked through the bedroom and into his massive bathroom and found Racheal on her knees with her face over the toilet. Her new weave was lopsided, her face was pale and her eyes were bloodshot red.

"Get away from me!" she yelled into the bowl. Her mouth was in the toilet, but her eyes were to the side staring at him. He rushed over and rubbed her back and she recoiled like a scared puppy. He held her hair, stopping it from dropping into the toilet before he said, "Come on, Ma. Let me put you to bed and get you better."

She slowly lifted her head. "You're going to get me better, Manny Black? *Really?*" She pushed away his hand of help. She stood, closed the toilet seat and then plopped down on top of the lid. "I need you to move away. Or maybe I need to move away. This is *your* house." She nodded like she had found a long, troubling answer. "Yes. This whole thing went really bad. Really-really bad," she mumbled to herself. "I never listened and violated."

"Violated what? And listened to who?"

She looked up, startled like she forgot he was even there. Then she waved her hand at him and said, "Shut up! I don't want to hear anything coming out of your mouth. It's all lies, Manny. The jokes on me." She put her palms to her face and started weeping.

Manny rushed to her side. "You know me, Ma. You know how real I am with you. I love you, Racheal. I really do. We gonna have our baby. You gonna be my wife. Everything I have will be yours, baby. Just let me show you."

"Bullshit, Manny. You only love yourself," she sobbed. "Now that you're facing a murder charge you love me? They have you, Manny. You killed that man while I was right around the corner? Waiting on you? Now I guess I'm your alibi?" She shook her head. "They have you on tape, Manny. It's you!"

"How do you know that?" he asked with suspicion. "Don't believe shit you hear. If they had me, would I be here right now? Would they give me a bail?"

She wiped the snot from her nose. "Don't' insult me." I studied law, Manny. I come from a family of lawyers." She stood with her eyes bulging and rubbing her stomach. "I'm having a baby from a complete *fucking* stranger! We don't even know each other...my gawwwd," she ranted.

"We're gonna have all the time in the world to get to know each other. I want to meet your family. I want to be your husband. Tell me, Racheal," he pleaded. "Tell me what you want? It's done. Tell me, whatever you need, and it's yours."

She sniffled, wiped her eyes and looked into his. "You sure, Manny? You sure you can handle what I want?"

"Anything."

"The truth, Manny. You won't give me that. Want me to be your wife? Please, I don't even know you. You're a sociopath, Manny Black."

He sighed. He knew that her and little Manny were the only things left in his life that was pure. "What do you need to know?"

Her head suddenly turned to him, and for a brief second she looked like she was ready to smile. "Did you kill Packy?"

Manny looked away. He shook his head with his gaze at the ground.

"You see? You can't—"

"Yes!" he mumbled. "Happy now?"

Her eyes almost popped out of her head. She quickly opened the lid to the toilet, opened her robe and sat on the seat just in time to avoid a mess from the diarrhea that was leaving her body. "Oh my god," she cried. Tears poured down her face as she stared at him. "Why, Manny? What did he do to deserve that? How many people have you killed?"

Fuck it, he thought. Based on what Alvaro told him, none of his deeds were a secret anyway. "Too many to pay attention to. I don't think about it, I just do what I gotta do."

Racheal screamed out while her insides poured into the toilet.

Manny grew angry. "Fuck it! You want to know? You *really* want to know?" he asked, stepping closer to her sobs and stench. "I killed men who knew what they were signing up for. You cross the line and live the life, you know death is around the corner."

"And you are death," she said, stating a fact.

"I'm what the fuck I got to be to survive. Only God can judge me, and I won't be seeing him. What else you want to know?"

"Did you start the M3 Boyz, like that officer…Baylor! Like he said?"

He shook his head. "That was Rico's thing and the shit just got out of hand. It's not like we said we were starting a gang, but I ended up being the leader. Wasn't my choice. The gang chose me."

"And Edeeks? Was he a part of the gang? Is that how you started the business?"

"No. Yes. Edeeks is too pussy for the streets. Me and his brother used to do robberies back before I met the Cubans. I needed somewhere to put all the money I was making and E taught me what to do. Then I used my own business ideas. I didn't know the shit was going to work so good, but I'm all legit now. You already know most of this shit!"

She stopped crying. Things were starting to make sense. "Did we leave Panama because of the Cubans? And were you involved with the incident in the Bronx? Is that what happened to Puncho?"

"How you know about that?"

She rolled her eyes. "The *news*?" Her sarcasm was back. "And Baylor said something to Larry at the office. So it's true," she said and looked off to the corner of the room. Now she understood him better. She nodded, accepting the truth.

"Anything else you need to know? What you need to focus on is that I love you, Ma."

"So you were the leader of the M3 Boyz, you killed people in that life, you started the company I work for with blood money, and you're still engaged in killing people because the Cuban's have a price on your head. Is that right, Manny?"

He shook his head—no.

"I can't hear you, luv. Speak up like a man. If you love me, be a man and say it."

"*Cono*," he cursed in Spanish. Confessing wasn't an option so he played it down the middle. "I did bad things in the past. Guilty! You happy now? Now you know me."

"And that man? Packy? Or whatever his name is. Why him?" she asked calmly like she was accepting his deeds.

Manny punched his palm and said, "Because he was no good! Rat bastard, cock sucker! If he would have kept his mouth shut, my boys would be home right now instead of in prison."

"So you killed a government informant, on the day you took me out? You dropped me off, drove around the corner, killed him and then picked me up like nothing happened?" She squinted and then asked, "But why did you smell like roasted peanuts?"

He was defeated. He sat on the edge of the tub and said, "They think I used the peanut butter jar to muffle the sounds of the shots. That's what Baylor told you right?"

"Who are you?" she mumbled. "What did I get myself into?" She looked over to him and asked, "How can a man who does all those things still be so affectionate and loving?"

"You judging me? Or you believing them over me?"

She shook her head and said, "No. Not me. That's not my job. I don't even know what to say."

He got down on one knee and said, "Say you love me and want to spend the rest of your life with a man who will always be real with you about everything. Say you gonna have our baby and help me make sense of my crazy life. I don't even know what I'm doing most of the time or what I'm supposed to be doing. I just know I'm not going to let nobody hurt you or my family. You are my family."

She looked out the bathroom window and mumbled. "I don't think you know the first thing about loving someone."

"Well…I'm asking you to be my wife so you can teach me."

She looked down at him on his knees. She had never seen Manny that humble or that serious before. Nor was she ever proposed to before. She stared at him for quite some time and then asked, "You want me to sign up for a life of danger, Manny?"

He stood. "Do you even love me?"

She started crying again. "More than you will ever know," she said between sobs.

"Yeah? Then what you think, everything is always good in relationships? Either you in this or you not. Either you gonna be my baby mama or my wife. We can end this shit now."

"I'm no one's baby mama, Manny! I'm a wife!"

"Then marry me."

She shook her head and yelled, "This is fucking insane!"

He turned to leave. "I gave you what you wanted and that wasn't good enough."

He headed across the room to his side of the bathroom and stripped off his clothes. Internally he had a war going on, and it was a reflection of how his life was externally.

Racheal had some damn nerves. He let the water run over his body thinking of the opportunity he was giving her and how she liked to throw his past into his face. It didn't matter to him that his criminal past was soiling his life in the present. The fact that he was facing a murder charge and couldn't be any good to Racheal or his children if he was rotting in prison wasn't a fact that he wanted to wrestle with. All that mattered to Manny at that moment was that he had a woman he declared his love to and she rejected him.

He walked out the shower and dried off as he entered the bedroom. Racheal rushed to him and stared into his eyes, but said nothing. Then she looked away and said, "I may have been a little too harsh."

"Ah huh," he grunted.

"Do you think you can really be a husband, Manny?"

"Do you think you can really be a wife?"

"Hmpt." It was her time to grunt. "When you propose, you're supposed to have a ring," she whispered.

He twisted his lips, and said, "Then get dressed so I can take you diamond shopping."

She stood in the bedroom and stared back at him. He was serious. Today could be the great day every girl dreamed of. Part of her wanted him to propose, but she knew too many things that Manny didn't that would separate them forever, if not getting her killed, and she didn't expect to receive the wedding proposal she dreamed about her whole life the way he did it.

"Things never turn out the way you expect them," she said to herself.

"What the fuck is that supposed to mean? Nothing can ever be simple with you."

She put her hand up. "Nothing can be simple with *me*, Manny? Take a look at your life and do not mess up my acceptance of your proposal."

He heard the words, but wasn't sure she meant them. There was no emotion to it, so he double checked. "So you're saying you want to be my wife?"

Racheal's tone was like she was closing a business deal when she said, "I'm saying I'll accept your ring and see where we go from there. Take me where you want to go. I need to get out the house."

Manny exhaled with relief. She didn't decline his proposal, and she didn't agree either, but before they left there was one thing he needed to clear up.

"Wait," he stopped her from entering the walk-in closet. "What the fuck is Ann doing in my house and wearing my shit like she run it?"

"Really, Manny? *Now*? Now you want to discuss this?"

Manny looked at her and grinned. That was another fight he wasn't going to win so he decided to open his mouth and fill it with his foot and remain silent.

*****

Pregnancy did not agree with Racheal and it was only the beginning. While Manny dressed, she complained about her physical changes and emotional feelings. She explained her doubts and continued to tell Manny all the things he would have to change to be a good husband. She made it clear that she intended on being a stay at home mom, she wanted to continue to collect her salary from his business, and she was going to need a full staff at the house to help with everything.

Manny agreed to everything she said because he didn't care and he had other things on his mind. He went to his garage, pulled the cover off his matte black Bugatti, unwrapping the million dollar car. The all black, deep dish rims and black tinted windows with darkened tail lights could outrun any Marielito, and the Kevlar padded doors would protect any bullets that tried to penetrate them.

As he and Racheal drove to the city, he was certain of one thing concerning the Packy case. Joe could string it out for at least three years before they went to trial. The alternative was Manny pleading guilty to a lesser charge if the evidence was overwhelming. By then, Manny would have Racheal under his spell. He could probably give her another baby, make her into the type of wife that could handle her husband being away, and the two of them could decide how to protect his wealth while she and the children lived in luxury.

With the Marielitos, it was better for Alvaro and his employers if Primo wasn't around anymore. So Manny was thinking, if he and his crew killed Mostro and Primo, then Alvaro's employers would be pleased. He wasn't testifying for, or against anyone. It was all politics, and his actions would save Puncho and everyone else. So if no one else placed him under arrest, as soon as he had Racheal pacified, it was killing time and he was finally going to put the war with the Marielitos to an end.

"What are we doing here?" Racheal asked when they pulled up to Mercedes Benz of Manhattan on Eleventh Avenue.

He pulled up to the side of the building, stopped at two huge gates, and beeped his horn. The gates lifted to reveal an underground parking garage. "You not a baby mama, right? So let me show you how my wife will get around."

Racheal looked over to him and smiled without showing teeth. He wasn't off the hook from her anger and mistrust, but he was doing a great job at convincing her to accept his proposal. He parked in the garage and most of the staff rushed out to feast their eyes on his brand new machine that they could only dream of owning.

"Mary Godek, please," he told a receptionist and she quickly called the sales department.

Within minutes a tall, blonde in heels and a miniskirt, who had breast and an ass that was younger than her sixty years, sashayed over towards Manny and Racheal. "Mannnnny," her raspy voice said with glee when she saw him. Then she looked over his shoulder, pointed to the Bugatti and asked, "showing off again, huh?"

"You must know him well," Racheal said before extending her hand. "I'm Racheal, pleasure to meet you."

Manny looked at Mary and said, "My wife. She needs a baby mobile. G-wagon. AMG."

Mary snapped her fingers with the extra-long nails and said, "Let's go down to the garage. I have just the one."

Manny and Racheal followed the sashay of Mary's ass and hips until they reached a red, box-like SUV.

"Have a seat inside," Manny ordered Racheal.

Racheal stared at the huge, four-door truck that was high off the ground and shaped like a box on wheels. She rubbed the crash bars on the front and the back of the vehicle and then opened the door and saw the custom leather. "This is *nice*."

"What's the best price you can do for me?" Manny asked.

Mary twisted her lips as she added numbers in her head. "Ahhh, about one-eighty after taxes and everything."

Racheal's jaw dropped. "Did she just say one hundred and eighty *thousand* dollars?" She quickly shook her head. "Ohhh, no. Manny?"

He twirled his finger and told Mary, "Wrap it up. I'll have Kevlar material put in the doors and custom wheels, but they'll come get it."

Mary kissed Manny on his cheek. "As usual. Nice to see you again. Stop being a stranger," and she walked away.

Racheal looked at the truck in awe. "Manny, I can buy another rental property with that type of money. I don't need that."

He took her hand and led her out the dealership. "It's not your money. Let me show you how much I love you. Don't get in the way of that. You want to see the difference between wife and baby mama, right? Now watch. Let's go."

"Okay, let's go," she surrendered.

She waited until they pulled out of the dealership before asking, did you always want to be a criminal?"

"That's what you see when you look at me?" he snapped.

She sighed, "I don't want you to ever think I'm judging you. When we first met and that officer barged into your office, you explained to me that you make no apologies about things you did. That was only a couple of years ago. You made it clear Manny that you're willing to handle whatever comes your way, correct?"

"Damn right," he answered, trying to contain his anger.

She nodded. "Right. That was my biggest attraction to you. Not the bad boy thing, but the way you have always been a man. The way you're ready for whatever. Call me crazy, but it makes me feel safe, and you're a great provider, but before I have any regrets about my entire life, I need to know a few more things."

He exhaled with exhaustion, "Don't mess up this day, please."

"I'm having your child," she reminded. "We will be connected for life. Don't you think I should at least know everything about you? I thought I did, but now that you're coming clean and telling me the truth." She rubbed her head and closed her eyes like she was in prayer. "I really need to hear the truth, Manny. I feel like we're starting all over." She looked at the stores go by her passenger side window. "And I like it," she said before leaning over and kissing his cheek.

Her sweet kisses removed all tension. "So what else do we need to do so we can put this behind us and start all over?"

She shrugged. "I mean, what caused you to feel that you needed to pursue a life of crime? With your mind, you could have done anything."

He looked over to her and said, "You should've been a cop. *Damn.*"

She smirked. "Answer, please."

After a pause, Manny said, "In Panama. We had no food. Pops got laid off and mom's was always crying. So, I robbed a man. It went bad, and it broke my family's heart. Almost killed my mother because of the shame she felt. She wouldn't even take the money. So I did what I had to do to come to America. Chilled at her girlfriend's house—Edeeks mother. I told you some or all this when we first met."

"*Wow,*" she uttered. "But you never—"

"We here," Manny said, stopping the car.

Racheal looked out the window and realized they were on Fifth Avenue at Tiffany's jewelry store. "Are. You. *Serious*?" she asked with glee.

He reached for her hand and looked into her eyes. "I *really* love you. I have to get focused. You're the best one to get me there, and I need you to be my wife. Not my baby mama. What I told you, nobody knows and you better not use it against me."

She studied him to see if he was threatening her. He was.

He pointed to the jewelry store. "I need you to go in there. Whatever ring you dreamed of having all your life, I want you to go make it yours. I want whatever's gonna make you happy and proud to be my wife."

Tears streamed down her cheeks. She stared out the window in silence much too long for Manny's taste. Then she took several deep breaths to summon the courage to do what she had to do. She leaned over and hugged him, "I love you, too, Manny."

"*Whew*," he let out. "That took you long enough. I thought you were going to hit me with your bullshit." He looked over to her and her eyes were staring up into the clouds outside the window. She was far away. Her body was with him, but her mind was somewhere else. He snapped his fingers to get her attention. "Hello?"

She blinked twice before snapping out of her trance. "Oh. Are we really doing this?" she asked like she was about to receive a dream come true.

He shook his head with amazement. One minute she could be as tough as a parole officer, and then the next minute she was as fragile as a small child. "Let's go before I start crying."

He rushed out of the Bugatti with all eyes on him. Racheal waited for him to walk around the car to let her out and they walked into the store where they were greeted at the door like they were celebrities. The lady employees looked at Manny's reserved demeanor and took a hold of Racheal.

Manny stood in a corner and watched the staff steer Racheal from one immaculate jewelry case to another. His cellphone vibrated. "Yeah," he answered.

"When can we talk?" Bobby Lee asked, not trusting the phone lines.

Manny looked across the room at Racheal's smile. He was glad it was back, because in the bathroom he thought he would never see it again. "I'm handling something important and trying to lay low.

"Need to see you soon. *Real* soon."

"Yep. Got my eye on Eddie's funeral to see who shows up."

"No need to," Manny assured.

"Why not?"

"I'll explain it all when I see you."

"Okay, we'll wake you?" Bobby Lee was asking if it was safe to come to Manny's house in the middle of the night.

"Yep. Early breakfast," he answered, telling him to come to the kitchen entrance.

"Say no more," Bobby Lee said, sounding more like Self as he ended the call.

Racheal walked over smiling while admiring the ring on her finger.

The saleswoman slid in next to Manny. "That's the Tiffany Embrace. Three carats. A modest stone."

"You like it?" he asked Racheal

"Yes!" she gushed. "Wow," she gloated, captivated by the diamond's brilliance. "I love you, Manny." She looked down at the ring again and said, "It's beautiful."

"And so are you, *Mami*," he told her, hoping she meant she was marrying him. "We'll take it," he told the saleswoman.

The woman smiled curtly and eased in on the side of Manny. "Ah. Sir. That will be close to seventy five thousand dollars."

Manny ignored the implication that he was unable to pay or didn't know the worth of the stone. He removed his Black AmEx card and looked over at Racheal while telling the saleswoman, "Yeah, whatever. I'll take it."

*****

"Wow," Racheal said in the car while admiring her ring. They were cruising down 42nd Street, heading to the Westside. "This is amazing," she said, commenting on her glimmering ring again.

"You sure you want to do this?" Manny asked with sincerity. He had been down this road before.

Racheal paused while gazing out the window. Then she answered, "I'm sure I want our child to come from my husband. I'm sure I want the fantasy of having a great family structure, but nothing really comes the way you want them to." She looked out the driver's window as they were approaching Park Avenue. "*Ciprianeeee's*," she said like a child passing an amusement park while pointing out the famous restaurant. "I always wanted to go in there."

Manny glanced at the establishment. He continued to drive when he said, "Call 'em up. Invite all your friends and let's do dinner as soon as we can."

Racheal smiled, "An engagement party?"

Call your family, fly them in. Set the whole thing up."

"For this weekend?"

He shrugged. "Yeah, why not?"

"Just like that?" she joked. "Just have an engagement party at a moment's notice at a restaurant that it takes months to get a reservation at?"

He sucked his teeth and said, "Picture you not getting something you want? All expenses paid. Just hand me the bills. Now I get to finally meet all of your family."

She eased closer. "You know. This morning I didn't want you near me ever again. Now I feel like I don't want you to ever leave my sight." She kissed his cheek. "I love you, Manny Black."

He glanced at her ring and said, "I love you, Racheal Black."

She glanced at her ring with admiration and said, "Damn right. Racheal Black it will be."

She kissed his cheek again while her hand eased between his legs. He swerved as they were approaching Times Square. Racheal unzipped his pants.

"Oh, you really like me now, huh?" he asked her.

"I think you're old enough, and experienced enough to know exactly when I'm liking you."

Manny rushed to get home. When he pulled into his large driveway, Racheal was stroking while panting, "Feed me this dick. Give it to me. Shoot that cum in my throat, *papi.*"

It had been a very long time since Manny had seen her as aroused as this. He knew it was the ring, the truck, and his declaration of love that did it, and at that moment, he felt that marrying her was the very best thing he should do with his life.

He quickly exited the car and dragged her across the driveway. By the time they were in the foyer, they were frantically ripping away each other's clothes.

"Yes!" Racheal yelled out when Manny pulled away her tights. "Fuck me all over!" she begged when he turned her around.

Instantly the click-clack of hard bottom shoes halted their passion. "Oh!" Ann said when she stepped out and found Manny with his pants rumpled at his ankles and Racheal with her tights down her thighs with her ass exposed. "You should take that upstairs," Ann angrily suggested.

"Whatever," Racheal huffed and avoided eye contact with her before grabbing Manny's hand to lead him to the bedroom.

"You can get the fuck out of my house," Manny said with a chuckle, but meant every word. He didn't like the energy Ann brought into his home, but right then wasn't the time to bring it up.

The newly engaged couple rushed to their bedroom and Racheal quickly killed the overhead light she left on. Manny pushed her back against the wall, grabbed at her tights, pulled them down, and ripped one leg off kneeling and sliding between her legs until her crotch was above his shoulders. The next thing she knew he was lifting her into the air. "Shit, yes!" she chanted, ripping off her bra. "Been a long time, *papi*."

Manny twisted her body until her legs were on his shoulders, her back was against the wall, and her fingertips were touching the ceiling. He slowly slipped his tongue between her wet slit.

"Sssssss," she hissed as he slowly rolled his tongue from her clit down to her split. "Your wife, your wife, your wife," she mumbled while his fingers gently spread her love lips apart. "Ummm. Hmmmm," she hummed when he sunk his tongue in and out of her hole.

Manny had a lot of making up and convincing to do. He pulled on her clit with his lips and then rapidly flicked his tongue onto her love button.

"*Whoa*," she grasped as heat traveled through her body. "Whoa. *Whoa.* Whoa.," she panted when his tongue was diving in and out of her wet crevice.

"You mine!" he yelled between slurps. "My everything. *Mucho mas, bonita.*"

Fireworks exploded behind her eyelids and an electric spasm ignited her spine and burst between her legs. "*Yes! Yes.* Ahhhhhhh," she exhaled as her legs trembled and her body shivered with spasms of ecstasy.

Manny eased her down to the floor, led her to the large canopy bed, and slid his tongue down her belly, ready for seconds.

"Feed me that dick while you eat me, *papi*," she begged.

Manny twisted his body until he was lying on her stomach with her leg bent back so her ass was in his face and his manhood was brushing her lips. Slowly he slid his stiffness between her lips and gently he stroked while rocking her hips closer to his face. When he couldn't take it anymore he began to feast on her wet hole.

"*Eyeeeee*," she squealed when he licked at her center like a mad man. "*Ohhhhhh*," she yelled too loud when his tongue played with her asshole and then dug deeply into her center. "Aye. Aye. You...da...*best*," she boasted as he gently pulled on her clit, nibbling, sucking with thirst and finally when he flicked the alphabet with the tip of his tongue.

"Whoa. Whoa-whoa...I'm....cha...*ummmm*. I'm *cum*...*ming*," she sang and Manny drank every drop.

Before the day was over Manny stroked her sideways, fucked her hard from the back, silk drilled her with her legs on his shoulders, and then spooned with her three orgasms later.

They lay in bed like they had no cares in the world, but as their eyelids dropped shut, they both knew better.

TEN

Manny dozed for less than five minutes before fear pushed him awake. Even when he was in a prison cell he didn't feel as trapped as he felt that moment. He had so much to catch up on, and put in motion so his life could be back in order and he could be around to raise his children.

He spent most of the night wresting with sleep while waiting for his guest. The thoughts that haunted him ranged from his brother lying in a hospital bed, to what he would wear to his engagement party that Racheal would be preparing for. With one of Manny's blank checks, he was certain she could pull off a miracle by having hundreds of people showing up to an engagement party at a moment's notice.

Manny heard a faint sound coming from downstairs. Someone was entering the sliding door in the kitchen, which meant who he had expected had arrived. Unable to be too safe, he held his HK sub-machinegun close as he crept down the marble steps. When he reached the kitchen, he exhaled in relief at the sight of Self, Rich and Bobby Lee.

"Nice place, Slick," Self said, his eyes bouncing around the ceiling.

"You got news?" Bobby Lee whispered to Manny.

Maybe Manny should have told them that he was arrested and someone from a Federal agency had information that put them all at risk, but he opted not to say anything. In his mind, he knew exactly how to make his predicament a win-win situation for his team. Heavy is the head that wears the crown. Manny was willing to carry the weight.

"I know who Primo is," he announced to his group.

Self stood. "Okay, Slick. Where Self gotta go and where Mostro?"

"I'm listening," Rich uttered.

"Jose Miguel Gomez. He's a politician from Florida. He's here in town," Manny explained. "He's the head of the Marielitos."

"And how you know this?" Self questioned with suspicion.

"Took the words out of my mouth," Rich added.

Manny looked away and paused before lying, "I paid someone to get me the info and I got it."

Self squinted, looking at Manny as if he knew a lie when he heard it. "You a'ight, Slick?"

"Why?" Manny asked with guilt, wondering if his deception was that obvious.

Self's eyes narrowed with suspicion. If anyone in the room knew Manny it was him. He shook his head. "Nothing."

Bobby Lee asked, "So you got a plan to handle this squirrel fucker?"

Manny shrugged. "Shit is complicated. Gotta take care of Puncho." He ran his hands over his head. "Plus Racheal is pregnant and planning an engagement party for this weekend."

"Really though?" Self asked unable to hide his sarcasm. His entire family and both his children were taken away. Now, in the middle of a war Manny wanted to have a party celebrating his new wife and a child on the way. "And that couldn't wait," Self grumbled, not asking a question.

Bobby Lee snapped his fingers. "Wait," he said before rushing out of the house. He returned a moment later with a small laptop in his hands. "Jose," he typed while talking. "Miguel. Gomez."

Rich eased into the picture and hovered over his brother. "Cuban politician," he read. "Affirmative," he nodded like he knew the missing piece to the puzzle had fallen into his lap.

"Says here that this scumbag is being honored tomorrow night. At an establishment named Asylum? Uptown in the West Bronx. Two hundred and second street and Ninth Avenue. Where is that?"

"That's off Harlem River Drive, by Dyckman," Self volunteered. "That's in the cut, nothing is over there."

"Manny!" Racheal called out from upstairs.

Before Manny realized what had just happened, he felt a draft, his head spun and Self was gone. Bobby Lee quickly backed into the pantry while Rich eased into a chair at the breakfast nook.

"Oh!" Racheal was startled by the giant sitting in their nook clad in military fatigues. She looked Rich over and then her eyes searched Manny's face for an explanation.

Manny looked over at his bride to be and said, "Oh. This is…um…"

"Allan," Rich lied, as he stood with his outstretched hand.

Racheal stared at his massive palm like it would attack her. Then she did a two finger hand shake and rushed over to wash her hands in the sink. "I've never met you before," she told Rich before turning her gaze over to Manny. "Is everything okay?" she asked, searching for a lie in his eyes. "I thought I heard more people down here."

Manny shook his head no. Then he and Rich stared at her, telling her that it was time for her to leave.

"Oh!" she blurted out. "Maybe your...um...friend, would like to attend the engagement party? It's this weekend."

"How you do that so soon?" Manny asked. "Not surprised at all, but how'd you do it?"

She shrugged. "Thank god someone cancelled. Like it was meant to be. Everyone is flying in." She rubbed her belly. "Everything is set." She yawned and waved goodbye at Rich, "Good night, sir," she told him before telling Manny, "See you when you come to bed. Please hurry."

Rich watched Racheal's curves sashay out of the kitchen. With each step she took with her exit, Bobby Lee took the same steps forward to re-enter the kitchen. As if on cue, Self eased back into the kitchen from outside.

Bobby Lee sat the laptop on the island and said, "We do this simple. Everybody. Armed to the skull, gonna go up to this event for Primo. When he and Mostro come out, we take 'em out, and head on over to Montana." He looked at Self and his brother. "Deal?"

"Indeed," came from Self.

Rich nodded. Bobby Lee looked over to Manny and said, "I need to go shopping. We need some two-way radios and Bluetooth earpieces. This time around we gotta set up a better perimeter. In case we get another surprise."

Self nudged his chin towards Manny and asked, "You riding with this, Slick?" He smirked. "Being that you got a wedding to plan, and an engagement party to get ready for."

Manny ran his hand over his head. He thought of his brother under police custody. He thought of all of Racheal's family flying into town to attend their party. If he was shot, captured or worse, there was no way he would be able to apologize to her or them.

"Well, Slick?"

Self pulled Manny from his trance. He looked at the doubt on Self's face, the anxiety in Rich's eyes and the disbelief in Bobby Lee's. Those sights were something new. "I started this war. I'm going to finish it," he promised, going against his better thinking. "If the ship goes down, I sink with it."

"Sounds like we gots ourselves a plan," came from Bobby Lee.

"And Mostro will die," Self added.

"Okay, tomorrow night," Manny solidified the meet.

Bobby Lee lifted his phone. "I'll let Chango and butt boy know what we gotta do."

"Butt boy?" Manny asked and nodded. "Oh, Culo. Yeah, do that."

Everyone was heading for the door when Bobby Lee stopped short and said, "I'll call you. Whatever you got on your mind, fix it. We need a clean head tomorrow night."

Manny nodded, closed the door behind them, and then killed the lights in the kitchen. "What the fuck am I doing?" he asked himself, knowing he wouldn't like the answer.

ELEVEN

The following morning Racheal was buzzing around the house, singing and humming. Manny played with his son, catching up on quality daddy time. As Racheal was making and answering calls for their engagement party, Manny's phone rang.

"*Jefe*, come down," Chango said on the other line and hung up.

"Come down where?" Manny asked himself while looking at the phone. Then his doorbell rang. "*Chucha!*" Manny cursed. "This dude is crazy."

Manny grabbed his robe and rushed down the stairs.

"Chango! Chango!" Manny Jr yelled and raced by his father to let him in.

"Baby *Jefe*," Chango called Manny Jr with endearment when the door opened. With dark shades on his face, he hugged the boy.

Culo walked in, shook Manny's hand and then hugged him. Manny looked behind Culo, searching for a driver. "How you get here?" Manny asked.

Chango looked up to the ceiling. "De spirits. They carry us."

Manny looked to Culo for a better explanation. Culo pointed to Chango and said, "Take him somewhere one time. He never forgets. He point, and I drive."

"And shoot," Chango said with a chuckle.

The two men laughed. Chango looked over to Manny and said, "*Jefe*, the water in the pool is water. Come see." He walked away beckoning Manny to follow.

While following through the hall that led outside, Manny looked over to Culo and asked, "The water in the pool is *water*? What the fuck?"

Culo shrugged and said, "I don't ask, Yo. All I know is...his crazy ass is never-ever wrong, Manny."

Manny was baffled. "Great," he said with disappointment and then reprimanded himself because he knew better than to ask Culo for an explanation when it came to Chango.

When they reached outside, Culo dragged his feet before quickly lying on a lounge chair. Chango walked to the edge of the pool and stood there until Manny arrived.

"What's up bro?" Manny asked, trying to understand what Chango was staring at in the pool.

Chango looked up and the jewelry in his mouth glistened when he smiled up at the sun. He was nodding rapidly like he was agreeing to orders that came from the clouds. When Chango's head came down, Manny stared at his own reflection in Chango's face. Chango smiled and pointed to the water."Water. *Agua.* It good, *Si?*"

Manny agreed.

Chango also nodded and said, "No good if it no move, right?"

"It's a pool," Manny offered. "Where do you expect it to move to?"

Chango smiled. Then he stopped, looked at the sun and spoke to it, saying, "Soon. *Bien.*" He looked at Manny, pointed to the pool and said, "But whatever go in, no come out. It no move. Not…" He made wave motions with his hands.

"Fluid," Manny offered a word, quickly growing tired.

"*Bien,*" Chango agreed, telling him good. "No fluid. It sit. No move. No new water flow. Not like ocean or river. Just pool. Water. Can't drink, no cook, just swim. Where? No where," he said and started to laugh.

"Yo. What's…up?" Manny asked, losing his patience with Chango's analogies.

Chango stopped smiling. He pointed to Manny's chest and said, "You *agua.* De water. You move, you good. You no move, like jail. You no good, but you never go to de jail. Dey no hold u."

Manny was stunned. *There was no way that Chango could have known about the arrest,* Manny thought. If Puncho was around, Manny would have understood where Chango's advice was coming from. He stood staring at Chango, giving his full attention now. Manny was all ears then.

Chango felt his lack of resistance and smiled. "You have de insurance for Manny?" he asked.

With the life he lived, Manny made sure that Manny Jr would inherit the world if something happened to him. "Yeah. Why?"

"Anything go bad. Little Manny safe with Chango?"

Manny realized that Chango was asking if he trusted him with his son. Despite the craziness, Manny did. "Yes," he answered with little apprehension.

Chango pointed to the sun. "You okay today." He said, telling Manny not to fret. He turned to leave. "I see you later, *jefe*".

Manny was speechless. He stood still, feeling something he was feeling all too often…fear. He watched Chango and Culo

155

leave his house by walking across his lawn and off his property line. Suddenly he felt someone touch him and he jumped—startled.

"You okay?" Racheal asked. "You look like you saw a ghost."

He nodded and turned to leave.

"Where you going?" she asked as he rushed into the house. "We need to discuss the party."

"Need to call my lawyer," he said over his shoulder. "And my accountant."

*****

Manny was sure he had the answer. He could personally put the tip of his weapon in Primo's face and end it all tonight. It wouldn't be the first hard target that he had to eliminate. If he could get to Pantera and cripple the Marielitos then, it should be no problem to kill the head and know for certain that the body of the gang would fall. Even if he personally had to find a plane to fly to Cuba and get it done.

As the sun set, he lay in bed with thoughts of what could go wrong later on that night and what he could do to avoid any errors.

Racheal came skipping into the bedroom humming the melody to Destiny's Child's *I'm a Survivor*. "Can you believe that I pulled this off?" she bragged.

He was concentrating on what he had to do later that night. "What?" he mumbled.

She grinned, looked at her soon to be husband closer as she approached. "I pulled it off," her smile faded. "The engagement party?" she asked with sarcasm and silently hoped he would give her praise for such a marvelous feat.

"Oh, yeah," Manny answered uninterested then sat up so he could hear her words more clearly. "Everything set?"

"What's wrong now, Manny?" she asked with skepticism. She knew him too well.

He tried to smile. "Oh, nothing. Tell me about the party," he said, trying to sound like the perfect husband.

Racheal dropped her pajama bottom to the ground, exposing her nakedness, and climbed into bed next to her man. Softly she asked, "Is something bothering you? Is it me? You don't like what the baby's doing to me?"

156

He smirked, knowing a host of questions were on the way. "I'm good. We good. Now tell me about the party."

She sat up, filled with new enthusiasm, bouncing her butt around the springy bed, and opening up her fist while she counted on each finger. "I have the entire menu done. My parents and family will be here. Ann has been wonderful, and I want you to wear your tux, and I have a gang of people I went to school with coming. I even invited your lawyer and he accepted. Is there anyone I left out? You really...ummm. You really don't have any friends," she said with apprehension.

"Just the way I like it," he said, calming her anxiety.

She sighed with relief. "Okay, then. We all set." She eased over so her eyes were inches from his. "So what's wrong with you?"

He shook his head, slowly, trying to avoid any questions she may have had.

She slid her palm against the smooth sheets until it rested at his crotch. After glancing at her new ring, she grasped his penis and stroked it. "You don't want to talk? How about feeding me and the baby?"

She dropped her head into his lap and kissed and pecked his tip, but nothing happened.

She looked up at him to find his eyes focused on the ceiling. She had no idea how bad he wanted to kill Primo and save himself, and hopefully create a win-win situation for Alvaro and his people.

"Oh, you're distracted?" she snapped with an attitude. "I know what you need." She popped up, pushed Manny onto his back, and slivered up against his body until her wet crotch was hovering over his lips. "You know what to look at now, don't you?" she asked seductively.

He sighed, then he closed his eyes, and nibbled at her clit, but she could tell there was something else on his mind.

She leaned back reaching for his penis, "I'm gonna suck this dick, daddy," she promised while stroking him and telling him what he needed to hear so he could stiffen, but it didn't work. "Get hard, Manny," she ordered.

It wasn't going to happen. Primo's face was at the forefront of his thoughts. Not sex. If he didn't play his cards right, he wouldn't be coming back home to please Racheal, suck her pussy or have sex ever again.

Racheal rolled off of him and continued until her feet were on the floor. "Who is the bitch?" She barked with her hands on her hips.

Manny was stunned. He looked around the room like she was talking to someone else.

"Are you serious? *Really?*" she whined. "I'm talking to *you*! Manny Black! The man who just had my pussy in his face and did nothing."

"Yo! What the fuck are you talking about?" he asked. He had way too much on his mind for an argument.

She pointed at him. "*You!* Ever since I told you I was pregnant you been acting different. I know someone else is on your mind."

"No time for this bullshit," he complained. "No other woman is on my mind."

She wasn't buying it. He had always responded to her seduction. To piss him off she asked, "So what? You got a man on your mind?"

"Yes!" he blurted out. Alvaro had gotten the best of him. "I mean...*no*. What the fuck?" he gave up.

"While I'm sucking your dick, and my pussy is in your mouth? You're thinking about *a man*?" She balled her fist and placed them on her hips. "Something I need to know, Manny?"

He smacked his forehead. The fact that he was being hunted by killers, been arrested, his brother was in the hospital dying and he could possibly spend the rest of his life in prison, probably never entered her mind. All she was concerned about was her issues and what was important to her.

He stood. "Not today," he begged.

"*Yes!*" she screeched at the top of her lungs. "Yes, today! Why not today? It's the day you don't want me and thinking of a fucking man while I'm trying to make love to you? *Really?* I don't even want to stretch my imagination to conceive what that implies."

"*Conceive what that implies,*" he repeated and chuckled with frustration.

"Is it too hard for you to comprehend?" she spat with venom.

He stopped short. It had to be the baby that had her acting this way, but he lost his patience. "Fuck outta here! Who the fuck argues like that? Shut the fuck up and find something to do."

"Shut the fuck up, Manny?" she asked, rushing to his side of the bed.

He thought of Xia's pregnancy and concluded that Racheal was too early in her pregnancy for her hormones to have her acting that way.

"Shut the fuck up?" she yelled in outrage and she reached under the mattress.

"What the fuck you doing?" he asked when he saw that her hand held his submachine gun. She checked the barrel, confirmed that a bullet was already registered in the short, black nozzle, and then flipped the safety off.

Where she learned to do that? He asked himself. He quickly remembered how Xia had done that same thing, and how it cost him eight years of his freedom. She was also pregnant with his child at the time.

"Now who should shut the fuck up, Manny?" she questioned, holding the gun like she had been doing it her whole life.

"Where you learn how to hold a gun like that?" he asked, calmly. He loved her, but if she shot at him and missed, she was a dead woman.

She lifted the deadly weapon and said, "From the best."

"*Tu habla espanol, puta*" he asked, wondering if another Marielito was sharing his bed.

"No, but who doesn't know that basic shit?" she snarled and shook her head like he was pitiful. She lifted the gun. "Now, you're going to tell me who's the bitch that has you not thinking of me? You think I'm stupid, Manny? Telling me you had a man on your mind when it's really some bitch? What happened to honesty?"

Again he was wondering if she had lost her mind. He couldn't make sense of her nonsense at the moment, and he didn't want to kill her, but he was losing his patience. "You overreacting, and just went somewhere I'm not gonna forget," he warned. When she didn't flinch or lower the weapon he said, "Do what the fuck you gotta do."

She lowered the gun a bit and screamed, "Why? You wanna kill me too, gangsta Manny? Huh? Wanna shoot another bitch that's having your baby so you can be with someone else?"

"*She's gone,*" he thought. *Loca*, he figured she had lost her mind, but he didn't like being vulnerable so he started moving. If she was going to shoot, he would have been shot. Instead of igniting the situation, or processing that she had just committed the ultimate violation, he rolled his eyes and walked into his closet.

When she didn't follow, he rushed to the snub nosed .44 he had hidden in one of his boots, quickly grabbed it, cocked it back into single-action and rushed to get dressed while remaining in the closet. Then he heard her crying.

"What the hell am I doing?" she bawled as he asked himself the same question.

He quickly threw on his Rockport boots, black Prada jeans, a bulletproof vest and a black Hermes sweater.

"I'm sorry, Manny," she wept when he walked out the closet.

"Me too," he uttered, heading out the room.

"We're still having the engagement party, right?" she asked in a state of panic.

Instead of saying the wrong thing, Manny kept his mouth shut and walked out the door. When his feet hit the last marble step in his foyer, Racheal rushed from the bedroom and ran to the top of the landing. "I love you, Manny! I'm sorry!" But it was too late. He was gone.

As Racheal stood at the top landing, staring at him walk out in anger, Ann surfaced from the guest room below and looked up at her in disbelief.

"*Really?*" Ann asked with her hands on her hip.

Racheal leaned her forearms on the white banister and closed her eyes before dropping her head in embarrassment. "Not now." she huffed

Ann quickly cuffed the ends of her jeans and then fought to put a yellow sweater on top of her white tank top. "Not now?" she asked like what Racheal was suggesting was insane. "Bitch. *Right* now."

"What's the problem?" Racheal asked like a guilty lover.

"You can't be serious right now," Ann snapped.

"Why not, huh?" Racheal barked back, giving Ann all the anger that was left over from Manny pissing her off.

"How much shit do you expect me to accept and for how long?" Ann yelled.

"Stop fucking yelling at me," Racheal yelled back. "I'm not in the mood."

"Maybe because you're having this fucking degenerate's baby?"

"You don't know what the fuck you're talking about!" Racheal corrected.

The sounds of feet pattering against the marble tiles in the kitchen and into the hallway stopped their argument. Macca turned the corner with little Manny right behind her.

"What happen, *Señora*?" Macca asked Racheal before glancing at Ann, who was just a few feet away. "I hear screaming."

"Somebody mad," little Manny concluded.

Racheal took a deep breath and then gave an equally heavy exhale. "Oh, no. It's nothing. We're okay." She created a plastic smile for lil Manny and said, "You okay, little man?"

He grabbed Macca. She eyed the women suspiciously. She cut her eyes between the two women like she was watching a tennis match, concluding that the energy between them was more like a lover's dispute than one between two sisters.

"Hokay," She said flatly while turning to leave.

"Byeeee," little Manny waved.

The moment the boy and the nanny cut the corner, Ann aggressively pointed her manicured finger up at Racheal and whispered, "You're very disrespectful!"

Racheal huffed. "Give me a minute and I'll come down."

Ann headed for the stairs, "No bitch, I'm coming up."

"Not today," Racheal said.

Ann took the stairs two at a time.

Racheal turned, heading for the bedroom. "Shush, before she hears you," she said over her shoulder.

Ann skipped at the top of the landing and scuttled to get closer to Racheal. "Bitch don't shush me."

From the recess and quietness of her bedroom Racheal said, "I'm only going to be but so many bitches Ann."

"As long as you're the *right* bitch, that's all that's important."

Racheal had no wins if Ann was too close to her. "What the hell is your problem?" she humbly asked, trying to avoid Ann's wrath.

Ann pointed out the door. "First of all you ask me to accept that you're pregnant! You violated every rule in the book with this shit!"

"You don't have to remind me," Racheal said in her own defense.

Ann stomped and yelled, "Now you're *engaged*? What the fuck! Are you thinking?"

Racheal folded her arms in protest and said, "No one else has a problem with it. Everyone is flying in. So what's the problem?"

Ann became livid. "Everyone? Everyone is not a co-conspirator to make you a millionaire. Everyone isn't pushing their heads between your legs and got you screaming how much you love them—according to what I know of."

That stabbed Racheal. She cringed, "I shouldn't have to tolerate your disrespect and abuse."

"*Abuse?*" She asked. She stopped, closed her eyes and held one hand up in the air like she was praising God. "I know this bitch just didn't use that word on me." She opened her eyes and they narrowed when she stared at Racheal. "Are you listening to yourself right now? Are you really tuning into your own broadcast this moment, cause you're lunching! I'm the one that loves every bit of you and has to put up with you falling for this degenerate, being pregnant and catching you fucking him."

"Whatever," Racheal said before walking off and flopping down onto the bed to text Manny.

"Yeah, whatever," Ann snapped. "Just remember when our mission is done, and Manny is dealt with that it will be you and I responsible for it. Go ahead. Make him believe there's going to be a wedding." Ann walked out the room and then doubled back to stop at the threshold. "*Viva la Marielitos*, bitch. Hold onto that reality, and don't expect me to show up to your fucking charade of an engagement party. I'll mail you my gift, bitch. A wash rag to wipe your tears with."

Racheal dropped her head in shame and started to cry. *You have an engagement party to plan*, she thought to herself, causing an emotional tug of war. She quickly wiped her tears and went into the bathroom to wash her face. She looked at the reflection staring back at her over the sink, and asked it, "You fool, what have you done?"

*****

Rage found a home in Manny's mind. He wondered if he could handle any more pressure, but his anger grew more and more intense with each moment. He headed to the garage ready to kill.

He was startled by a black, Chevy Camaro with black tints and black rims parked in his garage. He forgot he bought it. .The New York plates jarred his memory and he remembered putting it in his company's name. He shrugged and went to the rack of keys so he could be on his way. He had a man to kill.

Racheal's behavior was unforgivable, was all he could think of while driving out of his neighborhood. She was texting him over and over, but he didn't respond. After glancing at the phone one last time, he looked into his rearview mirror and a dark blue Nissan Maxima with tinted windows was trailing at the same speed. At the next red light, Manny made a sharp right. The Nissan followed.

"Maybe coincidence," he told himself, and he mashed the gas. The torque of the muscle car served him well. He was up to 90 in seconds and the Nissan was struggling to keep up. Then he saw the flashing lights in the car going off and heard the blare of the siren.

Fuck, he thought, grabbing onto the .44. That's when it hit him. Edeeks's car guys had installed a stash box. In that box was a Mac-10 mini-machinegun. "*Chucha*," he cursed. He was being pulled over and had two guns in the car. "Fuck it," he said before pressing the cigarette lighter three times and the stash box under the side compartment opened. He quickly tossed the .44 inside, closed it, and tapped the Aux button on the radio to seal it shut.

He pulled over to the side of the desolate thruway, but his foot didn't leave the gas pedal and his eyes didn't leave the rearview mirror. If a Latino stepped out of that police car, in or out of uniform, he was going to make a world record in speeding.

Finally the passenger door to the Nissan opened and a black man stepped out adjusting his badge and gun holster.

"Un-fucking believable!" Manny yelled and slammed his hand against the wood grain steering wheel.

Through the rearview mirror he realized that the Nissan had New York plates and carefully looked at the chewed cigar in the corner of the mouth of his nemesis. He couldn't wait for Baylor to reach the car. He had had enough. *First Racheal, and now this?*

Manny stepped out of the car wondering if Chango's words would come true. Was it Baylor who was coming to kill him?

"Get back in the car!" Baylor barked while reaching for his weapon.

Manny ignored him and slammed his door shut.

"Get back in the car!" Baylor yelled again, dropping his nasty unlit cigar in the process of backing away and yelling.

Manny was tired of playing president of a company. It was time for who he really was to surface. He had killed and almost died too many times to keep taking shit from a man he did not fear or respect.

"Fuck you, Baylor," he yelled, walking closer to the cop.

"I'll arrest your ass again, Manny. Stop where you are."

"Arrest me? This is Jersey!" Manny barked and kept walking towards him. Manny was pushed over the edge. "You ain't got shit to do over here. So fuck you and the rest of your pigs."

"Stand down, Manny," Baylor ordered, but he was the one who kept walking back with his hand on his gun.

Manny stopped, looked back at the short distance between him, the car, and him and Baylor. He looked at Baylor holding onto his weapon and said, "Keep reaching and I'm gonna gun your ass down right here, right now!"

Baylor froze. He was surprised. His hand quickly let go of the butt of the gun and he dropped it to his side. "Watch how you talk to me. I'm still an officer of the law."

Manny stepped closer saying, "All that means to me...today...is that bagpipes will be playing loud at your funeral and all the foul shit that you," Manny nudged his chin at the car Baylor showed up in. "And that other pig waiting on you do will be wiped clean after I gun you down, cause death makes you assholes saints and heroes" He looked at Baylor and then asked, "Wanna be a saint today, Baylor?"

Baylor didn't know this Manny Black, and Manny hadn't seen this side of himself in years. He thought the animal in him had died, but all the pressure he was under had burst the pipe of restraint.

He took a deep breath to calm himself. "What the fuck you want, Baylor? I know you coming across the Hudson is a violation."

"I want to know who you know," he firmly said.

"What the fuck you talking about?" Manny asked.

Baylor held up both hands, "Look. Let's start over."

Manny chuckled. "Start over?" He thought of the times Baylor put the cuffs on his wrist and sent him to prison. "*Oh*, now that you're out of your jurisdiction you want to start over? Next you're gonna beg and tell me you have a wife and kid." Manny spat. "*Puta*. Make it quick, Baylor. I got shit to do," he growled.

Baylor glanced back at his driver and then inched closer to Manny. "Okay. Okay. Peace then?"

"Peace?" Manny asked like he was crazy. "Never that. Say what you have to say."

Baylor couldn't scare, intimidate or threaten Manny, and since it could mean his job for being in New Jersey with a defendant he had already arrested, he knew Manny would have a clear cut case of harassment, so he didn't know how to proceed.

Manny didn't like the way Baylor was stuck. "You came here to tell me something, right?"

Baylor was coming back to reality. "Huh?" he asked. "Oh, who do you have on your payroll from the force?"

Manny chuckled. "What the fuck are you talking about, Baylor?"

"Either you have the greatest horseshoe up your ass, or you know someone *pret-ty* high up in police headquarters. I arrested you and now I got heat coming down on me, and they want me to retire all of a sudden, and since all this shit happened after I arrested you, I need some questions, for my personal understanding, answered."

"I can't believe this shit," Manny uttered. "The poe-lease coming *to me* to solve *all* their problems."

"This is how it goes, Manny. You get to a certain level in crime and either you, or the cops, want to play ball. That's what we have in common. So, you're at that higher level. Congratulations. Now, all I need to know is who was that man in the room? And are you an informant for the government? C.I.A.? Who? Because it's not the F.B.I, and I've been warned to stay far away from you by those who are affiliated with this powerful guy. So who was he?"

Manny chuckled again. "You know what's worse than a cop, Baylor?"

"A rat," he spat out and looked Manny directly in the eye.

"No. A black cop! A *Moreno* who forgets that, to the rest of the force, you just a nigger with a badge. You're useless. Get caught on the wrong night, doing the wrong shit, pull that gun and your cop buddies will gun your ass down while your badge is dangling from your neck."

"I know that," he quickly said. Now it was Baylor's turn to chuckle. "I joined the force with an agenda. I reached it, but that's my business. I only came to ask you who the man in the interrogation room was. That's it. I've been ordered to stay away from you when you were my primary target for years. I need to know who can do that."

"And that's why you in Jersey," Manny uttered a fact. "And you want me to help you?"

"Kind of. I know you're in the middle of a war with the Marielitos. I know they're growing, and maybe I'll retire knowing you're ahead of the game, but I need to know who that man is so I can get ahead of the game. You tell me, and I disappear from your life."

"Just like that?" Manny said with disbelief.

"Poof and I'm gone."

"And if I don't?"

Baylor shrugged and then smiled. "I got friends," he threatened.

Manny stared at Baylor. "Baylor. I'm gonna give you what you need, and make sure you tell all your police friends, deal?"

Baylor nodded with anticipation. He put a fresh cigar that he would never light into his mouth. "You tell me and I'll tell 'em. Scouts honor," he said, holding his hand up in a pledge.

Manny turned to leave. "What you need Baylor…is to suck my black dick, and tell your friends I said, 'Fuck all you pigs.' See you in hell."

Baylor spat out his fresh cigar. "Your grave, Manny Black. You just made your grave."

"Eat a dick," Manny answered before jumping into his car and pulling off.

As he made distance between himself and the police car in his rearview mirror, Manny knew the same thing that he knew when he was released from prison. If his life was going to stop from crashing, he needed to be in the driver's seat.

TWELVE

For two and a half hours Manny drove from the United Nations and up to the Asylum night club. Back and forth. This was how he had tracked down those he had lined up to rob back in the days. He was diligent. He needed the lead on Primo and Mostro. If he could catch either of them off guard, he could handle his business without putting anyone else at risk. 202nd Street didn't reveal any Marielitos so Manny headed to Bobby Lee and Self house.

Rich answered the door holding a 12 gage shotgun and greeted Manny with "Sup?"

"Ready. That's what's up," Manny said with exhaustion.

He walked into the spacious living room and found black garbage bags covering the windows. That was expected. What wasn't expected was a full box of grenades and smoke bombs on the floor. It was clear that Bobby Lee and Self hadn't lost their touch.

Self walked in behind Manny, sweating with his shirt off displaying a map of scars and bullet holes that were the result of Manny's war with the Marielitos.

Manny stared at his huge chest and then down at the twelve inch blade in his hand. "You good?"

"Self?" he asked, straight faced. "The God always good." He tapped Manny's chest with the back of his hand and said, "Take a lap."

In the big and small yards of any prison, anywhere, when a man asked you to take a lap, it meant that he wanted to walk and talk.

Self grabbed a flimsy tee-shirt and walked ahead of Manny until they were outside. He inhaled the brisk night air and then coughed—hard.

"You still ain't healed," Manny said.

Self led Manny over and across the New England thruway and into Pelham Bay Park. Manny could feel the tension, but this was his brother, the only man who had put his life in harm's way for him, over and over without asking anything in return, but Manny could never be too sure. "You good, Self? Really good?" he asked with suspicion. He still didn't know exactly how much psychological damage the death of his family had done to him.

Self stopped under a tree. It was so dark a passerby would have to take a second look to see the two men. "Self need to know what Self need to know."

If anyone could decipher Self's language it was Manny. "What you need to know?"

Self folded his massive arms and locked eyes with Manny's. "From day one. Self checked for Manny. From jump, Self held down the M3 crew."

"You don't need to tell me this," Manny said firmly. "I owe you. Probably my life. So what's the deal? I'm losing it."

"Self see that, but you ain't right."

"What you saying, Self?" he asked defensively.

"Self said what Self said." He pointed to Manny's chest. "You. Ain't moving right, thinking right, and too many blanks ain't getting filled in."

Guilt settled in. How could Self have known about the meeting with Alvaro? "What blanks?"

Self nodded. "You know. Self don't know. What you need to over-stand is, Self not coming back to the Apple. Self gone die killing Mostro. Gonna cut him into pieces. This ain't your beef no more, but one thing for sure. Self gonna end it this way before Self leave the Apple. Or Self gone die trying." He looked off into the distance. "Ain't no life without Peaches."

"That shit is killing me," Manny uttered.

Self smacked the tree. "Fuck all dat. Self gone ask you one time. Is there something Self need to know?"

There was his opportunity. Manny could confess about the arrest, tell Self all he needed to know, and the two of them could find better solutions to his problem, but Manny didn't want to show weakness. He was confident he could still end it all and save the day. "Nothing," he answered without enthusiasm. "Except that I'm going to kill Primo and Mostro. Finally end this shit."

Self shrugged. "There it is," he said before walking away. "It's on you, Manny, but one thing you forgetting to tell Self."

Guilt heated Manny's frame. He thought of Alvaro and asked, "What's that?"

Self walked off and added, "Tonight they all Self's. You see Mostro? Move out the way or get run the fuck over. He Self's."

Manny didn't move. He could tell that Self knew he was lying, but right then, he was grateful Self and him were on the same page. It was time for Primo and Mostro to die.

*****

"*Jefe,* tonight we dance. *Mucho* Marielito," Chango bragged over the headpiece that was lodged into Manny's ear.

From the small binoculars he held in his deadly hands, Chango viewed the spectacle in front of the nightclub across the street. Someone tried their best to make it look like a night at the Oscars. Red carpet, velvet ropes, photographers with their flashbulbs going, and huge lights circling the sky.

The corner of 202nd and 10th Avenue held a small electrical plant on the North corner, the Asylum club on the South corner, and closed food markets were scattered along the busy intersection. At the end of 202nd, headed east, Manny was parked in the dead end with Rich by his side. Further in the block, just a hundred feet from the entrance to the club, was Self and Bobby Lee. Directly across from the club, Culo was parked with Chango in the backseat of a stolen utility van. How Culo drove around New York with no driver's license and a cache full of weapons in a van they stole was beyond Manny's comprehension, but since they were there to hold him down, he had no complaints.

"Some real big shots attending this little soiree, huh?" Rich asked Manny as one limousine after another pulled up to the club.

"Yeah, this *puta* is really connected," Manny mentioned, hoping Rich didn't ask how he knew so much about Primo.

For hours they remained seated in their vehicles watching cars dropping off attendees. The occasional police car cruised by, and a handful of tuxedo clad, young Cuban's patrolled the perimeter—Marielitos.

"*Jefe,*" Chango called to Manny over the Bluetooth stream that everyone could hear. "Me go inside. Dance, and den dance outside," he said with a chuckle.

"You're not dressed for the occasion," Bobby Lee joked.

"Self need them to come now," Self said with impatience. "The God too close for comfort."

"Be patient," Manny whispered into the headset. "When we hit, hit 'em extra hard."

The amount of weapons Rich brought to New York was enough to arm a small army. Each man had their respective fully, auto machineguns. The difference between this time and the battle at the scrap metal yard was that Manny demanded that everyone wear full body armor and bring grenades. Rich demonstrated how to use them properly and insisted they only be used under circumstances of being outnumbered.

Another hour goes by before Manny sees the long, stretched Hummer that Mostro visited him in turn the corner. "Easy. *Easy.* Everybody be easy," he warned, knowing that if Self saw Mostro he could react and that wasn't according to the plan.

Just as Manny expected, a group of model-type women exited the vehicle, and after two henchmen exited and scanned the perimeter, Mostro exited wearing a black tux and huge smile. Manny remained silent. His heart went from 0-60 in seconds. He wanted to reach for his weapon, but he of all people had to contain himself. This was his war, his beef, the Marielitos just happened to invite everyone else to the party.

"Mostro!" Culo yelled into his headset.

"I take him now?" Chango asked into the mic.

"Where? He Self's," Self barked.

"Easy!" Manny said firmly. "We take 'em when they *come out.* Trap 'em in the cars and air it out. That's what we agreed on. Now we gotta wait for Primo." Manny stared at the truck Self was in, hoping the doors didn't fly open. "Bobby Lee?" he called, knowing Self would follow Bobby Lee's lead.

Bobby Lee looked over to Self, "He's good," he answered Manny.

Mostro and his entourage walked into the club while everyone looked on. Self was growling like a wild dog.

"Word is bond, nobody better touch Mostro. He belongs to Self," Self warned everyone. "Touch him and the hand of God gonna touch you. That's Self word."

Nobody spoke. Self wasn't going to get an argument. The determination in his voice said it all.

Just then, a long, white, stretch Lincoln limousine turned onto 202nd Street. It had diplomatic plates and on each side of the hood were Cuban flags flapping with the nippy wind.

"This is probably Primo," Manny warned his crew.

The car stopped and none of the doors opened. It just sat there. Suddenly a police cruiser with flashing lights turned the corner, slowed and then cruised down the narrow block. Immediately after the car passed, ten, well dressed men exited the club, rushing to the limousine.

"Keep your eyes open," Bobby Lee warned.

The young men surrounded the limousine. Their eyes glanced all around and their heads snapped from one side to the next searching for a threat.

"These guys watched the Secret Service work with the president one too many times," Rich complained to Manny. "Any particular reason why I just don't bomb the place and kill all of the gang in one swoop?"

"Too many innocent people," Manny said, even though he thought it was a good idea.

"Casualties of war?" Rich reasoned.

"They didn't sign up for this."

"Occupational hazard?" Rich argued, dying for an excuse to level the building.

Manny stared straight ahead. "It's not their war."

"Mine either," he huffed. Then he snapped his fingers and said, "Okay, how about we call it collateral damage, I level the place and we all go home? For good?"

"No," Manny said. He knew Rich was serious and capable of doing just that, but he didn't need Rich and Self on the loose, yet.

*****

Manny and the crew spent the next three hours watching every person and vehicle that entered and exited. Self had grown impatient long ago, and Manny's patience level had run its toll. Suddenly the sidewalk came to life. Marielitos started bustling outside, and then a camera crew reappeared aiming at the front door of the club.

"This may be it," Manny breathed into his earpiece.

"This *is* it. That's a promise," Self uttered.

The men from the large entourage that escorted Primo into the club were exiting into the street. In the center of their security circle was a smiling Primo, looking like a movie star, waving at his fans.

"When he gets in the car!" Manny reminded.

"And Mostro belong to Self," Self reminded.

From the safety of the truck, close to a block away from the entrance, Manny watched on as two of the men from Primo's security detail pointed at the van Culo and Chango were in.

"Heads up, butt boy," Bobby Lee broadcasted. "You got two coming your way."

Manny said, "If they cause any problems, just drive away."

"*Parrrrty* time," Chango sang while lying in the back seat.

"Chango, *suave*. Be cool. We still need Mostro to come out," Manny barked.

"*Definitely*, waiting for Mostro," Self added.

Meanwhile, in the van that was parked directly across the street from the club, Culo looked out at the two tuxedo clad men quickly approaching. He pushed the nozzle of his AK47 that lay on its side on his lap, right up to the door. Then he looked straight ahead while saying, "Yo, Chango. What I say?"

"Say we party planner," Chango chuckled. "We wait for party over."

Chango started whistling. Two, clean cut Cuban's approached, one stood in the middle of the street watching traffic while the other walked up to the tinted driver's side window and knocked on it for Culo to roll it down.

"Here we go," Rich said, slipping on his mask.

Manny's eyes were locked onto Primo. So close, but yet so far. Then he glanced over to Culo's van across the street. "Don't fuck this up, Culo," he warned.

"Yeah," Culo said into the Bluetooth. "We party planners." He slowly rolled the window down with his left hand as his right hand tightly gripped the trigger of the AK. "*Que paso?*" he asked the man.

"*Viva la Marielito*," the young man greeted him, probably thinking Culo was a member.

"Yeah, ok," Culo said annoyed. "Wha' sup?"

That was not the response the Cuban soldier was looking for. His head snapped at his partner, and then back to Culo. "Why you park here?"

"Ahhh. Umm. Party planner," Culo said with a smile. "We wait till party over."

The Cuban shook his head, telling the world that Culo wasn't checking out. He stepped closer, tried to look inside and Culo moved his head, blocking the nosey man's view of the AK47 in his lap and Chango lying in the back seat.

Over the Bluetooth all the men heard Chango chuckling and whispering, "Gonna be a party. Gonna be a party."

"Be easy," Manny whispered to him. "Primo will be in his car in a matter of seconds. We got this if we just be easy."

"Who you got in there?" The Cuban demanded to Culo as his eyes moved in the opposite direction of Culo's ever moving head. The other clean cut Cuban who stood in the middle of the street had a radio in his hands and was talking into it. He saw his Marielito brother's head dodging side to side and reached inside of his blazer for a weapon. Then he whistled to the others, warning them there was a problem.

Primo was on the sidewalk in front of the club, flanked with soldiers all around him. Even his attention went to the van across the street.

"What you hiding back there?" the Marielito asked Culo again.

Culo's eyes looked past the man, to Primo, and back. "Back there?" he asked the man with caution in his voice.

"Just drive away," Manny warned.

Culo tapped his ear, listening to Manny's orders. "Ahhh...just let me...um...pull off and get out your way," he said, reaching for the gear shifter.

The Cuban looked up and down both sides of the street, probably searching for the police. When he didn't find any, he quickly pulled a huge auto-magnum from his waist, pointed it at Culo and said, "Step out with your hands up."

"Mask on!" Self shouted from his ride while sliding his mask on.

"Be easy," Manny whispered.

Culo looked at the man and shrugged. "Ok, it's your way now, Yo."

Into the Bluetooth Chango whispered, "Surprise!" He chuckled into the headpiece before sliding his mask on.

"Something moving in the backseat," the Cuban yelled, pointing.

Culo watched the security detail scuttling over to him and Chango, reaching for their weapons. "Rich, oh yeah," he said.

"Ahh hell," Rich groaned, slipping on his mask and reaching to the back seat for his Barrett .50 caliber cannon rifle.

"Party time," Chango said before whispering to Culo. "Culo, start de party. Passenger side."

While the Cuban's looked on, Culo quickly turned his back to the passenger side door while raising the AK47 at the driver's door and squeezed the trigger. "Goodbye," Culo announced, sending bullets through the Cuban that stood at his door.

The Cuban was dead before he hit the ground.

"Fuck!" Manny yelled and quickly slid his mask on.

"Mostro belong to Self!" Self yelled before bailing out the truck and heading for the entrance.

"I'm on the roof of the truck," Rich said with his three foot rifle in tow.

The Marielitos had all hit the ground at the sound of Culo's gunshots, but now jumped to their feet with guns drawn.

"It's on!" Manny yelled into the Bluetooth as he exited the truck. Primo was his. He opened fire at the front of the club while sprinting at Primo with all the speed he could muster.

"Manny, I got you!" Bobby Lee said as he bailed out his truck with his sniper's scope to his eyes. "Squirrel hunting," he said before taking three Cuban's down.

Culo and Chango emptied their clips, causing bodily harm to the party goers at the front of the club.

In an organized fashion, Marielitos poured out of the club with fully automatic machineguns like they were expecting trouble. Primo was pinned to the ground. The door to his limo was open. Primo's men yelled for him to run to the limo.

There were too many men outside of the club. Manny saw photographers and well-wishers being shot down, but he had no time to care. From close to a hundred feet away, he wanted to cut off his enemy's escape. He ran faster. Getting closer. He aimed and fired at the tires, but nothing.

"Fucking bullet proof!" he yelled, ducking shots that came back his way. "Rich. Kill the limo!" he yelled.

Rich was trying to fasten the tri-pod onto the roof while sliding earmuffs over the ear that didn't have the Bluetooth. The same one he would need if he didn't want his eardrums to burst when he pulled the trigger.

"Done!" he responded.

Over the noise of the barrage of gunfire, the crackling of thunder burst loudly on the block and the entire body of the limo shook. Again the massive clap of the cannon's discharge made the ground tremble. A hole the size of a watermelon blew into the back of the bulletproof glass on the driver's side. The exit hole in the front windshield dripped with blood and pieces of the driver's head.

Self was playing leap frog. He shot at the Marielitos, ducked behind cars, and then repeated the process while inching closer. Unlike everyone else in the crew who reloaded their rifles and machineguns, when Self's gun was empty he tossed it, preferring the two handles of the .50 Desert Eagles.

"Hammer time, bitches," he said as he sent hot rockets of death into the bodies of men that ran down the block towards him. Suddenly, two Cubans in tight suits ran towards Self toting Glock handguns. Self dropped to one knee and aimed to the groin of the man closer to him, hitting his mark. "Can't touch this," he yelled, lost in a zone as the other shooter backed away to retreat when he unfortunately realized that Self ran to him instead of away from him like most sane people did.

"We come to party, cocksuckers," Chango yelled from behind the bullet riddled van that he and Culo used for shelter. Since he and Culo were the closest to the entrance, they received the majority of the Marielitos gun fire.

"Rich! Rich!" Chango called into his Bluetooth.

"Copy," Rich said.

"Kill deez mother...fuckers," Chango pleaded, exchanging gunfire.

"Roger that," Rich answered.

The thunder from Rich's rifle clapped and the van that Culo and Chango were resting their backs on shook from a direct hit on the opposite side.

"What the fuck, Rich!" Culo yelled into his mic. "Don't shoot us!"

"Sorry. Someone was coming up over the van."

Chango crouched down to look under the van and saw pieces of a Cuban's upper body splattered in the street on the other side of it.

Manny was pinned down with his ass on the sidewalk and his back was up against a news van, just twenty feet from Primo, but too many Marielitos were shooting his way.

Bobby Lee stood in the middle of the street down the block, fifty feet away from Self, popping heads off each Marielito that advanced on Self.

The Cubans had been prepared. The more the men rushed out into the street to attack Manny and his crew, the more they pushed Primo down and inched him back towards the entrance of the club.

The limousine was in a heap of smoking scrap metal by the time Rich was done with it. He aimed at the two red doors of the club and sent a hole through both. As he reloaded, he noticed the bravest man he laid eyes on that day, exiting the club spraying a fully automatic handgun in the direction of Manny, and then Chango and Culo.

It was Mostro.

"Self!" Rich barked into the Bluetooth, hoping he could hear over the gunfire.

"What da deal?" Self responded, trading shots with the Marielitos.

"Your mark. Entrance," Rich answered before slamming his second clip of .50 bullets into the cannon.

Self looked over at the entrance and spotted Mostro shooting all over the place, standing like an open target.

"I can take him," Rich said, watching Mostro in his sights. Suddenly a long stretch Humvee sped around the corner. "Got a new target. Talk to me Self."

Manny was pinned on the floor while the Humvee slowly crept right in front of him. He raised his weapon, shot at the driver's window and was only able to startle the driver. The thick, bulletproof glass stopped his shots.

"Mostro's Self's," Self answered.

"Copy," Rich answered and swung his rifle in the direction of the Humvee. "Manny, get out of there!" Rich yelled, but there was nowhere for Manny to go. He was too close with not enough fire power to keep his enemy back.

"Where I'm going?" Manny barked. "I'm surrounded."

Self saw Mostro and moved faster. The closer he got was the more Marielitos he had to deal with. His shots became more sporadic. More reckless, but still hitting its mark. There was so many of them he couldn't miss.

"Rich!" Manny yelled out. "Member I told you not to level the building?'

"Copy that," Rich answered. "And I listened!" he yelled in his defense.

"Man!" Manny yelled, "Fuck that! Clear this shit out!"

Rich didn't answer. Someone was firing at him from the roof of the club, but like Manny requested, he aimed the Barrett cannon at the windows of the club, and the swoosh of his huge bullet tore through them. Then he aimed right above Mostro's head at the canopy that covered the Cubans and fired into that, hoping to bring it down, but the old building was stronger than his new bullets.

The exchange of gunfire happened in a matter of minutes, but for the shooters in Manny's crew, time was slowing down.

With Rich shooting at several targets around the building, Manny was able to scurry like a rat in the street until he was on the same side as Chango and Culo. From where he stood, he could see the Marielitos pointing to the Humvee.

"Rich, kill the Hummer!" Manny yelled, but Rich couldn't hear him. Someone with a high powered rifle was peppering the top of the van with gunfire.

Manny waved his hand and got Chango's attention. Chango tapped Culo, and Manny pointed to the Humvee. Manny raised his rifle and fired towards the doors of the limo, preventing the men from running Primo to safety.

Suddenly a growling roar of heavy engines came around the corner. Manny heard that sound before. Two of the armored vans from the previous shootout sped by and stopped in front of the club.

Rich shattered the entire upper wall of the roof where the shots were coming from. He used his scope to watch Manny, Chango and Culo shooting towards the Humvee, and then quickly fired one shot after the other into the S.U.V, rattling it and causing a split into the body.

Self watched the armored vans arrive. "This mother fucker ain't getting away from Self," he declared, ready to sacrifice himself. He recklessly ran into the middle of the street and sprinted with his hammers raised high, gunning down everything he could.

Bobby Lee saw Self take off into the middle of the street and knew his brother was going to die. There were too many Cuban's with guns, and the armored vans at the end of the block weren't going to help the matter. Bobby Lee took off running, laboriously chasing behind Self while holding his sniper's rifle.

As Self ran up the block, the doors to the armored vans flew open. Bobby Lee was so focused on catching up to Self he didn't hear or see two police cars pulling onto the block behind him from the opposite direction of the flow of traffic. Bobby Lee ran as fast as he could. By the time he heard the roar of the engine behind him, it was too late. He was already hit and flying into the air.

Rich watched through his sight as the police car hit his brother from behind before screeching to a stop.

"Sweet Jesus," Rich uttered, aiming his sight at the police car's front grill and letting the trigger pop.

The radiator to the police car exploded and the loud blast of the engine block splitting in half startled everyone. The officer's in the car quickly exited and ran in the opposite direction of the gunfire. Self turned and stopped dead in his tracks at the sight of Bobby Lee sprawled onto the ground, ten feet in front of the police car. To Self's left was Mostro, shooting at him, and working his way towards the armored vans. To Self's right, was the one man who had always been ready to kill and die for him. The man who trained him over and over, embraced him and his family. The one who nursed him back to health. Self quickly unloaded his Desert Eagle in the direction of Mostro, and took off in the direction of Bobby Lee. "Bobby!" Rich yelled into the Bluetooth. There was no response.

Bobby Lee was face down and not moving.

Instantly the night lit up like the sun had come out. Up above, a police helicopter blasted its huge, bright, halogen light.

Self raced towards Bobby Lee but the end of the block was quickly growing with a police presence. He wouldn't make it to save him. It was suicide and that was already reserved for killing Mostro.

"Time to go!" Manny yelled.

"Bobby!" Rich cried into the mic. "Robert Custard Lee Fumble!" he yelled out his brother's full name. "Get up soldier!" he ordered into the mic, but there was no response.

Rich put his eye to the sight of his weapon, aimed it at the windshield of the police cruiser and blasted away. Then he shot into the crowd where Primo and Mostro had been standing. When his gun was empty, he rolled off the roof of the van, making sure his mask was secure. The bright light of the helicopter was blinding.

"Chango!" Manny yelled into the mic.

"*Toma*?" Chango replied in between the pot shots he took at the Marielitos.

Manny learned from the last shoot out that Chango was a better shot than he. "Shoot the helicopter light out. *Rapido*."

Chango chuckled. "*Bien*. Chango mi Chango," he sang. "Rougher than Rambo!" He aimed at the police helicopter, and sent a burst of three shots at the light. He didn't know if he hit it or not, but the operator of the helicopter tilted the iron bird, and quickly flew away.

With the spotlight gone, a heavy police presence, and the Marielitos swarming all over the place, Manny decided that he wanted to make it to his engagement party in two days. He ran to the passenger side of the van Culo and Chango were resting their backs against, dived over the back passenger seat, and grabbed as many grenades from the small wooden box as possible. He then exited the van and found Self standing there, also using the van for cover. Now all four of them were behind the bullet riddled van. Police sirens were everywhere like the entire police force showed up, and the roar of one of the armored vans was peeling away.

"We gotta go," Manny yelled out. "Rich?" he called, hoping Rich could create a diversion.

Self was stuck, staring down the block at Bobby Lee's body being surrounded by armed police officers.

"HALT! NOBODY MOVE!" came from a massive Police Special Unit vehicle that was the size of a fire truck.

All the gunfire stopped. The roar of the second armored van pulling off vibrated the scene.

Manny looked over to his brother and said, "Self, we gotta go. Gotta take the loss and work it out."

Self stared down the street at Bobby Lee. A part of his strength was helpless. His lips trembled as he groped two handguns. "That's Bobby Lee," he cried, filled with hurt. Then he rocked back and forth. "*Arghhhh*," he growled with his gun resting on his forehead. "*No*. Allah, no. Self need to go get him," he begged.

Manny grabbed Self's massive arm. "Gotta take the loss. These pigs is multiplying."

Bobby Lee was still face down, sprawled out on the south end of 202nd Street in front of four police cars that blocked the street.

Self, Manny, Chango, and Culo were in the middle of the block, stuck behind the van.

The front of the club was crowded with men screaming out in pain and other's crouched down behind the velvet ropes calling for ambulances.

The north side of the street was blocked by a police truck and the smoking Humvee.

"How the fuck we getting outta here?" Manny asked during the errie silence.

"Tonight we have a long drink," Chango said before chuckling and talking up to the sky.

Self reloaded his cannons and peeked around the van before crouching down. "Y'all ready to leave?"

Culo told Self, "Sometimes I don't know who the fuck is crazier, you or this nigga here," pointing to Chango. "At least Chango got the spirits telling him what to do."

Self adjusted his mask and held his guns up. "And Self the voice of God Chango be hearing."

Self rushed around to the back door of the van with his eyes searching for Mostro while opening the doors. He quickly looked behind him and saw the police making a perimeter at the entrance of the block. He placed his weapons flat on the back bumper, reached into the box of grenades, and like he was pulling the top of a lid from a bottle, he pulled the pins and launched them, three at the entrance of the club that was cluttered with Marielitos, and two towards the police cars at the entrance of the street.

"We ghost!" Self yelled, grasping his tools. He aimed towards the front of the club while the grenades went off, shattering car windows on the street and sending the police scattering for cover.

Manny didn't care where Self was going. He was following. Chango laughed hysterically as he and Culo scurried across the street while trading shots with the police.

Self ran across the street and didn't hesitate to shoot any of the Cuban's that moaned, groaned out for help or moved slightly. They entered the bright hall of the club and Self pointed to the exit signs that led to the rear.

"Manny!" Everyone heard over the Bluetooth headsets.

"Rich! Where you at?" Manny asked as they ran through the club towards the back door.

"In a cab."

"In a cab?" Manny asked in disbelief.

"Get the fuck outta here," Self uttered.

"Only in America," Chango huffed.

"That's what you New Yorker's call it, right? Gotta get Bobby…"

"I know," Manny sighed. Then it hit him. "Where you at in the cab? Look at the street poles and read off the sign."

"Dyckman. That's what it says."

"What about Bobby Lee?" Self asked over the headset.

"Gotta go get 'em," Rich answered.

Self opened the backdoor to the club. "Say no more," he answered.

THIRTEEN

The usual one hour trip to the Bronx was extended by the men putting the cab driver in the trunk, driving towards midtown Manhattan, and finally taking mass transit.

Rich rushed into the house and tapped away on the laptop.

"What's the deal?" Self asked, sliding up next to Rich.

"Gotta find out if he made it. In the hospital or where they have him."

Self raised his hands. "Be easy. Bobby gots no I.D. His prints ain't in that system, and if he can talk—"

"He's alive," Rich corrected.

Self sighed. "Self want him alive. Self need Bobby Lee alive, but what Self saying is, he won't talk cause of our sovereignty. We don't know what name he under so you gotta do some cold calling like you the media or some shit."

Manny said. "Check the precincts in that area, and then look at the check-in time at the hospital, or both." He kept looking at his watch and Self caught on.

"You getting the jitters, Slick?" Self asked Manny.

He had forty-eight hours to get ready for his engagement party. The fact that he was still alive was amazing, and now that he was, he wanted to satisfy all of his obligations. "Not jittery," he corrected. "just busy."

"Too busy for Bobby Lee?" Self asked.

Rich stopped typing and looked Self in the eyes. "The man got an engagement party in a few hours. When we make our move, he will be informed." He then looked over to Manny. "Get home to your wife to be. I'll keep you posted."

Self stared at Manny while leaning back in the chair. He nodded at him and said, "Last night, Slick? Was for nothing. No Primo. No Mostro, and Bobby Lee…well, we will see." He leaned forward and asked, "Slick, you ever think maybe you can't win this war?"

Based on the deal Alvaro gave Manny, the only way for everyone to be satisfied was to kill Primo and let the chips fall from there. "No. They hurt us too bad."

Self shrugged. "*Us*? Us ain't going to an engagement party." He yawned and looked away. "Self new occupation is killing

Mostro and Marielito. Gone bang hard until they drop Self or they all gone."

Chango was on the floor sleeping, but rustled awake and told Self, "Chango like dey job. Bang hard," he repeated before closing his eyes again.

Self looked at Manny, shrugged and then said, "There it is. Mostro mine."

Chango chuckled. "And Chango take the rest."

"Warriors go to war, Slick," he told Manny. "Go be the lover-businessman you always was. That's how it's always been for you and Self, and that's how it's gone be. Peace."

Manny nodded a farewell at the men, but looked at Self with regret before quickly departing, ready to keep up appearances and work on his alibi.

*****

"I'm sorry, Manny," Racheal said when Manny walked through his back door near the kitchen. "Are you still coming to the engagement party tomorrow?"

Manny looked at her like she had two heads. "Yeah. Why? You don't want to marry me anymore?"

She looked away, and then looked over at him while rubbing her stomach. "No, it's not that. I know how much I really messed up and I feel lousy." She walked over to him and put her arms around his neck. "I don't want to fight. I miss you. Won't even ask where you were all night."

"You can't," he said with a straight face. "I was sleeping next to you all night."

She stared at him with a blank stare. "Who? When...what are you talking—?"

"Me and you were in that bed last night, all night," he emphasized.

Ann walked into the kitchen wearing his pajamas. "Yeah right," she said before grabbing a Gatorade out the fridge and then walking back to wherever she came from.

Manny watched Ann walk out of the kitchen, but that didn't mean she was gone. He held Racheal closer and whispered, "We went to bed at nightfall, we made love and we slept until we woke up together. Say it! We were in bed all night."

Worry set into her eyes. "Okay. You were home in bed all night."

Manny pecked her lips. "Good. I'm hungry and where's my son?"

Racheal raced to the marble island and lifted the remote control, aimed at the TV, and turned on the. After a commercial her jaw dropped when she saw the crime scene in upper Manhattan and the caption read, "Cuban massacre. Dozens dead, twenty- one wounded, including police officers, one gunman captured and police hunt for the other gunmen."

She pointed to the TV, pointed at Manny, and then pointed back to the TV. "You? Did you? Was that where you…"

Manny stared at her for a long minute. Then he said, "I'm hungry. Are you cooking or what?"

Racheal's eyes narrowed as she stared at her fiancé before reaching for pots and fridge handles while darting her eyes between what she was doing and the TV screen. Manny watched the news attentively, waiting for some information on Bobby Lee and to see if they had any images of him and the crew leaving the scene. The images on the screen showed Rich on the top of the truck while lying on his stomach, turning over and shooting at the helicopter. It also showed Chango shooting at the helicopter and Self tossing grenades into the crowd.

Thank god for mask and gloves, he thought while eating poached eggs and turkey.

Racheal joined Manny at the breakfast nook and sipped tea and ate an entire bag of shredded cheddar cheese while they watched the news repeat the same footage until it displayed the image of four men running from behind a van, crossing the street, and running.

"*Ou,*" she jumped, startling Manny. She reached for the remote, pressed the rewind button on the DVR, and stopped it, and pointed at the image of the men running across the street. "See that?"

"See what? I'm watching the news," he sighed.

She walked over to the TV. "See that heavy shooter? The hood on his head, the mask, the sagging pants?"

"What about him?"

She pointed back at the same man on the screen, "See how a part of his shirt is sticking out of his pants?"

"What about it?" Manny asked with annoyance. "You losing your mind?"

She took a deep breath and said, "Manny it just hurts when you think I'm stupid."

He sighed, "Here we go with the bullshit."

She shook her head and then pointed to the man on the screen. "Remember I kept telling him to tuck his damn shirt in when we were leaving Panama?"

Shit, he thought as his heart sunk.

"See the rhythm in his walk? That's Culo." She pointed to the man next to him. "And Culo can't tie his shoes without Chango, so we know who that is, and the fool has two of the locks of his dreads hanging out the back of his mask."

It was Manny's turn to drop his jaw. He was speechless.

"Close your mouth, baby. You're looking crazy," she advised before pointing back at the screen. "This shooter here," she said, pointing to Self. "African American. Based on his stride he weighs over two hundred pounds, clearly over six feet tall and the way his right shoulder leans down indicates he either had a stroke before or he was shot multiple times and the body is trying to compensate by giving more work to his lungs."

Manny said, "You bugging the fuck out. You sound like some kind of crime expert. Who the fuck you work for 5-0?"

"I should," she said and then pointed to the screen. "Now this guy," she uttered while pointing at Manny on the screen. "He should've been home with his pregnant fiancée instead of trying to get himself killed." She slammed the remote on the marble floor, crashing it into pieces before yelling, "Fuck you for caring, Manny!" She walked off fuming.

Manny messed up. He knew it, but he figured that the only reason she was able to identify everyone was because she knew them. They all been in her house, spent time coming from Panama to America, and she was right about checking Culo about his pants. Lucky for Manny she wasn't the type who panicked and called the police. If she was that type, he would have been in jail long ago.

Instead of going upstairs Manny stayed watching TV so he could avoid Racheal's drama. Just as he was losing interest in watching the story again, a picture of Bobby Lee was posted. Manny rushed to the TV and manually turned up the volume.

The newscaster reported, "This, unidentified man, is an alleged shooter in the Cuban Massacre. He's being uncooperative with police officials and is currently being held at Roosevelt Hospital in Manhattan with a broken leg and a hip injury. He hasn't officially been charged, but stay tuned and we will give you an update."

Manny picked up his phone and called Self. "The God know already," he answered. "Roosevelt Hospital. We on it," he told Manny, and hung up.

Manny looked at the receiver and wondered if they were watching the same news broadcast.

He wasn't sure what he was going to do about Bobby Lee, but he was certain that when he spoke to his lawyer Joe at the engagement party that Bobby Lee was going to be added to the list with Puncho as someone else that he was ready to spend whatever it took so they wouldn't spend life in prison.

*****

High in the Oxbow Mountains of Montana was where Andy, Missy and William-Larry were preparing to build their new home. Montana was the refuge for the family, and the place where they brought Self to train and learn to live off the land. Now that they were setting up shop, and using the hundreds of thousands of dollars that Bobby Lee had stashed to make a new refuge, everyone was busy until Missy's phone rang.

"Howdy," Missy answered, breathing deeply into the phone.

"It's Rich."

"Where's Bobby Lee?" she panicked.

"Not good."

"What? Whatda' you mean, not good?"

"Had a problem."

She paused, thinking the worst before she asked, "What? Is he gone?"

"No, not that bad."

"And?" she huffed, exhaling with relief while waiting for the bad news.

"Gotta go get 'em."

"Well, all right then," she said with optimism. "When you need me there?"

"Missy," he growled with a warning.

"Shit no," she protested. "I couldn't come the first time, but if I had, he wouldn't be where he is now. I'm coming!" she demanded.

Rich decided to use common sense instead of force. He took loud deep breaths until she breathed in the same pattern. "Missy, you the woman in all this. If you're not around for us where does that leave us, sweety?"

She sighed before accepting her fate. "Alright. What cha need? We been on this phone too long already."

Rich cleared his throat. "Currency. Get Andy and Willie up here, and call Cooter to get it done."

"*Cooter*?" she asked with sudden alarm. "Is it that bad of a trap?"

"Get Cooter to stock 'em and drop 'em. At Fort Dix. I'll be there, and you take care of mama."

"Copy that," she answered and killed the line. She looked around the flat land in the mountain area and used her thumb and forefinger to whistle in three short burst.

Dogs barked loudly and came running from around the temporary structure they called home. Seconds later, a set of whistles resounded. One from below at the side of the mountain, and the other from within the woods where the dogs came running in from.

Andy came from the woods with a jar of moonshine in his hand. "What you gots in your drawers that's making you call us in such a hurry?" he asked.

Missy withdrew her knife, threw it down into a tree stump, and then spat a wad of tobacco onto the grass. "Just sit your ass down there. You goin' on a trip."

"Say what?" Andy asked and Missy just stared, holding back tears. Right then Andy realized she had serious news, so he sat.

Seconds later, William-Larry came over the ridge of the mountain with three wild turkeys dangling upside down. He walked over, stared at Missy and asked, "How bad is it?"

She sobbed. "They got him trapped."

"Who gots who trapped?" Andy asked between swigs of his poison.

William-Larry's eyes darted from his brother to his cousin-sister in-law. He spat his tobacco and asked, "Who got him?"

"Rich didn't say."

"Oh!" Andy said, the answer just hitting him. He quickly stood erect and dropped his jar of moonshine to the ground. "Who the fuck...do I have to skin...for having my big brother?"

"If I woulda known that, I'd be a freaking genius," Missy said with annoyance.

Andy argued, "Well woman, what did he say?"

"What did who say?" William-Larry wanted to know.

"Rich said to call Cooter—" She answered.

"*Cooter*?" Andy wailed, rushing off. "*Shit*! This is serious."

"Where you going?" Missy yelled out.

Over his shoulder Andy said, "If you calling uncle Cooter, then I gotta tell Mama bye. I might not make it back."

William-Larry spat and asked, "Is it really that serious?"

"Said for Cooter to stock you with enough guns for all of yall, and for him to fly you into Fort Dix and they'll be there to pick yall up."

"That's a full military assault we doing," William-Larry uttered, knowing what Rich wanted. He looked over to Missy and asked, "But who we hunting?"

Missy shrugged. "Does it matter?"

"Not at all. Don't you worry your pretty little head. We'll be back in one piece with him."

Missy looked down at the ground before pulling a large hunting knife from the small of her back and stabbing into the air. "You betta."

"Say no more," William-Larry said, sounding more like Self than his twin brother Bobby Lee.

*****

Racheal ignored Manny most of the day, but he knew how to deal with the elephant in the room. He ignored it too. She had already proven she could keep secrets. From the very beginning, when she found out that he was released on parole, that didn't separate them. Then after his criminal confession on the day he proposed to her, she still declared her love, so in Manny's mind, she accepted all of him. He knew she was right about him risking his life.

As night removed the day, Racheal started getting dressed and broke her silence in the confines of their bedroom. "Are you coming?" she softly inquired. "All of your guests confirmed they would be there, and a car is picking us up in an hour."

Manny was lying on his bed with the remote in his hand, wondering if the police would be knocking on his door again. He was also disappointed that he didn't kill Primo. He needed to accomplish that mission.

Racheal broke his concentration. He looked up and asked, "You want me as your husband?"

She looked away while putting in a teardrop diamond earring. "It's complicated."

"It's complicated?" he repeated softly, meeting her where her mood was.

"I don't want to argue with you, Manny."

"Then what's the sense of going tonight if you don't want to be my wife?"

She sat at her makeup counter and brushed away the flaws in her face. "Manny, I'm in way too deep," she said, almost at a whisper. "But...I never been a mother before, and I didn't intend on getting pregnant right now, plus I have no idea what I'm doing. I do love you, but..."

"Yeah, I'm waiting," he said sarcastically, starting to lose emotional control.

She turned to look at him through her mirror and confessed, "Loving you is much too complicated, but I signed up for this because I *thought*...well...I thought I could handle it." She sighed. "Now everything took a life of its own and I'm going to do what I have to do to make sure this baby has the greatest life."

"You make it sound more like a job or some shit."

Racheal mumbled to herself, "I will not cry, or lose control." She then told him, "We have a lot of people that flew in today to see you and me together."

At the end of the day Manny always had to do the honorable thing. He rolled out of bed and headed to his closet. His tux was ready, his shoes were shined, and he realized then how many steps ahead Racheal always was.

*****

While Manny was in the back of the Rolls Royce on his way to entertain family and friends, Missy was driving Andy and William-Larry to Oxbow Ranch Airport.

"Y'all member to move in, get my baby and come on home now," Missy encouraged.

Andy was in the back seat of the four-door pick up swigging away from his jar. "You know Missy, ever since Bobby Lee started plunging your pie hole you been yapping away like we didn't teach you everything you know."

"Jesus, give me strength," William-Larry mumbled from the front seat, knowing what was coming.

Missy turned onto the winding road of Oxbow Drive. She cruised under the shadows of damp trees and inhaled the moist air before yelling, "Just you remember mister, ever since your brother been plunging my pie hole everything in this family works."

"Amen," William-Larry mumbled.

"If this pie hole didn't tell you how to wash your ass good and proper, you'd be smellin' like a heated rascal on the eve of April."

"*A What?*" both brothers blurted out.

She waved them away and bit at her nails. Her eyes shifted from the rearview mirror to the road ahead and back at Andy. "Oh you just hurry up and never-mind, but you! Andy McArthur. Let that be your last glass of hooch."

"And why is that if I may ask?" he wondered.

"Cause I needs you to shoot straight, Andy McArthur, that's why. Cause you sittin' next to a satchel with a hundred thousand U.S. dollars that's gonna pay for your way there and back, and because I need your sober ass back here in one piece."

He smiled his wicked grin. "Oh that's so nice. I'm startin' to wonder if you got the eye for me while big brother is gone."

"Cut it out," William-Larry warned his brother. "Be drunk. Not stupid."

Andy lifted the last of the clear liquid in his jar. "I'll drink to that."

Missy pulled into the private airport that held small aircrafts and one in particular stood out in the middle of a desert road. It was an old, white Cessna 414A Chancellor with an American flag painted in stripes on the side and decals of P.O.W-M.I.A and others from the Vietnam War painted under the five porthole windows.

"There go my uncle!" Andy said like a little boy on his way to a joy ride, instead of a war. He quickly jumped out of the truck.

William-Larry put both his palms on his face and groaned, "I really don't have the strength to handle both of 'em."

Missy rubbed his back. "I know it, Willie, but you the only one on that plane with good sense."

"That's what I'm afraid of," he uttered.

"Just *please*," Missy begged in seductive tones, "Bring your brother back to me. Don't matter if he a little beat up or even wounded. Just go on over there and hurt them city boys before they hurt chu."

He leaned over and kissed her cold cheek before picking up the satchel with $100,000 and stepping out the truck.

"Yeeeeeeee hawwww!" was the echoing shout that pierced the damp night and alerted the whole airport that Cooter was there.

William-Larry was sure there had to be at least ten violations on the thirty year old jet, not to mention the amount of weapons he was certain Cooter had buried in the belly of the plane. He stopped in his tracks and stared at the mountainous man that was a few feet before him. Somewhere in the family gene pool, he and his twin Bobby Lee was skipped over when it came to size because their uncle Cooter was the twin to their father, and they were both 6'5", close to 300lbs of solid, healthy mass, but totally different in the mind. No matter what the weather, Cooter wore denim overalls, tall boots that rose up to his knees, and a flannel shirt with a tee shirt underneath. His glasses were thicker than magnifying glasses, his beard looked like he could hide a small person in it, but somehow he was still authorized to fly his plane. The things money could buy.

"God bless America," was how Cooter greeted folks for as long as William-Larry could remember, and he was going to show his uncle the respect he was taught to give by addressing him the way he had his whole life. "Land of the free, home of the brave," he answered.

Cooter walked over and hugged William-Larry and kissed his cheek like he was still a child. "Come on, come on. We got us a long flight and I want to tell you about the goodies I got."

William-Larry took a deep breath and stepped onto the plane knowing no one on this planet flew as fast as his uncle.

Andy bounced in the front passenger seat like he was a co-pilot while he sat alone amongst five empty seats. Cooter started flicking power buttons and stopped short to ask, "Did you bring the promissory notes?"

"In the back unc," Andy yelled, due to the large headphones on his head.

Cooter smiled and stretched out his arms and William-Larry knew what was next, Andy closed his eyes and Cooter bowed his head before saying, "Dear Lord, on this day of freedom, grant us the power of our forefathers as we take this journey. There is some tyranny down here lord that we must eradicate. Give us the vision to utilize our civil defense as the sovereign citizens of the United States of America, to purge the usurpations that violate our constitution and our land, dear God. On this day, father, allow us the might to defend our homeland against the foreign invasion that's transpired in New York. Protect us God, protect our country, and protect our Constitution and Second Amendment..."

"God bless America!" all three men said closing their prayer.

"Militia men!" Cooter yelled out while powering up the plane. "Let's show them what we're made of."

*****

Cipriani's on 42nd Street was the epitome of New York City high life. The grand hall was decorated in lavender silk. The fabric was shaped into whispering willow trees that rose up from the hardwood floors to the high ceilings. Crystal clinked, waiters moved to and fro with large serving trays of champagne, and the buzz of the guest's chatter halted when Racheal and Manny walked in.

A tall, older man with a short, salt and pepper Afro smiled widely and quickly approached Racheal upon their entry. "There goes my princess," the man joked as he hugged Racheal. *Her father*, Manny thought. Then he turned, stuck his hand out to Manny and said, "Mr. Manny Black. I know so much about you, yet we've never met."

"Mr. Gordon," Manny said flatly, but didn't see any resemblance to Racheal. As a matter of fact, the man looked more like Manny, maybe Panamanian or even Cuban.

He looked into Manny's eyes and smirked.

"*Daddy?*" Racheal warned with her tone.

The man placed his palms against his chest and innocently asked, "*Me?* What did I do?" He turned to Racheal, then back to Manny. "Call me Dickey. All my friends call me Dickey."

Manny smiled without showing teeth and shook the man's hand. "Okay, Dickey. We finally get to meet." Manny wanted to follow his hunch so he asked, "*Eres Cubano?*"

Dickey smiled, ignoring Manny's inquiry as to whether he was Cuban. Manny tried to looked the man in his eyes, but Dickey's gaze was on the other side of the room. Dickey cleared his throat, realizing that Manny was speaking to him and dismissively stated,

"Oh. Nice to meet you son, welcome to the family. Excuse me for a moment."

Manny was highly offended, but then someone else caught his eye. A glamorous woman, an older replica of Racheal, walked over and stopped in front of Racheal before kissing both her cheeks. *Her mother*, Manny concluded. Based on the resemblance, Racheal didn't inherit one drop of her father's genes.

The elegant woman looked over to Manny, stared and then cut her eyes back to Racheal. Racheal frowned, her mother frowned back and then an argument without words ensued. Finally the words came out and they debated, prompting Manny to ease closer. He had to know what was it about Racheal's family that had them hating him so much. He turned his back to them and looked off into the distance like he was preoccupied with the engagement of the night, but leaned his head so his right ear was facing them.

"How can you be pregnant and getting married to this criminal?" the woman asked Racheal in an aristocratic tone.

"Mommy, relax please. It's not what you think, and I haven't figured everything out yet," Racheal said in her defense.

"This is utter foolishness," her mother advised. "You're deeply involved, he probably won't stick around, and the one time you have a chance to do something to go to the top of your career you allow that man to get in the way of it?" she argued. "Now I have to partake in this fiasco?"

Racheal cut her eyes to Manny and realized he was looking their way so she smiled and then mumbled, "Mother, keep it down. *Please*." Then she turned to Manny and said, "Manuel!"

Manuel? Manny thought. *"When the fuck did I become Manuel?"* He walked over to Racheal and who he assumed was her mother with a giant, but not so genuine smile.

"So this is Manuel Black?" Racheal's mother said in a more subtle tone. Gone was the angry person from seconds ago. She patted Manny's hand affectionately and said, "My Racheal cannot stop going on and on about you. I do apologize for us not meeting sooner, but I'm a bit old fashion. I wanted the wedding to come *before* the baby…" she cut her eyes to Racheal and then back to Manny. "…but oh well," she uttered and Manny was still trying to grasp if it was the same woman who was talking to Racheal a minute ago.

A waiter with a tray of champagne walked by and her mother quickly grabbed two flutes of the bubbly. She gulped the first one, placed it down on the awaiting tray, and then nodded for the waiter to leave—she would sip the second glass.

"Well, Mrs. Gordon," Manny said with a smile. "We have a life time to get to know each other—"

"Mrs. Who?" she asked and then her eyes widened. "*Ack hmn*," her mother suddenly started to cough in spasms.

As Manny was getting ready to assist her with her coughing, Edeeks walked over, kissed Racheal and introduced himself to her mother.

"*Oh*, so we finally get to meet," she said to Edeeks in a much more pleasant tone than she did with Manny. Then without him suggesting, she kissed Edeeks on his cheek before cutting her eye at Manny.

What the fuck? Manny thought as he looked on, seeing Edeeks receive the type of love and affection from Racheal's mother that was better suited for the man Racheal loved, her soon to be son in-law.

When Edeeks was done passing on pleasantries to Racheal's mother, he turned to shake Manny's hand. "Congratulations," he said, greeting his best friend. A photographer walked over, pointed the camera and both men posed for the picture. Then Edeeks turned to him, but avoided eye contact. "Yo. Can we talk on the side for a minute?"

Manny looked around and motioned to one of the lavender silk trees near a corner. "Over there."

Edeeks looked all around at the black tie crowd that was growing in number. When he felt it was safe to talk, he eased too close for comfort and asked, "Yo, some Cuban's got killed last night uptown. Was that you?"

Manny looked into Edeeks' eyes and Edeeks shifted his gaze, looking around at the crowd of guests instead, "Yo, what the fuck are you asking me, E? All of a sudden you need a briefing if I'm in a beef?"

"You see? I can't just show some concern for my business partner?"

"That's what you call it now?"

Edeeks shook his head in disappointment. "Yo, I don't want to argue with you. I'm just saying, those Cuban's are not playing, and you need to lay low. We got things going every which way at the office, but..." he looked over at Racheal. "...we not here to discuss business. Congrats. Just be careful out there."

Manny didn't like anything about Edeeks that night. "That's why the fuck I'm standing right here, right now and them Cubans is dead. Because I know what I'm doing," he snapped.

Edeeks stopped short, "So that *was* you…" he didn't ask a question. "Be careful, Manny." He looked over his shoulder and grew a quick interest in walking to the opposite side of the room. "Enjoy your night. Just be careful, man."

As Edeeks stepped away, Racheal walked over and kissed Manny's cheek. "Most of the invites that were confirmed are in attendance. I did well."

"Yes you did," he said flatly, totally not caring about one word that came out of her mouth. He would address her nonsense later.

She smiled at someone that waved to her from across the banquet hall. "Ok," she said. "Time for us to greet our guests. Be patient, please."

Manny hadn't smoked a joint in years, but right there, right then, he wished he could take a puff.

FOURTEEN

For nine hours William-Larry had to listen to the rambling of Cooter and Andy discussing everything from the importance of the U.S. Constitution, the Vietnam War and the need to protect the world from U.F.O's.

As Cooter's plane was descending into the foggy New Jersey night, he yelled, "Wake up time!" He backhanded a slumbering Andy on his chest and said, "Nephew, get to the back and you boys change up. Your uniforms might be tight, your boots might be too big, but ah…get to the back, change and hand over the money while you're at it."

Andy looked at the military fatigues, yawned and then asked, "And how do we get to Rich again?"

"He'll be waiting," William-Larry answered.

Cooter pitched the plane downward and reached into the top pocket of his dirty flannel shirt and removed a joint. He lit the tip of his funny cigarette and said, "Grab the duffel bags out the belly. Everything there is made in America; Calico nine-fifty specials, ten with brass catchers and forty clips. One hundred silenced rounds. Flash bang and a few pineapple grenades. Full Kevlar body armor, C-four plastic explosives, handcuffs, a rocket launcher with six rockets and ten Glock, ten-millimeters. You got about a thousand rounds to boot."

"Yeeeee haaaaaw. We ready for a war," Andy celebrated while changing into his camouflage uniform.

William-Larry dropped the bag of money in the co-pilot's seat. Cooter glanced over at the bag and held up a hand while landing the plane with the other hand. As soon as the plane touched down, Cooter took a long drag from his joint. "Touch down," he exhaled with smoke.

He parked the plane at the end of the short runway where a military jeep was waiting and then pulled a stack of bills from the bag. "Hand this here ten grand to the fella in the jeep. When you're ready to go back, we'll be leaving on a cargo plane. Bobby Lee included. Dead or alive. Now you fellas go on ahead and get 'em. I got a party to attend and a whole bunch a shit to destroy if you run into a roadblock."

William-Larry adjusted the uniform that would give him instant access to walk down the restricted military airstrip and then grabbed two of the four heavy duffle bags before stepping off the plane with Andy close behind. His days of being in the Marines felt like yesterday. All around him were military planes and vehicles. He wasn't sure who was watching, but when he saw the flash of a green neon light guiding him to the men in the jeep, he knew his family's money was well spent.

"This way," Andy and William-Larry heard someone say in the darkness near the jeep. They approached and the voice said, "Drop the bags in the back, and then salute me like you're enlisted."

The brothers remained silent. They didn't need their voices identified if it wasn't necessary. They were in the process of committing a gang of crimes that would land them directly under a Federal Penitentiary. Only thing was, neither of them would ever allow themselves to get caught. Now that Bobby Lee was in that position, they intended on changing that.

*****

Manny did as Racheal asked. He posed for pictures, shook the hands of people he didn't want to remember, and exchanged business cards with others he never intended on calling.

While posing for yet another picture from a photographer who stalked his every move, he noticed just how packed the place had become. He was caught up in observing his guest when someone grabbed his hand and called for the photographer's attention. The flash went off as Manny turned to see who it was. To his surprise it was Alvaro Santa-Maria smiling by his side.

"Tsk. Tsk. Tsk, Manuel Black, a man of stature hanging out with these…these…*types of people?*" He looked around the room and said, "Something is amidst, Manny. I crashed the party and quickly realized two things."

"What's that?" Manny asked, not even concerned with how he got in.

Alvaro outstretched his arms with both palms up and said, "The party has been crashed on me."

"You said two things," Manny said calmly. He had no idea what Alvaro was talking about, but he refused to let Alvaro see him sweat.

Alvaro looked startled, and Manny didn't think that was possible. He looked around the room again and said, "Oh. I realized that you're going to need my help more than you think."

Manny was tired of playing games, plus he was in the middle of entertaining guests and making sure not to embarrass Racheal. "So, you're here for a reason?" he said with impatience.

Alvaro seemed totally displeased with the crows that came to Manny's party. He shook his head while looking at Racheal's father. "I wanted to see this fiasco in the making. This is history in the making. *Classic.*" He looked up at the decorations. "You're paying a pretty penny to be the meal at this feast."

Fiasco? Feast? Manny thought. "What the hell are you talking about?"

Alvaro used his thumb and index finger to grab his lips and twist like he was turning a lock. "Can't say, but..." he withdrew his business card from the inside of his tux and handed it to Manny. "In case you threw the first card away." He looked over his shoulder, then back at Manny. "At this point I'm the only one that's going to be able to help you. Help yourself, Manny and let's join forces."

"I'm nobody's flunky," Manny barked, too loud for his liking.

Instead of walking away like he was about to, Alvaro quickly pivoted and stepped in really close to Manny like he was going to kiss his lips. "Manny, that mess you made last night was not successful. My people do not wish for you to be a rat, as you say. We need you to be successful. He was right there, and when the foolish, on-line graduates of the N.Y.P.D, receives information that it was *you.* The same man they released on bail for a homicide. The same man who has the Attorney General so deep in his ass he can't tell the difference between a dick and constipation, what do you think is gonna happen to your future? Martyrs quickly become history, Manny Black. Save yourself."

"I'm not a fucking rat!"

Alvaro shook his head. "No. You're not, but I thought you were smart." He stepped off. "Maybe I was wrong," as he made his way to the exit.

"What the hell is that about?" Joe Tacopica asked while approaching, looking Hollywood tanned and dressed like an investment banker—a very successful one.

Manny took a deep breath, trying to regain his composure. "What was what?"

Joe motioned Manny to wait while pulling a Piaget watch case from his blazer. He handed Manny the case and smiled. "Congratulations on your engagement." He looked down at his watch, tapped the crystal and said, "I'm in and out. Just wanted to drop by and show my respect, but I have to go." He pointed to the case. "Open the case. Only twenty of them ever made."

Manny opened the case to find a shining, dark gold watch flooded with a diamond bezel. "Nice. *Bueno.*"

Joe nodded. "Nice, right?"

Manny shook his head with a smile.

"I did good with that, right?"

Manny shook his head again, still smiling.

"That was a token as your friend." He gently pulled Manny away from the photographer and said, "Now I want to talk to you as your lawyer and confidant, but I have to make it quick." He looked around with suspicion before asking, "What the hell do you and Alvaro Santa-Maria have in common?"

There was nothing Manny could say.

"That bad huh, Manny?" Joe asked when Manny hesitated.

"Who the fuck is he?" Manny asked with humility.

Joe smirked. "That's the best you can do?"

Manny shook his head. "No. No I didn't mean I don't know who he is. I mean, *who* the fuck is he? What does he do and for whom?"

Again, Joe looked around with caution like he had information to impeach a president. "Let me tell you something, Manny. I had a client years ago who *allegedly* embezzled part of the national wealth of Ireland. This guy was accused of stealing more than a billion dollars. *A billion dollars.* Now, that was during the time when American foreign policy was having a problem with Ireland due to the tax laws and evasion issues. So, Uncle Sam didn't want the case to get messy since my client was American. Do you know who they called in to clean it all up and make the whole thing disappear?"

"Alvaro," Manny answered.

Joe chuckled, "What? Oh, so you and this shit bag are on a first name basis?"

Manny shook his head. "Nah, Joe. Slow down," he warned, reminding Joe who was paying. "What I need to know is who he works for?"

Joe nodded while looking across the room. "Yeah. Sure. He's N.S.A. They take orders from the president and give orders to him too. Anyway," he paused and then changed the subject. "Puncho."

"What about him?" Manny asked with anxiety.

"I think I can get him a flat three years on weapons possession and not charged with any of the homicides. That crime scene was so contaminated words can't explain it. They're still trying to match ballistics, but it seems more than twenty guns were used, so it's a shell casing nightmare, not to mention trying to trace the trail from who's gun went to what bullet, and who's bullet went to what head and body. It's crazy, and guess who they have as an eyewitness to all that shit?"

Manny was afraid to know, but asked, "Who?"

Joe's Hollywood smile appeared. "No one. Not a single rat in the wounded bunch. I don't know who the hell has these Cuban's under pressure, but Manny..." he paused for effect "...I get it now why you and these guys have been beefing for so long. They don't give up, and the good news for Puncho is, they won't rat either."

Manny rubbed his chin. "Impossible."

Joe's eyes lit up. "That's what I said! But it's true."

"So what's the strategy to help Puncho?"

"If I move before the N.Y.P.D forensic guys can figure things out, with a stipulation to the D.A. that no further charges will be filed, we might be onto something."

Suddenly, an extra tall, strawberry blonde with legs and an upper body that looked like they were made to dominate anybody's walkway walked their way. The closer she approached, the more Manny was captivated by her beauty. She looked like she belonged on the cover of Sports Illustrated—forever.

Joe smiled and said, "My new assistant."

"Oh," Manny said in awe. "That's what they call them now?"

She walked over and shook Manny's hand. "Mr. Black. Heard a lot about you. Pleasure to meet you." She turned to Joe and tapped the crystal of her own watch.

"Well..." Joe told Manny. "That's my cue." He hugged Manny and said, "Try to at least *look* like you're enjoying this night. I'll see you in court."

Joe walked off, leaving Manny alone and not in the mood to socialize, but then Nzinga, Toki, and Larry showed up, all with big smiles and bearing gifts.

"Hello, Manny," Nzinga said with her British accent. "Congratulations. I predicted this and made a little wager when Racheal was hired," she said with a chuckle. She rubbed the side of his face. "She gets to take you off the market. Bullocks."

Toki nodded. "Hi, boss. Congrats. I'm hungry. I'll be right back to talk to you, okay?" She did a slight jog towards the table that had her reserved name tag on it and sat down.

Larry shook Manny's hand vigorously and handed him a box of cigars. "Cuban, No offense,"

Nzinga was about to walk away, but Manny grabbed her hand and gently pulled her back to him before telling Larry, "Larry, come back when she leaves. Please. I need you to handle something for me."

"Will do," Larry assured and posted himself ten steps away like he was Manny's personal body guard.

"How are things going?" Manny asked Nzinga.

She blushed and then replied, "Well, considering the circumstances. He's doing well."

Manny smirked, thinking of his imprisoned brother.

"His health is improving rapidly." She blushed and chuckled.

"Wait a minute," Manny said and started feeling good for the first time that night.

Nzinga looked away and blushed. "What's bugging you, Sir Manny?"

He backed away and tilted his head to the side while looking at her. "So you're falling for lil bro, huh? Is that what that blushing is all about?"

She blushed again. "Well you were taken."

"What about Edeeks?"

"Don't spoil my mood." She shook her head. "E is a married man. When his wife is good, he's great. When she's too much, he called me and I grew tired of being his safety hole." She looked over at Edeeks talking to Racheal and said, "E has other things he's pursuing."

"And Puncho?"

She smiled. "Like I said, you were taken. After that first visit I haven't missed one. It was our secret. He needs a wife and I need a husband. My eggs are not getting any younger and I need to get fat and have a bunch of Panamanian children."

"*Wow*," Manny uttered, realizing his brother just acquired a wife. Then he thought of what Joe told him. "And if he has to do time?"

"That's expected. I hope you'll accept my resignation? I know what I want, and he's it. So, where he goes, I go. Time flies, especially when you're in love."

Manny felt a hint of jealousy. He stood before the most unique type of woman, but the fact that she wanted his brother allowed him to rest easy. Puncho would be in great hands in case he's not around. He kissed Nzinga. "Thank you for everything."

She stepped closer, and kissed his cheek. "I should be the one thanking you. You're a great boss."

"Am I?" he asked with complete sincerity. He was willing to be vulnerable around her.

"Yes. You are. You just need to bloody grow up and understand that a business as big as yours means you're responsible for many lives and futures. If you had the attitude that people's lives were in your hands every day you showed up for work, then you would be more serious, because you would understand the severity of your position. One day you will. I do hope so."

Manny concluded that she was right. "You're right," he told her. "I promise. As soon as I handle a few more things I'm coming to take over the company for good."

Nzinga smiled wider this time. "Then scratch my request to accept my resignation. I'm due for a promotion and since madam Racheal will be home tending to crumpets, I feel I'm way overdue." She kissed Manny again and said, "Sir Manny. Please bloody smile more. You're looking like this gala is torture."

"I will. I promise," he said as she walked away.

Larry suddenly popped up without an invitation. He looked around the room with suspicion and then twisted his lips to the side before whispering, "What's up, boss? Have a mission for me? Gonna let me get a piece of the action with the Cuban's?"

Manny looked across the room at Edeeks hugging Racheal and laughing it up with her mother. Then he observed how all of her guests were on the other side of the room and he had no one standing by his side. He then turned to Larry and asked, "When was the last time you did a sweep at the office?"

Larry looked up to the ceiling, thinking of the last time he checked for listening devices planted by law enforcement. "About six weeks."

"Anything?"

Larry shook his head. "Not a one. I can't find them anymore."

Manny stared at Racheal talking to Nzinga. "Real soon. At a moment's notice, I want you to come to my house and do a sweep."

"*Whew*, this must be serious. Your home?" Larry was stunned. He rubbed his palms together. "I'll bring my whole kit. Got some new stuff too."

"I'll call at a moment's notice. Be quick. I need you to tear ass and get to my house when I call. Got it?"

"Need me to camp out in a tree for a few days before you call? Or maybe dig a foxhole on the property. I can cover it with camouflage and you'd never know I was there, maybe?" Larry asked seriously.

Manny looked into Larry's eyes, then at his crew cut and then down at his military shined combat boots, and thought of Self and Chango and wondered why he was a weirdo magnet. "No, sleep at home, Larry. Just please be ready."

Larry looked around and twisted his mouth to the side and whispered, "Yes, sir, and will you need me and my boys to take care of this Cuban problem? I kinda, couldn't help but hear it on the news."

At that moment Manny didn't feel alone anymore. He shook Larry's hand and then hugged him. "Thanks friend. Thanks a lot."

Toki locked eyes with Manny from the other side of the room. Her cheeks were stuffed with food like a chipmunk as she held a plate in one hand and a toothpick in the other.

"*Friend?*" Larry asked loudly with a huge grin on his face. "I never heard you call me that before." He shook Manny's hand vigorously and said, "I won't disappoint you, Manny."

"I know," Manny said and meant every word.

As Larry walked away, Toki scuttled over, trying to get some of Manny's time.

"Slow down," he told her.

She smiled with a mouth full of food and pointed to her plate and said, "This is *so* good." After she swallowed she dropped the nearly empty plate on a passing waiter's tray and brushed her hands together to remove the crumbs.

"You okay?" Manny asked, knowing how intense she could be.

She nodded and scraped food off her tooth with her un-manicured pinkie. "So!" she said all business like. "Might not be the right time to discuss this since it's your engagement party and all, but the company just lost like seven to eight million dollars. You fired Ann—who doesn't happen to be here, which is odd since Racheal is supposed to be her sister, and that's a *strong suppose*. I'm thinking, and hope you're thinking that somehow and in some way if someone in finance was more on their job—like the director—then maybe, *just* maybe, we wouldn't have lost all that money. Soooo! I think that position needs to be filled at once." She sucked her teeth and then looked at Manny nonchalantly.

"You do coke, Toki?"

She shook her head with indifference, "Nope," was all she said so he was relieved.

"So it sounds like you just asked me for a promotion."

"That's…about…right!"

Manny replayed everything she implied in her tirade and knew that she had always been loyal throughout all the year. Still noticing how Edeeks was chatting with Racheal and her mother, "You're hired," he told her. "But give me some time to sort out a few personal matters and we can make it official."

Cool." She replied.

Nzinga and Toki were the hardest workers in the company. It was no coincidence that both gave him ammunition to wake up to what was going on around him. He made his way across the room to Edeeks and smiled at the group and politely asked, "You mind if I speak with you for a moment?"

Edeeks excused himself, annoyed that he was being bothered by Manny and his attitude showed it when he asked, "What's up, bro?"

"What the fuck is going on in here?"

Edeeks rolled his eyes up to the ceiling and then sighed. "What now, Manny?"

Manny lost his patience. "Roll them fucking eyes at me again. That's my word I'll stick a knife in both of them. Stop fucking wit' me E."

"Yo, what's—the—*problem*?"

Manny pointed to the men in the circle and asked, "You know these people? Where you know them from?"

Edeeks checked to see if Manny was serious. "You got some type of mental problem, bro? Seriously."

"E, don't make me make a scene in here."

Edeeks put his palms up. "Let me get this right, I'm the *only* real person you can consider a family member here. I'm being sociable to *your* guests, representing *you*, and *you're* asking *me* where I know these people from?"

He had a point, Manny reasoned. "You know these people?"

Edeeks lost it. "These are *your* fiancée's, wife-to-be's guests! Why the fuck you don't ask her about these people?"

Manny looked at Edeeks and something deep inside didn't feel right. He searched Edeeks' eyes for weakness and asked, "So you saying you don't know any of these people?"

Edeeks looked at Manny like he felt sorry for him. "Do I have to ask your permission on who I speak with at a social gathering? Yes, I know some of them from school. Is that good enough for you Manny?"

This was not going the way Manny needed it to go. He walked away to stand by Racheal. He needed answers and was determined to get them before the night was over.

*****

After climbing into the military jeep, William-Larry and Andy were driven a hundred yards off base to meet up with a waiting Rich and Self.

"Brother," William-Larry greeted Self as he was climbing into the back seat of a new Avalanche pickup truck.

"It's just us. Self feel like the kid Chango is official, but you never know. This on a different level," Self said as they pulled off.

"How different than the scrap metal place?" Rich asked while his eyes were on the road. "How different than the night when—"

Self thought of Bobby Lee and cut Rich off, "Yeah, the God did the science. They came through, but this different. For Self it's all or nothing."

"Affirmative," Rich confirmed.

"Where is he?" William-Larry asked.

Rich and Self looked at each other before Rich answered, "Hospital prison ward."

"How many guards and what's going on with them squirrel fuckers?"

"Silence," Rich said and every man in the truck knew what that meant.

For about a half hour there wasn't a peep in the truck. Then Andy broke the silence when he said, "Drive by that place with all the lights."

"Times Square," William-Larry offered.

"We heavy," Self warned, reminding them of how much ammunition and artillery they were carrying. "Real dirty right now."

"We in the big Apple and I never seen it," Andy argued. "And I need a drink!"

"Never know when you're taking your last ride," William-Larry uttered, fully aware of the mission before them.

"Indeed," Self answered. "Let's take that ride."

William-Larry turned up the country music and the men rode unto the New Jersey Turnpike. As they were closing in on the George Washington Bridge, the New York skyline across the Hudson River started lighting up.

"Well, looka here," he blurted out, amazed at the skyscrapers. "My eyes have seen a great wonder of the world. How do they get them buildings to stand so tall? I'd be scared shitless to go way up in them towers."

Everyone laughed.

"Lemme ask you something?" William-Larry asked Andy, always the rational one. "How many confirmed kills you have?"

"Do you *gotta* go there?" Self asked with a chuckle.

William-Larry also chuckled. "*What?*" he asked with innocent humor. "They're confirmed," he stated, telling anyone who didn't know that Andy's kills were done in the military.

"Just answer the question," Rich barked. "I'm sure he's got some point to it."

"And you watch your tone," William-Larry warned Rich, showing who was the oldest.

"*Awwww,*"Andy let out softly. "They fightin' over me."

"Answer the damn question," Rich said, not too patient with Andy's antics.

"*Hmmmm,*" Andy thought. "Ok, thirteen, close contact. Seven hand to hand."

"And just how many men you beat in the ring when you were in?" William-Larry continued.

Andy's eyes rolled up into his head while he fought to think. When he was done counting in his head, his eyes rolled back down and locked onto his brother's when he said, "Twenty seven and one. Twenty four knockouts and the one loss was a fluke. I drank too much the day of the fight."

"*Exactly!*" William-Larry said, clearly making his point to himself. "And you're scared of a damn building? An unmovable object? Right, boy?" He shook his head in disbelief. "Stay off the shine."

The men laughed while cruising through the city.

Rich continued to drive while Andy "Oooo'd" and "Ahhhh'd" at the sights of the New York and New Jersey river views. When they turned onto 42nd Street with the bustling four lane traffic, tall buildings that sprung up on both sides of the street and bright lights that lit up the sky it took Andy and William-Larry's breath away.

"My *goodness*," William-Larry gasped. "They so *tall*," he said with his face pinned against the tinted windows. "But you can't be scared Andy."

"Then why don't your ass go run to the top of 'em since you're so brave?"

William-Larry was stumped.

Rich drove around Times Square until Self guided him back onto 42nd Street. As they were heading east and passing the overpass of Park Avenue, Self snapped his finger and said, "Pull over to your right. Want them to meet Self brother before they head out tomorrow." He picked up his secure phone and hit the number on the display.

*****

Manny's phone buzzed. "Yo," he answered, staring across the room, watching everyone party without him.

"The God need you outside," Self spoke.

"Right outside?"

"Indeed," Self answered. "In the tinted truck. Self and the other brothers."

Manny took a passing glance at his guests and quickly headed for the door. He had to make sure no one was watching his moves, but by the way the party was going, he wouldn't be missed. He stepped out of the ritzy entrance of Cipriani's and searched the sea of limousines and yellow cabs out front until he saw the Avalanche parked at the corner. He walked over, knocked on the front passenger window where Self was seated.

"Slick," Self said scanning Manny's tux up and down. "Ain't you looking dapper?"

Manny looked into the back of the truck and saw William-Larry for the first time and his head jerked back. "Damn, you and Bobby Lee are really fucking twins. I thought it was him." Then he nodded a greeting at Andy, who was still mesmerized by the sights of New York City.

"Yeah, that's why they here," Self butted in. "To help finish the shit you started."

Something wrong, Manny thought. Self was being sarcastic, talkative and his attitude had changed from love to hostility. *Ok, he lost his whole family*, Manny reasoned. "What's happening?"

Rich leaned over and said, "How's it going in there?"

Manny looked back at the entrance of Cipriani, sighed and then looked back at Rich.

"That bad, huh?" Rich asked.

"Later for all that," Self cut them off while his eyeing the police officers across the street at Grand Central Station. "Need a few stacks to handle expenses."

"How many?"

"Three hundred."

Andy whistled, leaned forward to Rich and whispered, "Does he mean three hundred thousand *dollars*? Just like that?"

Without hesitation, Manny asked, "Cash or check?"

Self answered. "Cash," realizing they were illegally parked. "By tomorrow if you can, Slick, and make sure you have an alibi." Self turned to Rich, and without saying his goodbyes to Manny, he said, "We out."

Rich saluted Manny, and Andy and William-Larry said their farewells as the truck pulled off.

Manny walked back into Cipriani's and found Racheal standing by the front door with panic etched into her face. "Where did you go?"

Her tone was a problem. A serious one.

He held a finger up in her face. "Check this out? Check that shit!" he warned. "Not tonight."

"This is how you want to act at my engagement party?"

Manny had enough. "That's the problem. Since it's *yours*, maybe you need to be here by ya damn self."

He stepped off and she rushed to his side. In a whisper she pleaded, "People are looking. Can we at least *act* like we're getting along tonight?"

He looked around the room, "Isn't this whole thing an act anyway?"

"I can't believe you." She said.

"And I don't believe you. I love you Racheal, but I'm not stupid."

The DJ announced, "Ladies and gentlemen, we ask that everyone focus on the center of the room where the bride and groom-to-be will start off the dance of love." Then "I Wanna Know," by R&B singer Joe started to play.

Manny and Racheal were caught off guard. They looked at each other for direction. He was afraid to do the wrong thing in front of all the guests and she didn't know how best to play her part.

She heard, "*Psst. Pssst*," coming from her right and turned to see her mother flapping her hands forward, whispering, "You two have to dance."

Manny put on his best theatrical performance to smile, approached his bride to be in a loving manner, and then asked her to dance. She smiled, curtsied and then they danced.

FIFTEEN

"Not to be in your business brother," Andy told Self as they were traveling East on 42nd Street.

"Now that's a sure sign to reckon that a man is about to be in your business," William-Larry butted in.

"Speak," Self answered.

Andy smiled at William-Larry. "See there?" he told his brother showing that he won a victory. Then he asked Self, "Manny? He can just hand over all that money to you, just like that?"

"That's Self brother. All he got cause Self believed. Self knew."

"And exactly how much is he worth?" Andy asked.

"You're pushing it," Rich warned, turning onto First Avenue.

"Probably, by now…" Self paused to think. "His company probably worth between twenty to thirty mil."

Andy whistled. "My god, sweet Jesus. And if you don't mind—"

"Yep," William-Larry uttered. "You're nosey as hell."

"Speak," Self uttered.

Andy smiled wider, he won another victory. "How'd he make that kind of money? How do somebody do that?"

Self was silent for a moment. His mind flashed with vivid images of the days when the M3 Boyz ruled. He remembered the huge amount of heroin and cocaine they sold and the murders he and Manny committed so they could both eat well. "Manny thought different," Self answered. "And he never thought he could lose. No matter how big the dream, he never doubted if he could make it or thought it was too big."

"But in the beginning, it was Self and Manny doing the dirty work," William-Larry answered.

"Hmpt," Andy grunted. "I got it."

As they were traveling uptown on First Avenue, Andy looked out the window to his right and was amazed by the massive, fortified compound with flags from all over the world in a line like a path. "What's that? *Gawww leee*, that building must take up a whole mile."

"That's the United Nations, fool," William-Larry added.

"Ohhhh," Andy let out. They stopped at the traffic light and Andy looked over to a stretch limousine and asked, "What diplomatic license plates mean?"

The light turned green and Rich pulled off while Self was looking straight ahead at the hill that led uptown.

Rich answered, "That means some representative from another country, or this one, receives benefits as the representative."

"And they can break the law and do foul shit while they in this country and they can't be arrested, detained or even questioned," Self added.

"Oh," Andy said. "A big shot from another country."

"Yeah, like the squirrel fuckers we need to deal with," William-Larry answered.

Andy wasn't finished. As the limousine was riding along side of them, two lanes over, he asked, "So the flags on the front of the diplomats' cars is the country they're from, correct?"

"Indeed," said Self.

Andy pointed out the window and asked, "Well, I may be wrong, but isn't that the Cuban flag?"

"*What?*" everyone else said in unison.

"Where?" Self asked with enthusiasm.

Andy pointed to the car that was making a left onto 57th Street. "The long white Cadillac."

Self turned to see the flags and discovered Andy was right. "Just like that? *Ahum du allah.*" He couldn't believe how lucky they were.

"Well I'll be," William-Larry blurted out. "That there is a limousine with diplomatic plates and Cuban flags on the front." He patted Andy on the back the way one would do an obedient dog and he told his brother, "You did good, boy. You smarter than you dumb."

"Put your blinkers on and ease across traffic," Self instructed Rich. "We going around the block." He then asked the passengers in the back, "Look for another car tailing them."

"I see a black Ford, but don't know," William-Larry answered.

Self un-tucked his .50 Desert Eagle handgun and checked to see if it was fully loaded. "Go around the block, but take it easy. We don't need no attention." He removed his black bandana from his pocket and tied it around his neck. "Y'all got your bandanas?"

"Does a redneck eat deer and shoot duck?" Andy asked.

"Gas mask from Cooter," William-Larry answered. "I like the gas mask."

Rich ordered, "Lock and load."

"I need a drink," Andy announced while removing two of the Calico sub-machineguns from their duffle bags. "Not gonna tell y'all again."

Rich followed all of Self's instructions so he could navigate through the city streets. They quickly made their way around the block and sped down 57th Street and headed west until they spotted the limousine on Broadway. A black Ford Escape was still traveling two car distances behind it.

"Get alongside of the Ford," Self ordered Rich. "Andy, when we pull up, look straight like you ain't watching."

"Yessir."

Rich pulled alongside of the Ford. The windows were pitch-black, so they couldn't see how many men were inside or if they were even trailing the limousine.

"Pull up to the limo," Self instructed and Rich stepped on the gas. They reached the limousine and again—all black windows, except for the front.

"One in the front," Rich stated. "Whatta we do now?"

"Follow," Self answered. "And wait."

"*If*, it's them," Andy added.

"Pin a lazy tail on 'em," William-Larry took over giving orders. "Stay five cars back. If need be, we do an assault maneuver."

The limousine made a right onto the hill of Eleventh Avenue. At 66th Street, it made a left and headed up a hill to the exclusive community of Riverside Boulevard. Massive architectural masterpieces created this small community of luxury apartments that looked over a large park across the street, and the Westside Highway and Hudson River was a stone throw away.

"Can it really be this easy?" Rich asked as the limo parked up ahead in front of a Trump building. The Ford was parked directly behind it.

"A humble is what we call it. Self used to catch mad shit on the humble. Just fall in Self lap. *Insha-Allah* Mostro in the back of that limo."

"If so," William-Larry interrupted while making sure the barrel to the Calico machineguns was clear. "Self and Andy take the limo, and Rich, you take the Ford. I got your back."

The limousine and Ford sat idle before the Trump building and no one exited. Then a beautiful brunette stepped out of the entrance of the building and the back door to the limo opened. His tanned face appeared first, and then his custom tailored suit was in full view, smiling at the woman he helped get into the car.

"Bingo!" Rich uttered.

"Primo," Self declared. "Cover your face. Drive ahead and make the first right."

Rich quickly pulled ahead and eased pass the two vehicles. They had no idea what was waiting for them, or how much artillery was in the vehicles, but they didn't care. The leader of the Marielitos was right in their grasp.

"We have rocket launchers," William-Larry volunteered. "We can just end it all now."

"No," Self responded. "We need to get Bobby! That comes first. So we need to keep this quiet. In this community? The S.W.A.T. team will be here the minute we start banging out."

Rich made the first right and they parked at the steep hill. The shade of the towering buildings above added to the darkness they needed, but the bright lights from the parking garage across the street was going to be a problem.

"Park here," Self advised. Rich placed a .44 revolver into his lap, slipped on his gloves and waited. When the headlights to the limousine slowly made its way around the corner, Self said, "Pull out into the street. Pop the hood and lift it. Tap the hood and we rush 'em." He looked over his shoulder and asked, "Andy you ready?"

"Besides needing a drink?" Andy asked. "Yessir."

Rich quickly pulled into the roadway and followed the plan. The limousine slowed and he popped the hood of the truck. "Tap. Tap. Tap," he knocked.

"Move!" Self said and all three men exited the truck with weapons high.

Andy did a full sprint, moving faster than everyone else. He leaped onto the hood of the limousine. Then he ran across the roof until he reached the back and kicked in the moon-roof.

"Don't move!" he yelled to the petrified man and woman in the back seat who had their hands up in surrender.

Rich and William-Larry were on either side of the Ford, weapons drawn. Rich stopped in front of the driver's window at an angle while William-Larry slowly took baby steps backward, moving further into the shadows and lining himself up for a better shot.

Self came around and put the big nozzle of the Desert Eagle to the driver's window of the limo and said, "Open the door!"

The driver obeyed and Self yanked the door open before hitting the button to unlock all the doors and reaching in to search the driver.

"I'm clean!" the Latino yelled. "I got a wife and kids, man," he pleaded.

"Good, make it home to them. Hand over your wallet!" Self demanded. "Hurry!" he ordered like he had done in many of his robberies. The driver fumbled for his wallet and dropped it, and Self picked it up and opened it. He flashed the license to the driver and said, "You see nothing. We know where you live."

"Take whatever you want!" the beautiful brunette screamed, looking up at the nozzle of Andy's gun in fright.

Andy's eyes were fixated on a crystal decanter of brown liquid that was in a bar rack inside of the limousine.

"Stay where you are," Rich barked to the passengers in the Ford. So far, no one inside moved and Rich didn't like that. He didn't know if they were on the phone or what they were doing. He looked over to William-Larry on the other side of the truck and shrugged.

William-Larry didn't like the circumstances either. He was certain Rich could kill anything that moved in seconds. With that surety he quickly inched forward, taking small steps, and smashed the back window out with the butt of his gun. "Open the door!" he ordered the two Latino's. "All phones and guns out! That was your warning!"

"Two minutes!" Rich announced to Self.

Self nodded and ran to the back door of the limousine. He opened it, ducked his head and then his weapon inside and told the passenger, "Bitch, move over." He hopped in, looked up to the sunroof and told Andy, "Come in. Tell 'em to follow!"

Andy turned to his brother. "Follow!" he said before dropping in through the sunroof.

"*Follow?*" Rich asked in disbelief while looking over his shoulder. He looked over to William-Larry and shrugged.

"*Shit,*" William-Larry grunted and then rushed into the back seat of the Ford while Rich ran to the truck. He slammed the door shut and pointed the nozzle of the Calico to the back of the passenger's head. "Follow."

Rich looked around at the empty street and quickly put his gun away. He rushed to close the hood of the truck and then hopped inside and pulled out of the limousine's way.

Self read the name on the license and yelled it out. "Alex! Drive up Riverside drive and don't stop until you reach the GWB."

"Take what you want and just leave us alone!" the brunette yelled.

Self and Andy sat on the lounge chair across from Primo and his date. Andy stared at her.

"You beast!" she spat at him. "Take what you—"

Andy planted two, quick, deathly punches to her chin. Her head snapped back and then slowly leaned towards him. Her eyes closed and then her head flopped forward into his lap. "*Whoa, Becky*," he uttered and looked over to Primo, who was across from Self with a grin on his face. He then grabbed the crystal decanter and lifted it while staring at Primo.

"Congac," Primo offered.

Andy bounced his eyebrows and lifted the decanter to Primo in gratitude. "Not my brand, but it'll do."

As Andy tilted the liquid courage to his lips with the unconscious woman's head in his lap, Self aimed his weapon at Primo's face.

Primo lifted his right palm like he took an oath. He closed his eyes and in Spanish he prayed, asking God for forgiveness. When he opened his eyes he looked at Self and asked, "You're Manny Black's henchman?"

"Where Mostro?" Self asked, fully focused on what he was there for.

Primo exhaled slowly. "Which one? He has no home."

Self raised his gun a little higher. "Not gonna ask you again."

"He doesn't sleep!" Primo insisted. "He has no home. Each day he goes to a different place. He is everywhere and nowhere. Sometimes he's in two different places at the same time. He may be watching us now. This is how he operates," Primo explained and shrugged, telling Self to believe what he wanted.

Self admired that. Mostro was indeed a worthy opponent, but he still had to die. "The God need you to take the God to him."

"Would you take me to Manny Black?" Primo asked as he grumbled his frustration. "Manny and these foolish battles he creates. He was just a pawn."

"What's Mostro's weakness?" Self asked.

Primo put his hand back up. "Excuse me sir, I think we started off on the wrong foot. I'm Jose Gomez, Ambassador to Cuba and—"

"A dead man if you don't answer the God question.

Andy looked at the empty decanter in his hand that just held a fifth of cognac and announced, "This some pretty good drink."

Primo looked at Andy in fright, certain that the drunk before him was a psychopath. "Okay, okay," he pleaded calmly. "Do you have a name?"

"Abdulla."

"What I need you to know Abdulla," he said in a whisper. "Is that Mostro is in the way. He's a rock in my shoe. I'm indifferent to his demise."

"What. Is. His weakness?" Self asked through clinch teeth.

Primo dropped his head and answered, "Mostro's weakness is blood. The shedding of blood and his love of Cuba. He is too idealistic. Which has become a problem."

"So you will sell him out? Cross him?" Self asked. "To survive?"

Primo sat back and adjusted his suit like that would return his dignity. "I'm his general. He is my soldier," he answered calmly, stating the facts. "Soldiers win the wars while the general does the thinking to get the best out of the soldier. Like you and Mr. Black's relationship. I don't see him, and how did you find me here?"

Self said, "Not hard. So you can give him orders to come to the God? He's your pet?"

"He is a savage beast," Primo boasted about Mostro. "But yes, some feel I am his master, but I know better. This is about politics. As the leader of this organization we stand to create a level of influence beyond our dreams, if we stick to the agenda. Unlike you, Abdulla. Your motives move you, and Manny influences you. Is he your master?"

"I Self am Lord and Master,"

"Hmmm, then peace to you," Primo added, clearly understanding Self's culture.

"Wise man," Self complimented him.

Primo grinned. "Knowledge of self."

Self quickly lowered his gun. Primo was wiser than he seemed. "So why shouldn't Abdulla destroy you?"

Primo smiled. "Third person," he uttered, finally understanding Self's speech pattern. "Kill when it's to your advantage. You're deaf, dumb and blind to why we are enemies. When we can be allies."

"Build," Self encouraged him to continue as Primo made the foolish error of starting to relax.

While the driver crept through the shaded streets of Riverside drive, Andy's head moved back and forth from Self to Primo like he was watching a good movie.

Primo adjusted comfortably in his seat and volleyed with his answer when he said, "We have no beef. Every time some new player gets ambitious, he uses others to try to dismantle Los Marielitos. The chiefs may change, but the Indians will always remain. This is politics—war without bloodshed, but in our case, the U.S. government engages weaker men to spin the minds of other men, and they attack. One of those men is Manny Black. Another you may know of was Pantera—Mostro's brother, and of course, Gato. We have reason to believe that Manny Black is a government informant and a paid mercenary. How do you explain him being apprehended the other day for murder and yet he still walks the streets?"

"Apprehended?" Self asked with suspicion as his face twisted like he tasted something sour.

Primo's face came alive with joy. "I see Manny is a man of many secrets. You're willing to put your life on the line for him. You think he would have mentioned that? Unfortunately for him, information is everywhere. This is how I found out."

Self's mind was spinning, but he maintained his composure. If it was true, he would deal with Manny accordingly.

Primo was on a roll now. "How else does he evade the law, maintain his wealth and arbitrarily wage war on the Marielitos? Why would a man with so much money pick up a gun unless someone else, who is more powerful, is pulling his strings? I would love to discuss this with him. I'm actually perplexed by this anomaly to patterns."

"Patterns?" Self quizzed.

Primo stopped short and looked at Self like he was the student and wasn't paying attention to the lesson. He placed his palms together like he was praying and said, "Let me explain. People, based on their behavior and habits, they create patterns. These patterns—"

"Ab, know patterns," Self cut him off. Primo was teaching the instructor of human patterns and Self was thrown off by how much he and Primo had in common.

"Oh," Primo said. "Well, I would love to discuss this with Manny personally."

Self smirked. That was highly unlikely. "Who waged war on Ab family?"

Primo looked confused, "Ab?"

Self tapped his chest.

"Oh, yeah. The way you speak..." Primo looked down and mumbled, "Your family. I'm sorry for your loss. That was Mostro's doing. He wanted to *'purge'* all who opposed us. It was a military exercise to gain loyalty amongst his soldiers."

"And you approved it?"

"I found out after the fact, but in a situation like the one you have me in now, you know that the average man would tell you whatever you want to hear to survive, but I'm telling you that it was Mostro's doing. His love of blood, with the revenge factor for his brother's death, especially on U.S. soil was what he considered a major victory."

"Did you agree with it?"

"Abdulla, you sound as if I have some personal or an emotional attachment to the action of my soldiers. As the leader there is a certain modicum of action I must keep reserved. Where is Manny Black, right now? Is he out dining like I intended to? Or is he in the trenches? Again, I don't see him here. So forgive me, Abdulla, but my days in the trenches are long gone. I need to dictate. It's just a job with tremendous rewards that has the benefit where I have no emotional attachment to my soldiers."

"You not getting Ab closer to Mostro."

Primo turned in his seat and looked at the men trailing in the Ford. He pointed a trembling finger out the back window and said, "They know. They drive for him."

There was one thing that was bothering Self, humbling him. "Why we enemies?"

"A misunderstanding," Primo answered. "Pantera wanted to run Los Marielitos. He wanted Manny to eliminate the other leaders in the organization. Manny, and who I later learned was his wife, did that."

Self was there and his gun ended many of their lives too.

Primo continued, "Then Manny and your crew were rewarded, and then there was yet another player, Gato. He gets bright ideas and someone pulls the strings every time. This time it's Mostro and the U.S. government who Gato worked for and maybe Manny too. That's for you to figure out."

"Alex!" Self yelled. "Pull over." The car stopped in the darkness of 160th Street. Self turned to Andy and said, "Let's go."

Andy smiled, grabbed a bottle of scotch from the bar and told Primo, "You have some good booze. *Adios*, squirrel fucker."

"You don't have to kill me," Primo begged.

"Abdulla won't," Self promised. "But the God gun won't cool until Mostro is in pieces."

"I will forever be grateful. If you need anything, I know you know how to find me. Peace be unto you and yours. *Salaam*."

"*Wa laikum*," Self responded in Arabic as he was stepping out of the car.

"Ahh. Umm," Primo got Self to stop short and whispered, "It doesn't look right if they run back to Mostro and tell him I lived after seeing you."

"They know his trail?"

"Yes, I'm certain. As current as today they drove for him."

Self nodded. "You won't have to worry about it." He stepped out the limousine and told Andy to jump back into the truck.

Andy walked away to join Rich in the pickup while Self jumped into the back seat of the Ford where William-Larry had the nozzle of his Calico pressed against the ear of the passenger.

"Which one you think is the leader?" Self asked William-Larry.

He nudged his chin towards the man he had at gunpoint.

"Meet you in the truck," Self told William-Larry. He looked at Self, asking without words if he was going to be okay. "The God got this," Self said, and William-Larry eased out of the back seat.

"What chu gonna do?" The passenger asked Self with fear laced in every word.

Self looked into the man's eyes, lifted his cannon, extended his arm towards the driver; and let the hot slug free, splattering the driver's brains all over the dashboard.

"What! *The fuck!*, Man!" the passenger balked while reaching for the door handle.

"You got one time to answer," Self warned. "Where's Mostro?"

"Jamaica, Queens!" the Marielito squealed.

"Where?"

"I-I-I drop...dropped him off at...at a house in Jamaica Estates. One-eighty-eight, twelve, Aberdeen Road. Brick house, big windows. He goes after like—like one in the morning. Oh Jesus, please, Jesus save me," the Latino begged with his forehead resting against the dashboard.

"You believe in God?" Self asked the praying man as they inhaled the pungent scent of burnt brain matter.

He nodded with his eyes tightly closed, refusing to look at the mess in the seat next to him. "Yes, I do. Please don't kill me," he begged.

"If you love Jesus, tell him Self said 'peace to the God,'" Self advised before squeezing the trigger, splitting another skull.

He stepped out of the Ford and walked over to the awaiting pick-up truck. When he slid into the front passenger seat, Rich asked, "Primo?"

Self shook his head. Primo would live that day. "Self got a new way to end this war for good."

Rich put the truck in gear. "And the two in the Ford?"

Self looked straight ahead as they were driving onto the entry way to the Cross Bronx and the Major Deegan Expressways. Self nodded. "Warm up for tomorrow when we go get Bobby."

SIXTEEN

The night at Cipriani's was going to be a night to remember for everyone except the bride and groom to be. They couldn't agree on anything. After bundling up the few gifts and saying their farewells to their guests, they both jumped into the back of their awaiting car, fuming with anger.

"You Cuban?" Manny asked her as they approached the Holland Tunnel that would take them back to New Jersey.

"Your paranoia is starting to disturb me. The enemy you were sleeping with was the other wife, honey, and I'm not in the mood for an interrogation."

"Oh, you the only one that can try to get confessions, huh?" he asked in frustration.

She smiled and sighed, "I can't believe tonight of all nights is when you want to do this?"

"Yeah, better now than later. What's up with your pops? I thought your last name was Gordon?"

She turned back to him as she looked out the window. "I introduced you to my father already."

"Your father's name is Gordon?" he asked. "When I called the man's name he acted like I was talking about somebody else."

"Umm," she paused. "I never told you that's his name."

"Then why he let me call him Mr. Gordon?"

"He's hard of hearing."

"Oh shit," Manny said with disbelief. "I can't believe you hit me with that bullshit."

Racheal remained silent for too long. Then she asked, "What do you think his name is, Manny? Since you're making a big deal out of nothing."

His intuition was gnawing at him. "What's the man's fucking name!"

She looked towared the driver to see if he was paying attention. When her eyes locked with his in his rearview mirror, she looked over to Manny and barked, "Don't you dare use that tone with me."

"I already know what I have to do," he grumbled to himself.

Racheal eased closer to him. "You wanna kill me, Manny? Huh, killer? I'm not gonna go so easy, big boy," she whispered.

He didn't know if it was the pregnancy that had her losing her mind, or if it was the anxiety from the wedding, but he was certain he did not know the woman next to him.

As they were exiting the tunnel Racheal started sobbing. Manny didn't care. There was too much that went wrong at that dinner. There were too many pieces to a new puzzle that created too much doubt for him.

"How do you love someone that you can never have to yourself, Manny? How do you have a child for a husband, but know your child will be a bastard? How do you risk it all because you get caught up in love? Have everyone in your world condemn you for your decision, yet tell you to do a good job with the circumstances before you? How does a simple human being do that?"

"Is the man's last name Gordon?" Manny asked, not interested in her questions.

She softly replied, "You see? You missed the whole thing. Right there before you. Like always."

"Fuck all that. Answer me!"

Her pause lasted too long for his liking, but then she said, "His name is Wright. You probably heard a few people calling him Jasper or Dickey, so now you're all paranoid for no apparent reason and really messing up my engagement bliss to boot. I have my mother's last name."

Now that she was opening up, he wanted to see what else she would tell him. "Speaking of your mother. What does she think about me? About *us*?" There, he asked it. He knew the answer well, and felt the negative energy all night.

"My mother is very idealistic. Appearances matter to her and her ideal son-in law is not one who gets dragged away in handcuffs." She rubbed her belly. "And I can't undo this." She paused another long moment before she almost whispered, "Mother had to change her life and move from Silver Springs because of you—us."

"Why?" Manny snapped back.

"Long story and you're mad enough as it is." She looked at him with love in her eyes, but her tone was all business as she said, "Anything else you need to know?"

"Yes." Manny had the million dollar question. "Are you Cuban?"

Tears streamed down her eyes and she softly answered while shaking her head, "No."

Manny had a silent sigh. His emotions were quickly settling. She had spoken the truth, but that wasn't going to stop him from following the intuition that was nagging at him.

Racheal looked at him and then looked away. "There's so much that's right in front of you that you don't see, Manny," she said like she felt sorry for him.

The driver pulled up to the front of the house. He had been slipping. Too much was on his plate at one time. The pressure of everything he had to juggle was just too much.

Racheal walked ahead while he and the driver moved all the gifts into the house. Once the gifts were put away, Manny headed to the kitchen where Racheal was sitting, hoping to enjoy an ice cold beer. He heard the squeal of the closet to the suite on the bottom floor and watched as Ann walked by. She was dressed in his pajamas again and had the nerve to stare at him with contempt.

"Ann," he beckoned her with a soft tone. She didn't stop her stride or even stutter-step to acknowledge him.

"What?" she snapped with her head inside the refrigerator and her back to him while digging through his food.

"Get the fuck outta my house."

"*What?*" Racheal gasped. "*Why*...wait—Manny!" she protested.

Ann turned ready to fight. "What did you say to me?" she asked, like she was the one paying the bills and daring him to repeat it.

Manny dropped his jacket off of his shoulders and said, "I asked you. To. Get. *The Fuck*. Out of my house. *Mucho rapido*." He pulled his shirt off and was down to his tee-shirt when he said, "Next time I'm not asking, and take my shit off too."

"You *really* lost it," Racheal snapped.

Ann moved her lanky frame side to side, gathering her thoughts. Then she ran her chocolate hand through her close cropped hair before sarcastically asking, "So I'm a moocher? I don't have to be here."

"How long you worked for me before I fired you?" Manny asked her.

Ann put her hand on her hip and stood before him, facing him down. "Too long," she answered.

"I come across like someone who will allow you to take my kindness for weakness?"

"You come across as a murdering, low-life criminal who thinks he's doing good to hide all the evil shit that he does. It doesn't make you the worst guy," she said. "But to me, you come across as a piece of shit! Now you know how you come across to me."

"Good bitch, then leave my house. Make it quick and leave all my shit here, and in the future, when your sister needs help, I'll hire another maid, so you don't have to stay over and live with a piece of shit like me."

Ann didn't move. She looked at Manny then at Racheal with extra confidence.

"Manny what are you doing?" Racheal demanded.

He flipped through TV channels and that's when it hit him. "You expect me to explain myself?"

"Yes, I do."

Manny had enough. The way he was being undermined and overlooked at the engagement party, especially since he was the one financing it all started to torture him. He steps closer to Racheal as he said, "Baby, *I'm* Manny fucking Black!" He twirled his finger around and said, "I own all this shit. My name is the one that's on the check that you and that *puta* cash. If you think I'm going to explain myself to somebody that lives in my house rent free, then you just as crazy as this gay bitch!"

"*Gay?*" Ann and Racheal said in unison.

Manny turned to Ann. "Bitch I'm busy, not blind or stupid, and I'm wondering if y'all even sisters cause you don't look like Dickey, whoever the fuck he is. You didn't show up to your only sister's engagement party, and you certainly ain't the child of her stuck-up, extra uppity ass mother."

"*No,*" Racheal gasped. Her eyes wide open. She hadn't seen this Manny Black since they first started dating and she didn't like it. "Do not talk about my mother like that!" she yelled.

Ann was silent.

Manny snapped his fingers and pointed it at Ann. "You see that? I disrespect your mother, and you don't say shit, but I say something about Racheal and you lose your mind until you homeless?" Manny nodded. "Yeah, you funny bitch, and y'all probably are fucking. Won't be the first bitch I had that liked pussy on the side."

"Fuck you, Manny," Ann spat.

"Manny this is me you're talking about," Racheal bawled.

"I know," he said and walked out of the kitchen.

"Yeah, big shot, Manny Black," Ann sung like a melody. "Just remember this face when you're begging me. Real soon."

He rushed up to Ann, looked into her eyes and promised, "Threaten me again bitch and I'm a change your life."

She stepped closer to him. Her lips close to his chin. "What you gonna do, Manny, blow my head off too?"

Manny leaned forward and whispered, "Yes."

Ann quickly stepped back. The determination in his eyes proved that he meant it.

Racheal looked over at Ann, and then she saw the death in Manny's eyes. "Ann, let me help you pack."

*****

Early the next morning Manny rose from the bed in the guest room. He hurried to shave, shower and put on one of his best business suit. When he walked down into the kitchen Lil Manny was with Macca eating while Racheal sipped tea staring at the television.

"Going somewhere?" Racheal muttered, sounding like she didn't care if he answered or not.

"I got a company to run," he answered flatly.

"Hmpt, all of a sudden?"

"Yes, like you, a lot of shit been getting out of hand."

Racheal kept her mouth shut. Then her lips parted like she was going to say something.

"Just sip your tea," he ordered, ready to show her the gangster side once again.

And that's what she did.

Manny kissed his son, wished him a great day and rushed to his all black, custom Jaguar XJL in the garage.

"Larry!" Manny yelled into his Bluetooth as he was speeding through his neighborhood, trying to get to the office quickly.

"I'm here," he answered.

"You ready to get busy?"

"I'm in motion. Going to Jersey now," Larry answered.

"Okay, on my way to the office," he told him and clicked over to make another call.

"*Jefe*," Chango answered the phone.

"*Tienes las bolsas,*" Manny asked if he had what he needed.

"*Si,* we have the bags, *Jefe.*" Chango chuckled. "Today good day."

"It will be even better if you do what I need you to do. On time, *comprende?*"

Chango chuckled before saying, "We no control de time. We control de *nada,* but okay. Chu late," he mentioned before ending the call.

As usual, Manny shook his head in disbelief. Chango was right out of a movie, but the man gladly put his life at risk for him, so what more could he ask for.

*****

"Mr. Black?" the head of security at his office building said in surprise when he saw Manny walk through the door. "Funny seeing you here so early."

He didn't know if he was having a complex of insecurity or if it was obvious to everyone besides him that he had become a push over. "Why?" he asked calmly. "I do still own my company don't I?"

The Irishman turned beet red and instantly came down with a case of humility. "Yes, you do, sir. I didn't mean anything by it. As a matter of fact, I root for the underdog, regardless of what everyone else may say."

Manny shook his hand. "Good, if they ask about me tell them I'm giving interviews upstairs."

He nodded vigorously and said, "Will do."

Manny needed the exposure on this day more than any other. He rode the elevator up to the office wondering if there was another area he overlooked for things to go well that day, and he couldn't think of any.

On the floor where MB Enterprises were located, the chime to the elevator rang, and all eyes at the receptionist desk looked up. When the two women behind the desk saw that it was Manny, they both reached for the phone. Manny knew they were either notifying all the other employees to be on their toes, or notifying someone outside of the building that he was there, and for the plan he hatched, he needed exactly for that to happen.

"Good morning, Mr. Black," the receptionist greeted and then she pointed to the lounge area. "Two ahh...gentlemen are waiting for you?"

"Where?" Manny panicked. The security didn't mention that someone was there, and Larry was on his way to New Jersey, so there was no telling what could be waiting for him. His paranoia told him to rush to his office for a gun first, but then Baylor popped into his mind.

Manny walked into the lounge area and heard, "*Jefe*, chu late." Like Manny requested, Chango and Culo were there early, dressed in business suits, but what he didn't expect was for Chango to be wearing a tight ass, bright red suit, British style with multicolored socks, and shiny red shoes with a matching suitcase on wheels. He also didn't expect Culo to be sleeping on his lounge chair in an oversized tan suit with his pants hanging off his ass.

A million things began formulating in his mind, but he held his tongue instead and said, "Follow me."

As he and his new entourage were passing by the desk, the receptionist asked, "Should I inform Mr. Gonzalez that you're here?"

Manny was counting on that. He did a drum roll on the marble counter with his palms and said, "*Yes.*" He looked at his watch. It was only eight fifteen, but time waited for no one. "As a matter of fact, please inform all senior staff and their assistants that there's a ten o'clock meeting. Ms. Gordon included. Tell her that I need her here on time."

The receptionist's head snapped back with confusion. She probably wanted to know why he didn't just pick up his phone and call her since they lived together, but that wasn't what he wanted. He wanted as many people as possible to know where he was and what he was doing.

"We're good?" he asked in an effort to pull her out of her trance.

She awoke and nodded. "Yes. At once."

Manny rushed away while Chango and Culo followed. They entered his office and he quickly ran to his desk and thumbed the remote to his TV. He hit a button under his desk that was installed his very first week there and fast forwarded and watched security footage of everyone that entered the office while he was gone. There was only one person—Racheal.

Since no one planted any recording devices while he was out, he rushed to the large wooded column near the floor to ceiling window and hit a lever down at the bottom and the hinges in the column clicked.

"Bring the suitcase," he told Chango as he opened the full length door to the hollow column he installed.

Chango rushed over and Manny pulled two heavy duffle bags from the hidden compartment and dropped them to the floor.

"Take fifty out of that," he instructed, pointing to the bags of cash. "Put it in one bag. Give Self three hundred and you and Culo split two hundred thousand."

"*Ju serious?*" Culo yelled like a child on Christmas day. "Yo, dog. You know how I'mma be the man in Panama wit' dis?" he asked, spending the money before he had a chance to touch it.

Chango smirked. The money would change nothing in his life. Like all he stole, earned or extorted, his wealth went to feeding the poor kids in the slums. "*Gracias,*" he said, showing his gratitude.

"Yeah," Manny said, always liking the feeling of giving instead of receiving. "The girl out front will call the car service. Take it to Harlem and change over to another cab. Take that one to the Bronx and then take another cab to the park where Self will be waiting."

"Got it," Culo said as his eyes widened from the sight of so much cash. "We got it boss. We got it."

After the suitcase was packed, and Chango was ready to go, he stopped short before exiting the office. "Chu move like water?"

"*What?*" Manny asked, not in the mood for Chango's antics. He was caught off guard. "Yeah," he answered.

Chango heard the answer and looked up to the ceiling and smiled and nodded. "I tell chu he listen, *Santo,*" he mumbled to the ceiling. He slid on an oversized pair of red Chanel designer shades and said, "Today, sunny sky. Nobody cry today." He looked at Manny and said, "Chu pray for Chango, okay?"

"Pray?" Manny asked in frustration. It had been a long time since he did that.

"Okay?" Chango was persistent.

Manny shrugged. "Whatever. Yeah, okay."

"Okay!" Chango celebrated and beckoned for Culo to follow.

The moment Chango and Culo walked out of the office Manny's line rang. It was the call he was expecting.

"Hey baby," he said when he answered.

"*Hello?*" Racheal asked in shock. "This is me, Manny, Racheal."

"I know. My wife," he said softly, smooth talking himself into the perfect plan coming together.

"*Really?* Oh *kay*," she let out with suspicion. "I don't know what you're up to, but can you please tell me why I'm being summoned to the office by ten o'clock?"

"Executive meeting. You're usually here by now anyway, so I didn't think it would be a big deal."

She sighed. "I was still helping Ann pack her clothes."

"Ann is unemployed and unless you plan on joining her in unemployment I suggest you be here by ten." He knew she would call his bluff so he quickly changed tactics. "Nah, babe. I actually really need you here because everyone says you got soft since your pregnancy, so I want to show them that we're a team. You should get here before them."

"*Who?* When did they say that?" she asked defensively with new interest. It was confirmation that Manny's methods were working.

"You know I have my spies."

"Yes, I do know that. Do I have to put on business attire?" she asked like she was rushing. "As a matter of fact I'm on my way. I'll give them something to talk about. Yes, I'm coming."

All he had to do now was quickly get everyone else out of the house. "Oh, tell Macca to take Manny out to the park for a lil while. He needs to run around. Hurry up and get Ann outta my house and come over."

"Why do you need the house empty?" Racheal caught on.

Shit, Manny thought. "I can care less," he lied. "It's just that with everything going on, Manny Jr. needs to get out more, we have work to do and Ann just needs to get out of my house."

"You're right. I'll be right over to the office," she said and ended the call.

He leaned back in his chair and thought of new ways that he could be seen by as many people that day as possible so he could have an airtight alibi for what was about to take place.

SEVENTEEN

"So here's the layout," Rich said, kneeling down and drawing a diagram of Roosevelt Hospital's prison ward in the dirt of Pelham Bay Park. He, Andy, William-Larry, Chango and Culo were in a small huddle looking down. "Based on our observation, lunch time is best. Staff is short, ambulance traffic is low and we're in and out."

"Heck," Andy butt in. "Getting in and upstairs is not the problem. Getting out? Now that's another story."

Rich looked down at the square diagram in the dirt that looked almost exactly like the image of the hospital on the laptop screen in his hand. The square, red bricked building in Manhattan was surrounded by the large, major thruway of 10th Avenue, the cross blocks of 58th and 59th Streets, andNinth Avenue. An "E" was drawn to show the patient emergency room entrance, and an "A" was on the opposite side of the building where the ambulances had their own emergency room parking.

Rich pointed to the A. "Ambulance to the car. Car to tunnel. Tunnel? We on our own," he reiterated the course that led to the getaway cars they parked the night before.

After they were done with Primo the night before, they drove to a parking garage in Connecticut and forced the parking attendant into the trunk of a car. They removed the keys to cars that were in long term parking, dismantled the tracking devices, and each man drove off with a vehicle that was going to help in getting Bobby Lee home.

"Dey no see," Chango said up to the sky. "Dey no see."

"What's that racket you got going?" William-Larry asked Chango. "And who in tar-nation are you talking to?"

"He's talking to the spirits," Culo offered. "Don't even worry about it, Yo."

"Whew," William-Larry said and then grunted looking at Chango. "We sho'got us an outfit here now don't we."

"Can we start shooting now?" Andy anxiously asked. "I'm sober, horny and homesick. All the illnesses a man should never have. Especially at the same time."

"Ju need *distraccion*," Chango said.

"A *what*?" William-Larry asked.

"A distraction," Rich answered. "Something to occupy—"

"I know what a damn distraction is, fool," William-Larry barked. "Since you were born you been a distraction. Like that red get up he got on is a distraction."

"Speak," Self told Chango.

"Hospital have *mucho policia. Distraccion* stop police. Ju go up, while *distraccion* keep them down."

"Okay, so what do you suggest?" Rich asked him.

He paused, "Dragon," he answered and then plastered a wide grin on his face.

Culo smacked the side of his face, shook his head and then said, "*Nah.* No, Yo! The *dragon*? You ain't been the dragon in *years.*"

"Somebody wanna fill me in?" William-Larry mentioned.

"I'm hip," said Andy.

Self asked, "The dragon?"

"Well, I done heard that," William-Larry snapped at Self. "What in tarnation is the dragon?"

"I'm confused," came from Rich.

Self shrugged and shook his head, just as confused.

"And we running out of time," William-Larry told the group while looking at his watch. "Need to get the helmets and go. So what's this dragon fandango?"

Culo explained, "The dragon is what he used to do to eat. You ever see those guys that blow the fire out their mouth and shit?"

"A fucking fire dancer?" William-Larry balked.

"I done heard it all," Andy said. "But if Chango here wants to join the party, then why not let him?"

"So will this distraction isolate the police?" Rich wanted to know—all business.

"*Si,*" Chango answered.

"What do you need?" Rich asked.

Chango looked up into the trees and said, "Wood, cotton, and gasoline."

"You meet us there. You go in at twelve-twelve," Rich instructed.

"Then what's to yap about?" Self questioned. "Chango go in first, and do…"

"What Chango do," he answered. "When de fireman come. Ju come."

Andy smacked his legs and said, "All righty then. Now can we start shooting and go get my pain in the ass brother?"

Rich asked, "Is everybody on the same page?"

All men nodded then hugged.

"Let's get her done," William-Larry said as the men walked off, hoping things went according to plan.

But they hardly ever did.

*****

At 10:00 a.m. Manny was pacing back and forth in his boardroom while the executives of MB Enterprises mulled in with apprehension on their faces. Usually when Manny called for these meetings, heads rolled and the company was shaken up to increase productivity.

When half the members were in, Edeeks walked into the room and did a head count. Then he sighed heavily, walked over to Manny and asked, "What happened now? What's this meeting called for? And you think you could have given me a heads up?"

Manny looked down at Edeeks wingtip shoes, his stiff slacks, window pane blazer and yellow shirt. "Yo. What happened to us?"

"*Us?*" Edeeks eyebrows came together into a frown. "Us, Manny? I don't know, what happened?"

Manny crossed his arms across his chest and looked into Edeeks's eyes before he whispered, "We used to sleep on bunk beds and bug out in one bedroom when your brother moved me in. You had all these dreams, E. Big dreams with no money. I brought the money, and look at us now. You got a couple mansions, expensive cars, and you ain't never happy. You banged a hundred broads while you married, and what it got you?"

He glanced at Manny and quickly looked away. "You judging me or giving a speech, man?"

"Nah, I'm giving a history lesson and trying to get you to listen."

"Do I need to tell you my version?"

Manny didn't care what Edeeks had to say. He needed to kill time. "Yeah, tell me your version." He looked down at his watch and asked, "Where the fuck is she at?"

"Racheal?" Edeeks asked. "She running a little late. Baby got her sick, but she's on the way."

Manny's eyebrows rose with surprise. "So you know what my wifey is doing? *Chucha*," he cursed in Spanish.

"We're friends, Manny," Edeeks offered as an explanation.

Manny had something new on his mind. He didn't like how Edeeks and Racheal were all touchy-feely at the engagement party. He looked Edeeks in his eyes and asked, "E, you fuck my girl before? Keep it real. Between us. Tell me."

Edeeks looked at Manny as he turned red growing anger. "What the fuck is wrong with you," he said too loud. "Then you wanna know what happened to us."

"Yeah, what happened? Give me your version. I'd love to hear this shit before everyone gets here."

It was Edeeks turn to cross his arms across his chest. "Real life happened, Manny. While you were gun totin', fighting wars, going to prison and being a part time boss, everything fell on my shoulders. I had to pay all the bills…"

"But I put things in motion to make the money to pay the bills," Manny said in his own defense.

"Yeah, you did." Edeeks stretched his arms out and said, "All this was your idea, but I had to implement it. Had to take care of it, watch it grow. Like a baby while you was off doing time like an absentee father. Then I had to clean up all your bullshit. Had to take the heat that you caused, for what, Manny? What was all that shit about? Bullshit! I lost my wife—"

"Cause you can't keep your dick in your pants."

Edeeks grew madder. "So what!" he yelled and then looked at all the employees as they watched the commotion between him and Manny. Then he whispered, "When the fuck do I get to enjoy life and take the fucking edge off? When the heat comes down we all can't pick up a gun to solve it. Real life is fucking hard, and all this expensive shit we buy is only pretty gift wrapping to hide the foul shit we do to keep an image we call life."

"You want to die, Edeeks?"

"You threatening me, Manny?"

"You know I don't do that. It's just…you crying like a bitch cause you rich? Get a fucking grip!"

Edeeks shook his head. "I knew you would never understand." He looked at Manny with pity in his eyes and then he softly stated, "Just remember, everything I did was for the best interest of this empire you built and all the people who we support and the families that rely on us to eat."

"You sound like you saying goodbye or some shit," Manny whispered while most of the staff filled the room.

Edeeks turned to leave. "I have some papers for you to sign. Nothing important."

Manny nodded in agreement while taking a head count. The only person who was missing was Racheal, and then she walked in and announced, "I'm here. What's this about?"

Manny's phone vibrated. He looked down to see that Larry sent him a text that read, "*I'm in.*"

He smiled, knowing that if his house was bugged, Larry would find them. Then he smacked his hands together and announced, "Thank you everyone for coming. Please take the time to clear your calendars for the day and inform whomever you have to that you'll be spending the next few hours with me. We have a lot to discuss."

Everyone started to grumble and shift awkwardly in their chairs. They were certain that their jobs were on the line. Why else would Manny bring them all in one room? Tensions flared and Manny liked it that way. His only concern was that his alibi was secure.

*****

At noon Self, Andy, William-Larry, and Rich were parked in a stolen pick-up on 10th Avenue in front of John Jay College of Criminal Justice, twenty feet away from the entrance of the emergency room. At 12:12 p.m. Culo pulled up in a green Subaru Forrester. The passenger door opened and Chango stepped out wearing nothing but a pair of red briefs, red paint on his face with his dreads covering his eyes, and Vaseline petroleum jelly all over his defined, slim body. In one hand he had a red ketchup squirt bottle filled with gasoline. In the other hand were long sticks with gauze pads wrapped around the ends.

Three ambulances were parked at the entrance to the emergency room. Chango walked inside and all eyes focused on him. The tall, black, security guard that was posted at the entry door lifted his eyes from his phone and looked at Chango not interested, he had seen worst. Then Chango squirted a pink liquid from the bottle onto the sticks, and pulled out a lighter.

"Sir," the guard said stepping forward. "Sir! You can't light that in here. Sir, don't do that!"

Chango danced from side to side like he was listening to Salsa.

"Sir!" the guard called out with his eyes locked on the lighter that was sparking the flame on the stick. "Don't do that either," he demanded, his hand was still his cellphone.

Chango squirted the liquid into his mouth.

"Fuck!" the security screamed before reaching for his gun—big mistake. Chango turned his face towards the hand that was reaching for the gun, and let the dragon come alive by blowing out a stream of fire. "*Arrrrghhhh*," the guard screamed as he ran away like a ball of fire.

"He-he-he-he," Chango laughed. His gold smile cheesed for the nursing assistants who were fleeing their post in all directions.

Pandemonium made room for opportunity when the hospital staff ran out the building in fear of the fire breathing man.

"Hit it!" Self told Rich as the sirens in the distance were drawing closer.

Rich pulled off 10th Avenue, made a left at the corner, and cruised to the entrance of the hospital. Each of them had on all black helmets with tinted shields, gloves on, full body armor, and tall boots with a short Calico machine gun in hand and different grenades dangling from their black jackets. All four doors to the truck opened at the same time. Rich didn't intend on using it to leave with, but he kept the engine running just in case.

As they rehearsed, Rich took the lead. With his deadly quickness and skills as a marksman, he had the job of securing the lobby. Since Chango had most of the security detail running to handle the fire breathing madman, there were only two guards seated at the security desk in the middle of the floor.

"Oh my *gawd*!" an elderly white woman gasped as she saw the four gunmen walking by. It took the majority of the people walking through the hospital longer than expected to realize what was going on.

Rich ran ahead, then stopped, skipped once like a high jumper on the tiled floor and then skipped again before his feet left the floor. When the two white guards looked up from their newspapers, one received Rich's foot in his face. The other attempted to stand but the butt of Rich's gun crashed into his chin, knocking him out cold.

Self took off into a full sprint to catch the closing elevator door with William-Larry close behind breathing hard, trying to keep up. Andy aimed his gun at the door that led to the emergency room while Self and William-Larry hopped on the elevator.

"Nine," Self said as he hit the button on the elevator to go up. He looked over every bit of ammunition William-Larry had on, and then he removed two grenades, one flash-bang smoke grenade, which is mainly used to cause a diversion, and a more powerful one to take down any barrier between them and Bobby Lee.

"Five minutes," William-Larry said as he watched the clock that dangled from his neck.

The chime to the elevator rang when they reached the ninth floor. The doors opened and Self released the handle to the flash grenade and tossed it towards four correctional officers that were huddled near a security desk.

"POP" the blast went spreading smoke everywhere.

Self peeked out to his right and saw the four officers standing in front of a huge steel gate covering their mouths and milling about in confusion. Behind that gate were two other bulletproof glass doors.

William-Larry opened the shield to the helmet and did the family whistle. Then they waited. Nothing. He whistled again, and Bobby Lee answered. The faint whistle was blowing over and over from behind the glass doors.

Self nodded, pulled the pin from the other grenade and threw it through the slots of the steel gate. The small black ball rolled, stopped where the doors joined, and exploded.

"Go!" William-Larry yelled. "Four minutes."

Self stepped out the elevator with his gun high. An officer stepped in Self's line of sight and Self planted two quick burst of gunfire into his armored chest. Another officer reached for his gun while covering his face with his forearm and Self sent a bullet through his forearm that exploded his nose and blew out the back of his head.

"Move!" William-Larry yelled at one of the officers who were crawling beneath him. When he didn't move fast enough, William-Larry shot the man in his leg, kicked away his gun, and then knelt down to do a frisk, making sure he didn't have a back-up weapon. "Three minutes!" he yelled to Self.

Self rushed over to another officer and planted a right uppercut to his jaw and stunned him. He grabbed the officer by his collar, spun him around and pushed him towards the steel gate. Then he lifted his visor. "Open it!" Self barked.

The officer yelled, "I have to find the..."

Self pushed the nozzle of his gun under the officer's arm and sent three heavy slugs into the man. When Self looked over his shoulder, the last correctional officer near the gate sitting on his ass, kicking out in an attempt to back pedal away from the masked gunman who shot first and asked questions later.

William-Larry yelled. "Two minutes!"

Self ran over to the officer. Time was ticking and the entire N.Y.P.D. would be there in four minutes. He grabbed the officer's tie, yanked, and the clip-on flew upward in his hand. That made him mad. He then grabbed him by his collar and dragged him across the floor and didn't stop until they were at the steel gate.

"One time! Open it!" Self ordered.

With no hesitation, the officer fumbled with the keys, twisted it into the lock and the electronic gate squealed as it opened. Self dragged the officer with him to the shattered glass door and stepped through it.

"Don't kill me, man..." he pleaded. "...I got a family man, *please.*"

"One minute!"

"Good," Self told the officer. "Then they can miss you if you don't open these doors. All of them.'

William-Larry and Self didn't want the authorities to know who they were coming for so freeing all the prisoners gave them more distractions to use to their advantage.

Self aimed his weapon and ordered the officer to open all eight doors.

With a cast on his leg up to his knee, Bobby Lee stepped out of the secured room. He looked out into the smoky hallway and hobbled to the elevator while picking up the guns that belonged to the other officers.

"Time!" William-Larry yelled, letting Self know that in two minutes they would have a major shoot out on their hands.

"Inside!" Self yelled, ordering the officer into one of the rooms that once held many of his prisoners.

Fright entered the officer's eyes. With a trembling lip he mumbled. "I can't go in there."

"Say bye to your wife and—"

"Okay! Okay!" the officer quickly changed his mind. "Just don't shoot me."

Self thought of all the cells he had lived in. He remembered how prison guards thought they were gods on the inside, but lived like peasants on the outside. He did a round-house kick that sent the officer into the cell and locked the door. "No fun when the rabbit has the gun."

"Move! Move! Move!" William-Larry yelled from the open elevator. Clutched in his hand was the collar of the lame officer Self knocked out earlier.

Self turned his machinegun to the side and used it like a bar to push the backs of six prisoners until they were all cramped into the elevator.

"Oh, shit, man!" an oversized, white prisoner with a long beard celebrated in the elevator. "Y'all got a gun for me?"

"Keep your mouth shut," Bobby Lee warned.

"Who died and made you boss?" the newly released prisoner asked before the hot nozzle of William-Larry's weapon was pointed into his groin.

Bobby Lee clutched the two guns in his hands tighter and pointed to his brother before saying, "Him!"

The elevator door chimed at the lobby and Self pulled Bobby Lee to the corner near the call buttons and placed the correctional officer in front of the door. William-Larry was squeezed in the opposite corner. Then he dipped low, quickly bent to the side to peek out the door, and just as quickly ducked back into the corner. Less than a second after William-Larry moved his head, a bullet entered the head of the correctional officer, killing him on sight. Then more bullets entered the other prisoners in the elevator.

"Sniper fire!" William-Larry yelled from the elevator, pinned down from an N.Y.P.D. sniper a hundred yards away on 10th Avenue.

"Got it!" Andy yelled, crouching down on the outside of the security guard's station.

He raised his Calico, aimed at the glass doors on 10th Avenue and squeezed the trigger. Bullets poured from the gun, shattering all the glass from the doors and sending whoever was on the other side of them running for cover.

While Andy sent slugs out the exit, Self, William-Larry and Bobby Lee ran from the elevator and made a quick left, then another left towards the emergency room. Rich was securing the cuffs of the two officers he had face down on the floor of the security booth.

From each end of 10th Avenue, two police cars raced up to the emergency room entrance. Rich looked over at Self, William-

Larry and Bobby Lee heading for the emergency room, then to the opposite side where Andy was up ahead reloading a hundred round cartridge, and took off running towards Andy. With the police cars coming to the front, it was only a matter of time before the police had the place surrounded. He needed to buy time.

Due to the helmet, Rich was unable to call Andy over a radio. He was praying that he wouldn't get shot for startling his brother. He ran up behind Andy, removed two grenades from his jacket and removed the pin off one while holding onto the pin of the other. He raced to the entrance, avoiding sniper fire by standing off to the side, and tossed one grenade under the chassis of one police car. A snipers bullet instantly chipped off the top of his helmet, sending a cloud of white dust up into the air. Rich dropped down onto his belly and tossed the other grenade under the chassis of the other police car.

The sniper's gunfire peppered all around Rich, blocking him in. Andy spun the loader to the Calico, sought cover behind the security booth, and watched the sniper's trail. His brother was trapped and there was only one way out. He aimed his gun at his brother's head, moved over six inches, and fired two burst in the snipers direction.

Rich was trying to locate the sniper based on the shooter's line of fire. From the flow of the trajectory Rich knew the sniper was higher up. As Rich concentrated and watched the police car flip onto its side from his grenade, he felt a rush of wind move past him from behind, and saw the shatter of the window near the corner where he was crouched. He knew someone was shooting from behind.

Andy watched Rich's head turn and waved at him before holding three fingers and indicating that he was going to provide cover. Then he tapped his wrist to signal they were running out of time.

Bobby Lee limped through the double doors of the emergency room, saw a security guard on the phone and shot her. He hit the woman in the leg, sending her sprawling to the floor, and all bystanders followed her movements and hit the floor too, making a clear path to the exit.

They were a few feet away from the exit when they heard Andy's gunfire. Bobby Lee stopped.

"Keep Moving!" William-Larry yelled. "They can handle themselves."

Bobby Lee nodded. They trained and trained constantly for years to prepare for the end of the world as they knew it. A shootout in a hospital was nothing in comparison to what they were prepared for. So he kept moving.

As William-Larry and Bobby Lee pressed forward towards the exit, Self walked with his back to their backs, slowly moving backwards in case any of the ailing patients in the waiting room decided they wanted to play hero and die. He had what he came for, but the hard part would be getting out of there alive.

They were met by a surprise when they burst through the emergency room exit. The back door to an ambulance was wide open. Inside, two EMT workers and two hospital security guards were struggling to subdue Chango into a straightjacket and strap him onto a gurney while another EMT worker was trying to stick a needle into his neck.

In front of the ambulance, Culo blocked the entrance with his stolen car, cursing at the motor with the hood up. To a bystander, his engine failed in front of the hospital. To the crew, Culo had an AK47 on that front seat and they were going to have to kill him before they drove away with Chango.

William-Larry hopped into the back of Chango's ambulance, catching the civil servants off guard. The butt on his rifle went into the face of the needle toting EMT worker, sending her face forward out of the ambulance.

Self yanked the driver from the ambulance, dropping the man's back onto the asphalt.

"Whoa!" the driver yelled out. Then Self commenced to bashing his face in with the heel of his boot until he was unconscious.

Bobby Lee struggled to get into the ambulance and when he did, he raised one of the guns he took from the officers upstairs and said, "Everyone outside, face down on the floor and you'll live."

"You ain't got to tell me twice," the guard said before rushing to get out of the ambulance and plant his face into the ground.

The EMT worker didn't hear so well. His freckled face squeezed into a frown. "You can't take this ambulance. This is my job, and—"

Bobby Lee shot him too. Dead center in the chest. Nothing was stopping his freedom and he was too close to waste time.

After dumping the corpse of the EMT worker out of the ambulance, William-Larry helped Chango with his restraints.

"No. No," Chango told William-Larry when he tried to completely remove the straight jacket. "Chango no finish yet. Go!" Chango hopped up, jumped out of the ambulance and slammed the doors behind him.

Culo dropped the hood of the car, jumped in and quickly reversed, making way for the ambulance to flee.

Suddenly the bang of a grenade went off inside the hospital, causing everyone to look back. They stood frozen, looking at each other, wondering what was going on, but knowing they had to get out of there. Self jumped into the driver's seat of the ambulance, but a police cruiser was speeding into the parking lot, not knowing who was in the ambulance.

"Cocksuckers," Self grumbled as he reached for the door handle. He jumped out as the police car drove in and sent shots into the windshield.

*****

Inside the hospital, Rich raised his hand telling Andy to wait. From where he was peeking he could see where the shots were coming from. Then the shooter moved. The situation took him back to Iraq where he had waited ten hours for a sniper to move before he shot the sniper with a bullet through the scope. The difference between now and then was that Rich didn't have his sniper's rifle this time. This time he had a machine gun that was made for close quarters combat, but bullets flew fast and far if the shooter knew what he was doing.

He waved at Andy, pointing at the window and then gave a thumbs up, Andy was too far away. To buy time, Rich removed a smoke grenade and released it in front of the door. The smoke would blind the sniper of his location for at least a moment.

Following his brother's lead, Andy pulled the release from his smoke grenade, launched it a hundred feet in front of him where Rich was lying, and took off on foot, hugging the wall so the sniper couldn't see him.

After a huge cloud of smoke filled the entry way, Rich was able to stand without drawing fire from the sniper. He pulled a standard grenade from his jacket, removed the pin and tossed it outside, needing a bigger distraction. Then he pointed up to the window in John Jay College of Criminal Justice.

The grenade exploded, sending police, pedestrians and the media who gathered running frantically for their lives outside the hospital doors.

Andy lifted his weapon, and Rich did the same. Together they unloaded more than sixty rounds into the window across the street. Rich grabbed Andy and they immediately hugged the wall, turned, and took off running. Racing across the tiled floor of the lobby, they moved as fast as they could into the doors of the emergency room.

As they burst through the doors, they saw a security guard tip-toeing to take aim at the ambulance doors where the crew was held up. In one movement, Rich raised his massive forearm while running and clothes lined the guard by slamming his forearm into the back of the man's neck, sending him crashing face down. Andy quickly picked up the Glock 9mm that skidded towards the exit, and they both ran outside and hopped into the awaiting ambulance.

Self hopped back into the ambulance, put it in drive, and pulled off, making a left up the one-way street of 58th Street.

"Hit the siren," William-Larry instructed and the race began.

Sirens screamed as Self made his way across the busy intersection of 10th Avenue. He looked into his rearview mirror and was caught off guard by the sight of two unmarked police cars on his tail. Suddenly another ambulance barreled between the two unmarked cars, pushing one of them off the road. Self hit the gas faster wishing Rich was driving, but Rich didn't know the streets of New York.

As they approached the right turn to head down 48th Street, they all looked out the window with their guns aimed and discovered it was Culo behind the wheel of the other ambulance with Chango in the passenger seat. From the quick glance over to the other lane of traffic it appeared that Chango was dancing in his seat.

Together the two ambulances raced down the busy street with their sirens blaring. The crawling traffic was quickly moving out of their way. For Culo and Chango it was a joy ride. For Self and his crew it was life or death, and they needed to get to the Lincoln Tunnel at warp speed.

"Road block," Self said, idling on the avenue and looking across traffic at a two car barricade the police made on 11th Avenue.

Rich opened the door, jumped out of the passenger seat and unloaded a hail of bullets at the police, who planted their faces into the pavement. He quickly jumped back into the ambulance and ordered, "Make a way when there is no way."

Self glanced at Culo in the ambulance at his side and checked his side mirror to find a line of police vehicles with flashing lights behind them. In an instant he decided to take the sidewalk. He gunned the engine, and maneuvered onto the side walk and sped pass the police barricade. Culo was right behind him with Chango firing calculated shots at the police in pursuit.

"Do not stop!" William-Larry ordered when they reached another police presence on 42nd street, but instead of blocking off the road, they were parked on the side of the road, letting the ambulances go through.

Rich flipped his visor and asked, "Why they do that?"

"Midtown!" Self yelled. "All the rich folks moving around. Can't risk them getting hurt."

"Good reason!" Andy yelled. "I need a drink!"

"Soon!" William-Larry shouted. "God willing."

Self veered left into the road that led to the Lincoln Tunnel. None of their efforts would be worth it if the plan for the tunnel didn't come through.

Culo raced pass Self, knowing the plan, but making one of his own. He went ahead of Self, veered across the two lanes of traffic and then made a U-turn, blocking all traffic that was coming their way. Then he stopped, allowing one lane of traffic to pass the way Self needed. He counted ten vehicles before a sea of police sirens were headed his way. Quickly he parked the ambulance to block off both lanes of traffic.

"Let's go!" he told Chango before racing through the back door.

Chango ran to the front of the ambulance where police cruisers were parked in an arc and danced with only his red briefs on his body and his straight jacket dangling off his shoulders. He stomped, put a curse on the gang of officers and then ran into the darkness of the tunnel, catching the police off guard.

Self and the crew abandoned the ambulance as planned, and Andy rushed to the first passenger vehicle that passed in the caravan of ten cars. It was a Peter Pan travel bus. He raised his gun for the driver to stop, and the driver did. The driver held his hand up. Then he followed Andy's hand gestures and opened the door.

"Get to the back with your face down!" Rich instructed before getting into the driver's seat.

William-Larry, Bobby Lee and Andy got on and rushed to the back of the bus with the driver leading the way. They dropped to lie on their backs and pulled the driver down with them.

Self didn't wait for the bus to pull off. The plan was for him to take this part of his journey on his own, but he had company. While racing across the road he stripped himself of the body armor. He climbed the railing of the tunnel and rushed to the fire exit that they had opened the night before. Soon thereafter Culo approached gasping for air, trying to keep up until Chango caught up and passed him. They rushed into the exit, slammed the door, barricaded it, and then entered another steel door. Self led the way as they ran straight about twenty yards before coming to another door that led to the traffic entering New York.

Self cracked the old steel door and peeked outside. Traffic was flowing. The police were looking for gunmen who entered the tunnel heading for New Jersey. The video cameras would later reveal how they escaped, but if Self timed it perfectly and got the ride he needed, he'd be back in New York so he could kill Mostro and finish the war with the Marielitos.

For sixty seconds the car they needed to escape hadn't driven by. Then he peeked further down the tunnel and saw it. A long, silver limousine with tinted windows was easing towards them. Self rushed out the door, jumped over the banister and landed on the hood of the car, sending the driver into complete shock and causing the car to come to a complete stop.

"Move the fuck over," Culo told the driver as he entered the driver's seat. He got behind the wheel of the car, yanked the driver's cap off his head and put it on his own while Chango and Self entered the rear doors. The carjacking took less than a minute.

"My goodness gracious," a male passenger said when he stared at Chango, who sat across from him with his back to the limousine divider.

"Shhhhhh," Chango quieted him by putting one of his fingers to the stranger's thin lips.

Self ordered the man, "Turn around. Put your face in the seat and your ass in the air, and don't move."

The passenger hesitated and Chango backhanded him. Quickly, the man changed his mind and did as he was told.

Culo crept by the police barricade that was rapidly waving cars coming into New York to pass freely. When they reached 42nd Street on Ninth Avenue, Self and Culo kicked the two passengers out and then Culo made a left to the West Side Highway where Self had a car parked on the service road at 96th street.

EIGHTEEN

At the conclusion of the meeting Manny quickly left the boardroom and headed into his office. It was a quarter to one. Larry had to be finished and he needed to know if Bobby Lee had escaped successfully.

"Breaking news," was what Manny heard when he cut the TV on in his office. A ring of terrorist has launched an attack on the Roosevelt hospital prison ward where this man…" A photo of Bobby Lee popped up, "Known as John Doe, was being held on many charges that involved gun violence in front of a club in upper Manhattan. The prisoner was uncooperative and refused to identify himself. Our last update indicated that masked gunmen had successfully escaped based on their ability to penetrate a flaw that the N.Y.P.D. had never encountered. Our sources tell us that this was an inside job, and that the gunmen were military trained and possibly linked to Al Qaeda. More when we come back."

Images of the shattered glass at the hospital's entrance were on display. Then images of a large police presence in front of one tube of the Lincoln Tunnel popped up on the screen. Police dogs, helicopters and a S.W.A.T, team were combing the area and randomly stopping cars. Then an image of the Peter Pan bus on the side of the road with all the passengers being questioned by police and New Jersey State Troopers appeared.

A New Jersey news reporter then came on TV and said, "*It is clear to everyone involved that these gunmen were military trained. The men high-jacked the bus within the tunnel where cameras captured them moving so quickly that it only took a matter of seconds. By using the passenger vehicle they avoided detection by state authorities. After clearing the area, the men stopped the bus at an underpass and instructed the driver to get to the back of the bus. Authorities believe that they later fled on foot to an awaiting vehicle.*"

Manny couldn't move. He had a silly grin on his face rejoicing that Bobby Lee had actually escaped. A new image of the Lincoln tunnel appeared. The reporter came on and said, "*Breaking news. Cameras from the tunnel revealed that three of the gunmen— including this man*"-A picture of Chango dancing and lighting the emergency room on fire appeared on the screen—"*were not on the passenger bus to New Jersey. Instead, these three bandits used the emergency exit of the tunnel and ran to the New York bound tube. Witnesses state that the gunmen carjacked a limousine and re-entered our great city. These fugitives were well organized and it appears their plan has worked. Please be advised that these criminals are highly trained, armed and dangerous. If you see something, say something."*

Edeeks barged into the office with three packets of paper. He dropped them onto Manny's desk like he had done many times before and then marked several areas with an X. "Sign, there," he told Manny. "There. There and...there."

Manny stumbled over to his desk. His eyes were on the screen, but his feet were walking. When he saw the stack of documents on the desk, he assumed they were the same as they had always been over the years.

"What are these?" he asked.

Edeeks rolled his eyes and sighed. "It's all for legal. Structuring for your new venture. What? You don't trust me?" Edeeks joked.

Manny broke his glance from the TV and answered. "As long as I don't grow a pussy, *papi chulo*, then you're the only man I trust." Manny signed the documents.

A huge grin came over Edeeks' face and he looked at the documents a little longer.

"You okay?" Manny asked because he was still staring at the documents. "Did I forget to sign something?"

"Oh!" Edeeks was startled from his daydream. He quickly scooped the papers up. "No. No." He started to the door and turned to Manny. "We really built an empire."

Manny looked at Edeeks, who now had tears in his eyes and asked, "What the fuck is wrong with you lately, bro? I swear you acting like you pregnant. Your emotions are all over the place."

Edeeks wiped a tear, nodded quickly, and tucked the papers under his arm before leaving.

As Edeeks walked out, Racheal walked in with a smile on her face. "What was that malarkey meeting about?" Her smile turned into a frown at the sight of Manny.

Manny cut off the TV and shrugged, "We needed to clear the air and see where we are going as a company," he lied.

Her eyes narrowed with suspicion. She stood silent, wondering what he was really up to.

Manny's phone vibrated. He looked down and a message from Larry came up. *Back at the office. Coming up.* Manny slid his phone into his pocket. Then he looked over at Racheal. "You wanna put a day in at the office and then we go home together?" Her suspicion didn't die. "Yes. That sounds good. I have some work to do anyway." Then her phone rang. She held up one finger for Manny to wait. As the person was on the other line talking, Racheal's eyes looked up at Manny with alarm in them. "Yes. Okay, immediately," she said into the phone before ending the call. "You know what?" she asked. "I think I'll head home now. I'm starting to feel nauseous."

"Oh. Oka—" Manny stopped short when Racheal quickly rushed out of the door. Her behavior was odd, but lately he was feeling like he really didn't know who he was getting ready to marry.

*****

With Racheal's quick departure Manny used the time to cut the news back on, hoping he wouldn't hear that one of the men from his crew was captured. What Rich and William-Larry had done was historical. Never in the history of the N.Y.P.D. had anyone committed such a brazen act of disregard of police authority. Manny felt like his favorite team had won the Super Bowl.

The phone on his desk buzzed. "Mr. Black," one of the many receptionists said on the other line. "Larry from security is requesting to meet with you?"

"Send him in!"

Larry entered Manny's office. "Not so good news, boss," were the first words he told Manny.

"What?" Manny didn't know if he heard him right.

Larry's eyes darted around the office with suspicion. "When was the last time you checked your surveillance system to see if anyone was in here?"

"Every day."

"Including today?" he double checked.

Manny nodded with assurance. *"Yes,* even today.*"*

"Too bad we didn't think of doing the same for your home." Larry stopped short and tapped on the desk. "Nice place I might add. Whoever did your decorating deserves an award, especially the—"

"Larry," Manny sighed, trying to get him to stay focused. Larry's eyes opened with excitement. "Do not! Go. Into. That house again," he warned. "And if you do, don't say a word once you walk through the door."

"You found something?"

"Yes I found something."

Manny sighed. This wasn't the first time he had been under surveillance. As a matter of fact, he couldn't remember when he wasn't under someone's watch. Either through Baylor, the special unit of the N.Y.P.D. and, or possibly the F.B.I, but someone wanted him and Larry always found the bugs. "How bad?"

Larry shook his head over and over extremely fast. He couldn't hide his excitement. "*Bad.* Ohhhh, so bad. Bad-bad-bad! I mean, it was awful." He reached into his pocket and dropped three tiny pieces of metal onto Manny's desk.

"What's that?" Manny asked. He had seen recording transmitters before, but nothing like what was on his desk.

"That my friend," Larry said like he was gloating. "Is as high-tech as it comes. That's what I found in your home, boss. *Unbelievable* craftsmanship. It was like, if you took a dump they could hear the piercing of your anal muscles releasing the—"

"I get it," Manny stopped him. "But how?"

"How? You want to know?" Larry asked with sarcasm. "The question is who? How is not the issue. They could have been in and out within minutes depending on *whom.* I tell who I know it's not."

"Who?"

"Who?" Larry was confusing himself. "No, what. Who it could never have been in a million years is the N.Y.P.D." He pointed at the devices on the desk. "Those would cost them their annual budget."

"F.B.I.?" Manny wondered.

Larry shrugged. "Maybe secret service. Maybe S.E.C. by way of F.B.I, but I doubt it. This is a national security type, Osama bin Laden type clearance. James Bond type, double oh-seven type—"

"I get it," Manny said, holding his hand up. "So now what?"

"You don't go home," Larry answered as a matter of fact. "You don't drive any cars from your home. You don't wear any clothes from your home. Or you throw them off by knowing you're being recorded as a precaution."

Manny nodded, liking the sound of that.

"Ever wonder if the bug is being planted by someone in your home?" Larry asked.

Manny looked down at a staple glistening from the carpet. He thought of Ann, but said, "Macca maybe, but she's too loyal. She's like a mother to me and my son."

"Anyone can be compromised," Larry interjected.

"Yeah, but she has her own quarters and takes care of my son like he's her own."

Larry repeated, "Anyone can be compromised."

"I get it," Manny said, knowing the truth when he heard it.

Larry glanced over to the TV that was looping the *Breaking News* reel all day. "Militia men," he said with pride.

Manny glanced at the TV and then back at Larry wondering how he knew. "What you say?"

Larry stared at the TV with admiration and slammed his fist into his palm before saying, "How in Jesus, Mother Mary and in Joseph's name do I wish I could have been a part of that jail break. Gotta be militia men. Long gone by now, with forty or so ex-admirals, generals and well respected military brothers that will verify that those men were with them at the time of the incident."

"And how do you know this?" Manny asked wanting to hear Larry's version.

"There was no hesitation. The weaponry was all the same. Cheap, but all the same. They moved in formation, was in and out in minutes, and they penetrated the clowns in the department for who they are. *Definitely* military trained and use to working with each other. Maybe even trained together for years."

"And if you were down? What would you have done different?" Manny quizzed the action junkie.

Larry shook his head. "*Absolutely* nothing. Would have been back to work this morning like any other day. Resume normal activity and you stay off the radar." He stood, towering over Manny. "But *you* need to keep your eyes and ears open." He put a finger to his lips. "*Shhhhh.* Do not talk in that house. I'll sweep it again in a week. We find something, then the nanny has to go."

Manny slumped lower into his seat. As soon as he thought things might get better, it was starting to get worst.

NINETEEN

"Everything is everything brother," Bobby Lee told Self over the phone. "On my way home. Waiting for you up in the heavens," he said and they both knew he was talking about Montana.

"Yeah, if the God get there," Self said while crouched down in the driver's seat of a stolen funeral hearse.

With the help of Culo, Benta's Funeral Home in Harlem was short of one, long, black hearse. It was the one vehicle Self never expected the police to pull over. After dropping Culo and Chango off at the Hilton Hotel in Times Square, Self pointed the vehicle towards the Queensboro Bridge. Now that his top priority was out of the way, he had a new one.

"Don't accept defeat, my brother," Bobby Lee said.

"No surrender. No retreat. See you at home, brother," Self answered and ended the call.

It was midnight and he was parked in front of Aberdeen Avenue in Jamaica Estates, Queens. The desolate neighborhood filled with mansions and estates of all shapes and sizes was just a few blocks away from the 'hood, but a total different world and major property tax difference. With Bobby Lee and his brother's homeward bound, every chance Self had taken and the lives he ended were for the greater good of his brother being free. Now that he was parked a block away from the home of his only sworn enemy, a few more deadly deeds would put everything to an end.

At one o'clock Self exited the hearse and stepped onto the sidewalk of the residential community. By his observation, a police car patrolled every five minutes, and an escape from that community would be a difficult one, so it was time to make his move.

Dressed in all black, he slowly walked like he had a dog, but instead of a leash being in his hand, he held his two .50 Desert Eagles with sound suppressors on the tips to guarantee silence. He reached the address Mostro's driver gave him and silently walked to a side door. As expected, the small lens to the hidden camera was stuck in the corner of the doorframe. Self slammed the butt of his gun into the lens, crushing it and then froze right there, waiting.

Depending on how secure the alarm system was, someone from the house should have come to check, or worst, the police, but no one showed. He tucked one of his tools of trade into his waistband and removed the sixteen inch Tanto blade from the side of his calf. He inserted the blade where the door met the door frame and tried to jimmy the lock. When that didn't give quickly enough, he decided to handle things the old fashion way—he kicked the door in.

"Jose!" someone from upstairs called down to Self. "Jose?" the baritone called again.

Self took long strides across the huge living room floor, stopped at the end of the stairs, and quickly unscrewed a dimmed wall light.

A second later the voice called out again, "Marco! Marco? *Problema*," he warned that there was a problem.

Self didn't move.

The baritone rushed down the stairs and in an instant he stopped. Frozen. It was like an animal in the wilderness who could smell the predator. He looked around into the darkness, waiting for something to move, breathe or make a peep.

Self had done this too many times before.

"Marco!" the man yelled upstairs, with a bit of fright cracking his voice.

Self took two long strides until he was facing the man.

"Marco!" he yelled out while raising the gun in his hand.

"Polo," Self whispered and violently swung his blade at the baritone's hand, chopping it off at the wrist.

The man eyes looked at his hand on the floor still clinching the gun and then looked at the stump that was still attached to his body. That's when it hit him. He attempted to scream, but Self silenced him by sliding the crimson blade into his windpipe.

"Shhhhhh," Self advised.

"Bana!" someone yelled from above.

Marco, Self thought.

Marco ran down the stairs. With each step Marco descended, Self skipped upward. When they both reached the middle landing, Marco stopped. In shock he looked into Self's eyes and asked, "*Bana*? You not Bana!"

He raised his gun and Self grabbed his wrist with one hand and plunged the sharp blade into Marco's heart with the other. As Marco's body slowly dropped, Self eased his blade from his chest cavity and then flicked the dripping blood onto Marco's face. He was just warming up. Instead of quickly moving around the house he ran back down the stairs and did what he did best. He stood still. In his profession as an armed robber, what allowed him to survive was the ability to be patient and catch his victim off guard. The element of surprise was half the work, but this time something was wrong.

From the hallway that he stood in, a kitchen was to the left of him, and the front door was to the right. The night light outside the door quickly went off and the power to the clock on the cable box went dead.

Somebody killed the power, his experience told him. So he waited.

With a gun in one hand and his blade in the other he inhaled deeply while slowly inching his way into a crouch. He placed his back against the wall with his wrist rested on his knees, and he waited some more. He inhaled the aroma of shampoo, olive oil and cheap cologne. The cologne belonged to Marco. The olive oil came from the kitchen. To his left, and from above, lingered the shampoo. He was definitely not alone.

Ten minutes passed and Self didn't budge. Then the sound of cars pulling up outside surprised him. Suddenly footsteps ran across the floor above. Someone else was upstairs. His ears followed the footsteps from directly above him. The owner of the feet stopped at the top landing, the voices from outside grew closer to the front door and, Self knew it would be seconds before he was outgunned and outnumbered.

"Who is here?" Mostro's voice growled from the top of the landing. "Self?" he growled and then chuckled.

The man he came for was here. Self quickly slid his blade into the sheath at the side of his leg and raised both his cannons at the front door and squeezed. The silent slugs put grapefruit- sized holes into the door. Self ran towards the steps and spotted Mostro at the top with an army issued M-16 machinegun.

Without hesitation Mostro squeezed the fully automatic assault weapon down in Self's direction and recklessly into the floor.

As the hot slugs rained down, Self ran back to the hall.

"*Fuck!*" a gunman yelled when he saw Self through a hole in the door. He quickly raised his revolver and shot at Self, just missing him.

Self fired back, letting his hammer blow. First at the front door as he moved back towards the stairs, and then up into the ceiling, hoping he could kill his trapped opponent. One thing he knew for sure, one of them was not leaving there alive. Someone yelled in pain outside. Self's bullets had hit its mark. It was only a matter of minutes before the police would have the place surrounded.

Self rushed to the steps, taking them two at a time. And saw Mostro standing at the top landing with his machinegun nestled at his hip. Self stopped, slammed his back against the wall to avoid the gunfire that Mostro sent his way, and then he dove off the stairs, head first over the banister.

Like he had trained to do a hundred times before, Self tucked and rolled onto the floor. When he stood, he felt the numbing sensation that told him that he was hit. From his shoulder down to the tip of his fingers tingled. Then he felt the pulse of the pain he would ignore throbbing from the back of his right arm.

There were heavy footsteps above, which were quickly followed by more gunshots coming through the ceiling, missing Self by inches. He glanced around searching for a camera, wondering how Mostro knew where he was.

"Self!" Mostro called out and chuckled. He sounded like he was at the top of the landing again. "Say goodbye."

You just fucked up, Self thought, removing a grenade from his jacket pocket. He quickly pulled the pin and lobbed the explosive upward. He heard it roll across the floor above and ducked for cover.

The house shook like a wrecking ball had hit it. The men outside were heard scurrying away in their cars. Self jumped up the stairs two at a time, and when he finally reached the top landing, he discovered that the remnants from his grenade had destroyed huge pieces of the wall and floor. A cloud of dust filled the air. A bloody heap was pinned in the corner with the M-16 lying a few inches away.

"Ack ack ack," Mostro coughed with his back slumping down the wall, his ass on the floor and his broken legs spread wide.

Self rushed to the machinegun and kicked it away as his platinum smiled appeared.

"Ju can't win," Mostro laboriously uttered.

Self examined his enemy and knew something was wrong. The man in front of him had the same face as Mostro, same gold teeth, and same grimace, but his eyes didn't have the thirst for blood, and his face was more apologetic. He was defeated.

After many attempts at gasping for air, Self's victim muttered, "Mostro. He cut ju in pieces. Like he do ju family."

Self quickly removed his Tanto blade. The images of Joy, his baby dying and the lost of his family made him more determined. He gripped the handle of his blade with both fists and slammed the edge into his enemy's throat before dragging his thrust, along with the body through the room while ripping Mostro's chest cavity open.

"Mostro!" Someone called from below.

"*General*," another man called up.

While Mostro's men called with uncertainty from below, Self was sawing through Mostro's chest until his heart was separated from the rest of his body. Self dug in, removed it, and then quickly began beheading his enemy.

"Mostro! You okay, *general?*" came from below. Then someone started climbing the stairs.

Self stopped sawing through Mostro's neck and pushed the bloody corpse to the edge of the stairs. He kicked Mostro's hip and sent the corpse tumbling down to the men.

"*Arghhh*," the men gasped in unison, witnessing the impossible. Mostro was dead.

Self sheathed his blade, removed his cannons from his waist, and with each step down he let his silenced hammer blow again, piercing the bodies of the Marielitos that were looking down at their dead comrade. One of the men rushed from the house and Self was on his tail, but the Marielito's speed far exceeded a wounded Self.

Outside, a white Infinity M35 sedan was parked in the driveway with the engine running and the driver's door open. The prestigious neighborhood had awoken. A Chevy Camaro was parked in the middle of the street and the runner was fighting to get into the car. Self aimed, lined the Marielito's head in his sight, and then lowered his weapon. Who he came for was dead. It was just a matter of seconds before the police arrived.

Self rushed to the Infinity.

Suddenly the roar of two Cadillac Escalade trucks turned the corner. Self stopped short. Both passenger doors opened and Self didn't wait to see who was inside. He sent two shots into the door of the truck furthest away. When he went to aim at the truck that pulled up first, Mostro jumped out the passenger side blasting a long .41 Revolver, just missing Self.

"What the fuck?" Self muttered. It couldn't be. He just killed the man in front of him upstairs. The body wasn't even cold yet.

"*Shataan*," Self reminded himself before running around the hood of the car for cover.

Mostro wasn't playing. He was a marksman for sure. His aim was missing Self by centimeters and if Self wasn't well trained, he would have been dead long ago.

Self quickly glimpsed over the hood and then ducked.

Mostro smiled, bearing his gold teeth with his arm extended while quickly limping his way to Self. Self was trapped between the car and the garage, but that didn't matter. He dropped down on his back, leaned closer to the front driver's tire, and tried to fire, but Mostro's bullets were bouncing off the floor too close to his body.

"I kill ju once! I kill ju again and again!" Mostro yelled. "You may kill me hermano, Self, but never me!"

Twins! Self thought. Motherfucker. Now everything made sense. He had the ability to be in two places at the same time, Self remembered Primo telling him. Fuck it then. Both gotta go, Self concluded.

From the corner to his left, a siren was blaring and quickly approaching.

"General!" someone yelled before one of the trucks pulled off.

Mostro shot into the car Self was behind, then around the car, and then attempted to lean under the car to kill Self, but Self fired back.

"*Uggh*," Mostro growled before spinning and hitting the ground. With a loud thud he rolled onto his back and then painstakingly hopped back up.

Self knew when his slug had found a home. He remained crouched down at the front of the car. The sirens were cutting the corner. He quickly ejected both clips and reloaded. Then he rose to finish the job. Mostro was back on his feet and fired off two shots at Self, emptying his revolver. Self moved instinctively, ducked from getting hit, and stood to take aim as the first police car was pulling up.

Mostro tucked the revolver, removed a Mac 11 sub-machinegun that dangled from inside his jacket, and he turned to the police car.

Self had to get out of there. He could sacrifice his life, fire on Mostro, killing him dead, or he could remove the threat to his freedom. He turned one of his cannons towards the passenger door of the police car and dumped each slug from his weapon into the door, window and windshield while Mostro did the same to the opposite side. The officer on the passenger side wasn't making it home.

The human will to survive overruled police training and the driver of the patrol car quickly reversed and sped off until he recklessly ran into a sprawling lawn a block away.

Self turned firing on Mostro and one of the Marielito soldiers fired on him from the back passenger door. The slugs hit the car door instead of his body. Self raised his hand over his head from behind the car door and fired until he heard the roar of the truck pulling off. He then quickly hopped into the running Infinity, slammed the shifter into reverse, and peeled off heading for Mostro with red lights flashing in his rearview mirror.

Mostro's truck sped down the two lane, tree lined street of Midland Avenue. Up ahead was the overpass of the Grand Central Parkway.

With sirens blaring and police on both their trails, Self decided to leave Mostro to deal with the police. He sped ahead of the roaring truck, made the first right onto the service road of the Grand Central Parkway, and pushed the throttle to the max until he sped onto the highway. The police couldn't keep up, but others would be up ahead.

Self fumbled with one hand to reload his cannons. After several turns, he slowed his pace. Police cars zoomed by two blocks ahead. He slowly turned onto the heavy traffic of Utopia Parkway. He gently eased into the dark cavern, and didn't stop until he saw the brake light of a red minivan parking.

Quickly, Self parked the Infinity, hopped out and raced to the driver's door of the minivan.

"Oh my *Gawd*," an Asian girl, who probably borrowed her mom's car, screamed at Self when he suddenly appeared. "You scared the shit out of me!" she yelled again and punched his chest in frustration.

Self sighed and turned his head towards the entrance of the garage where sirens were blaring. He looked down at the Asian girl, stealthily planted an uppercut to her jaw, and watched her eyes roll into her head before she slumped into his arms unconscious. He didn't know if a hostage could buy him time, so he quickly threw her into the back seat before pulling off. Like a soccer mom with a van full of children, Self cautiously eased out the parking garage, turned onto traffic, and obeyed all traffic laws as police cruisers drove past him from all different directions.

TWENTY

After Larry delivered the news that Manny shouldn't go home, Manny sat at his desk replaying the defining moments of his life. Hours slipped by as he replayed images of being poor in Panama. His father was injured and couldn't work so he robbed and killed a man to feed his family. After shaming his family he fled to America. Shortly after moving in with Louie and Edeeks, his mother's girlfriend's children, Louie showed him how armed robbery was really done in New York. Louie got caught slipping, and was ultimately killed by one of his robbery victims.

For Manny, one robbery and homicide led to more, until the night Manny went to rob Pantera's henchman. A botched robbery turned into an illegal job opportunity and the saga with the Marielitos started there. Now that he had more money than he could spend, a son he never spent time with and a fiancée his intuition kept nagging him not to trust, Manny realized he was never truly happy. One tear fell from his eyes and opened a deluge of other tears. Regret had gotten the best of him. Crime indeed, did not pay.

By 3:30 am, Manny was disrobing to sleep in the pull-out bed. He heard the vibration of his phone on the desk and figured it was Racheal calling to ask about his whereabouts so he ignored it. It wasn't until he was under the covers that he realized he had two phones. He jumped out of bed, rushed to his desk, and saw that it was his secured line buzzing.

"Yo," he whispered into the phone.

"Need something, Slick," Self said in rushed tones on the other line.

Manny closed his eyes and exhaled with joy. "Thank God. *Anything.*"

"A mil. In cash."

"No Problem. When?"

"Now."

Manny tallied up all the cash he had at his disposal, but was short. "Gotta get E on it during banking hours."

"Do that."

"Where?" Manny wanted to know the drop off.

"E's crib."

"Okay. By the morning, you get there and I'll make E work it out."

Self ordered, "Call him now."

"No prob. How long before you get there?"

"Tell him I'm eating in his kitchen," Self answered and ended the call.

Manny smiled from knowing Self was okay and up to his old tricks.

*****

As he was about to call Edeeks, Manny's phone buzzed again. He rushed back to his desk certain it was Self wanting to tell him something else.

"Yo," he answered again.

"Manny Black," Alvaro Santa-Maria said on the other line. "I'm in a black truck across from your office. You mind if I get a moment of your time? Or the Secret Service and I can barge in to speak with you?"

"Whoa," Manny huffed. "Give me a minute."

Alvaro had the audacity to feel that Manny was at his beckon call. Manny dressed and was composing a long line of words that would make matters very clear to Alvaro. He was nobody's rat or soldier and he intended on letting the special agent know it for the very last time. He stepped out into the nippy air where two tinted black trucks were parked outside. The back window to one of the Chevy Suburban's opened up and Alvaro's tanned hand waved him over. Manny jogged across the street, opened the door, and was surprised that the truck was unconventional. Inside was customized with a lounge chair, a computer station and a huge flat screen that made the divider between the passenger and the driver. Manny sat with his back to the divider, and cut his eyes at a black attaché case sitting on the seat next to him.

"Office on wheels, huh?" Manny asked.

"Thank you for accommodating me on such short notice," he told Manny.

"How'd you know that I was here?"

He smiled. "Because you're not aware of what's going on at your home." He shrugged. "So, I have my resources."

"You bug my house?"

Alvaro shook his head. "Not I said the cat, but since we're asking questions, allow me to ask a rhetorical one. Did your guys, your *family*, raid a hospital, launch government issued grenades, injure police officers and brazenly do a prison break while killing several employees of the Department of Health and Corrections?"

"I was in my office," Manny offered.

Alvaro chuckled. "Do you know what type of threat your friends caused to national security?"

"What?" Manny asked.

Alvaro snapped his fingers, pointed to Manny with a smile and said, "Not once did you deny it was your men."

Manny shrugged.

"The threat to national security is zero. Not a good idea to use grenades, though. It gives a direct link to federal ammunition inventory. Pipe bombs? That's okay. You can make those in your basement."

"So no one cares?" Manny asked.

Alvaro shrugged this time. "Money and power Manny. That's all that matters. I don't need evidence to convict anyone, anywhere. Even the president of our great country, but you're a man in demand, so it doesn't matter who did what. You have serious people who want to have serious business with you, and it's a win-win situation for all parties involved. Whoever else is interested in indicting you, charging you, or your family, will quickly go away if you agree to form a partnership with us."

Now was the time for Manny to tell Alvaro what he needed him to know. Manny leaned forward and rested his elbows on his knees. He looked Alvaro in his eyes and said, "Listen. I'm nobody's bitch, rat or soldier. I'll play the cards that I was dealt."

"Mr. Black. I don't mean to insult you, and I'm certain you're not trying to insult me or my employers. We all have jobs to do, and if you look into that attaché case next to you, and arrive at the restaurant at the precise time, Primo will be there. When he leaves with a full stomach, you do what you do best. My problem solved, and all your problems solved. I can have your brother home twenty four hours afterwards, and you can live a long prosperous life spending your millions. Or you can choose the alternative, and it was nice meeting you." Alvaro assured him.

This was déjà vu. Manny was in debt to Pantera because he gave Manny an address and a gun to eliminate someone. When Manny did, he was caught on video, and it took years and a total war with the Marielitos to get it back. Now Alvaro was asking the same thing, but with a greater reward.

Alvaro saw Manny's hesitation and whispered, "What's one more homicide? This organization sent you to prison, killed your family, your child and threatens everything you are. You kill the head and the body falls. Not to mention not spending the rest of your life in prison."

He's got a point? Manny pondered.

"No one is asking you to take the stand against people you were engaged in crime with. *That* is a rat! My employers are not asking you to compromise your integrity or honor in the name of us. We are simply asking you to eliminate your enemy. Manny you're smarter than this, and I'm done with this conversation. The case is yours. Or not."

Taking the case meant doing one last job that would make everything in his life okay. Leaving it meant going to prison and dying a slow death. Manny grabbed the case.

"Excellent choice," Alvaro said and opened the door. His job was done.

Manny stared at the man wondering what it was that Alvaro was not telling him. With nothing to say, he stepped out of the truck, and before the door slammed shut, the driver was pulling off. Manny stood in the middle of the street with no one but his decision.

Primo was a dead man. He needed everything to go well. He walked into his office, opened the attaché case and found a sheet of paper that read "Gomez, 105 Reade Street between Church Street and Broadway, 6 PM." He removed the paper to reveal a Walther PPK-S, .380 automatic handgun with a silencer lying in black foam. The small, sexy gun was made for a spy or a woman, but if that's what Alvaro wanted for Manny to escape all indictments, then that's what he was going to get.

He looked down at the name of the restaurant and wondered if he was being set up. Could he trust Alvaro for sure? He didn't know, but the alternative was spending his life in prison, and that wasn't looking so appealing anymore.

*****

At 7:00 am Edeeks strolled into the massive kitchen of his New Jersey estate, sleepy eyed wearing boxers and a N.Y. Knicks tee-shirt. He met eyes with Self, who sat on the stool at his marble island, and turned to open the fridge. He reached in, grabbed a container of orange juice, put it to his lips and then suddenly dropped the bottle. Then he spun around quickly, looked over at Self again and ducked low while raising his hands high.

"Oh *Jesus*! Don't kill me, don't kill me, don't kill me," he yelled. He dropped down into the fetal position on the checkered floor on the other side of the island and out of Self's view. "Oh shit! *Self*? I'm dead! Sorry man. I didn't even see your face. *Please, please, please*, don't kill me, Self, don't kill me. They made me do it! Arghhhh, fucking Racheal, that bitch. Tell Manny I'm sorry, I'll leave right now and go to Puerto Rico and you will never see me again, I'll give you six million in cash right now, Self, Manny's going to jail he won't know."

"Stand up!" Self barked.

Edeeks was weeping hard. "Naw man. I can't move, I pissed myself."

"Stand up, Self not gonna say it again."

"My kids are upstairs, man. Don't hurt 'em. I did it. Don't kill me."

The aroma of human waste entered the room. Edeeks had shitted on himself as well.

"Self don't care."

"I know, I know, I know," Edeeks wept like a child. "I fucked up. Manny sent you over here because he found out that the baby is mine and I robbed him of the company. Plus the federal shit. I knew he would. Fucking bitch, Racheal. Her and that bitch Ann was freaking off and then I started fucking her and she got pregnant. She's keeping it. Maybe I deserve to die."

"Manny didn't send Self. Self don't care."

Edeeks remained silent. His weeping suddenly stopped. After a few sniffles, he asked, "*What*?"

"Self losing patience. Bitch, stand the fuck up!"

Pots rattled from below the kitchen island and Edeeks, slowly rose with a frying pan covering his entire face with the exception of one eye and a sauce pot covering his chest. "Manny didn't send you?"

Self shook his head with a slight smirk on his face.

"Then why you here?"

"Self need your car, and a mil in cash. I want Manny's cash, but since you got more, you can give Self what you want Self to have."

"*What*?" Edeeks asked again.

"You didn't hear the God?"

Edeeks shook his head and quickly nodded. "Yeah. No. I mean, I heard you." He put the pots down, wiped his nose and sniffled, slowly gaining his composure. "Manny didn't send you?" he asked in disbelief.

Self shook his head.

"So I'm dead for telling you what happened?" he said with remorse.

Self shook his head and held up two fingers. "Self came for two things, and Self need them now."

Edeeks held up both his hands like he was under arrest. Then he looked up like he could see through the ceiling. "My kids are upstairs, Self. Don't kill me here. I don't believe you."

"Self gone do you if you keep wasting Self time."

It finally hit Edeeks that Self was serious. "So you broke into my house?" Edeeks looked at the freshly washed dinnerware on the island. "Ate, and waited on me because you need a car and Manny told you to see me for some cash?"

Self nodded—slowly.

"*Fuck!*" Edeeks smacked his head and raised his hands while his eyes widened with anticipation. "The cars are in the garage. Take anyone you want. Take the Ghost if you want. You can have all them shits if you want 'em." He held up one finger. "Wait right here. Give me about ten minutes. Don't move."

Self nodded again. He didn't even make an attempt to decipher Edeeks's guilt. Nothing mattered anymore. His only concern was chopping Mostro into pieces, and he knew what he had to do to end the war, and find Mostro. Time was going to be on his side, and money for his army was going to be necessary. The total annihilation of the Marielitos would be done if that's what it took to chop off Mostro's head.

More like twenty minutes later, a freshly showered Edeeks came into the kitchen with a Gucci suitcase in each hand.

"That's two million Self. If you need more, you know where to find me," he volunteered. Then he waved his arm in the direction of the six car garage and said, "You know where the garage is. Keys are on the hooks. Help yourself. Please, but just so you know," he said with his hands raised like he was under arrest. "I'm flying out to Puerto Rico today. I'm gone for a while. If you say never come back, so be it!"

Self walked up to Edeeks. He looked into his fearful eyes and then down to his trembling lips. He leaned in close, kissed Edeeks on his cheek, patted him on his ass, and said, "Damn shame," before walking towards the garage with the two suitcases.

At the garage door, Self examined the Maybach, Rolls Royce Ghost, a black Ferrari, a Mercedes SL65, and a midnight blue customized, Mustang GT. He walked to the rack of keys, removed the keys to the Mustang from the hook, and pressed for the trunk to open. He dropped the two suitcases in, hopped in and quickly bought the engine to life. The garage door opened with Edeeks at the control, waving goodbye. Self put the car in drive and allowed the powerful engine to take him to the destination that would end the war.

*****

By 7:30 am, Nzinga buzzed Manny's phone.

"Yeah," he said over the intercom.

"Your attorney is on the phone," Nzinga said. "He doesn't want to call your cell phone."

Manny frowned, looked at his cell phone and smirked from being confused. "Patch him in."

The line switched on and Joe started the call off by saying, "Are you sitting down?"

"I don't need any bad news, Joe," Manny warned. "Yeah, I'm sitting down. Whatssup?"

"It's been gnawing at me like mice in a cheese factory about why the U.S. Attorney's office was so interested in your case. So I did some homework and I got bad news."

"How much is it going to cost me?" Manny wanted to know. Money had a way of making legal issues go away.

Joe remained silent on the phone and then said, "This time my friend, you can keep your money. Before me is a dossier, copies of top secret stuff. Listen…" he said as he shuffled papers. "Manuel Black, kingpin of the M3 Boyz, a corrupt organization, along with the money laundering enterprise of MB Enterprises. They're charging you with running a Racketeer Influenced and Corrupt Organization. R.I.C.O. Manny. They have years of you on tape, and two key witnesses. One of which is your brother and business partner Edeeks. From what I know he's been given full immunity and allowed to keep all his earnings from the business. The other is identified as Rose Cardozo, an undercover agent who has infiltrated your business."

"That bitch, Ann!" Manny blurted out. "I'mma kill that bitch! And Edeeks? You sure, Joe?" he asked as his temper was brewing.

Joe shuffled papers and said, "This is a pretty heavy superseding indictment. Your finance department was compromised, a long line of tapes was collected with you talking on it, and you're also being linked with the Marielitos as a paid assassin. This investigation started four years ago by the F.B.I. The C.I.A. offered help and Uncle Sam is linked in as an agency on the case. The I.R.S. will want blood."

"So why didn't they arrest me?"

"They're coming for you today."

By tomorrow, Primo would be dead, so the indictment Joe is talking about would be meaningless, Manny thought to himself. All he had to do was avoid being captured, and the office would be the first place they came looking. He had to go. "Okay," he answered.

"Okay?" Joe asked in shock at how cool Manny was about it all. "Okay? Manny, as your *friend*—not as your lawyer, who could make a ton of money fighting this case—but as your friend, I'm telling you that you need to disappear. Walk away from everything and just *go!*"

Manny knew what Joe didn't know, and that was Alvaro's deal. Once Primo was dead, he wouldn't need a lawyer or ever have to worry about being indicted again. Getting out of the country was a good idea, but before he left, Edeeks would have to die.

"Okay, Joe. Thanks for the heads up."

"These are serious charges, Manny. They can sentence you to several life sentences for this…if they can find you," Joe warned before they ended the call.

The pressure was too much for one man to handle, but Manny Black wasn't the average man. At that very moment, the only thing he could think about was protecting his son. Quickly, he reached for his cell phone and dialed Racheal's number.

"Come on!" he was hoping she picked up on the first ring.

"*Chucha!*" he yelled when it went into voice mail.

He rushed to his private compartment behind the television and removed a silencer. On that day, he intended on using two of them on three different people. Edeeks had to go, then Ann, and then Primo, and in that order. He grabbed a small duffle bag of cash worth $250,000 and rushed out the door with his gun tucked in his waist, while calling Edeeks' phone number.

"Fucking faggot!" he grumbled when a voice service said the number was no longer in service. "Fuck you gonna cross me?" Manny screamed out loud as he walked down the hall to Edeeks office. "I gave you the world and you cross *me?*" He reached the receptionist desk, looked at Nzinga and asked, "Where *the fuck* is Edeeks?"

It wasn't the first time Nzinga had witnessed Manny's temper, but in an effort to save her boss, she pointed to the gun that was clearly showing for everyone to see. "Manny, perhaps you should gather yourself?"

He looked down at the gun, then back at her, and in a snarl he yelled, "I don't give *a fuck!* Where is he?"

Nzinga shrugged. "I don't know, but you're scaring me, Sir Manny."

Those words brought him back from the edge. "Motherfucker!" he said in a rage.

Suddenly his phone rang. His head snapped down at the screen hoping it was Edeeks's or Racheal. Someone was calling him from his house phone. He sighed with relief certain it was Racheal.

"Hello?" he answered with hope.

"*Senor*, chu must come home now!" Macca cried.

"What happened to Manny?" he asked frantically.

"Please, come home. Come home now, please," she begged before hanging up.

Manny wondered if Mostro or the Marielitos were in his house. Since Macca didn't tell him what was wrong, he assumed she was being held at gunpoint and couldn't speak. He lifted his phone and called Culo's number.

"Yo!" he answered.

"Yo, I need y'all to go to my house. Right now!"

"What's wrong?" Culo asked. "We in Jersey right now."

"Jersey?" Manny quickly grew suspicious.

"Yeah, *jefe.* Some place called Paramus?"

"Why?" Manny needed to know. They were just a few miles from his house.

"At the Holiday Inn Express, we needed to change up".

"I need y'all at my house," he said, and then the words that would get Chango there immediately came to mind. "Tell Chango I think Lil Manny is in danger. I'm on my way."

"*Si*. Be there in ten minutes, Yo."

Manny ended that call and tapped the phone for another.

"Speak," Self answered.

"Yo! When you go get that paper from E, set his ass free," Manny yelled.

"Word?" Self asked with indifference.

"He violated to the utmost."

"Patterns," Self answered, but Manny didn't want a lesson right then.

"He gotta pay," Manny responded.

"E taken care of," Self promised.

"Whoooo," Manny exhaled and then thought of Edeeks no longer being alive. Guilt eased into his mind and he pushed it away by saying, "He had to go, but yo I need you to meet me at my place. Somethin's up."

"Already in the neighborhood," Self answered.

"Yeah," Manny wasn't surprised. He and Edeeks only lived a mile apart. "See you there."

"Indeed. Down in the back, across the lawn by the lake," Self instructed.

Manny hung up feeling more secure that his help was on the way. "Shit!" he yelled while hitting the speed dial for Racheal. When she didn't answer he stared at her number and shook the phone in his hand, ready to slam it.

He stopped at the entrance to his office, looked around the massive foyer, and then turned to Nzinga. "Take care of Puncho," he told her, not sure if those would be his last words to her.

TWENTY ONE

Manny dashed into the street, waved a yellow cab down and then hopped in. "Alpine, New Jersey," he told the driver.

The Arab whistled. "Must be nice," he said.

Manny wasn't in the mood to talk. His mind was filled with questions about his future. What would happen to his son? Was Racheal capable of having the baby and raising it on her own? He had some answers to those questions, and they all ended with killing Primo. With the help of a large tip, the Arab driver delivered Manny to his home in record time.

"What the fuck?" Manny asked himself as he entered the sprawling driveway to his estate. A small moving truck was parked at the right. "What the fuck is this?" he asked, mostly to himself.

Manny stood still, but everything was spinning in circles around him. He was in a daze. His eyes darted around and he stutter stepped and almost stumbled from shock. The three movers nodded at him as they carried boxes of his property into the truck, making it clear that Manny wasn't the first husband that was surprised that his woman was moving out.

Macca came running out the house with her pudgy legs working to get to Manny. Behind her was Manny Jr looking confusion.

"*Señor*, I no know," Macca cried. "Wha' happen?" she asked, not realizing that Manny was just as confused as she was.

"What happened?" Manny replied.

Macca held both palms to her face like she was hiding from him. "I no know. *Senora* Racheal! She wake up. Truck come. Big men come and move de furniture?" She stepped in closer and frowned with a grimace. "She no love you. Me no know she no love you."

"Me either," he answered knowing his whole world was coming apart one thread at a time. "Macca, take Manny in the house!" he said, defeated.

Manny took baby steps until he reached the side door of his home. He walked into his kitchen and flopped down at the breakfast nook. He couldn't believe Racheal was leaving him. He replayed all the good times and romantic getaways he and Racheal shared, but what he was most disappointed in was ignoring his intuition. His gut told him she was no good. Puncho told him not to trust her, but he let his intrigue distract him. His head rose from the roar of the moving truck pulling off, then he felt something at his knee and looked into the eyes that favored his.

"Papa, you okay?" Manny Jr asked softly.

Macca walked in behind his son and said, "Manny, leave papa alone."

Just then, Manny looked at his son's eyes come alive. "Chango!" Manny Jr yelled.

Manny snapped his head around. Chango and Culo were walking from across his lawn wearing suits and ties. Chango's dreads were shaved off and facial hair was gone, and Culo was well groomed. They both looked the total opposite of the wanted pictures that were circulating on the news.

"*Que sucedio jefe?*" Chango asked what happened.

Manny exhaled heavy and then shook his head. "I don't know."

"Cuban's was here?" Culo asked.

Manny shook his head. "No." "Racheal moved her shit out when everything is crashing down."

Culo slammed his fist in the palm of his hand. "Puncho said that bitch was no good." He looked over to Chango, who was with Manny Jr. "Yo, we gotta head to Cali right now."

Culo smacked his forehead. "Here we go with this shit."

Chango looked up to the ceiling and said, "He general," talking about Manny Jr. "We raise him to be king of Panama. *El jefe, numero uno.*" He looked down at Manny and asked, "I raise him in Panama, *si.* "

"Not now, Chango," Manny begged. He was too stressed and plotting on how to kill Primo so he could fix everything.

"Yes! Now! We need to go," Chango demanded in a threatening tone.

Manny looked up at him with a frown.

Chango looked up to the ceiling and said, "Yes. Puncho plane."

Instantly it sounded like a good idea. Manny stood and told Chango, "Take Little Manny and Macca."

"To where, *senor?*" Macca questioned.

Manny looked at her with pleading eyes. "To Panama. All the staff is there. They can help you with Manny until I get there. Don't take any clothes. Just grab your papers and go." He turned to Culo and said, "Follow me." As he rushed to the basement door he yelled out, "Chango, get Manny ready for the trip!"

"Yeahhhhh," Manny Jr celebrated about leaving with Chango.

Manny hurried down his basement steps with Culo stumbling down and rushed over to a hot water tank and shoved it over.

"Cool, Yo," Culo responded when he saw Manny's fake hot water heater. Under the heater was a flat, iron plate. Manny removed the plate to reveal several bags. "Let me guess. Cash?" Culo asked.

Manny nodded. "A million dollars. Take it with you. If anything happens to me, make sure Manny is okay."

"Chango got that, but I got you too," Culo said with a smile. "What can happen to you, *jefe?*"

Manny didn't have time to explain the world of trouble he was in. "Nothing," he lied. "Let's go."

Together the men made two trips until all the cash was in the trunk of Culo's car. Culo sat behind the wheel with the engine running while Chango stood in the driveway talking to the heavens, only this time he wasn't smiling. He walked up to Manny, held him tight and then looked into his eyes. "See you on the other side, *mi hombre*. Manny Jr. will be okay. This is the way."

Manny looked into the car at the son he never spent enough time with and didn't teach enough lessons to that would someday make him a better man. He regretted so much at that very moment and would have traded everything in to just be able to raise his son. He sighed as Chango climbed into the car.

Primo gotta go, he thought to himself as Culo drove away. The death of Primo was the answer to all his problems. His phone rang as he started towards the house. It was Self.

"Outback," Self told him, and Manny switched directions. He turned and headed to the back of the house and met Self at the end of the road that circled his property.

*****

As soon as he cut the corner of his house, two Ford Taurus's led a fleet of dark sedans, followed by a dark passenger van with tinted windows sped onto his massive driveway. The two front doors to both Fords opened and out jumped four officers wearing dark blue jackets with F.B.I in yellow letters on their backs, and gold badges dangling from their necks. Their guns were drawn.

Two Latino's exited one car. A black woman with short cropped hair and an older Black man with a salt and pepper Afro exited the other while the occupants of the other vehicles wait for their orders.

"Go! Go!" one of the Latino started pointing to the house signaling agents to run into the house.

The black couple stayed outside, covering their underlings. The black man turned to the woman and asked, "Ann. You sure he's in there?"

Ann turned to her supervisor for more than ten years and said, "Dickey. We watched a cab roll up, and only four people roll out, including the boy. Trust me, that scumbag is in there."

"Well, we came for him, so." He smiled and said, "He was such a nice fellow at the engagement party."

Ann shrugged. "You think that was nice? Try working for him for four years. Manny gave out the best bonuses, great perks, company vacations and his Christmas parties were the shit!"

Jasper turned to Ann and jokingly asked, "You sure you weren't compromised?"

Ann smirked and put one hand on her hip. "Now we both know there is only one person that could have been compromised."

They both turned and looked over their shoulder at the passenger van.

*****

Manny walked through the woods and Self stepped out from behind a tree, just up a hill from his car in the road below. "I fucked up."

Self nodded. "Indeed," he agreed and then looked over at the massive lawn. "Take a lap."

Walking and talking was exactly what Manny needed. He was going to tell Self everything. Then Self could help him put an end to Primo and the Marielitos, and hopefully the rest of his life could come together.

"Self know how to end the war," he told Manny as they were a hundred feet away from the house.

Anxiously, Manny said, "Yeah. Me too. I know how to bring all this shit to an end."

"We been following your plan, right?" Self asked.

"Yeah, but this is different."

Self shook his head. "Patterns. We followed your plan to get money. We followed your plan to get on video and body Pantera.

We followed your plan and cousin Kev and Carmen and Lil Rico got murdered. You see where Self going?"

"Nah, this different," Manny tried to explain. "I gotta do this one thing tonight, and then everything will be good."

Self stopped short, close to the end of Manny's property line. "You a rat, Manny?"

"What?"

Self shook his head. "You Self closest brother. Don't go out like that. Answer the God."

Oh shit, Manny thought. *Self knows about Alvaro.* "Nah. It's not like that."

"No need to explain. You didn't tell the God about the case. No good."

"You right."

"Now the broad and bitch ass Edeeks making moves, and E gonna be a rodent for the feds."

"How the fuck you know this?" Manny asked. "I just found out an hour ago."

"Patterns. Told you years ago about patterns," Self said as his eyes scanned to see if they were being watched. "Joy gone, Manny. Not once did you shed a tear. That monster bodied Self seeds. Self *only* seeds. Right in Self face. You know Self gonna get real messy with that, right?"

"For sure," Manny answered with certainty.

"You know Self gotta end this war, right?"

"Me too."

"But you slipping too hard for us to follow your plan."

"I know, but—"

"But you not listening. *Your* broad pregnant by Edeeks. Edeeks was fucking your girl. Then the broad somehow got his mind fucked up and they got all your cash. A lot of cash. All your fucking money." Self waved both hands downward at Manny and said, "You all fucked up. Your mind hurting and we all gonna go down, fucking wit' you."

"How you know the baby is his?" Manny asked.

Self shook his head. "You see? On this chess board you still trying to protect the queen, instead of sacrificing the bitch to win. Your chess game would be much better if you took your bitch off the board before your opening. Patterns."

Manny was crushed. "This bitch lived in my house. Had my son loving her. Was swallowing my nut and running my business all while she was fucking Edeeks on the side? I'mma kill that bitch too."

"First you gotta find her, but that's irrelevant."

Manny looked up with surprise. "How you know I can't find her?"

Self shook his head. "Man, you really fucked up," he said with remorse. "Patterns!"

Manny shook his head. "Fuck it! The war ends tonight."

Self nodded. "Indeed. The war ends with you. They want *you*! Want you to be they henchman while Self do the wet work. No more, Manny. They want you to be the pawn while Self protecting every queen except his own."

Manny was amazed at the sight before him. Self was crying. Actual tears were streaming down his face.

"Joy was better than Self, Manny. She was Self foundation, and the baby? Self prince was making Self human again, but no more. Monster against monster. It's on."

"I'm with you," Manny said with enthusiasm.

Self shook his head. "Nah, you the beginning and the end. If there ain't no you around, then there ain't no war, no ratting, and nobody knowing Self."

Manny nodded, knowing what he had to do. "Okay, so I'm out. I sent Lil Manny to Panama. I just gotta do this one thing and I'm heading to Panama and just disappear."

Self nodded repeatedly. "Indeed. You need to disappear," said Self as he removed the cannon from his waist. He turned to Manny, aimed at his hip, and let his gun blow.

The shot hit Manny and flipped him over into the dirt. He fell on his side with his leg behind him.

"Self!" Manny groaned. "*Self*? What you doing, brother?"

"Ending one war, and starting another," he said, standing over Manny. "See you on the other side."

"*Nooooo*," Manny Black let out his last breath.

Self looked away before squeezing his gun two more times, sending heavy slugs into Manny's face.

Self turned his back on him and tucked his gun into his waist. "Time for Mostro," he said and headed for the car.

*****

The two Latino's rushed out the house when they heard gunshots in the distance. "You heard that, Dickey?" they asked their supervisor. "No one was ordered to fire shots."

Ann looked over to the passenger van and waved the occupants out. The doors opened, and an older white man with rosy cheeks and a huge belly ran over with his gold badge dangling on his sloppy chest. Behind him was the one woman who was most familiar with the case.

"Did you get him?" she asked the crowd as she removed her badge from the inside of her shirt.

"He's not in there," one of the Latino's said.

"Search the house again," she ordered, slipping on her F.B.I. jacket.

Dickey tightly gripped his gun with both hands. "Rose."

The woman didn't move. Her eyes were fixated on the house.

"Agent Cardozo!" Dickey said her last name, but she didn't respond.

Then Ann barked, "Racheal!"

The woman snapped out of her trance. "*What*?" she barked back.

"Snap out of it, Rose," Dickey ordered. "This case has come to a close. We won't be calling you Racheal anymore. Your suspect is missing Rose and we need you focused. Possible gunshots came from behind the house."

The woman Manny knew as Racheal quickly drew her weapon and held it tightly. "No more Racheal, sir. It won't happen again."

One of the Latino officers ran from behind the house and yelled, "Across the lawn. Come on!"

The entire force of Federal Agents ran across Manny's lawn. They frantically searched the property for a clue, until Ann pointed to a shallow break in the woods and said, "Over there."

They ran harder towards the man who was lying with his back to them.

"Is that him?" Agent Rose Cardozo yelled, before stopping in her tracks.

Ann ran faster and was the first to reach the body. She knelt down and shoved the shoulder to look into the face of the warm corpse. "Shit!" she yelled loudly.

"Do not compromise the crime scene!" Dickey ordered.

"Is it really him?" Agent Cardozo questioned from the distance.

"Four years of investigation for this shit!" Ann complained.

The first Latino that walked over and looked back at Agent Cardozo and nodded. "Affirmative."

"D.O.A." the chubby, winded white man announced.

Everyone huddled over the dead body, staring. Agent Cardozo inched closer. Her eyes were locked in a trance as she stared at the corpse. All eyes left the body and looked at her pitter patter her way over. When she arrived, she looked down at Manny and her lips started to tremble. For more than a minute her face was etched with pain as she stared down at the man who proposed to her, gave her a new life, and did his very best to provide for her every need. He was truly the only man that ever loved her and showed her what it meant to be cherished. Manny Black was going to be her husband in a perfect world, but now he was dead, right there in front of her. Maybe because of her.

"Are you okay?" her supervisor Dickey asked.

For more than a minute she stared again, her mind twirling with too many thoughts. Then her true feelings came to the surface. She sniffled, wiped her nose, took a deep breath, and on the exhale asked Dickey, "Do I still get my promotion?"

THE END

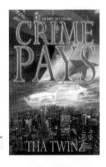 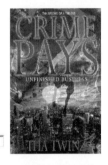 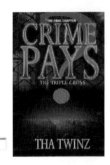

SPECIAL OFFER: $13.00 Each **S/H $4.00 PER BK**

FORMS OF PAYMENT:

Cashier's Checks, Institutional Checks, & Money Orders

Prestige Communication Group, PO Box 1129, NY, NY 10027

Credit Cards: PRESTIGECOMMUNICATIONGROUP.COM

Total Title(s) Checked _____   Amount enclosed_____

Name/ID #_____

Address: _____

City/State/Zip: _____

Made in United States
Orlando, FL
21 March 2022

15994794R00167